Shooters and Chasers

SHOOTERS AND CHASERS

LENNY KLEINFELD

FIVE STAR
A part of Gale, Cengage Learning

Alameda Free Library
1550 Oak Street
Alameda, CA 94501

GALE
CENGAGE Learning™

Detroit • New York • San Francisco • New Haven, Conn • Waterville, Maine • London

GALE
CENGAGE Learning™

Set in 11 pt. Plantin.
Printed on permanent paper.

LIBRARY OF CONGRESS CATALOGING-IN-PUBLICATION DATA

Kleinfeld, Lenny.
    Shooters and chasers / by Lenny Kleinfeld. — 1st ed.
        p. cm.
    ISBN-13: 978-1-59414-739-5 (alk. paper)
    ISBN-10: 1-59414-739-6 (alk. paper)
    1. Police—Fiction. 2. Assassins—Fiction. 3. Murder—Investigation—Fiction. 4. Vintners—Fiction. 5. California, Southern—Fiction. I. Title.
    PS3611.L455S56 2009
    813'.6—dc22   2008039749

First Edition. First Printing: January 2009.
Published in 2009 in conjunction with Tekno Books and Ed Gorman.

Printed in the United States of America
1 2 3 4 5 6 7 12 11 10 09 08

For the woman who sang "Simple Gifts" in the sentry tower of the Manueline fortress at Belém.

ONE

August 2002

Luxury. A motel room, king-size bed with a mattress didn't feel like it was older than he was.

TV with porn cable.

Food, good food, and two six-packs of *cervezas*—in a cooler. Fuck, that fucking Oscar thinks of everything.

Boom box and CDs.

Weed.

A dark heavy Nine, serious gun, serial numbers gone, two extra clips loaded and ready, oh yeah, serious gun, gift from Oscar 'cause this was the big time, this was the real shit. *Professional.*

And some product. Oscar said it was okay to snort a sensible, *professional* amount of blow if Meelo wanted.

Meelo wanted. His job was to wait in that room till Oscar got back, which could be any time between right now and noon tomorrow. Meelo had been there three hours already. The porn was all gringas with blonde nylon hair and plastic tits, and some Asians with plastic tits. All shaved. Meelo switched to Mexican League reruns and cranked a Kinky CD. Did a few lines. A few more.

He was not to leave this room, not for a second. Oscar had been real clear about that. Like *Fuck-this-up-and-I-put-a-cap-through-your-brain* clear. Do not leave the room.

Meelo was annoyed something so easy was so hard. All he

had to do was chill. But what he wanted most was to get out, just a couple of minutes. Then Meelo realized, even with all this luxury, this was not chilling. This was waiting. This was work. Worse. Half of him was like, this is the sweet dream come true, success, money, respect, my slut sister dumping that stupid ugly boyfriend and apologizing to me and begging me to take care of her. . . . Half of him was like, what if this goes wrong, my stomach hurts like there's this big lump of dirty slush inside, how deep is the shit I'm into here?

Meelo sat at the little built-in desk alongside the dresser. Unzipped the grass stash. Filled his pipe. Then took half the bud out of the pipe. Then put it back. Then took half out. Fuck. Oscar never said what he meant by "sensible," what a *professional* amount of high was. Meelo had thought of asking, but it was a faggot question. Fuck it. Meelo filled the pipe. He was too wired not to do some more weed. And beer.

Meelo clenched the pipe in his teeth and flicked the lighter. Nothing. Piece a shit was out of butane. He threw the green plastic piece a shit lighter at a framed poster above the bed, picture of some weirdass old buildings under big fancy red letters that said THE MAGIC OF THAILAND. The empty piece a shit lighter decided not to risk offending the magic of Thailand, missing low and clanging off a wall-mounted reading lamp.

Meelo panicked for a minute as he wrestled with the competing impossibilities of doing without weed or leaving the room to get a lighter. Then he remembered the extra lighters Oscar stashed with the weed. Oscar was big on backups. *Professional.*

Meelo fished out a new lighter and sat on the bed. Flick; we have ignition. Astronaut Meelo grinned and adjusted the flame so it maxed out. Good three inches long. He liked the soft *hiss* of the burning gas. He touched the long yellow-blue flame to the pipe and took a deep hit. Kept the lighter going, *hissing* along with his triple-XXX primo bud rush. Then took another man-size hit. Then a monster toke—

"*Fuck!*" Meelo yelled, fingers burning—he'd held the flame to the metal pipe the whole time—

He simultaneously dropped the pipe from his blistered left hand and yanked his right hand away, the one holding the lighter, accidentally shoving it into the box of tissues he'd taken from the bathroom and placed on the bed while he was watching pornos, unaware his thumb was still clamped on the butane lever so the lighter was still doing its baby flame-thrower act—

Meelo screamed as the box of tissues his right hand was jammed into caught fire. He leapt up and frantically snapped his right arm, flinging the burning tissue box to the floor. The box burst, tissues fluffed out, oxygen rushed in and with a sharp *bap!* the tissue box went mini-nova, erupting in an orange fireball that launched swirling shards of smoldering institutional-grade Kleenex across the room. Shrieking what started out to be curses but never made it all the way to language, Meelo stomped on the charred remains of the tissue box—and found bubbling, smoking acrylic carpet beneath. He grabbed a *cerveza* from the cooler, smashed the neck, and doused the carpet.

Victory . . . *Shit!*

He saw glowing fragments of tissue float down and settle on the pillows, on the carpet, on his weed stash. He rushed around the room, lunging and flailing, smashing the life out of the little orange fuckers, whimpering at the astonishing pain each time he slapped an ember with his burned hands.

But at last all the smoldering tissue fragments were snuffed. Meelo took a long, slow look around, making sure there were no glowing orange specks, nothing, not nowhere.

Okay. He had it under control. Except his heart was pounding like it wanted out of his chest.

Take a slow breath, he advised himself.

Meelo took a slow breath. Another. He closed his eyes, willing himself to relax—

A knock at the door. As Meelo whirled to face it, his elbow clipped Oscar's boom box, which went flying off the dresser, smashed into a chair leg, and landed with a crunch. The CD kept spinning but skipping—BUP-BUP-BUP-BRRRP! BUP-BUP-BUP-BRRRP!—an electro-jackhammer attacking at party volume. Meelo's fingers were stinging so bad he had to kneel and awkwardly press the STOP button with his elbow.

The person knocked again. Meelo froze. It wasn't Oscar's secret knock. Just a regular knock.

It happened again. Whoever it was said, "Hello? Are you all right?"

A woman.

"I'm okay," Meelo said.

"You sure?"

Meelo almost told her to go away. But in his mind he suddenly heard a replay of what the last few minutes must have sounded like to whoever was on the other side of that motel wall.

He decided the thing was to talk to her a minute, chill her out. 'Cause otherwise she might go to the manager. And she was, you know, a woman. Maybe him and her could hook up, after.

"Minute," Meelo called out. He got to his feet, went to the door, undid the chain. Opened the door only halfway. Filled the opening so she couldn't see into the room. *Professional.*

Betsy at first thought the Mexican kid looked like trouble. Shaved head. A lopsided two-inch wide scraggle of beard sticking off the end of his chin. A frayed black muscle T with the sleeves torn off to better display a tattoo of a lurid green and red rattlesnake. The tat began with the rattle on the back of the kid's left hand, wound around the length of his arm and continued up under the T-shirt, where the snake's head emerged above the collar on the kid's neck, mouth gaping, fangs bared. As if the snake were about to launch a savage attack on the kid's earlobe.

"I'm okay," the young man assured Betsy in a dull, vague murmur. "It was just, um . . ." He shrugged. "Nothin'." After a moment he seemed to notice how lame that sounded, so he added, "I uh, cut my hand."

Betsy decided what he looked like was a kid desperately trying to look like trouble. "Musta been a pisser, the way you were yellin'. I got a first aid kit," she said, and gestured for him to show her his wound. "Lemme see."

He yanked his hand out of sight. "Sorry if I woke you or something. No more music or noise tonight. I, I 'pologize, really."

"That's okay." She sniffed the air. "Smells smoky." She gave him a small shrewd conspiratorial grin. "Little fire damage you'd just as soon they don't find till after you check out?"

"No fire, nothing burned, I . . ." He shrugged again. Then snuck a sniff, and paled as he realized his room did smell fucking torched. "Oh, that. I, I uh, um, burned a letter from my girlfriend."

"You cut your hand burning a letter?" Betsy teased, warming up her grin from conspiratorial to sympathetic-inviting. The kid was a loser, dumb as a door, but harmless. Fine for scratching a one-night itch. Way better than the alternative of spending the next three hours trolling some crappy bar and ending up with this dumb loser's grandfather.

Betsy saw the kid recognize her invitation and be tempted by it. She saw the kid wonder if she was too far beneath his dignity.

He ran his eyes up and down her, one last quick body-scan. He made his choice. "Thanks for checking if I was all right. I uh, won't make a lotta noise no more . . . G'night," he murmured. Genuinely regretful.

Shit. She was like forty. Pasty-white pudgy. Clumpy thin hair like an old woman. Dressed in a baggy sweatshirt and jeans, like a man or a dyke.

But she wasn't a dyke. Shit, she was begging for it. And she wasn't disgusting wrinkly-old. If he could get her in and out of here before Oscar got back . . . Fuck, even if he did, and Oscar found out . . .

Meelo promised the woman not to make no more noise and said goodnight.

She didn't leave. Just stood there, looking kind of amused, like she knew he was running dirty movies of the two of them in his mind, like she knew if she just stood there while he imagined her pudgy tits, he'd cave.

Shit.

Meelo closed the door all slow and careful, so she'd know he wasn't slamming it in her face.

Shit. Besides not leaving the room for a second, Meelo was not to let anybody but Oscar in, no matter what. Nobody, no matter what. That was the other thing Oscar had been real clear about.

Fuck shit.

TWO

Naguib Darwahab almost had an excellent night.

Between the meter and tips he'd already cleared three hundred dollars, and it was only ten-thirty. Darwahab decided if he made it to four hundred he'd buy his grandson new basketball shoes. If this really was a night of nights, if he made it to four-hundred-fifty, he'd buy his wife . . . something.

Four-fifty wasn't impossible. The Loop was promisingly crowded; it was a Tuesday night in late August, three weeks of Midwestern boiler-room humidity had just broken, and Chicagoans do not waste good weather.

From now till eleven p.m. diners would continue to roll out of the restaurants. After eleven the theaters would empty. From midnight on there was the bar trade, assuming Darwahab had the stamina to work the overtime, or wanted to. Those were the risky hours.

Probably wouldn't be necessary. He hadn't been empty more than two minutes in a row all night, and wasn't this time. He picked up his next fare, on Dearborn.

About twenty middle-aged, expensively dressed men were milling on the sidewalk in front of an expensively dressed Italian restaurant. The men were exchanging hugs and shouting alcohol-effusive goodbyes as parking valets fetched their cars.

A tall man with an impressive plume of silver-white hair, the dramatic V-shaped crest of his widow's peak crowning the middle of his skull with the flamboyant authority of a Roman

13

officer's helmet, was being urged by a friend to get into the friend's yellow Targa.

The tall man dismissed that notion with an amiable but firm wave, and hailed Darwahab's taxi.

At first Darwahab didn't like the fare, who seemed friendly when he got in and gave an address, but then issued detailed orders about the route Darwahab was to take. As if Darwahab needed instructing on how to get from here to there, a man who'd been driving these streets twenty-three years. A man who'd driven a taxi in Cairo.

Darwahab sneaked quick, practiced glances in the rear-view mirror, assessing this passenger who so needed to have his own way in every tiny thing and was so obviously used to getting it. The fare was wearing a loose summer suit, of muted pale green silk. Underneath he wore a collarless shirt, open at the neck, made of soft, weightless cream-colored linen; Darwahab had never seen an American wearing linen of that sophistication. The fare was probably about Darwahab's age, fifty-seven, but looked younger.

Darwahab looked older. He was mostly bald, and the strip of hair clutching the sides of his head was a grizzled mix of black, gray, and white. His eyes were surrounded by crow's feet and had sunk a little into their sockets the way an old man's do. His cheeks and jaw were clouded in dull gray stubble no matter how recently he'd shaved. His shoulders were thin and slightly hunched from decades of slouching behind the wheel. His clothes were not silk or linen or new. He looked like his life, which had been much harder than the fare's, but had not broken him.

The fare noticed Darwahab looking at him in the mirror. Smoothly, as though that had been his intent, Darwahab inquired, "All right to play some music?"

"Absolutely."

Darwahab popped in his favorite tape. Favorite because it was the music he'd grown up with. And because it was a reliable test of his fares' attitudes, more than ever since the Israelis had blown up the World Trade Center and blamed it on the faithful.

At least half his American fares were surprised when their Egyptian-born cabbie played Egyptian music; they'd furrow their brows as they tried to decide whether it was annoying, or insulting, or blasphemy, or torture. "Would you please turn that"—they'd pause, as they searched for an adjective that wouldn't sound bigoted—"*music* off?"

Young fares would often think the music was cool. Some would ask if he'd ever heard Dead Can Dance. Or Led Zeppelin's "Kashmir." "Rock the Casbah," maybe?

This fare was attentive as "Nar" wound its way out of the cab's speakers, the singer's mournful yearning riding the sensual syncopated pulse of an ancient, un-rocked casbah. This fare broke out in a small satisfied grin, closed his eyes, and began nodding his leonine head to the beat. When the song ended, this fare gave Darwahab a thumbs-up.

"You liked it," Darwahab said, less a question than a careful stating of interesting data.

"Who wouldn't," the fare wondered, bouncing an index finger in time to the next tune. "This the same singer?"

Yes it was. This tape was a collection of Abdel Harim Hafez hits, Darwahab explained, a big star, huge star, back home when he was a kid. Radio, movies, everything.

"Elvis," the fare said.

Darwahab shook his head. "Sinatra."

The fare acknowledged the distinction with an appreciative grunt, and asked where home was. Darwahab told him. Turned out the fare had been to Egypt four, five times. In fact, he'd gotten his shirt in Alexandria.

15

"Yes, of course." Darwahab nodded, pleased. "I spotted that immediately."

The conversation took off. Darwahab did most of the talking, prompted by the fare.

The fare never asked the first question most did: When and why did you come to America? This fare wanted to know about Darwahab's boyhood and teen years. What Cairo had seemed like to him then, what his favorite things about that city had been.

Darwahab was describing his first time behind the wheel of his uncle's taxi, in 1960. A pre-war Renault whose doors were attached to the frame by leather hinges . . .

They arrived at the fare's destination, a leafy one-way street on the Near North Side, a few blocks in from Lincoln Park.

Most of the block was lined with townhouses. At the center of the block, at the fare's address, was a freestanding home, wide as three townhouses. Tall hedges blocked the ground floor from view. Soaring above the hedges was a wonderment of a building, a collection of simple rectangular shapes jammed together in some complicated modern way, but Darwahab didn't hate it.

The fare tipped well, wished him *Salaam aleikum*, and got out.

"Wait, wait," Darwahab insisted. "One moment." He yanked the cassette out of the dash and handed it out his window. "For you."

Touched, the fare held his hands up, protesting, "That's very kind, but I can't take your only copy."

"This tape I can find in a dozen shops, and my grandson can steal it off the Web. You must. Please."

The fare accepted the cassette and shook Darwahab's hand. "Thank y—"

A hedge behind him broke with a loud *crack* as a man who'd

been hiding behind it pushed his way through, tripped, yelling "GWWWAAAHHH!" as he stumbled across the pavement and banged into the taxi's rear fender. "Fuck shit," he muttered, then levered himself upright and raised his free hand, the one holding a gun. "Don't move," he hissed, trying to be forceful without getting loud enough to alarm the neighbors.

The fare didn't move. Neither did Darwahab.

The mugger was Hispanic, young, with a shaved head. Stupid little beard dangling off the tip of his chin. Black sleeveless T-shirt. Wrapped around his left arm and crawling up his neck was a tattoo of a green and red snake. His eyes were glassy and his hands were way past trembling, they were vibrating. The last time Darwahab had seen a kid that high was two years ago, when he'd made the mistake of driving a crackhead to the ER, running red lights in a failed attempt to get there before the kid puked, all over the passenger-side window, which of course dripped down inside the door.

"Your wallet!" the mugger shriek-whispered.

"You got it," the fare assured him, pulling the wallet out and offering it.

Wildly nervous, the mugger reached for the wallet as if it were a real snake. When he got close enough to touch the wallet, his hand twitched, flinched away. Embarrassed, he grabbed the wallet with a sudden sharp swipe and the gun went off, a muzzle flash bright as fireworks and a bang that sounded like a cannon to Darwahab as the fare sagged against the front fender and fell onto his back, clutching his midsection and groaning.

The mugger moaned "Shit," frantic with dismay, about to cry. He leaned toward the fare as if about to beg forgiveness. Then Darwahab saw the mugger's expression change to anger, blame, rage at the old fuck who'd done this to him.

The mugger put two more slugs into the fare. He pointed the gun at Darwahab and yelled "Out!"

Before Darwahab could move, the mugger yanked open his door, grabbed him by the collar and dragged him off the seat. Darwahab clawed at the mugger's arm, but the guy flung him to the ground and shoved the gun in his face.

Darwahab closed his eyes.

A couple of days later he heard the taxi door slam. The cab being put into gear. He opened his eyes and saw his taxi screech down the street, bald tires smoking. The tires didn't blow out and kill the bastard in a fiery crash.

Darwahab, dimly aware of a sharp ache flaring in his elbow, crawled to the fare. He took the man's face in his hands. It was pale, slack, and now looked much older than Darwahab's. The rear left side of the skull being missing didn't help any.

THREE

The Cubs went into extra innings, so Doonie, without asking Mark, notified Squad they were going on meal break.

Mark was fine with that. He could do with a half-hour of baseball decompression. He still let himself get pissed off at stuff his crafty old partner shrugged off. Not real pissed off. But still. Mark needed to, as Doonie advised, "Stay more disin-volved."

Detectives Mark Bergman and John Dunegan had wasted the last hour trying to reason, cajole, shame, flirt, and bribe Ms. June Dockyer into not recanting her claim she could ID the perp in a fatal hit-and-run.

Last night, a little after eleven, an SUV had hit a fifteen-year-old who was out skateboarding in black clothes. Ms. June Dockyer, walking home from a friend's apartment, had been about twenty feet away, looking straight at it. She began to give a statement to the cops at the scene. But upon figuring out that being a witness would impose unacceptable uncertainties on her busy schedule, the high-octane young commodities broker trainee realized she hadn't actually gotten a clear look at the driver. By tonight Ms. June Dockyer had gone into such deep, delayed-reaction shock over the whole horrible nightmare she was not even sure any more what color the black Explorer had been, if it was in fact an Explorer.

Ms. June Dockyer was, however, happy to let the detectives sit in her Ikea-cheerful studio apartment and beg, for as long as they cared to. Mainly because the younger cop charted well into the hottie zone. Thirtyish. Good-looking. Not model good-looking, intelligent good-looking. With observant, instantly intimate gray eyes. Long jaw. Fair skin contrasting with stark black eyebrows and hair, which was kind of longish, un-cop-like. And he was well-spoken in a sophisticated, un-cop-like way. But he had that very cop-like physical thing, that . . . he could do violence.

The young cop was the reason Ms. June Dockyer had told them the only convenient time to speak would be nine p.m. at her place.

Eventually the detectives played their trump, made her look at photos of the victim. Goofy teen snapshots. Heartbreakers, considering.

Ms. June Dockyer was touched, but remained resolute in her devotion to the truth, which was that she'd been in shock when she'd given her initial statement at the scene. She could not in truth identify anyone or anything.

Okay, Mark thought, as the pretty-but-pinched sorority-trained blonde continued to stonewall on the ID and assess him as a potential acquisition, *Nothing else is gonna work. This won't either. But here goes.*

He glanced at the American Ballet Theater poster hanging in Ms. June Dockyer's breakfast nook and asked, "You catch their new *Bayadère* last spring?"

Ms. June Dockyer shrugged and shook her head; cute, pouty.

Doonie recognized his cue, stood up, and asked could he please use the facilities.

"Of course," Ms. June Dockyer told him, though she didn't exactly hide her dismay at having to disinfect the toilet once this paunchy, rumpled, low-rent, beer-breath, nicotine-stained, fiftyish Cro-Magnon had been in contact with it.

She focused on the hottie. "You like ballet," she said to Mark, taking care to sound intrigued and not surprised.

"My college roommate is a lighting designer. His first couple of pro gigs were dance concerts; I went, just to show the flag, but, holy shit, some of them turned out to be cool. Hey, pound for pound, ballerinas are the best-conditioned jocks I've met."

He's a cop who's met ballerinas.

Mark saw that one register. He leaned forward a touch and said, quietly, just between the two of them, "He's resident designer for ABT now. Next time they're in town I should be able to score some house seats, and get us backstage."

" 'Should be'?"

Mark gave an ambiguous shrug.

A shrewd grin from Ms. June Dockyer. "Detective, are you attempting to suborn perjury?"

"Never. But I have been known to try to suborn truthfulness." Friendly, frank, playful.

Ms. June Dockyer took a moment to study her options. "The ABT won't be back till next year. Maybe we should discuss this sooner, like, this weekend . . . Dinner?" Friendly, frank, businesslike.

"The deal is, I can't have a social relationship with a witness until the trial is over. Not that these cases go to trial that often—they usually get pled out."

No sale. Ms. June Dockyer stood up. "Good night, Detective."

Mark stood and handed her his card. "Just in case—"

Ms. June Dockyer ripped the card in half and purred, "Fuck off."

The toilet flushed.

Doonie waited till they were back in the car to burst out laughing. He socked Mark in the shoulder to make him feel better.

"Fifteen-year-old kid gets splattered and she can't be

inconvenienced to nail the fuck," Mark muttered, annoyed he let himself get annoyed. Amnesiacs were as common as donuts.

"Shoulda said yes for this weekend, man. She was warm 'n wet."

Mark looked at Doonie. "If she'd have stood up, I'd have treated her to the ballet and a good meal, then taken her home, shook her hand, and thanked her for a pleasant vehicular homicide conviction."

Doonie was appalled. "You ain't curious about lizard sex?"

"Wonder how the Cubs did," Mark said and tuned into 'GN.

So, what with a tenth inning coming up and Wrigley six blocks away, Mark, who rarely took so much as a cup of coffee on the cuff, was fine with badging their way in and visiting the press box. Doonie always had a couple of sportswriter pals who were glad to soak up Homicide gossip and invite the detectives to help themselves to food and beers. Which was another thing Mark liked about dining at the press box; beer was the hardest drink Doonie would be able to get his hands on for free.

Cubs reliever Nick Lettweiler got through the top of the tenth without giving up a hit, much to the surprise of Doonie, the sportswriters, and most of the thirty-some-odd-thousand fans.

Not Mark. Victory was miniscule but his. He nudged Doonie. "Told you Lettweiler was settling down."

"Yeah," Doonie nodded sagely. "He's the perfect Cub—stinks the joint out till he's about to get sent down, then pitches great just long enough so they'll keep him around to stink some more."

"Yeah? Season bet: I say Lettweiler finishes the year with an ERA under six-point-oh," Mark deadpanned.

"Too easy taking your money. No fun." Doonie went to get a refill.

Leading off the tenth for the Cubs was a thirty-nine-year-old fading slugger with bad knees, who'd spent most of the season on the DL and had yet to hit his weight since being acquired last fall to boost an alleged pennant drive. And yet Mark's mood was improving, just being here. The mystery of baseball.

The batter dug in. The pitcher went into his windup. Mark's radio squawked.

Mark keyed the mike and said "Bergman" just as the seven-mil-a-year power cripple poked a curveball into right for an opposite-field single, the first pitch all year he hadn't tried to pull, so Mark was drowned out by the delirious roar of the happily surprised crowd.

"Bergman," he repeated, louder, as the organist started playing cavalry calls and the crowd screamed *Charge!*

"Enjoying dinner?" the dispatcher asked.

"We're at a hot dog stand," Mark explained. "Who's dead?"

The sportswriters loved that one.

FOUR

They'd almost gotten all the way out of their car when a uniformed cop urgently informed them, "The vic is a Wilson Willetts, famous architect or something."

No shit, Mark thought. He shot a look at Doonie. "Gonna be a circus night."

The uni nodded. "Looie ordered us to lock both corners. Bodies, brass, and media liaison are on the way."

Doonie leaned down, scoped the corpse. "Never heard of him."

Mark joined Doonie. "Pro job?" Re the head wound.

"Messy. If it's pro, it's amateur pro."

Down at the corner a cop was having his first argument with the first media van that would try to force its way onto the one-lane residential street. The first juddering eggbeater thud of an approaching news chopper could be heard.

"It was a mugging gone bad," the uni eagerly informed the detectives. They straightened up, looked at him. "Got a witness, was here for the whole thing, cabbie who dropped the victim off."

The genius pointed to an old guy perched on the rear seat of a squad car, the door open, his legs outside the car. Ignoring a paramedic begging to treat him. The old guy was cradling a bloody elbow, rocking gently and fingering beads. Studying Mark and Doonie.

★ ★ ★ ★ ★

While Doonie made the introductions and asked the opening questions, Mark read the cabbie. Middle Eastern, small, kind of shabby. Not that old; had a geezer-before-his-time quality. Quietly distraught—less about himself than about Willetts. Tough geezer. In shock but ready to suck it up. Not interested in having his torn-up elbow bandaged before he took their questions. Good witness. Determined witness. Let's hear it for revenge.

These were the two men who would have to catch the killer. Have to.

Naguib Darwahab needed to be certain they *knew* what happened, exactly, all the details, and soon as he started talking he realized he'd never get them to *know* if he had to rely on words, let alone English. So Darwahab acted it out, all of it.

Darwahab had them park a squad car exactly where his cab had been. He stood on the exact spot where the fare was standing when Darwahab handed him the cassette.

He showed them how the crackhead stumbled out of the hedge, then straightened up and pointed the gun.

Darwahab described the crackhead in detail. His looks, tattoo, clothing. And the crackhead's frantic, slippery mood. And the gun, a revolver, with a four-inch barrel.

The older detective asked if he was sure the snake tattoo was on the left arm.

Darwahab held up his left arm and pointed to it. Yes, I can tell which arm is the left. The older cop signaled an apology and gestured for him to continue.

Darwahab described the shaky grab at the wallet and the first shot, an accident, absolutely, then how the crackhead suddenly hated the fare, stood over him, stuck out his arm and shot again, on purpose, then again, holding the gun in both hands, bang.

Then he pointed the gun at me and yelled—

The young detective, the one with the name that may have been Jewish, wanted to confirm the killer held the gun with both hands for the third shot.

Yes, Darwahab explained yet again, I was sitting in my cab, right here, I saw everything, tattoo on the left arm, third shot with two hands, just so.

Darwahab acted it out again. Just so.

That shot was to the head?

Darwahab nodded. A good point, he'd forgotten to specify which shot hit where. The young cop gestured for him to continue.

Darwahab showed them how the crackhead dragged him out of the car, a wild beast. The cabbie pantomimed how he'd scratched the crackhead's arm—the left arm, the one with the snake. Scratched across here—indicating the biceps—with this hand. Holding up his left hand. Identifying the limbs firmly, defying any dispute: his left arm, my left hand.

The young detective glanced at an evidence tech, who nodded. *Yes I'll get a tissue scraping.*

Darwahab lay down on the pavement, demonstrating how he'd landed on his elbow so hard it tore half the sleeve of his jacket, when the crackhead threw him down . . . and pointed the gun at his face, just so. Darwahab closed his eyes. Relived the wait for the bullet. Relived the sounds of the crackhead stealing his taxi and fleeing.

Darwahab opened his eyes. The young cop helped him up. Darwahab started to tell how the first thing he'd done after that was crawl over there, to *him*—Darwahab pointed to the corpse.

An evidence tech holding a camera was standing next to the body but wasn't taking any pictures; she was watching Darwahab. So were other techs, unis, and paramedics. And a small delegation of stern-looking senior officers, to whose arrival Darwahab had been oblivious.

Darwahab looked around at the circle of cops watching him.

"Thank you, Mr. Darwahab," the younger detective said, with respect. "Let's take care of that elbow."

Darwahab shook his head and gestured, Not yet.

He went to the evidence tech with the camera, a young woman wearing a blue jumpsuit and serious glasses. Darwahab quietly instructed her, "You must be certain to take a picture of that."

He pointed to Wilson Willetts' bloody hands, which were clutching the Abdel Harim Hafez *Classic Hits* cassette.

Then Darwahab turned to the detectives and told them, "After we see to my elbow you must bring me some coffee and show me the mug shots."

FIVE

Local news dickwads interrupted Letterman's monologue. Annoying. Wilson Willetts got shot by a mugger. Like she couldn't wait till tomorrow to find that out. And like even tomorrow it'd have squat to do with the price of April pork bellies.

Ms. June Dockyer clicked to Leno. The NBC dickwads had also gone live to the dead architect. She was about to press GUIDE, see if she could find a *South Park* or *SNL* rerun, but the dickwad news flash stopped her cold.

It was a grainy, telephoto shot in bad light—reporter on the scene explained/bitched how the police wouldn't let the press within a half-block of the crime scene—but there they were. A trio of executive cops—the gold braid decorating the brims of their hats was heavy enough to see in a long shot in the dark, and maybe show up on satellite photos—were huddling with a couple of plainclothes cops. She recognized the plainclothes guys right away, even though they were mostly in silhouette: the hottie and the Cro-Magnon.

A uniformed cop intruded on the huddle, said something and left. One of the braid hats nodded at Bergman and What's-His-Name. The detectives walked away as if they had something important to do.

Shit. He meets ballerinas and gets TV-sized murders. Maybe she should fish the pieces of his card out of the trash . . .

Nah. No need. He's interested. Clearly. So there's no need to call him. No need to testify. No way this future futures broker is going to

28

overbid on Detective Bergman. It's not like he's even close to being marriage material.

SIX

There wasn't much to brief the brass on; they'd seen most of Darwahab's performance. The brass needed to hear an APB had gone out on the taxi and someone had gotten on the horn to Gang Crimes to see if Snake Boy's description rang any bells. In Deputy Superintendent Marcus' opinion, half of Snake Boy's neighborhood would be calling in leads. Thank fucking Christ this one wasn't going to be hard to clear.

The media liaison officer, Commander Riles, suggested the immediate problem was the press statement. The hyenas needed to be fed, right now. The thing was to not let them badger Marcus into giving out details or confirming speculations. The hyenas were gonna be more rabid and specific than usual because tapes of Darwahab's performance were already on the air. The choppers hadn't gotten any usable footage because the trees blocked their view. But videocam-armed neighbors shooting from their porches and windows had taped Darwahab and were already e-mailing and uploading copies—

A uni broke in with the news the taxi had been found. Abandoned.

Mark and Doonie got back to work.

Cubs won, 5-4, in eleven.

"Fuckin' omen," Doonie predicted. They were tear-assing southwest to where the cab had been found, on a side street off Cicero. "We're golden. Cubs win, we close this fucker tonight, tomorrow we're on TV—national TV. You believe the coverage this Willetts is drawing, like this was the second killing of Princess Di?"

"He designed the Central Fidelity building on Wacker," Mark explained. "The new media campus at Northwestern. A museum in France. Christ knows what else."

"Central Fidelity building is huge," Doonie conceded. Playing the dumb Mick was Doonie's art form.

"Wouldn't get your hopes up about TV, though," Mark teased. "Don't think we're gonna impress anybody, clearing a no-brainer."

"We're golden," Doonie insisted with cosmic gravity. "In all areas. If a bum like Lettweiler can go two perfect innings and get the win . . ."

A third-generation Sox fan, Doonie preferred riding with a partner who was stuck loving the Cubs. More entertaining.

Darwahab's taxi had been dumped at the south fringe of Austin, an ongoing disaster of a ghetto, perhaps the only Chicago neighborhood that hadn't felt a drop of the money shower that drenched the city during the nineties.

No designer town homes on this block. Just some sorry brownstones with sagging front steps, and a couple of crumbling brick four-story walk-ups, punctuated by empty lots, on both sides of the street. The one tree on the block wished it was dead and was working on it. The cab was parked by a rubble-strewn moonscape at the corner.

Eleventh District unis were canvassing the block. More amnesiacs. No one saw the cab arrive or anyone get out of it, despite the fact it was probably the only licensed taxi to risk this block in living memory.

Beat patrols were cruising the area, stopping to talk with everyone on the street, checking for green and red rattlesnake sightings. No results.

Following procedure, the unis had given the cab's interior only a quick look, leaving it as pristine as possible for the detectives and techs.

Mark and Doonie pulled on the gloves. Doonie opened the driver's side door. Ten seconds later he found, on the floor alongside the driver's seat, a matchbook.

He looked at it. Handed it to Mark.

The matchbook was pink with black lettering. It said THE GOLDEN DOOR MOTEL.

The address put it less than a mile from here.

Doonie pointed to the word GOLDEN. He looked at Mark and intoned, "Lottery tickets."

The Golden Door Motel was on Cicero Avenue near Roosevelt Road, at the cusp of the Austin and Cicero neighborhoods, of black and brown.

The motel was late-sixties vintage, two stories high, facade of glazed brick that had once been a color. Twenty-two rooms. L-shaped parking lot. Run-down but scrubbed. The door to the Golden Door's office was pink but the doorframe had been slathered with metallic gold paint.

Chatusiphithak Nomsilp, the owner, was at the desk. He had a Thai accent, wary eyes, a smooth fortyish face set in a neutral expression that was just short of anesthetized, and a fondness for precision.

He told the cops his wife, Mrs. Nomsilp, had been at the desk when the Hispanic guy with a shaved head and the snake tat checked in. At 4:32 p.m. Oscar Lopez. Cash. Brown 1991 Chevelle. Room Eleven.

Nomsilp had been at the desk since 7:33 p.m. Didn't know if Mr. Lopez went out; his car was here the whole time. But at 11:36 p.m. Nomsilp saw Lopez in the parking lot, opening the trunk of his brown 1991 Chevelle—rusty, broken shock absorbers, he don't take care of it. It's parked over there by Room Eight—don't know why—then he went round the corner to where his Room Eleven is. No, you can't see from here—ground floor around to the right, last unit on the end. You have to go outside to see from here.

Mark sneaked a look. The lights were on in Eleven and music was coming from the room.

While Doonie radioed for backup Mark called Room Ten, the room next to the suspect's.

Room Ten was registered to an Elizabeth Hackenmeyer. Room Ten was dark and Ms. Hackenmeyer's truck wasn't in the lot, so she was probably out despite the hour. Nomsilp hadn't seen Ms. Hackenmeyer drive away, but that didn't mean she hadn't; Nomsilp pointed at the computer on his desk and explained he was taking an online course. Tax preparation. Very interesting.

Mark let the phone ring eight times. No answer. So it was a good bet there was no one in Room Ten right now. And the room directly above the suspect's, Eighteen, was vacant. So all that was left was to get the backups in place and assure Nomsilp the city would pay to repair Room Eleven's door and any other damage.

They waited, hoping maybe the suspect would fall asleep.

A little after two a.m. the lights were still on and the music was still going.

A *Chronicle* reporter named Bob Gilkey showed up. Gilkey had been monitoring scanner chatter. Drove by to see what was up. First thing he asked was if this had anything to do with Willetts.

Drug bust, Mark informed the reporter. Promised him an exclusive if he'd stay out on the street in a cop car with the

Nomsilps and keep quiet till this was over.

With the reporter temporarily stowed, Mark, Doonie, and the entire chain of command agreed right now was the time to go in, before other hyenas caught on, the media vans showed up, and the suspect turned on his TV and discovered he was a celebrity.

In fact the TV was on, and the boom box was playing (radio, because the CD was fucked), and Meelo was out cold on the bed, 'cause he had to smoke enough dope to take his mind off his burned hands, Oscar's fault, 'cause Oscar didn't think of everything after all, didn't leave no aspirins in case of an accident like this that could happen to anybody . . . Meelo had just drifted from marijuana-float reverie into dead sleep when a crashing noise jolted him upright and terror juice lit up his nervous system and he went straight from unconscious to flung-through-the-windshield awake and crazed screaming cop animals with guns were about to shoot him then someone tried to tear his arms out and somehow he was down on the floor hard with his hands cuffed behind him. A voice was reciting something Meelo wasn't listening to or making sense of until he heard that "Right to an attorney" movie cop shit—suddenly Meelo whimpered and went rigid—he thought he had been shot. Because his pants were warm and wet. Front and back.

Mark was Mirandizing when the stinks from the suspect's double squirt began to perfume Room Eleven. Several cops groaned. Mark had one of those moments where he thought, *I turned down a scholarship to grad school.*

What he said was, "I love my job."

"Good," Doonie said, "you put him in the shower."

Mark hauled Snake Boy to his feet and handed him to a couple of unis. One almost mouthed off but a hard look from

Mark made the uni decide to lodge his complaint elsewhere, so the uni glared at Snake Boy and snarled, "Tough guy."

The kid began trembling, sure he was about to be beaten to death, or worse.

"Don't worry, Oscar, it's just a shower, you're not gonna get Louima'd," Mark assured him.

"I'm not Oscar."

"You were when you signed the register."

"Oscar made me do that," the kid protested.

"Can you two chat later?" Doonie pleaded.

"What's your real name?" Mark asked the kid.

"Emilio, Emilio Jesus Garcia, I swear."

Mark nodded to the cops and they marched Emilio Jesus Garcia into the bathroom, holding him at arm's length.

Evidence techs arrived. Mark told them to get the suspect's jeans and go through the pockets.

"Hey," Doonie said. He showed Mark the gun he'd just found under a pillow on the bed.

Gagging noises from the bathroom.

The gun was a 9mm automatic. Mark and Doonie traded a look. Maybe Darwahab got it wrong about the shooter using a revolver. They both doubted it.

Doonie sniffed the barrel. Shook his head. Hadn't been fired recently.

The shower was turned on. There was a sharp yelp, then Garcia's plaintive "Fuckin' freezing, man!" followed by a "Shut the fuck up!" from a cop.

Mark and Doonie gave the room a quick toss. No other weapons.

The tech brought Mark a wallet and keys. Mark pulled a driver's license out of the wallet. Emilio Jesus Garcia.

While paramedics wrapped Emilio Jesus Garcia in a blanket and treated his burns, Mark and Doonie went out to the

Chevelle. In the trunk, under a greasy, mildewed swatch of carpet, they found a revolver. Four-inch barrel. Recently used.

And a wallet. It was made of soft, supple, burgundy-colored leather. Inside, one corner was stamped with a logo that identified the maker as GONCALVES/LISBOA. A driver's license and several weapons-grade credit cards identified the owner as Wilson Willetts.

SEVEN

"Murder?" Meelo was stunned, confused. An act lots of perps were good at. "You busted me for *murder?"*

"Uh-huh." Mark nodded. "Remember when we met, I was kneeling on your back, saying, 'You're under arrest for the murder of Wilson Willetts'?"

Meelo shook his head. Then hastily added, "I ain't calling you a liar. I just . . ." He shrugged helplessly. Skinny, scared, confused. Wearing some old sweats of Doonie's, which looked even larger on him than the blanket had. Seemed younger than his age, twenty. Not a street-hard kid, practiced at shooting architects.

Doonie tapped a file on the table in front of him. They were in an interrogation room in Area 3, where he and Mark worked. "You got a nothing sheet, Meelo." On the ride over, the kid had given up his nickname.

Doonie shook his head; the disappointed but empathetic uncle. "One Andy Hardy purse snatch, didn't even buy you time. No gang affiliations. No assaults, not a single weapons charge . . . Forget murder, this was your first armed robbery, wasn't it?"

Meelo shook his head. "No, no, I didn't do none a that shit, never."

"Till tonight," Mark suggested.

"No!"

"It's your first time, you're nervous, this isn't really your

37

thing—and you're a little too high, right? Fucked up and oh shit, this is not as easy as I expected. You're way jumpy about getting in this guy's face with a gun because you're basically a good guy, and . . ." Mark let it hang there a moment, "Bang . . . That first shot, it's like the gun had a mind of its own."

"No no no no, man, I never left the room all night, I-I-I-I . . ." He stammered to a halt, unable to make any more words.

"Can you prove you never left the room?" Mark asked.

Meelo desperately pondered that one. Finally gave one helpless shake of the head, No.

Mark and Doonie traded a glance. The kid was still doped up, and terrified, and not a Mensa candidate to begin with.

"Take your time," Uncle Doonie told him. "Drink your soda."

Meelo dutifully picked up the can of Diet Fresca and sipped.

"Excuse me," Mark asked, "can I see your arm? The left one?"

Mark went to Meelo, gently took his wrist and inspected the kid's left biceps. Then the right one. No scratches on either arm.

Mark and Doonie traded another look. Darwahab might have only imagined he scratched the perp. Must have. In any case, the forensics on the tissue scraping from under the cabbie's fingernails would settle that question in a couple of weeks.

"All right, Meelo," Mark coaxed, "we want to hear your story, all of it. Take your time, don't leave anything out, just tell the truth. Everything. From the beginning."

Meelo gazed worriedly at the two cops for a long moment. "Like, from, when like I was born?" Not smart-mouthing. He really wanted to know.

"From when you checked into the motel, at 4:32 p.m."

"I go to this Golden Door, just like Oscar tells me."

"Who's Oscar Lopez and why'd he make you use his name?"

Meelo thought about telling, then nervously shook his head.

"He'd kill me, man, kill me."

"Why?"

Meelo wouldn't say.

Mark and Doonie held a brief telepathic debate about which way to go here. Doonie gave Mark an imperceptible nod, indicating for Mark to take one more shot at it before Uncle Doonie morphed into Godzilla Doonie.

"Meelo, we have a witness who described you as the shooter, and a witness who saw you outside the motel, putting something in the trunk of your car after eleven p.m. Both of them will ID you in a lineup. Detective Dunegan and I will bring their statements, and the victim's wallet, which we found in your car, along with a gun, which I'm betting ballistics are gonna show was the murder weapon, we will bring all this to the State's Attorney and you will be indicted for first degree murder. Unless you tell us what really happened. All of it."

The ball of icy slush that had been in Meelo's gut all night began to churn and grow and he thought maybe it was gonna gush out his nose and ears and explode and kill him. He couldn't decide which he was more scared of, Oscar or going to the joint for fucking ever.

As the kid sat there, stalling, Uncle Doonie stared holes in him and began to take deeper and sharper breaths, building up to his transformation into Godzilla Doonie . . .

No point. Meelo was too preoccupied to notice.

Meelo was having deep thoughts. There was only one way to make sense of all this. Oscar had framed him. Fucking shit.

Meelo started talking, certain it would make sense to the cops too.

EIGHT

Mark was too tired to eat. Not hungry anyway. And even if he were, the idea of loading his stomach right before crawling into the sack for what he hoped would be total stone-cold sleep . . .

"C'mawn," Doonie nagged. "We ain't ate shit 'cept coffee and vending crap since the top of the tenth at Wrigley last night. Just stop over for a bite on your way home."

Mark's way home was north; Doonie lived southwest, in Beverly, at the other end of the city.

"You ain't seen Phyl and the animals for weeks. They all miss ya. 'Specially the little one," Doonie added, in a tone that combined flattery and guilt.

Mark shrugged, surrendering. He was so weary-dense it had taken till now for him to realize what this was about: Doonie was too exhausted to drive himself home. But Doonie would do it anyway, and maybe wrap himself around a phone pole, before he'd ask for a ride.

Mark could respect that. Which made him wonder if he'd been on the job too long, after only eight years.

"Yeah, okay," Mark said, careful not to come right out and offer to drive.

They'd just knocked off. Been awake about thirty hours. Been on the clock for most of it.

Meelo's story had been nearly as long, detailed, and plausible as the Warren Report. Though, Mark conceded, Meelo's story

40

featured a meandering, stoned, passionate sincerity that beat shit out of mid-1960s Federal prose.

Meelo met Oscar about three months ago. Older dude, like thirty-five, forty. From out of town, wouldn't say where. Meelo thought maybe Miami—Oscar's accent wasn't exactly *cubano* but he had a style. Straight dark hair. Silver streaks coming in on the side of his head. Moustache—no, goatee—flat, neat goatee . . . Oscar is maybe couple inches shorter than Meelo, like five-nine.

They meet 'cause this amazing beautiful really high-class whore gets the hots for Meelo, who is spare-changing tourists down near the Water Tower, being cool, not doing nothing wrong or bothering nobody, when this woman, like she's dressed like she belongs on Michigan Avenue and she ain't streetwalking so there's no way he can even tell she's a whore, she goes in her wallet then smiles and tells Meelo he's a lucky man, smallest thing she got's a five.

Latina, but like does the American accent perfeck. Long dark brown hair, like way down, middle of her back. She gives Meelo the five and talks. Just stands there and talks. Asks his name. Tells hers. Heather. Heather, but she's definitely Latina. And Heather asks what kinda work he does, maybe she can hook him up, and he tells her about his bad luck with jobs so far, and she asks if he's hungry, she's in town for some convention so she can buy him dinner and put it on her company card. Says she's gonna write him on her expense thing as a potential Chicago recruit, and she laughs. She had this really sexy laugh. She had the hots for Meelo like he couldn't believe.

They go to her hotel—that bigass Sheraton down on the river by the bridge—its got like what, ten restaurants? But they get there and there's like a million people in the lobby and Heather's, man, all the restaurants gonna be crowded and noisy, bad as the lobby—let's get room service.

So they go up to like, some floor, she's got this cushy room got shit in it like, oh man, y'know? And they start looking at this menu but they never get to order anything because, 'cause Heather can't wait . . .

So, they're on this super king-size bed got these blankets that you sink into them like he does not know what, oh man, and they're swapping spit just getting started, taking their time, and Heather gets on top, she's like sitting on Meelo and looks down at him and pulls off her sweater and she hasn't got a killer set just average, but they're in this incredible shiny bra, like Meelo knows this is the most expensive bra he's ever—

That's when the electric lock thing goes clunk and the door opens and this serious-looking dude walks in, suit and tie, and this little briefcase. And he's just standing there giving them the bad eye thing, man, and you just know.

But Meelo can't move 'cause Heather is on top of him with her average *chichas* out there in that big-money bra and she's not moving, she's just looking at the guy—who's y'know, Oscar—and finally she says like, "You're early."

And for a minute he just stands there like deciding if he's gonna kill both of them, but he takes out a bunch a hundred-dollar bills and throws them at her and waits. She grabs up the money and books.

Meelo asks if it's okay can he leave. The guy opens his jacket, shows Meelo a Nine and tells him don't move. Has these nasty eyes, black, him staring like that at you quiet is scarier than guys on the street waving a piece and yelling.

Dude asks, Meelo works for Delgado, don't he?

Meelo shakes his head.

Dude asks, He work for Luis One-Eye?—tell the truth, gonna find out anyway.

Meelo says he works sometimes at his uncle's laundromat, only job he's had lately.

The guy tells Meelo close his eyes and if he opens them he dies. Meelo closes his eyes. Hears the guy do something maybe in the closet, like he's checking if something's there.

Guy tells Meelo open his eyes. Nobody moves. Just looking at each other. Meelo says he's sorry, didn't know Heather was somebody's girlfriend.

Dude smiles and says forget it, Heather's just a *puta* with a college degree. Not Meelo's fault. Dude says sorry he got a little heavy just now, had to, business, you understand. Name is Oscar. Shakes Meelo's hand.

They go get a drink. Dinner. Oscar says Meelo's okay, Meelo handled himself okay back there, that fuckin' stupid thing at the hotel, that five-grand-a-day superwhore coulda got someone killed.

So here's what. Oscar's gonna check Meelo out. Oscar does business in Chicago, he can use somebody local, somebody can handle himself.

Meelo nods, doesn't say nothing. Never asks what the business is.

Oscar approves. Tells Meelo him not asking faggot questions shows he's got the *huevos.*

Three, four days later Meelo's coming out of this alley where he scores shit, off Homan near Humboldt Park, you know where that is? And shit, there's Oscar in this car, just, like who knows how he got there? Oscar's a *professional.* So Oscar's like, you got a car, man? And Meelo's, sure, my sister gave me her Chevelle, yeah, I got a car.

You got a piece?

Yeah, a .38, Meelo tells Oscar—but not about how he stole it off his uncle. (Hey, you gotta understand, Detectives, Meelo ain't never done no armed robbery, no gangbanging, you understand, none a that shit, swear to God he never shot the .38 at nobody, like, he was like this close to maybe pawning it for some dope, y'know?) But now Oscar's got this work for him. Needs a man to watch his back. With a gun. Man Oscar can trust, man who can keep his mouth shut not tell nobody nothing never.

So like maybe once a week Oscar's in town and Meelo does these jobs for him, which turn out like kinda easy, y'know, but mysterious? So you know this is the real shit.

Like Oscar goes in some fancy hotel or restaurant and Meelo has to hang outside, sometimes in his car but mostly just hang out on the street, and watch for Oscar to come out.

So when Oscar comes out—how long? Like maybe fifteen, twenty minutes most times, once it was like an hour but Oscar told Meelo up front, however long it takes, Meelo don't come in and look for him. Never. Like that's a sin, give away he's Oscar's secret backup, y'know?

No, Oscar never tells Meelo what he's doin', all these places he goes in. In this business each man only knows what he absolutely gotta. That's how you know this is *professional*. As if you couldn't tell right away from how Oscar does all his shit.

So like when Oscar comes out he gets in his car and Meelo waits to see no one's up Oscar's ass, then follows in his car just to make sure. And when Oscar's like walking it's the same, except they're walking not driving. Then they meet up and he gives Meelo fifty or a hundred, cash. And sometimes he gives a little extra, like some weed or coke, man, and it's always triple-XXX-primo, y'know? He says a man needs to get high, time to time. Thing is a *professional* knows just how much and just—bam—stops doin' up whatever shit he's doin' up, so he's never too wasted to do the fucking shit he has to, man. So they talk shit like that, Meelo and Oscar, then he don't see Oscar till the next time Oscar needs him.

How's he let Meelo know? Oh that's so cool, man, he gives Meelo this number to call in every day, like this phone service shit, and it says there's no message or there is, and if there is it's Oscar and he says where and when, y'know?

How does Meelo get from that to bein' in the motel?

Turns out all this other shit was like tests, see if Oscar can trust Meelo, and Meelo's perfeck, he only fucks up maybe once. So one night Oscar says let's go eat, this nice place, fancy food and these like awesome smooth old tequilas they're pounding down, straight, and Oscar tells Meelo he's ready for a big job, some serious money, he's shown Oscar something here. And Meelo says anything for you, man, and Oscar says there is one thing, like, today there were two other dudes on the street with shaved heads and for a second Oscar couldn't tell which one was Meelo, and in this business a second is like life or death, so how about Oscar treats him to a little tat or something, so one look and Oscar will always know it's Meelo got his back.

Hey no fucking problem, dude, and on the drive down to this little tat place they do a little blow, so like they're both in this real great mood when they get there. So Meelo is lookin' for a design maybe on his shoulder, but Oscar's all no, man, you want somethin' people can see, like Oscar's goofing far as the guy runs the store knows, but Oscar's like saying this to Meelo looking him right in the eye so Meelo knows this is them talking as *professionals,* which this big Anglo tat dude doesn't pick up on at all, just, like, awesome, triple-XXX primo cool.

So Meelo says how 'bout this snake, which was this snake thing that kinda goes around just the top of your arm here, and Oscar laughs and says snakes are the coolest oldest power symbol, but why you wanna settle for such a small one? Want women to think you're the small snake guy? And they're all laughing, even the big Anglo tat dude, and, man, next thing he's workin' on this shit starts here and goes to, well shit, look at this shit, am I the monster snake man or what?

Tat place was way the fuck south, man. Hammon', Hammon'

Indiana. Big tat dude's name was Ralph. Place was called Ralph's. Hadda go back three times, like in between doin' parts of the tat, like when the snake's just partway done. During which Meelo's sister's all up in his face, man, "You're stealing my money for that ugly tattoo, big ugly worm on your arm you sick little *pendejo.*"

But Meelo just tells his sister what Oscar told him to: The tat don't cost nothin', some gringa tat girl got a case on Meelo and is doin' this just to get at his real snake.

No, his sister don't believe him, fact she just laughs at him which works out perfeck: Meelo gets mad and walks out and didn't come home a few days so she didn't say nothing about it again.

Yeah, he lives with his sister. His mother died when they were little, and his father got bad lungs when Meelo was like fourteen, checks into County Hospital and dies. So Meelo and his sister lived with Tio Mannie for a while but Meelo's sister and Tio Mannie's new wife fuckin' hated each other. So soon's Meelo's sister was eighteen she got a job and with that and the government money Meelo got for being under eighteen with both folks dead, him and his sister got an apartment.

It's Angela. Angela Garcia . . . What was he telling you guys about before his sister Angela and her name and shit? Oh, right.

Like he gets the big snake tat, and Oscar's like, you are ready, Meelo, you are ready. You're gonna hole up in this motel and wait for me, I'm gonna show anytime between like eight that night and maybe noon tomorrow, I'm gonna show up with some serious product, then we just keep it safe a couple more hours, then this other dude's gonna come check it out and take it away.

And then, then Oscar is gonna pay Meelo ten thousand dollars. Cash.

Only thing, Meelo has to keep a serious eye on this other

dude while he's in the room. Can Meelo shoot? Like it ain't gonna go down like that, not one time in a million, but if this is like the million and one time, can Meelo shoot?

Fuck yeah he can shoot.

But Oscar has to check this out—Oscar don't take no chances, Oscar don't forget nothin'—well, except the aspirins—so last night they go to the landfill and shoot rats. Meelo don't—fuck, you know how quick those little fuckers are—Meelo don't hit one rat. But Oscar says Meelo shoots good enough to hit something big as a man standing right across from him, y'know?

Then Oscar squeezes Meelo's shoulder and says, only thing, you gonna be a *professional*, you need a pro piece. Something take a man down with one shot.

Grins and says I'm gonna trade you mine. Oscar takes Tio Mannie's lame old .38 outta Meelo's hand and gives him his Nine. His own gun. This like Glock, comes from, uh, y'know, like the Volkswagens, man.

Meelo can't even say thank you, he's workin' so hard not to cry, and Oscar just pats him on the cheek, um, kinda like his old man used to . . . Right there, like that minute, was like the only time in his life Meelo felt like he had a brother.

So, uh, next day he hooks up with Oscar, gets the motel money. Rents the room, goes and picks up the supplies and shit from Oscar, then back to the room, about seven, goes in and stays there just like he's told. Never left the fuckin' room, man, never, all night. Till you guys brought him here. And he didn't shoot nobody. In his whole fuckin' life.

No, nobody but Meelo never saw Oscar—hey, Meelo did everything perfeck, so a course nobody else never saw Oscar.

Right, 'cept Ralph the big Anglo tat dude. Ralph saw Oscar. That one time.

Why'd Meelo park his car over by Room Eight when he's in Eleven?

Oscar, man. Dude says at motels you always park three, four rooms away, so anybody tries to surprise you they go to the wrong room. That Oscar, there is nothin' he don't fuckin' think of . . . You gonna bust me for the drugs, man? They was all Oscar's stash.

Meelo talked for three hours and forty-nine minutes, yawned once, and nodded out, content the detectives were now clear on what really happened.

For a moment Doonie and Mark gazed at him enviously, then pushed back their chairs. Quietly, so he wouldn't wake up and talk some more.

They went through the preliminary forensics and field reports that had come in while they were in the room.

They checked on their witnesses. Darwahab and the Nom-silps had given preliminary IDs of Meelo from his booking photo; all three would come in tomorrow to view a lineup.

Mark dialed the alleged Oscar's alleged voicemail; got a recorded message saying the number was not currently in service.

Doonie found a number for Ralph's Body Ink in Hammond, Indiana; got a recorded message saying the number was not currently in service.

They made a list of those and the many other parts of Mee-lo's fantasy they'd have to run down.

They called his sister, Angela Garcia, and left a message on her machine.

They made appointments to interview Wilson Willetts' family and co-workers, to find out if there was anybody besides Meelo out to get him.

They got called into the squad room to catch a national news spot of Chicago's Superintendent of Police, Elvin Blivins, informing the press the prime suspect had been apprehended within hours of the crime. Charges would be filed soon as all the i's were dotted and t's crossed. Which the Superintendent expected would take place in the next twenty-four to forty-eight hours. Behind him on the podium Commander Riles, the press liaison maven, suppressed most of a wince.

Next they watched the first part of a longer story on Naguib Darwahab, featuring one of Willetts' neighbor's grainy home-video footage of the cabbie reenacting the crime for Chicago PD homicide detectives. The story cut to an interview in Darwahab's living room. Surrounded by three generations of his family (only the teenagers were delighted to be on camera), the old man gave stone-faced, monosyllabic answers—he'd been cautioned by the cops not to discuss details with the press. But Darwahab started to choke up when he described how Wilson Willetts died clutching the music cassette—Doonie turned the TV off and said, "Wonder who'll play us in Darwahab's movie of the fuckin' week."

They briefed Lieutenant Husak. A happy Lieutenant Husak. Downtown was pleased with the rapid results and great press.

Mark and Doonie's briefing made Husak even happier.

Paraffin test was positive. Emilio Jesus Garcia aka Meelo had fired a weapon in the past twenty-four hours. He says at rats. Cabbie says at Willetts.

Ballistics matched the lead in the victim to the .38 found in the trunk of Meelo's car. Gun was wiped down, no prints.

Same with the victim's wallet, also found in the suspect's trunk.

Driver's side of the taxi was also wiped, inside and out—not a single latent. But the cabbie puts Meelo in the cab.

Meelo says he never left the room. Motel owner says Meelo

was in the parking lot and opened the trunk of his car, approximately forty minutes after the murder.

"Slam dunk," Husak declared.

Doonie nodded. "We're golden."

Mark tried not to feel like an idiot.

They left Husak's office and got the paperwork started.

They bonked. Both of them were cross-eyed exhausted. And Doonie's back was stiffening up from the all-nighter crammed into that goddamn Steelcase interview room chair. They agreed to call it a day-and-a-half. Which is when Doonie started nagging Mark to come by for dinner, meaning Doonie was too tired to drive home, but couldn't admit it.

They left work about 5:30 p.m., which meant driving straight into the teeth of Chicago's rush hour, which in recent years had swollen to a Manhattanesque ugliness.

As they walked to their cars in Area 3's parking lot Doonie stopped and said, "Shit."

"What?"

Doonie grimaced, rubbed the small of his back. "Forgot, my tank's dry. I'm too fuckin' hungry to waste time stopping for gas—I'll ride with you. Phyl can drop me back in the morning."

"Makes sense to me," Mark said.

NINE

They'd been inching south on Ashland. Hadn't said a word since they got in the car half an hour ago, both men too tired to crank up a conversation.

Until, seemingly out of nowhere, Doonie informed Mark, "You're fuckin' nuts."

"Yeah," Mark agreed. He wasn't surprised Doonie knew what he'd been thinking about. "Forget the scratch on the biceps. Darwahab could have imagined it."

"Good bet, considering Meelo ain't scratched."

Reluctantly, Mark asked, "You think Meelo's bright enough to make up a story that size?"

"Drugs."

"You see Meelo being *professional* enough to remember to wipe down the cab, gun, and wallet—and get it right?"

"Adrenaline."

"Yeah . . . Not to mention, if you assume Meelo's telling the truth . . . The implications, just in dollars and personnel, are even more fuckin' nuts than I am."

"No shit," Doonie said. "Like the Superintendent told the world—one, two days more and we got this sucker nailed down. Don't worry, soon we're gonna be back working that hit-run."

They rode in silence another minute. Then Mark asked, "You think in the middle of freaking out, Meelo would use a two-hand grip and make sure the last slug was a head shot?"

Doonie shot Mark a sour look. He reclined his seat-back and

closed his eyes. Muttered, "Wake me if we ever get there."

Mark wondered if "there" referred to Doonie's house, or the point where the shooter's two-hand grip would have fuck-all to do with clearing this case.

Probably both. Doonie was kind of a poet.

Mark figured he'd save that observation for some time when he wanted to really piss Doonie off.

TEN

Most of the housing stock in Beverly was single-family homes, nicely maintained. Many of the owners were cops, firemen, and small businessmen. The majority ethnicity was Irish, the culture was Catholic, and the religion was the Cook County Democratic Party.

Castle Dunegan, as its mortgage-holder liked to call it, was slightly larger and spiffier than the typical Southside brick cottage-style home. When complimented, the mortgage-holder would shrug and claim the renovations had "fallen off the back of a truck." What that meant was Phyl's cousin's brother-in-law was a contractor who'd work at cost, because he knew the value of family, and of being owed favors by a veteran cop.

Mark, Doonie, and Phyl were alone at the big kitchen table.

Kieran, the nineteen-year-old, was having dinner at his girlfriend's house.

Seventeen-year-old Tom had gobbled his food and retreated to his room to resume his spiritual quest to reach and destroy the highest level of *MechWarrior* 4.

Patty, twelve-almost-thirteen, would stay at the table as long as Mark was there, but had been ordered by her fascist mom to bring a pie to her friend Noelie down the block, who was stuck at home with a leg she broke at the summer-league soccer championship last weekend.

Phyllis Dunegan was a tall, ruddy, robust woman whose

ancestors had obviously been visited by Vikings. Phyl was as generous as she was formidable. She ran a cheerful, well-organized household, maintained the healthiest garden on the block, was an office administrator for a Loop real estate broker, was vice president of the high school PTA, refereed the hormonal warfare between Doonie and two teenage sons, was raising a sweet, pretty pubescent daughter who was still as interested in soccer and science as in makeup, hosted more than her share of extended-family social events, and waited till she was done nagging Mark about not having dessert before she started nagging Mark about the latest very interesting girl she wanted him to meet.

Mark had been Doonie's partner three years, which meant he was an unofficial member of the family. Which meant he was official family property. Mark enjoyed how cheerfully the Dunegans barged in on each other's personal decisions. His own family was just as manipulative but pretended not to be, preferring to communicate via convoluted, surreptitious waves of tension.

Phyl had given Mark fair warning he had till age thirty to settle down. He was now thirty-one and not even slightly engaged. "She's just your type," Phyl informed him; a definitive statement whose veracity could not be challenged. "Drop-dead gorgeous, and brainy. A graduate student—in Philosophy."

"Ah, gibbim a break," Doonie groaned. Slurring a little.

Phyl arched an eyebrow at Doonie. He threw up his hands in apology for having forgotten his place, and retreated to the fridge in search of another beer. Phyl returned her attention to Mark.

"Would it kill you this once to say yes?"

Mark nodded.

"Look," Phyl reasoned, "you turned down my blueberry pie, you owe me this one."

"Your logic is flawless, but I am not," Mark confessed.

"How 'bout a little after-dinner shot," Doonie suggested, gesturing toward the den, where the whisky lived.

Mark shook his head. "It's a day past my bedtime."

"So have a few snorts and crash here tonight," Doonie urged.

Right. Stage Two of Doonie's plan: *get me to stay the night so I can drive him to work in the morning.* Mark shook his head. "Thanks, I gotta get home."

Mark stood, bent down to kiss Phyl and thank her for dinner.

"He's turning us both down for the same reason," Doonie confided to Phyl. "He's got some action lined up on the way home."

"Tonight," Mark sighed, "I'd have to find a woman who wouldn't mind me sleeping through it."

"See?" Phyl assured Mark, "you already know the secret of married sex."

"That's it," Doonie warned Phyl, "your old man dies and leaves you some money soon or I'm outta here."

As always, they walked Mark to his car and stood at the curb watching till he drove out of sight.

Mark's place, thanks to a small inheritance from his grandfather, was a one-bedroom condo on a high floor of a building just past the north end of Lakeshore Drive. Indoor heated parking, only way to get through a midwestern winter. Unobstructed view of the lake. Not enough closet space for a live-in girlfriend.

Mark dumped his mail on the coffee table. Played his messages; only interesting one was Carrie, she was dying to know about Willetts, there was gonna be trench warfare over who got the case, call late as he wanted, she'd come over. Mark considered it for a millisecond. Realized he'd barely pass the physical and surely flunk the verbal.

Mark peeled off his clothes, took a leak, glanced at his

toothbrush, and sagged into bed.

He got his stone-cold sleep, till a little before dawn, when an ambulance siren woke him just enough to start dreaming. He was at a body shop, found a black Explorer with a crumpled fender. Phyl wanted to fix him up with Heather. Every Explorer in the city had a crumpled fender. He was driving down Ashland, eyes closed, asleep at the wheel, traffic was flowing slow and smooth, and he tried to wake up, felt driving asleep should feel wrong but it didn't, traffic was flowing slow and smooth. Carrie was naked. He was aching-hard. And he had to piss. He resented having to decide which.

The phone rang, for real. No, it was his clock radio. No, it was both.

Good morning.

ELEVEN

Ralph's nose got stuck in the tote-bag zipper. Arthur assumed he'd pack the hands on either side of the head, but Ralph's head and luridly decorated hands were really big. Cutting the fingerprints off made no difference in volume. Only one hand could be squeezed in alongside the head. And with the other hand underneath the head, the nose stuck out too far to zip the bag shut.

Ralph's nose poking out of the tote should be the last stupid complication on a stupidly complicated job.

Arthur always booked hits through his agent. Never met with a client, or disclosed when or how the hit would happen. This control-freak client had demanded both.

Arthur refused.

The control-freak client backed off on meeting Arthur in person, and grudgingly agreed no pro would risk his life by giving a client prior knowledge of his plan. But the control-freak client did insist Willetts' death be an accident.

Arthur, through his agent, pointed out Willetts had no regular schedule—or any health problems, or dangerous hobbies—that would make an accident scenario feasible.

Arthur proposed a misdirection hit. The control-freak client agreed, on condition it was not just a random, unsolved killing. There had to be a fall guy. Willetts' death had to be a "closed book."

Arthur turned down the job.

The control-freak client persisted, offering a staggering fee.

Normally the agent never told the client and the shooter each other's names. Arthur told the agent, an old friend, that he wouldn't resume negotiations unless he knew who this control-freak client was and why the price was so much more than right. The agent thought that was, in this rare, suspiciously lucrative case, reasonable. He gave Arthur the control-freak client's name and motive.

Talks resumed. The control-freak client upped the already massive fee. Arthur agreed to set up a patsy and make Willetts' death a "closed book."

The final detail of closing that book was disposing of Ralph the tattoo artist. Ralph was the only witness who could confirm "Oscar's" existence and link Oscar to Meelo. So Ralph Garn, who was guilty of nothing worse than believing Sword & Sandal illustrations were humanity's finest artistic achievement, was dead.

One more corpse, one more chance for Arthur to get caught.

Arthur couldn't blame the client, though. He blamed syrah. The syrah was why Arthur, for the first time in his life, hadn't done the sensible thing and walked. Arthur, at forty-seven, was solvent enough to retire. But the upfront money from this job meant he'd been able to stop renting space at the winemaking co-op in Santa Maria and buy a sweet little vineyard/winery in the hills west of Paso, complete with a state-of-the-art German crusher and French steel tanks. And still have cash left over to put a winning bid on a couple of tons of Napa's most brilliant syrah grapes. (The Paso winery was planted in zinfandel, but Arthur would sell those grapes; his passion was Rhône wines.)

So here was Arthur wrapping Ralph's nose and the unzipped side of the bag with duct tape, God's handiest gift since fire. No end to its uses. Arthur wouldn't be surprised if the first men on Mars arrived packing an ample supply . . .

Get real. Duct tape on Mars? That was about as likely as him making a syrah that got served at the White House . . . Actually, he was going make wine that good. Why the hell else bother? . . . Okay then. New career goal. His syrah poured at a White House dinner. Why not. A man needs a dream.

Arthur put the tote in double garbage bags and taped them shut.

The garbage bag containing the tote containing Ralph's head and hands went into a dumpster outside a sausage factory outside Kankakee. Even if the garbage truck somehow missed next morning's scheduled pickup, this was a neighborhood that took no notice of primal odors.

The rest of Ralph (headless, hand-less, but handsomely inscribed—the tats covering his own body were done by other people, all of whom were better needle-jockeys than Ralph) was slit open to permit buoyant gases to escape, wrapped in a tarp, weighted, and deposited in a deep toxic pond southeast of Joliet.

The pond was in a fenced, restricted site—a marsh where runoff had gathered downhill of a munitions factory. The factory had done reasonably well during the Civil War, extremely well during World War One, phenomenally well during World War Two, Korea, and Vietnam, then had abruptly gone bankrupt in 1981, one week before losing a final appeal on an environmental judgment.

The marsh was now an official EPA Superfund site. Federal budget shortfalls after 2001 had resulted in A-list Superfund sites, scheduled for immediate cleanup, getting put on hold for ten to twenty years.

The marsh was a B-list site.

TWELVE

The news Mark woke up to was a radio reporter interviewing print reporter Bob Gilkey, who was touting his exclusive coverage of the hair-raising assault on the gunman's lair, which was on the front page of today's *Chronicle: The courage of those cops who went through that motel door was awesome, just awesome* . . .

Shit—Marta, the maid, had as usual switched the radio to AM. Mark switched it back to FM.

Simultaneously, Mark's answering machine took a phone call. It was from a local TV news reporter, asking what would be a convenient time and place for Mark and his partner to do a quick interview.

The phone rang again. This time the voice on the machine was from the Department's media wrangler, Commander Riles. Here's the deal: Mark and Doonie were too busy to make any comments to the press today, but that would have to change what with the *Chronicle* story playing them up big. Riles would set up a photo-op Q&A for sometime tomorrow or next day. Contact him ASAP, he needed to walk them through what they would and wouldn't say to the hyenas.

Phone rang again. Carrie. From her car, driving south on Sheridan, almost at Mark's place. Was he there? Did he mind if she stopped up?

Mark picked up the phone. Told her she was welcome to stop up, but he had to be out the door in thirty minutes, there would be no juice, coffee, or talking.

Assistant State's Attorney Carrie Eli said those terms were acceptable.

Mark got to Area 3 before Doonie but after Angela Garcia.

When Mark arrived there was a young Latina seated on the bench in the squad's waiting area. Mid-twenties. A little too hefty for what was probably her best plain black cardigan and slacks. Soft brown eyes, red-rimmed; more tears than sleep last night. Composed now. Fiercely. Hands gripped tight on her lap, nails of her right hand digging into the left.

Seated next to her was a gooey, penguin-shaped man Mark correctly assumed would be Meelo's attorney, a PD named Paul Obed. Aka the Prosecutor's Pocket Pal. What Obed lacked in trial skills he made up for in willingness to accept lousy plea bargains. Obed was the chill that went down defendants' spines when they heard the words "Public Defender."

Obed was about to stand and ask Mark if he remembered him. Obed started every conversation by asking if you remembered him. Was relieved and grateful if you did. Mark wondered if Obed started every lawyer-client conference by asking if the client remembered him.

Obed was gathering the energy to haul himself off the bench when the young woman sprang up and planted herself in front of Mark.

"I'm Angela Garcia. My brother Emilio didn't do this. He didn't kill anyone. He *couldn't*," she said, as if it were an unarguable truth, as if it were something a murder cop had never heard before.

She's here alone, Mark thought. *Boyfriend didn't come with. Not unusual. No family, though, which is. Especially for Hispanics. She didn't want them here. They think Meelo's guilty.*

"Thank you for coming in, Ms. Garcia. I'm Detective Bergman," he said, extending his hand.

Angela didn't want to shake Mark's hand but was too polite not to. Once she gripped his hand she hung on to it, asking, "When can I see—"

"I uh, dunno if you remember me," Obed said, smiling wanly and offering Mark his hand. "Paul Obed."

"Yeah," Mark said, chummy, scoffing at the notion anyone could forget Paul Obed. "Representing Mr. Garcia?"

Obed nodded.

Mark looked at Angela. "Your brother's in a holding cell downstairs. I'll send word, and an officer will escort him up here in about twenty, thirty minutes. In the meantime it'd help if we could talk—"

"Uh, Miss Garcia," Obed interjected, apologetic, "I suggest you wait unt—"

"Yes," Angela told Mark, "we need to talk."

Mark gave her an approving, complicit nod. Looked at Obed. "Counselor, you should know your client has agreed to stand a lineup."

Obed sighed regretfully and shook his head. "N-uh, I'm afraid that may have to be, um, off the table until he and I have a chance to discuss—"

"Meelo will do the lineup," Angela declared, staring defiantly at Mark.

Angela Garcia was as composed, lucid, and precise as her desperate urgency allowed her to be.

She confirmed Meelo's account of their family history. She was twenty-four. Been raising her kid brother since she was eighteen. Waitressing. Though she was going to bartending school. Better tips, and more respect . . . She frowned and shook her head once, silently reprimanding herself—*No, wrong topic, you're not here to talk about yourself.*

Meelo had been out of the house a lot. He didn't get along with Angela's boyfriend. They—maybe it was her fault, letting the boyfriend stay over so much.

No, she hadn't seen Meelo since a couple of days before the murder.

Last couple of months Meelo hadn't been hitting on her for cash so much. Maybe she should have asked him more about how come. But it was just such a relief.

Far as she knew he didn't have a job. Maybe *Tio* Mannie would slip him a ten or twenty for running an errand or wiping up around the laundromat. But no real job . . . Meelo's story about the gringa tattoo artist must be true. Meelo said there was this woman who had a thing for him, gave him that— thing—for free. Maybe the woman tat artist also gave him money.

When Angela's boyfriend got a new car, Angela got his old one and gave Meelo her Chevelle. Free and clear, he didn't steal it. She wanted Meelo to have it, hoped he'd want to make money, keep the car up.

Tio Mannie's gun got stolen six months ago. If Meelo had it she never saw it. If Meelo had a gun it was for protection. This is the point. Meelo never won a fight, not since third grade. When he was fifteen, sixteen, he tried to get in a gang, they wouldn't take him.

He did a couple of stupid things, getting high, stealing, but lots of boys do that, and he was all alone too much, but she needed to work a lot of extra shifts, maybe that was a mistake.

But she's not wrong about this: Meelo is a dumb, scared . . . child. Sweet child. Everything that happened to him, he still never turned mean. Every year on her birthday, even the ones where they're fighting and Meelo won't talk to her, Meelo leaves her a flower. Meelo, he does not, he does not have the stomach to walk up to a man and shoot him. Not once, forget three times. Meelo does not have the meanness or the *cojones* to shoot anybody in this world.

And if he did, it would be her boyfriend.

THIRTEEN

Meelo and the other four wore long sleeves, so the snake tat wouldn't be an issue.

Standing with Naguib Darwahab on the cop side of the two-way mirror were Mark, Doonie, Lieutenant Husak, Public Defender Obed, and Assistant State's Attorney Harrison Miller; ASA Carrie Eli had lost the competition for the assignment.

Soon as the shade went up Darwahab pointed and said, "Number three, that is the crackhead who did it. He is the one who killed Wilson Willetts."

Obed cleared his throat. A sound less like a cough than a whimper. "Um, Mr. Darwahab, sorry, I have to ask this: Are you absolutely su—"

"Yes," Darwahab declared. "I saw that man, number three, shoot Wilson Willetts, this far from me." The old man held his hand eighteen inches in front of his face. "This far."

Darwahab's expression remained implacable but there was a note of commiseration in his voice as he put a hand on Obed's forearm and said, man to man, "He is guilty."

Mrs. Nomsilp picked Meelo. No hesitation.

"Not here. None of these is him," Mr. Nomsilp said a few minutes later, in the same room, to the same men, looking at the same lineup.

"What?" Obed asked, wishing he didn't sound so shocked.

Nomsilp gave the lineup another glance and said, "None of these men is the man who opened the trunk of the 1991 brown Chevelle."

"Please, Mr. Nomsilp, take your time, look at each of them carefully," Doonie urged.

Nomsilp looked again. Shook his head. "Number three looks just like him—"

Lieutenant Husak lunged for the intercom: "Number three, step forward."

Meelo stepped up, looking pleased, ready to be vindicated.

"Mr. Nomsilp," Doonie asked, "Is this the man you saw in the parking lot?"

Nomsilp shook his head no.

"Mr. Nomsilp," Mark reminded him, "number three is the man whose photo you identified."

"In a photo he could fool me, but not now, in life," Nomsilp explained. "If I had seen you arrest him I would have told you he wasn't the one, but you made me stay safe back in your car, with the reporter."

"But number three looks 'just like' the guy?"

Nomsilp nodded. "Almost exactly, but not. Like brothers. Maybe number three's the guy's kid brother. The guy looked just like him but a little, you know, bigger, maybe a half-inch more tall, more muscles. Older, maybe two-and-a-half years."

"But you're sure—*sure*—number three is *not* the man you saw in the parking lot?" Obed asked.

"Yes."

PD Obed gave ASA Miller a look daring him to dispute the weight of this exculpatory testimony. ASA Miller didn't seem to notice.

"Mr. Nomsilp," Mark said, "if you can't identify the face, perhaps you can identify something else for us." He keyed the intercom. "Number three, please remove your shirt and turn so

66

your left arm is facing the mirror."

Meelo did as asked. Mark asked Mr. Nomsilp if he recognized the tattoo.

Nomsilp nodded. "Exact same tattoo. But not the exact same man."

"You've never seen this man? Anytime, anywhere?" Mark asked.

"No. Same tattoo, same bald head, same looks, same ugly little beard, different guy," Nomsilp insisted.

During the lineup Harrison Miller never said a word or varied his expression from the cold analytical Gaze he'd cultivated during his thirty-one years as a prosecutor. When he was younger he'd practiced not blinking, because he believed The Gaze rattled witnesses. A gaunt man with large bony extremities and an incongruous pot belly, Miller was the senior ASA in the Chicago office, a lifer.

Mark figured Sy Vytautis, the State's Attorney, had assigned Miller because the primaries were coming up next spring. Miller, an uninspired but experienced, relentless prosecutor, could be trusted to win the slam-dunk case, but no amount of favorable publicity could turn Miller into a viable candidate who might run against his boss.

After Obed and Mr. Nomsilp left the room, Husak looked at Miller and said, "I don't think Nomsilp's retraction hurts us."

"Hurts us? Tonight I'm going to dream about the Pocket Pal trying to sell the Half-Inch Taller Lookalike defense to a jury," Miller gloated, flashing his Flynn Grynn. In his youth, before developing The Gaze, Miller had been just as diligent in copying Erroll Flynn's most charmingly arrogant grin.

It was the first time Mark had ever heard Harrison Miller make a joke. First time for Doonie, too. And Doonie had known Miller since typewriters and dial phones.

Mark was impressed. Nailing Emilio Jesus Garcia was going to be so easy Harrison Miller was, for the first time in his career, going to have fun. Or whatever twisted approximation of it Miller's queasy little smirk was supposed to indicate.

Mark and Doonie did a quick follow-up with Meelo.

You said Oscar was shorter than you?

"Uh-huh."

Not taller?

"No way."

Oscar shave his head?

"I told you, he got hair."

Tats?

Meelo shook his head.

Know anybody who has the same snake tattoo you have?

"Fuck no." Offended at the notion.

FOURTEEN

He tossed the black wig and shaved the goatee. Back to his usual self; balding, bland oval face, unremarkable little moustache; the third accountant from the left in an office photo. Arthur Reid flew out of Indianapolis to Albuquerque. Retrieved his 4Runner from a self-storage facility. Spent a few days unwinding in Taos. Drove home.

Arthur's junior partner, Dina Velaros, flew St. Louis–New York–Milan. Had a world-class stylist remove the long brown hair extensions, give her a new do. Shopped the Via Della Spiga boutiques. Took the train to Venice. Shopped the Murano galleries. This last job paid unbelievably well.

Hector B, the Meelo-look-alike shooter, flew Milwaukee–Miami–Belize. Swimming. Snorkeling. Skin-diving. Spending as much time in the warm Caribbean as it took to make him believe that fucking snake was totally washed off his arm. The scratches he got from that fucking rag-head, though, were deep enough to scar. He needed to find out what plastic surgery would cost. He should get health insurance anyway. One serious trip to the hospital could wipe out every dime he made, even on this gig; Bill and Heather were right about that.

Even if Hector B didn't believe Bill and Heather were their real names.

FIFTEEN

Mark and Doonie did a ten-minute standup in the headquarters media room.

They were convincingly modest about going through the motel door. Said they'd been well-trained. Pointed out four other cops went in with them.

They were polite but firm about refusing to discuss any details of the investigation. Referred the questioners to the official spokesman, Commander Riles.

Riles was pleased with their performance. Doonie had a solid, reassuring veteran vibe, wore a sport coat that fit well enough to stay buttoned, and the only alcohol you could smell on him was aftershave. Bergman was relaxed, conversational, didn't do the grim, tight-jawed cop thing; Riles liked the guy's potential as a persuasive, contemporary camera presence for the Department.

But Riles wasn't nearly as pleased as Bob Gilkey was. The *Chronicle* reporter was knee-wobbling ecstatic. Gilkey had spent the ten minute Q&A rigid with fear, pen poised over notebook but not moving, as he waited for a nightmare moment that never came, one where the cops disputed some detail he'd described about the arrest, or pointed out Gilkey hadn't actually seen any of it.

The detectives wrapped up on schedule. Riles took the podium as though it were his side of a tennis court and deftly returned serves.

No, he could not say when the preliminary phase of the

investigation would be complete. Superintendent Blivins' mention of twenty-four to forty-eight hours was not a prediction, it was an estimate. Riles could affirm the investigation was making good progress, proceeding in a careful, thorough, professional manner.

No he could not discuss what evidence the detectives were looking into.

Yes, he could confirm that the weapon found in the trunk of the suspect's vehicle was the murder weapon.

He could not predict when an indictment would be filed; that was up to the State's Attorney.

No, there was not at this time any other suspect. Or reason to believe there would be.

SIXTEEN

The chairs in Wilson Willetts' office were burgundy leather, the same color as the victim's wallet. Distinctive, angular, strikingly modern but comfortable the instant your butt made contact. Consistent with Willetts' architecture. His buildings were boldly sculpted but designed for the real needs of actual humans. Even when it came to himself. Willetts & Associates was located in a remarkably un-flashy renovated warehouse in Bucktown; Willetts was such an international archi-god he didn't need to prove his status by locating in a pricey lakefront skyscraper, or designing himself a radical statement building that screamed LOOK I'M AN ARCHITECT'S OFFICE. Which was consistent with everything Mark and Doonie were hearing about the man.

Helen Rowan, Willetts' longtime secretary, explained the distraught staff had been given time off until after the funeral. But more than a few people had come in today because they were working projects where any delay would incur significant avoidable expense for the client; Wilson wouldn't have wanted that.

"Like any great architect, Wilson was the undisputed commander in chief, but he was never a tyrant, a megalomaniac." Rowan, a tiny, sharply focused woman of forty-five, was explaining to Mark and Doonie why she was sure none of Willetts' past or present employees might have wanted to kill him. Rowan was wearing a severe black skirt-suit. Her hair was pulled back tight. Her eyes were red-rimmed but clear. Her spine was vertical.

"Did he have any enemies—competitors, dissatisfied clients, anyone?" Doonie asked.

Rowan shook her head.

"Again, we're sorry we have to ask—" Mark started to say.

"You have to be thorough and correct," Rowan said.

"Just one more question," Mark said, proceeding gently. "I understand Mr. Willetts has been a widower for seven years. Are you aware of him having had any romances since then that ended badly, or involved any unstable personalities?"

Rowan shook her head. "Wilson was my friend as well as my employer, but he was always a gentleman. He didn't discuss . . . those kinds of things." Rowan stopped, but didn't seem finished. She wasn't. "Women, beautiful, intelligent ones, of all ages, constantly make—made—themselves available to an artist of Wilson's prominence. And attractiveness. But, I am fairly certain, Wilson never cheated on his wife during their marriage. Twenty-eight years." Rowan looked about to cry. Instead she took a sip of coffee. "After Karen died . . . Wilson was all over the world, all the time . . . I know he dated, and I'm certain there were affairs I don't know about, but the relationships I was aware of were brief and amicable . . . The last two years he was—I believe—seeing only one woman. More a friendship than a torrid romance. A very stable woman. In her mid-forties. You may know the name—Tomoko Kamitsubo."

Yeah. As in Judge Tomoko Kamitsubo. Federal bench. Mark and Doonie had a brief telepathic discussion in which they agreed there was no hurry, absent the collapse of the case against Meelo and the discovery of a death threat to Wilson Willetts signed in her own blood, to be dropping in on Judge Kamitsubo to chat about her sex life.

Helen Rowan tracked down Willetts' senior associate, Carlton Bass.

Rowan escorted the detectives into an elevator and down to the ground floor, to the model shop. A huge room. Walls lined with cabinets and bins, work tables, power tools, art supplies, taping-gluing-soldering supplies, and a mini-kitchen with a coffeemaker whose pot was almost empty, next to which was an open, one-third-empty bottle of Delamain cognac.

In the middle of the room was an enormous table. On it was a twenty-by-fifteen-foot model consisting of four buildings, of different sizes and shapes but sharing a family resemblance, connected directly by ramps and bridges, and indirectly via walks through parkland.

Carlton Bass was at the table making a minute adjustment to the sloped roof of one of the buildings. Bass was in his late forties, African American, hadn't missed many meals, was utterly absorbed in what he was doing and would have seemed professorial if not for the bespoke English dress shirt, slacks, and shoes, and French necktie, a nubby-textured psychedelic pattern of handwoven silk shot through with threads of real gold and silver.

Bass was being watched by three young colleagues. Two were newborn architects, a boy and a girl. The third was the chief model-maker; blond handlebar moustache and stained T-shirt. All three were gazing at the model buildings. All three had damp eyes and were holding coffee mugs.

Bass stepped back from the table. Studied the model. Nodded at the others. Said, "Okay." A satisfied, pained, serious, resigned *Okay.*

Bass turned his attention to the newcomers. For a moment he and Helen Rowan looked at each other, old friends sharing a few tons of sadness.

Rowan introduced the detectives to Carlton Bass and the others. She let the youngsters know Mr. Bass would need the room. They left, taking their coffee mugs.

Rowan said individual goodbyes to Mark and Doonie, urging them to contact her if there was anything she could help with. She left.

"That one of his?" Mark asked, going to take a closer look at the model.

Bass nodded. "LAFAM."

Doonie raised an eyebrow at Bass.

"Los Angeles Fine Art Museum," Bass explained.

"Hope it gets built," Mark told Bass.

"It's one of three finalists in the competition," Bass said, not sounding optimistic. "What is it you need to discuss?"

The cops explained to Bass why they were there. Took him through the boilerplate questions. Got the same answers Helen Rowan had given. Got the same sense of enormous loss, as if Willetts had been family. As if Willetts had been a modern Leonardo, and none of them were going to get to work alongside anyone his size again. Like Helen Rowan, Carlton Bass had to pause and work on not crying.

While Bass composed himself, Doonie asked, "Mind if I grab a cup of coffee?"

"Please."

Mark thanked Bass for his cooperation and apologized for having to intrude during such a painful time. Bass told Mark he had nothing to apologize for.

As if putting official business aside for a moment, Mark gestured at the model, asking, "Does Mr. Willetts being gone hurt the chance of this winning, even if it's the best design?"

Bass nodded.

Mark shook his head. "But, even with him gone, LAFAM would still be getting a Wilson Willetts design. The Last Wilson Willetts."

Indicating the model, Bass said, "This is, in architectural terms, a conceptual sketch. After LAFAM's design committee chooses and the full board approves a winner, there will be a two- or three-year tug-of-war over details and modifications before final blueprints are approved. If the committee picks Wilson's entry they'll never be sure the modifications are the same ones he would have come up with. What they *are* sure of is, if they make Wilson the winner they won't get to spend the next few years working with a world-famous architect."

"Which also means socializing with," Mark said.

"Uh-huh," Bass confirmed. "On the one hand, the design committee will in fact be tempted by the cachet of owning the Last Wilson Willetts. On the other hand, live architects make better dinner guests." Bass saw where Mark was going. His voice dropped to a quiet, no-nonsense rumble. "I know the other two finalists, Detective Bergman. Neither of them would kill for this job. Not even the one who's an asshole egomaniac."

"Good."

During the conversation Mark had circled the table so that in order to face Mark, Bass had to turn his back to the kitchen. Giving Doonie a chance to slip some cognac in his coffee. Mark figured one shot would leave Doonie mellow enough to get drawn into a brief speculation about some idiotic possibilities.

Bass frowned. Very quietly asked Mark, "Detective, do you have any reason to suspect the man you arrested was . . . hired . . . to shoot Wilson?"

"None," Mark declared. From the heart. Meelo was lucky someone would hire him to clean a laundromat; *Tio* Mannie must've held his breath every time the kid picked up a mop. Messing up an easy mugging, turning it into a murder, and getting caught the same night was a much more plausible form of employment for Meelo.

Fucking Nomsilp and his fucking retraction.

SEVENTEEN

The sky had been clear and blue when the detectives arrived at Willetts & Associates. During the last twenty minutes the light coming in the windows had gone pale. By the time Mark and Doonie left the building, the city was twilight-dim, as a gang of surly dark gray clouds took over the sky. Stiff gusts sent stinging swarms of insect-sized debris swirling across sidewalks. Thunder pealed, and, as if a switch had been thrown, fat drops began to fall. In the few seconds it took the cops to walk to their car the rain went from scattered to steady. By the time they'd pulled into traffic, wind-driven torrents were pummeling the car, rattling the sheet metal. Raindrops practicing to be hailstones when they grew up.

Neither cop commented on the weather. Typical midwestern thunderburst. Blow over as quickly as it blew in.

"We gotta check out that list," Doonie said.

"Soon as we're done with this," Mark replied.

Doonie was suggesting it was time to move on; "that list" was a computer file of driver's licenses from the hit-run case.

Ms. June Dockyer's initial statement at the scene had pegged the vehicle as a late-model black Explorer. The cops posted an alert to all the body shops in the area to report any black Explorer in for work on its grille and/or right front fender. Eighteen responses had come in so far; all the owners had alibis, none of the fenders had been coated with dried bits of fifteen-year-old boy.

In her initial statement Ms. June Dockyer also said she'd gotten a glimpse of the driver. She made him a white male, thirty-five to forty years old, light brown or dark blond hair. On the chance the driver was also the owner, the cops did a DMV data search. First, the names of any males in the tri-county area who owned a black Explorer. The owners' names were then run to find those who were registered white male drivers between thirty and fifty. Once the detectives got that list they pulled up the driver's license photos, sorted them for drivers with light brown or blond hair.

It was when Mark had called Ms. June Dockyer and asked to her look at the license photos that she announced her astonishing memory loss. Said she'd been meaning to call the detectives and tell them the bad news but she'd been too embarrassed. Mark could almost hear her fluttering her eyelashes over the phone.

"Got any ideas for how to make another run at the lizard girl?" Doonie asked.

"No. Get to that once we close Willetts," Mark said, countering Doonie's attempt to avoid the topic.

"This case? The one my partner calls the 'no-brainer'? "

"Just for the entertainment value," Mark said, "I've been thinking what it would take for Meelo's alibi to be true."

Doonie sighed but didn't interrupt.

"I figure three people, minimum," Mark continued. "Heather the Advanced Placement hooker, Oscar the Grouch, and the look-alike shooter."

"No one makes a plan where they gotta find an exact twin patsy for the shooter," Doonie pointed out.

"Doesn't have to be that exact. Same general ethnicity, age, size, features. Witnesses are gonna fix on the big markers like the shaved head, the snake tat, the teen disaster beard. Plus nobody gets more than a quick look at him."

"Okay," Doonie wearily demanded, "where do they find a patsy who is only almost an exact twin of the shooter?"

Mark admitted, "I don't know. Got a couple of long-shot theories, but . . ."

They arrived at their destination. The scene of the crime. Wilson Willetts' house, where Mark and Doonie would be interviewing members of Willetts' family.

Mark cut the engine. He and Doonie didn't open their doors. The downpour hadn't slowed any. Their slickers were in the trunk.

Mark was sure the puddles he and Doonie made in the foyer weren't really the size of small ponds. Not that it mattered. The floor was of locally quarried limestone. As utilitarian as it was splendid. Just like the rest of the mansion. Just like Nina Willetts-Monfantino, twenty-six, PhD candidate and working photographer, who had flown in from Italy the day before with her husband Ugo and their three-year-old son.

Jet-lagged, grieving, and very much her father's daughter, Nina had answered the door and greeted the sopping detectives herself. Nina pooh-poohed Mark and Doonie's apologies, asked Ugo to fetch towels for them, tried to talk them into accepting dry socks and slippers, and ushered them into the kitchen where she could make them something warm to drink.

Mark and Doonie sat at a large kitchen table with Nina and Ugo, who taught physics at the University of Bologna, and held his wife's hand all through the interview. Also at the table were Wilson Willetts' older brother Ted, a craggy retired anesthesiologist who'd driven in from Lake Geneva, and Marshall Solwitz, Willetts' attorney and lifelong friend.

Neither the daughter, the brother, nor the lawyer/friend could think of anyone who had a motive to kill Willetts. None of them knew of any threats. None of them had noticed any changes in

Willetts, or sensed anything had been troubling him. His affair with Her Honor, Tomoko Kamitsubo, had been more companionship than romance; mature, relaxed, utterly un-tumultuous.

Solwitz did most of the talking. Mark suspected the attorney had been born wearing a three-piece suit and a bowtie and speaking like a dictionary with sharp teeth. Solwitz assured the detectives the financials of Willetts & Associates were unassailably secure. Likewise, Wilson's personal pecuniary situation had ceased being an issue several decades ago. To Solwitz's certain knowledge Wilson had no debts.

Solwitz could also detail Willetts' movements the night of the killing; he'd been with Willetts at the dinner Tuesday night at Trattoria Maggio.

"It's an annual event," Solwitz explained. "A stag dinner. The majority of the attendees have known each other since we were undergraduates at the University of Chicago. Each year we gather for cocktails, red meat, and a raunchy limerick contest, on a specific topic . . . Wilson had been abroad during the last three dinners, he was delighted to be able to attend this one . . ." The attorney's precise, measured voice thickened. "Wilson's final evening was . . . anachronistic, incorrect, juvenile . . . and among friends." Solwitz stopped, swallowed, tried not to continue, but, to his surprise, was too moved to control himself. "I offered to drive him home, did my not inconsiderable best to persuade him, but he . . . I should have insisted. *Insisted.*"

"Then what, Marshall?" Ted rumbled. "You drive Will home and we have *two* funerals."

Nina went to Marshall, put her arms around him, and kissed his bald spot.

Mark was picturing white-haired, gnomish, bow-tied, three-piece-suited Marshall Solwitz behind the wheel of a yellow Targa. Mark decided it was time to go. He looked at Doonie, who agreed.

Mark was delivering his and Doonie's thanks for the co-operation and an apology for the intrusion when the front gate intercom burbled. Someone in another room answered it. Ted glanced at his watch and muttered, "Shit."

Nina, Ugo, and Solwitz walked the detectives to the door. Ted headed the other way, fleeing deeper into the house.

As they entered the foyer the housekeeper opened the front door and a dry—the rain had stopped—lanky, aristocratic silvered-haired matron wearing a severely tailored black silk suit blew into the room, black scarf fluttering behind her. She spotted Nina, moaned, "Oh Nina," as she swept across the foyer and enveloped Nina in a hug, kisses, and sighs. After a while the woman loosened her grip, looked Nina in the eye, shook her head sadly, and wrapped Nina up again.

Then, with only slightly less fervor, the woman embraced Ugo. Then Marshall Solwitz. Then she turned to Mark and Doonie and might've tackled them as well if they hadn't been total strangers wearing moist clothing.

Mark didn't think it was an act. Her pain and her flamboyance were genuine.

Nina took the woman's arm and made introductions. "Gentlemen, this is Florence Brock, one of my parents' dearest friends. Mine too. Florence, Detectives John Dunegan and Mark Bergman."

"The officers who caught the killer!" Florence exclaimed, squeezing Doonie's hand in both of hers, and then Mark's. "Thank you," she whispered. "Thank you—I'm so glad I got here in—I got to my plane hours later than I planned, I am so pleased I'm here in time to meet you, excuse me, I'm babbling, this is such an unspeakable, I met Wilson and Karen when he designed my home, the year Nina was born, my late husband and I have been crazy about all of them ever since, oh Nina, Nina, I wish there was something, what can I do, tell me what I can do . . ."

"You already did, Aunt Flo," Nina said, pulling her closer. "You showed up. Like always."

"Always will, Neen." Florence's eyes glistened, but the rest of her face went tight with anger and purpose. "I swear I will go to war for him like never before—I will go public, I will go dirty, do *whatever* it takes to make sure they choose his—" Florence gritted her teeth. "Ah, Neen, I can't promise we'll win—but I swear to God if those bastards don't honor him, if they don't build Wilson's final masterpiece I'll quit the committee, quit the board, and never set foot in that goddamn museum again—and then, *then* I will nail every member who voted against him, I will wreck those people, swear to fucking God," Florence snarled, and burst into tears.

Mark and Doonie were headed back to their office, inching along in dense traffic. The curse of the unmarked car: Drivers don't slide out of the way like they do when they spot a squad car. And you can't run red lights.

Mark didn't mind. The traffic would give them time to do some blue-skying.

Florence Brock. Widow, inheritor of a small petroleum services empire. Based on his own gut feeling, and his continually growing respect for Wilson Willetts, Mark figured Florence Brock was okay. Willetts wouldn't have let Florence get that close to his family if she were just some pushy patron out to adopt a pet architect. Nina wouldn't have promoted her from Florence to Aunt Flo.

If Aunt Flo turned werewolf at the thought of her boy not getting the LAFAM commission, Mark wondered how other, less sweet billionaires on the design committee might take defeat.

"I've been thinking about Florence Brock," Mark said.

"Me too," Doonie admitted, with a small, wistful snort.

"What you think?"

"Oh man," Doonie sighed, "that old broad is sexy when she's angry. Jesus." Doonie shook his head, enjoying how turned on he was.

EIGHTEEN

ASA Harrison Miller was waiting for them in Lieutenant Husak's office.

They briefed Husak and Miller.

Miller stood, Flynn-Grynned, and extended a bony hand. "Good work. I'm on my way to the grand jury. Got papers drawn and witnesses waiting."

"Okay," Doonie said, shaking Miller's hand.

"We still haven't checked out the tattoo artist," Mark reminded them.

Miller stiffened. "Say it turns out the suspect *was* at Ralph's Body Ink—*and* say he *was* accompanied by a five-nine, fortyish guy with a goatee, named Oscar. Would that make any of the rest of Garcia's story true?" Miller sneered. State's attorneys didn't love having their indictment decisions second-guessed by cops. "How about, would that make any of the rest of his story even remotely believable?"

"Yes," Mark replied, "remotely."

"That's my phone," Doonie said, recognizing the ring, and left to pick up the call.

Harrison Miller didn't dignify Mark's arrogance with a response. Miller just gave the little shit a blast of The Gaze, then thanked Lieutenant Husak and marched off to battle.

When Miller was out of earshot Husak warned Mark, "Don't ever get between an ASA and a TV camera."

Mark shrugged. "This was Vytautis' decision; he'll announce

the indictment himself."

"But Miller will get camera time once the trial starts."

Mark nodded. Point taken.

"Besides," Husak continued, "the whole fucking city, including the Department, wants to get on with it."

Yeah. Waiting another couple of days would mean Wilson Willetts' funeral would have been splashed over the international airwaves, and there'd still be no indictment, and the world would be wondering how long the clumsy assholes at the Chicago PD needed to nail down a case against a suspect whose gun was the murder weapon he was seen killing the victim with by an eyewitness.

Mark nodded again, resigned.

Husak, a decent boss, studied Mark for a moment. Asked, not unsympathetically, "You got anything real?"

Mark shook his head no.

"Hey," Doonie said as he walked back in to Husak's office, "that was the Hammond police. Ralph's Body Ink, owned by one Ralph Garn, burned down two nights ago. Fire inspector says it started in the basement, caused by a standard-issue, small-time home-cooking meth-lab explosion."

"And Ralph?" Mark asked.

"Garn's gone. Him and his van. Hammond's checked family and friends, nobody cops to seeing him since the fire. Got an APB out."

Mark looked at Lieutenant Husak.

Husak shook his head. "That ain't real. That's a tweaker having a bad day and getting the hell out of town."

"Yeah," Mark said. What he meant was "Probably," but you don't give lip to a decent boss.

It was a no-nonsense grand jury. Stayed late so Harrison Miller could present his case in one session. Went right to work when

85

Miller finished. Miller's coffee had just cooled off enough to drink when he got called back into the courtroom. Eight minutes. God, what a night. Thirty-one years in, Harrison Miller finally caught a case that generated joy. He went out and had one-and-a-half beers.

Every local station broke into prime-time programming—including the Cubs and Sox games—for a live cutaway to State's Attorney Sy Vytautis' press conference, at which he announced the indictment of Emilio Jesus Garcia for the murder of Wilson Willetts. Vytautis had a deep, authoritative baritone and a great jaw. Some of the regulars were projecting him for governor.

Sy was aiming at getting reelected by a fifteen-or-more percent blowout in the next State's Attorney race and heading straight for the U.S. Senate.

NINETEEN

Mark fell asleep with Carrie Eli and woke up with Paul Obed.

Mark was tired of talking and hearing himself talking about the Willetts case, so, instead of Carrie, he'd been thinking of calling one of the other two women he'd been seeing lately.

Two problems kept him contemplating the phone instead of picking it up and dialing one of the other women.

The first problem was that both relationships were even more casual, and far less stable, than the one with Carrie. Both were approaching the evaporation point; might not make for the simple night of rest and recreation he needed.

Molly, Mark's long-ago ex-fiancée, had recently turned up because she'd broken up with her new fiancé. Molly was seeking comfort and revenge; she wasn't looking to get back with Mark, she was just flossing between serious romances. And Mark wasn't looking to get back with Molly.

They'd met when he was twenty-five, she was twenty-three. Molly was getting a PhD in Comp Lit, after which she'd become a professor, or the marketing director of her family's chain of shoe stores. Mark was a uniformed cop who'd casually reached in and removed the key from the ignition one night when Molly and two girlfriends had wobbled out of Metro and piled into her Miata. Molly was as all out on the surface all the time as Mark was reticent. They amused the hell out of each other. They got infatuated, fast, and got engaged, momentarily.

Lying awake a couple of hours after she'd said yes, Molly realized she couldn't really tell her parents, or herself, that she was marrying a cop. She woke Mark up and spent the next twenty-four hours trying to talk him into quitting the force and having a life. When that didn't work she tried a few hours of weeping and accusations that Mark didn't really love her. When that didn't work she stormed out and waited for him to call.

Two years later they bumped into each other at O'Rourke's, had a drink, decided they could be friends. Which meant they traded a phone call or two a year.

Last month Molly showed up in person, tearful and horny. At first they hooked up every couple of nights so Molly could fuck out her rage at her latest ex-fiancé. It worked. Molly had cooled off and Mark hadn't heard from her in over a week. Mark guessed that meant Molly's thirst for revenge was giving way to her thirst for true love, and kids, which she wanted to start having, soon.

Then there was Janvier, who was attending grad school at the Art Institute and waitressing at a hip restaurant that featured a Japanese-Peruvian fusion menu and painful chairs. Janvier was tall, striking, spirited, and fond of recreational drugs. She was too polite to do them in front of Mark, but there was no way she qualified as a long-term girlfriend for a cop. In fact Mark should've broken it off by now, but sex with Janvier was so much more ecstatic than it had been with anyone else in years . . .

Well there it is, Mark thought, *being a cop disqualifies me for a life with a straight, upper-middle-class girl or with an edgy, upper-mind-expanded artist.* He wondered what that left him. He wondered how addicted he'd become to carrying a badge and gun.

Which brought him to problem number two with calling Molly or Janvier, the real problem: He didn't want to talk about the case, but needed to. Which meant Carrie.

Mark and Carrie had been good friends since college. Neither had been unconventional in popular conventional ways. Carrie Eli was an attractive, brainy workaholic; Jewish, liberal, good-natured, and determined to become a prosecutor. And as pragmatic and mercenary about sex as a man. Carrie and Mark were never lovers; they were pals who periodically fell into bed over the years when nothing else was happening. During the times when either of them was seriously involved with someone, Carrie and Mark stayed pals who didn't fall into bed.

Like Molly, Carrie heard her biological clock ticking and liked the idea of kids, but then Carrie also liked the idea of having a dog, which she no way had the time for. She was wedded to her career and her independence. Which was probably why her few truly passionate affairs had been with married men, and once with a married couple.

"I don't think you're an idiot," Carrie told Mark. It was a little after two a.m. They were in bed, snacking on sections of navel orange. "That museum commission is plenty of motive; people kill for a lot less."

"But given what we've got on Meelo, there's no way we spend time on some purely theoretical alternative," Mark said.

Carrie nodded.

"What about the rest of it?"

"Well." Carrie munched thoughtfully. "The two-handed head shot to finish Willetts is maybe kinda minorly hinky, but . . ."

"Doesn't by itself mean shit."

Carrie nodded again. "And the motel owner, Nomsilp, insisting the guy going into the trunk of Meelo's car wasn't Meelo? Doesn't play. Not with Nomsilp contradicting his own original ID of the photo. Especially not with Mrs. Nomsilp IDing Meelo as the guy who owned the car and rented the room."

"Yeah," Mark admitted.

"Which leaves Ralph Garn the tat artist burning down his store and disappearing, which only even qualifies as microscopically hinky because it happened so coincidentally with the murder."

"Okay, tell me this: If you were a mugger, you hide in an upscale hedge and hope a victim comes along?"

"A mugger with the IQ of a mugger, imagine that. What does Doonie say?"

"He keeps changing the topic."

Carrie winked. But then she added, "Hey—alone, none of these things mean shit, but together, you're sensing some vague gestalt of hink."

" 'Vague gestalt of hink'?"

"Precisely. Thing is, you're not going to be comfortable sending the guy up till you've nailed shut every doubt. That's you being a good, semi-obsessive cop."

"Thanks," Mark said. "That sounds better than 'idiot semi-obsessive cop who's lost his perspective.' "

"Is *that* what this is about?" Carrie asked. Becoming a little more alert, a hunter sensing movement in the bush.

"Huh?"

"You having doubts about staying a cop?"

Shit, she didn't even try to hide the eagerness in her voice. *Great. It's official. Even Carrie has the bug.* Now every woman Mark knew, from Mom on down, had a problem with his career choice. Well, except for the Dunegan women; Phyl didn't care what Mark's job was as long as he got married, and Patty didn't care as long as he didn't get married until she was old enough to qualify.

"No," Mark sighed, "I was wondering what you thought about the Willetts evidence."

"Bull," Carrie insisted. "You're gonna do what you're gonna do no matter what I think."

"Carrie, listen to yourself: I ask for an opinion about whether my doubts about this one case are reasonable, and you've got me quitting the job."

"So that's all it is, huh?" she inquired, giving Mark's dick a squeeze.

"Yup."

"C'mon," Carrie urged, as she leaned closer and began absentmindedly brushing her nipple with the tip of Mark's erection, "tell the truth."

Scouting parties of sunlight were infiltrating the blinds, the radio was offering three possible weather forecasts, the other side of the mattress was empty. Carrie had gotten up an hour earlier, gone home to put on unwrinkled clothes in which to represent the People's legal interests.

Mark started the coffee. He showered and toweled. He put on pants. It would be a while before he was dry enough to put on a shirt; the breeze off the lake felt good and Mark didn't feel like turning on the AC to cut the humidity. He poured coffee. Checked his e-mail.

Six messages. One mattered.

From: PAUL OBED

I'm Emilio Garcia's attorney—I know you remember, but it never hurts to make sure. Especially on official business. My client wants to speak with you and Detective Dunegan ASAP. There is a witness who can put my client at the motel at the time of the shooting. We need to find her ASAP. Please contact me ASAP.

TWENTY

"You never asked me that, man," Meelo whined. "You didn't ask where I was at some exact minute. You asked could I prove I never left the room, and she couldn't prove that, she only saw me there for like a couple of minutes when she knocks on my door."

Back in the interrogation room for this morning's episode of Meelo's Adventures In Logic. This one was a little painful, because the kid had a point. They'd never asked if he could prove he was in the room at the time of the murder. 10:55 p.m.

"Okay," Mark conceded, "our fault."

"Absolutely," Doonie pretended to agree. "What made you think to tell us about her now?"

"I forgot all about that motel woman, y'know, till yesterday afternoon, when I called my sister Angela like I promised her, and we're talkin', and Angela asks me did anybody, y'know anybody at all see me at the motel that night, so I'm, No, then like wait—Yeah!"

Angela asked? Mark resisted the urge to look at Obed.

Doonie didn't. He gave the PD a sour, disbelieving grin.

"I-I uh, I—*chhm!*" Obed sputtered, and cleared his throat. "I was going to cover that with my client at our next meeting," he assured Doonie.

"So the woman from the room next door came over to ask about the noise. How long did you talk?" Mark asked Meelo.

"A while, a couple of minutes maybe . . . It, it was kind of a

92

thing. She came over 'cause of the noise, but she just didn't wanna go away, she was like . . . coming on to me, man."

"That just keeps happening to you," Doonie noted.

"Yeah," the sex god agreed, trying not to gloat.

Mark asked the sex god, "You're certain about the time?"

"Yeah, man, yeah—I mean I didn't check out my watch or nothin'. But it had to be right around ten-thirty, eleven, eleven-thirty. I'm sure about that."

"Once you've located this um—" Obed checked his notes—

"Elizabeth Hackenmeyer," Mark offered.

"Right. Once you find her," Obed assured the detectives, "we're confident Ms. Hackenmeyer can fix the time she saw Mr. Garcia in his room."

"Yeah, yeah," Meelo told the cops. "She'd remember. She was real organized. She had a first aid kit."

What Elizabeth Hackenmeyer didn't have was a fixed abode. Her registration form at the Golden Door Motel listed a post office box in Catawba, Wisconsin. Which Mark was able to find on the map, halfway between Rhinelander and Rice Lake.

Doonie wasn't impressed by Mark's cartographic acuity. Doonie was busy running a BCI on Ms. June Dockyer, looking for some leverage to pressure the lizard girl to check out the photos of possible hit-run suspects. Doonie was done with Willetts.

Mark wasn't. Elizabeth Hackenmeyer was the only motel guest who hadn't been questioned about Meelo sightings. Apparently she'd been out all night. Mrs. Nomsilp said Hackenmeyer showed up the next morning at 11:50 a.m., just before checkout time, collected her belongings from her room, and left; she'd paid—cash—when she'd checked in.

Hackenmeyer had drawn a line through the box on the registration form that requested a phone number. She had, however, filled in the make and plate number of her SUV. Mark ran the plates; got the same Catawba PO box address, but there was a phone number. Mark tried it.

He got the Little Fry Daycare & Preschool, Miss Janet speaking. No, Betsy Hackenmeyer was not affiliated with Little Fry. The school had been assigned this phone number when it opened sixteen months ago. Betsy had left town a while before that. Miss Janet didn't know Betsy all that well but knew Betsy had sold her house, what was left of it, and hit the road about a year and a half back. Betsy had gotten a terrific settlement from a freight company, some say in the middle six figures, some say lower, but terrific. This was after one of the freight company's drivers got drunk and pulled off Route 8 for a snooze but didn't stop till his truck was halfway through Betsy's house, which was nothing fancy, but it did get totaled and Betsy did get put in the hospital and might have died, and she said she had some terrible nightmares—and Miss Janet had no reason to believe Betsy was lying.

No, there was no Hackenmeyer family left in Catawba. Betsy was married once. Guy ran off. No kids. Lived alone. Worked at the mill till it closed. Then sales clerk, that sort of thing. Betsy did have two close friends but Miss Janet doubted they'd heard from Betsy because neither had said. Miss Janet had to excuse herself for a sec to separate a couple of Little Fries who were acting out. When Miss Janet got back she told Mark that Betsy did have an older sister who'd married and moved to Tomah over a decade ago. Miss Janet heard Betsy and Christine didn't get along so well. Miss Janet thought Christine's married name was Burdeen, with two e's, no i. Husband's name was something like Harry.

Mark called Betsy Hackenmeyer's two friends. One had the key to Betsy's post office box, collected what little mail Betsy got, forwarded it when she heard from her. Last time was five months ago: Vermont. Betsy didn't have e-mail.

Mark contacted Mrs. Harold Burdeen of Tomah, Wisconsin. Christine hadn't heard from her sister Betsy, who was piddling away her settlement living like a gypsy. Betsy claimed she wanted to see the world. Live life. Sure, Betsy'd had a terrible shock, deserved some time off, but seriously. Betsy thought as long as she lived frugal, and maybe went from flea market to flea market and turned just enough profit to cover some expenses, the settlement could last the rest of her life. There was no reasoning with Betsy. No, Betsy didn't have a cell, no way to call her. Used payphones and disposables, just so she could stay out of touch.

Mark put out a national tracer on Betsy and her truck.

Mark checked Betsy's credit statement. Her savings and checking accounts were at American Fedbank, which had branches nationwide; made sense, given her plan to roam. Mark got a list of Betsy's recent withdrawals.

Yes. Ten-thirty-seven this morning, two-hundred-dollar ATM withdrawal at a branch in Cape Girardeau, Missouri, at the southern end of the state, right off the I-55. Mark alerted the local cops and the highway patrol.

Doonie came up dry on Ms. June Dockyer.

Meelo was arraigned. Pled not guilty.

TWENTY-ONE

Mark traced the disconnected phone mailbox number Meelo claimed he called to hear Oscar's instructions. The last renter disconnected it two hours after Willetts was killed. The last renter used the name Dan Smith and paid with a postal money order. Which did not in any way confirm Meelo's story. Or contradict it.

Initial forensics came back. The scrapings from under Naguib Darwahab's fingernails consisted of human skin, blood, and a chemical, probably dye or ink; color couldn't be determined till they separated it out from the blood.

Preliminary results indicated no DNA match with Meelo. And the blood was Type A; Meelo was Type O. And in any case Meelo had no scratches.

Mark contacted Darwahab, who indignantly denied the possibility he'd clawed anyone but the shooter that day.

There were no traces of fresh blood in Darwahab's taxi. If Darwahab had scratched the shooter: A) It wasn't Meelo, and B) This guy had covered the scratches mighty fast and/or arrived prepared to wipe down the cab with some sort of solvent. (*That Oscar, he thinks of everything?*)

The lab results ended Doonie's boycott, partially. He stopped changing the topic. And, Doonie conceded, if the dye under the cabby's fingernails came back a tattoo ink the same color as Meelo's snake, he would waste some more time working the case.

Mark suggested Doonie be the one who called to inform Harrison Miller of the new hinks in the evidence.

As he dialed Miller, Doonie admonished Mark, "You stay disinvolved, you don't make more enemies than you're going to anyway."

Miller listened politely, thanked Doonie for the information, and hung up.

No cause for concern, Miller thought. *All the other evidence says Meelo did it.*

Far as that motel guest who will allegedly alibi Meelo for the time of the murder—first we have to find her, then she has to credibly confirm Meelo's story. For now it's just Paul Obed blowing smoke.

The forensics on the scratches . . . Obviously the cabbie scratched someone besides Meelo and for some reason refuses to admit it. Maybe because it was a woman—or a boy . . . But if the cabbie wanted to keep it a secret, why'd he bring it up? . . . Maybe . . . Darwahab had scratched someone else that day, and the shock of witnessing a murder and having a gun shoved up his nose made him displace the event, so Darwahab really does believe the shooter is the one he scratched. Miller could hire a shrink who'd testify to that.

Though once you open that can of worms, any defense attorney, even the Pocket Pal, is going to point out the prosecution wants the jury to think the cabbie's a reliable witness when he IDs Meelo, but a wacko when it comes to remembering whose arm he tore open.

Best if the cabbie backed off, said he never scratched the shooter.

Yeah. Gotta talk to Darwahab, face to face, alone. Find some—careful, deniable—way to let Darwahab know if he wants this guy convicted, he needs to let go the idea he scratched him.

And Darwahab did want this guy convicted, big-time.

TWENTY-TWO

With the crime solved and the killer indicted, the Wilson Willetts story lost its national heat. All three network news shows covered the funeral with a two-sentence mention at the end of a segment.

The cable news shows, with a full hour to fill, gave the funeral sixty seconds, showing montages of Willetts' best-known buildings.

PBS did ten minutes. A three-minute reporter piece, starting with a stand-up in front of Fourth Presbyterian Church on North Michigan Avenue as mourners filed in, then cutting to a bio of Willetts and an overview of his work. Then the host did a seven-minute discussion/evaluation of Willetts with two experts: the brilliantly constipated dean of the Yale School of Architecture, and an emphatic Dutch architecture critic who managed to make three references to his recently published book.

Local news shows gave it two or three minutes. Began with a recap of the crime, using the murky amateur footage of Darwahab impersonating the shooter, followed by professional close-ups of the bloody sidewalk taken the morning after. Cut to the funeral, which was private, so the coverage concentrated on quick shots of cultural and Machine heavies exiting the church. Those included the Mayor and his wife; Willetts had been a key member of Mrs. Mayor's committee to beautify the city, which had been a smashing success. Mrs. Mayor delivered a brief eulogy, which made this a hot-ticket event; any major pol who'd been at one cocktail reception with Willetts decided Wilson had been a dear friend, and tried to wangle invitations to his interment.

"Damn." State's Attorney Sy Vytautis shook his head, frustrated. He was in his office, watching the funeral coverage, his door closed and the sound low.

Half of that funeral crowd was the city's big-money Fundamental Forces, folks who built skyscrapers, folks who funded foundations, orchestras, and political campaigns. Other half was a good chunk of the Machine's officer class, the folks who'd fucking decide who'd fucking run for the U.S. Senate. Vytautis took a sip of MacCallan.

Being there would have been good. But having to recuse himself from involvement in the case because he was claiming friendship with the victim would not.

In fact it was time to let the public know how closely he was supervising this prosecution. Vytautis pondered whether it would be better to have his aides leak some chatter, or to just book an interview with some columnist and flat out say so himself.

Twenty-Three

Molly called Mark and invited him to dinner. Said it was her treat. Not hard to guess what that meant the occasion was; Molly was done flossing.

Mark and Molly behaved well, discussed it frankly, no bullshit. Enjoyed the evening. At the end, standing at the curb, she kissed him goodbye. Soft, sweet, then a quick touch of her tongue on his, as if she were giving and collecting one last carnal sense-memory to be stored for use at a later date.

Molly ended the kiss. Thanked Mark for the past month. And for not, years ago, back when she broke their engagement, not once turning her accusation around and saying she didn't love him enough to let him be a cop.

After he put Molly in a cab Mark thought that, as failed engagements went, this one had turned out okay. It had just taken six years for them to get around to saying a civilized goodbye. Which, at the time, they'd been too young and pissed off to have been capable of.

TWENTY-FOUR

The government official, Mr. Miller, had personally phoned to invite Naguib Darwahab to a private meeting in his office. Came out to the reception area to greet Darwahab and usher him in. Ordered his secretary to hold all calls. Poured the tea himself.

Then asked Darwahab to lie in court.

Oh, Mr. Miller was a man of the world, he knew how these things are done so they are not being done, said so they are not being said.

But it was clear. It was about the scratch.

Darwahab told the truth. This Garcia was the one he'd seen shoot Mr. Willetts. This Garcia was the one whose arm he'd scratched.

Mr. Miller showed him photographs of Garcia's arm. No scratches. Mr. Miller said Darwahab must have scratched someone else.

He did not.

"Then why did Garcia have no scratches?" Mr. Miller asked. Quietly, sympathetically.

Darwahab didn't know.

"Emilio Jesus Garcia is not the man you scratched. The skin and blood we took from under your fingernails is not his; we have scientific proof."

Darwahab couldn't argue with science. But he knew this Garcia was the one he'd scratched.

"If Garcia is the man who shot Mr. Willetts," Mr. Miller said, *"he cannot be the man you scratched."* Mr. Miller tapped the photo to emphasize his point. Squeezed the cabbie's shoulder like an old friend, looked him in the eye.

Mr. Miller asked Darwahab, "What is the important thing here? What is the important thing?" Looking him in the eye, that way.

Should he lie to make sure this Garcia is convicted?

Darwahab's mind whirled. Darwahab had seen this Garcia kill. True. He'd scratched this Garcia's arm. True. Yet the police found no scratches. Also true. *This is impossible. This defies sense. Yet it exists.* Darwahab could not explain this. But that was not a reason to lie about it. But if he did not lie, this Garcia might get away with murder, and it would be Darwahab's fault. So a lie might be the right thing . . . But when he testified in court he would be taking an oath on the Book.

Darwahab told the government official he could not explain the mysteries of photographs and science. He could only tell the truth.

Darwahab thanked the official for the tea. Told him it was excellent. Which wasn't a lie; it was good manners.

TWENTY-FIVE

Mark and Doonie burned a morning talking to fair-haired guys who owned black Explorers with blameless fenders.

Back at the squad Mark found a message from Janvier on his voicemail. First time she'd ever called him at work.

Said she knew he'd been working insane hours, not to mention being a TV star for a coupla minutes there, but hey, it'd been over a week. She missed him. She missed him in a sultry, insinuating voice. A stoned voice.

Well. Shit. Yes. No. Maybe. Maybe this one last . . . No.

Mark figured he'd call Janvier back and tell her the case was keeping him too busy . . . Hey, how's that for chickenshit? Don't leave her dangling and wondering and interpreting silences. End it. End it face to face.

Get one definitive, undisputed fact established today. This week.

Mark called Janvier and asked if she could meet him for a drink when he got off work.

There was a brief silence. Janvier asked, "Was it me or the roaches in the ashtray?"

Mark's professional life was riddled with amnesiacs, his private life with psychics. He wondered if he should point out it wasn't only the roaches, he was psychic enough to have noticed the times she'd had that coke tightness in her voice, and that she'd been tripping on X one (incredible) night.

After a moment Mark said, "Let's blame Congress."

"So you think drugs should be legal?"

"I think you and I have contradictory priorities—Christ, now I sound like a congressman—listen, can we have this conversation in person, so we have some time and I'm not in a room full of detectives?"

"Nah, not necessary. 'Bye, Mark," Janvier said, and hung up.

Well that was definitive. Probably.

Mark checked in with Hammond. No Ralph Garn.

Mark checked in with Cape Girardeau. No Betsy Hackenmeyer.

Mark imagined Ralph and Betsy picking each other up at a swap meet in the Ozarks. Ralph's van and Betsy's truck snuggled side by side. Barney Fife running their plates, hitting the witness jackpot.

Mark tried to imagine what Ralph would say when asked about the existence of Oscar. Tried to imagine what Betsy would say when asked if she'd seen Meelo at the motel at 10:55 p.m.

Couldn't.

Mark stopped off at a cop bar with Doonie after work and got disinvolved.

Yeah, right.

TWENTY-SIX

Betsy hadn't seen the photos of Meelo that appeared in the newspapers and on the tube. Betsy had missed any mention of Wilson Willetts' demise. Her sole source of news was talk radio, where (so far) no one had called in to ask if the murder of a Chicago architect was linked to the Democrat conspiracy to suspend the Constitution and bring back Clinton for a third term so the Saudis could buy Bin Laden a pardon. The last couple of years Betsy had mainly been listening to music anyway.

Since that night when Death's eighteen-wheeler had whizzed past her sleeping nose and brought her house down on top of her, Betsy had lost interest in the world's transient, trivial distractions. She'd spend whatever time she had left embracing life's meaningful ones. Lying there in the hospital during her recuperation, trying to count how many actually happy days she'd had, Betsy realized she'd never had a whole happy day. What she'd had were happy minutes. Maybe an hour here and there.

She wasn't going to miss out on any more of them. Betsy pulled off the interstate at Cape Girardeau because it was a college town. Missouri State University. She'd been nagged by the thought of a night with a young one, ever since her near-thing with the Mexican kid with that adorable clunky snake tattoo.

After spending the morning reconnoitering the campus area Betsy decided to rethink her college strategy. Better to find an all-male school, someplace where there wouldn't be so many perfect nineteen-year-old girls wearing tiny clothes. Have to do a little research.

In the meantime Betsy fired up her truck and headed down into Arkansas. She'd heard about some cool flea markets.

Betsy didn't get back on the I-55, just meandered down any country road that sang to her. She'd heard good things about Arkansas scenery. And if Arkansas wasn't incredible enough she'd just keep going till she got to New Mexico.

TWENTY-SEVEN

The biker didn't enjoy ratting out a brother Mongol to the Joliet cops, but it didn't keep him up nights, either. Big Cecil had been clipped on a dealing charge, nickel-dime stuff, couple pounds of grass. But they got him cold and it was his third strike. So he gave Snark to the cops.

Snark's own fault. Asshole was bringing down the club anyway. And Big Cecil couldn't have nailed Snark if Snark hadn't run his mouth.

Snark had inherited a Luger from his grandpa. Asshole executor of the estate won't turn the Luger over unless Snark signs for it. Asshole Snark wants the Luger so bad he autographs the dotted line, his real name, I have taken possession of this Luger firearm serial number blah-blah-blah.

Snark is so fond of this Luger he carries it. Says it won't be a problem, comes to a hassle, he'll remember to pull his regular piece.

Right. One night Big Cecil gets jumped by some Angels in the lot behind this roadhouse, Snark comes running out of the bar and drills an Angel in the back. Drops him. With the Luger.

Everybody grabs their hog and scatters. Snark's tear-assing down this little country road, knowing he's gotta break up the Luger and scatter the pieces, but he loves this fucking Kraut iron so much he keeps dicking around, trying to decide where would be the best place to do this, but Snark's just stalling. So this fuckwit is riding around packing the murder weapon and pretending to think, when he hears this siren, looks back, and sees party lights coming his way.

Snark kills his lights and bumps off into the woods. The bike dumps, Snark runs. Bashes into a barbwire fence, goes down, just in time to hear the cops blast by on the road. Snark just lays there eating dirt a while. Waiting to hear if the cops come back.

They don't. Snark stands, looks around. Sees the barbwire that fucked him up is attached to a gate. Just enough moonlight to read the sign on the gate.

Goddamn. He has found the spot.

Snark climbs through the wire. Snark tosses the piece. Can't bring himself to break it up, but he's not worried. The Luger has had a proper Viking burial, gone where no man can follow.

Couple days later Snark shows up. Everything's cool. None of the Angels saw who threw the shot. Only one who got a good look at the badass was his Mongol brother, Big Cecil. And Big Ceese ain't talking.

Until now. Now Big Ceese gives the cops Snark. If they make his third strike go away, Big Ceese will testify he saw Snark do the Angel.

And tell them where to find the Luger. That's the key. So it's not just the word of Big Cecil, who's trying to slip a third strike; it's a ballistics match plus written proof of ownership.

Can't believe asshole Snark got so dipshit sentimental about a gun . . . Maybe it was about his grandpa. Well, shit. Fuck it. Snark's own fault.

The Will County cops couldn't afford hazmat diving gear, let alone a specialist qualified and fucking nuts enough to use it. Most they could get authorized was an EPA dredge crew and some surplus entry-level FEMA hazmat suits. Good luck fellas, try not to poison yourselves while you're at it.

Eventually they did come up with Snark's Luger, but by that point it was an anticlimax. The interesting thing they'd pulled out of that pond, dripping with six kinds of corrosives and liquid cancers, was a large canvas tarp. Lead weights attached. Large tattooed body inside. No head or hands.

TWENTY-EIGHT

Useless. One more intriguing, useless tease. Just what Mark needed.

Even as corpses go, Dead Headless Ralph was uninformative. The M.E. couldn't fix a cause of death. Posited a head wound; couldn't prove it. Couldn't establish if the amputations had been a murder cover-up or a postmortem art project on a guy who died in his sleep.

The only thing linking Ralph Garn's death to Wilson Willetts' was timing—and that link existed only in the minds of those willing to posit the reality of Meelo's invisible friend, Oscar.

Instead of calling or e-mailing, Mark delivered the file to Harrison Miller's office so Miller couldn't avoid a discussion.

Mark noted the timing and manner of Ralph's death were consistent with Meelo's story. Ralph could identify Oscar, a professional killer. The removal of Ralph's head and hands in order to slow identification, and the well-thought-out disposal of the body, said Ralph had been treated to a pro hit.

Miller concurred about the quality of the work, but had a simpler theory about who to credit. Just a wild guess, but—considering Ralph had blown up a meth lab, maybe Ralph had been hanging around with and pissing off some people in the meth biz, people who have a real extensive background in murder.

Mark's only response to that were the tox screens on Dead Headless Ralph, which came back negative for meth. But, Mark

111

had to admit, negative for nearly everything else, too. That Superfund pond had pickled Ralph pretty good. Maybe Ralph had meth in him when he died. Maybe not. They'd never know.

Mark went down to Hammond to see if he could clear up some amphetamine ambiguities. Talked to the cops, and Ralph Garn's family and friends. Unanimous verdict: Ralph didn't like speed. Hadn't touched it since high school.

Harrison Miller, Mark knew, would believe the recent explosion in Ralph's basement suggested otherwise.

The family and friends all were sure the meth lab in Ralph's basement wasn't Ralph's. Most of them were sure Ralph *was* dumb enough to have rented the space to some dealer. None of them had any idea who that dealer might be.

A seventeen-year-old girl who'd hung at Ralph's and done shit for him in exchange for tats said she'd seen Meelo there— his last visit, night the big snake got finished. Meelo showed up alone. Meelo didn't say anything about any Oscar. Ralph didn't, too.

"Useless," Mark muttered. In a booth in a tavern in Beverly, near Doonie's. Doonie had told Mark to call on his way back from Hammond, meet him here. Better to talk shop in a crowded noisy joint than in the rec room at Dunegan's House of Nosy Teens.

"Fuck no," Doonie disagreed. "It ain't real yet, but it ain't useless."

" 'Yet'? " Holy shit. Doonie's about to join the idiot-lost-perspective club.

Doonie scowled. "Finish that," he instructed Mark.

Mark chugged the remains of his first drink and ordered another round.

"Look," Doonie continued, wishing he weren't saying this,

112

"when's the last time you heard some low-level crank dealer—only kind this Ralph would know—whacks a guy and bothers to remove the face and fingerprints, then guts him, gift-wraps him, and drops him down a poison well?"

Mark played ASA Miller, complete with Miller's sour little smirk. "So in your expert opinion, Detective, a speed dealer would lack the energy to butcher and hide a corpse?"

"Fuck you, Bergman," Doonie snorted. "Only witness who might verify Meelo's story gets a fancy pro sendoff, I fucking gotta believe it's . . ." Doonie furrowed his brow. "Probably." He tossed back his bourbon, sucked thoughtfully on the ice.

"Yeah," Mark sighed. "Fuck."

"Fuck," Doonie agreed.

Mark raised his empty glass. "Welcome to the Vague Gestalt of Hink."

"The fuck is a, a Vegas Salt of Hink?"

"It's what you got under your skin."

Doonie eyed him suspiciously. "*Vegas,* because . . . why?"

Mark shrugged.

"Stupid fuckin' expression," Doonie said.

"True . . . But you got Vegas Salt so bad, here you are back wasting time on this case before we find out if that was tattoo ink under Darwahab's fingernails."

The waitress arrived with the new round. After she left, Doonie told Mark, "Ain't a waste. It's a reasonable risk. Upside is, if we find out Meelo's being framed, means we gotta look into those architects and the rich fucks on that L.A. museum committee. To get the dirt on them . . . we have to go talk to Florence Brock some more." Doonie eased back in his chair, a sweet, contemplative leer on his face.

Mark shook his head sadly. "Angry older woman, dressed in black . . . jeez, Doon, tell me this ain't about getting turned on by some hot schoolboy memory of enraged nuns."

"Hey," Doonie protested, "I'm not the one who goes around in public saying shit like 'Vague Gestalt of Hink.' " Pronouncing it perfectly.

Mark laughed for the first time since . . . he wasn't sure. Couple of days. Maybe more.

Twenty-Nine

Until now Obed hadn't talked to the press. He'd had Meelo plead not guilty and left it at that. Made no mention of his client's claim of being a fall guy; Obed wasn't sure, if he couldn't avoid having this thing go to trial, that he wouldn't be using some other defense. Obed didn't want to risk tainting the credibility of this possible other defense by first putting out some elaborate, fevered tale of being framed, and then retracting it. Makes the defendant look like he's shopping for alibis.

The pushy sister, Angela Garcia, had argued passionately in favor of telling Meelo's story. Maybe someone who heard it would recognize the people who set Meelo up, call in with information. It was the only chance they had to track these people. Because no way could she hire a private investigator. She had checked out a bunch of them, sat up all night crunching numbers. Wouldn't compute. No way she could pay a private eye and her rent. And none of her family would loan her a dime for Meelo. So Meelo had to at least get his story out there and hope for the best.

Obed and the pushy sister went around on this for hours.

Angela finally backed off. She thought she was right. But she might not be. She might just be naïve, stubborn, and crazy with worry. So she wasn't willing to risk hurting Meelo by going against his lawyer. Not when she couldn't afford a better one. All she could do was pray this lawyer knew something.

Paul Obed did know something. He knew enough to assert

his client was being framed when one of his client's alibi witnesses turned up decapitated. He just wasn't secure enough to go ahead and do it, until his superior at the public defender's office gave him step-by-step instructions and threatened to fire him if he didn't start stepping.

Obed sent e-mails to the media trumpeting an important development in the Willetts case, related to the grisly discovery outside Joliet. Linking a headless, handless, 100-percent-tattooed alleged meth dealer to the Willetts murder should attract a decent number of reporters.

"I'm Paul Obed," he apologized, squinting into an intimidating number of harsh lights. "The um, attorney representing Emilio Jesus Garcia, the defendant in the Willetts—the Wilson Willetts case."

His voice trembling as if this were his first time in front of the cameras, which it was, Obed announced, "Emilio Jesus Garcia is the victim of a conspiracy to frame him for the murder of Wilson Willetts. There is a witness who could alibi Mr. Garcia for the time of the murder—the police have that witness's name and are searching for that witness as we speak.

"The police have also been searching for a man who could have verified a key element of Mr. Garcia's story. That man was Ralph Garn of Hammond, Indiana, whose incredibly . . . disturbed . . . remains . . . were recently uncovered and identified. The implic—"

A reporter interrupted, pointing out that the Hammond police believed Garn's murder was linked to the explosion of a meth lab in the victim's tattoo parlor. Did Obed believe the Hammond police were wrong about that?

Obed pointed out the Hammond police had a theory but no proof. And no leads.

Then he got back on message. "The implications speak for

themselves. My client has only two witnesses who can confirm key elements of his alibi. Both witnesses disappear the day after Wilson Willetts is killed. Now one of them has turned up, obviously the victim of a professional hit. Was Ralph Garn's gruesome death a coincidence? Was it unrelated to Garn being a witness in the Willetts murder case? I don't think so. I believe I'm justified in connecting these dots."

Obed paused to think, to breathe, to make sure he phrased his brainstorm exactly the way he'd rehearsed it. Okay, here we go.

"And if anyone thinks my theory is improbable, I ask you to recall Dallas, 1963: An important man is shot. A suspect is arrested within hours. The next day key witnesses began being brutally murdered—well, not mutilated like Mr. Garn, but—murdered, so . . . The implications speak for themselves."

After a moment of stunned silence, the reporters erupted in an enthusiastic barrage of questions. Especially the TV reporters; this was a slim story but a lethal hook. *Defense claims headless tattooed corpse proves Willetts murder cover-up; cites possible link to Kennedy assassination. Tape at ten.*

Obed slid through the Q&A in a daze of pleasure. It had worked, it had worked. They were excited, they didn't think he'd wasted their time. Swept along by the reporters' loud, needy attention, Obed started handling questions as if he didn't fear them. Built steam, got smoother, projected something that resembled confidence.

Then Bob Gilkey asked if Obed had any information, any theories who the real murderer might be.

Obed thought about it. And thought about it. Shrugged. Finally said, "No."

THIRTY

Arthur Reid gave up trying to nudge the brix-measuring contest into the realm of rational, civil argument. Waited it out, his mind half-elsewhere.

Arthur and the whiz-kid winemaker he'd hired, Chip Bozeman, were with Fred Kaamp, in the rustic-baronial office of Kaamp's home, on the ridgeline above Kaamp's legendary vineyard.

Fred Kaamp was a big, swaggering, pig-headed son of a bitch whose Empire Slope vineyard produced some of the lushest syrah grapes in Napa, in all California, in all the known goddamn universe.

Chip Bozeman was a sharp, passionate five-foot-six bantam, a young artist whose pig-headedness took a back seat to no tall man's, especially after Bozeman's first two syrah micro-bottlings (less than four hundred cases produced) had been sanctified by several uber-critics and snapped up by collectors (Arthur Reid among them). Chip was more than ready to rise to the bait when Kaamp started getting abusive, about thirty seconds into the discussion.

Arthur sat patiently, letting the bantam and the middle-aged schoolyard bully work their way through that wine-head classic, the war between vintners and growers over who'd decide the exact moment of crush—the picking and mechanized stomping of the grapes.

Determining the perfect moment was the hugest, most

scientific, mystical, personal, make-or-break crapshoot in the wine biz. There was no argument involved if a winemaker grew his own grapes; Arthur would have that luxury if he ever decided to make zin from the grapes grown on the vineyard he'd recently acquired. But there just might be an argument involved if you were intent on making great syrah from great grapes you had to buy from a great shithead thug of a grower, through a contract loaded with out-clauses.

Bozeman and Kaamp were approaching the point of physical violence because Bozeman wanted to hold off on crush until the grapes reached 26 brix. Kaamp insisted his grapes were perfect at 24 brix—which is where they were now—and he was going to pick tomorrow, or the next day at the goddamn latest.

Brix is the index of sugar content in the maturing grape. With the right grapes, higher brix makes for a heftier taste and a thicker, more viscous mouth feel. These were the right grapes, from Empire Slope's uppermost parcel, best of the best. Chip wanted to wait for the very last moment, when the fruit had maxed out. Kaamp wanted to get the crops in soon as they were decent. Waiting was risky; the grapes could pass their peak, dropping in flavor and total yield. One hot or cold or wet or earthquake day could wreck the vintage and leave the grower with raisins. Or less.

"I'm talking a week, ten days at most—here's the long-term forecasts for the next two weeks," Chip snarled, slamming a fistful of papers on Kaamp's desk. "There's nothing coming going to hurt our grapes."

"They're *my* goddamn grapes and I can't believe some goddamn child is standing here telling me he wants me to risk my goddamn crop 'cause he believes in the Tooth Fairy and weather reports!" Kaamp bellowed.

"I cannot make the wine I can make unless those grapes are at twenty-six!"

"My goddamn grapes are goddamn perfect at twenty-four! I know what the hell works for my fruit! We pick tomorrow!"

"Fuck no!"

Kaamp looked at Arthur, who was the money. "I pick tomorrow. You don't want my goddamn grapes, say so. I pick up this goddamn phone and I got five buyers kissing my ass."

True. Winemakers would kill for those grapes. Arthur might have, if it wouldn't have created more problems than it solved. He never did anything as stupid as killing someone he was publicly associated with.

No, he merely did something as stupid as accepting the contract to kill Wilson Willetts.

The Great Brix War was the noisiest but not the primary vexation on Arthur's mind. During the drive north to Napa from his new vineyard home near Paso Robles, Arthur had stopped at a cyber-café in San Jose to check the online editions of the Chicago papers; he never used his own computer to keep tabs on his hits.

Arthur had been waiting for the other shoe to drop since God had played that little joke on him and spat Ralph's corpse out of its toxic waste pond. Frustrating. But Arthur had trained himself to let go of frustration. It was depressing and inefficient. So he waited and watched; contemplated his options.

The Hammond police had of course chalked up Ralph's death to meth-gang petulance.

But Meelo had of course told his attorney about Ralph and "Oscar." The attorney had gone public.

Now the Chicago police would of course have to dig into Ralph's death.

Two paths might lead to Arthur. The first was Ralph. The second was that the police might now take a harder look at the possibility Meelo didn't kill Willetts. Which might lead to the Meelo look-alike. Or to Arthur's client. Either of whom might lead to Arthur.

Too soon to take any measures to shut those paths down by removing Hector B and/or the client. And the odds were Ralph's death would remain a mystery, unconnected to Willetts; there should be no clues to who killed Ralph, or how . . . But then the odds were the discovery of Ralph's corpse was an event that should have taken place sometime between three decades from now and never. Hell, the odds were, not even Meelo would find a lawyer who'd stand there and compare this case to Dallas in '63 . . .

"Hey Reid, what the hell you smiling at," Kaamp fumed. "Think this is funny? Think I'm kidding? 'Cause you can just drag your sorry—"

"Fred, I apologize for letting the discussion get out of hand. I was keeping quiet because I'd never presume to get in the middle of a technical debate between experts," Arthur said, his tone as mild as his looks. "I think we can settle this amicably. If you agree to hold off on crush until—"

"Are you goddamn deaf?!" Kaamp thundered. "We . . . pick . . . tomorrow!"

"I will guarantee to pay the full price of our contract no matter what shape the grapes are in. You don't lose a penny no matter what."

Kaamp chortled derisively. Chip's shoulders slumped, knowing what was coming.

"I don't lose a penny?" Kaamp sneered. "If Empire Slope craps out on a whole vintage because I bend over for this pissant wine genius"—jabbing a thumb at Chip—"the reputation, the reliability of my grapes is damaged *for years* in this goddamn bitchy business so I lose *billions* of pennies, *plus* I get to eat shit from every grower in this valley 'cause I got jobbed by a dilettante dipshit like you who thinks he's a *winemaker* 'cause on a good day he can tell red from white!" The veins in Kaamp's temples were vibrating. "You taking the grapes I'm picking *tomorrow?!* Yes or no!"

Arthur touched Bozeman's shoulder. "Chip, would you please excuse us," Arthur calmly requested.

Chip nodded at Arthur. Threw a hard stare at Kaamp. Resisted the urge to tell Kaamp if those grapes were picked tomorrow he and Arthur would go buy grapes at a supermarket and make better wine out of it.

Settled for slamming the door.

Chip Bozeman was leaning on a fence gazing up at the sinuous parallel rows of dark green vines marching across the face of Empire Slope's fabled Vespasian Patch, the stalks bowed by the weight of the fat grape clusters Chip knew, dead knew, he could shazam into true magnificence, juice that would rival the finest Hermitage or Cote-Rôtie, if only he could get them at 26 brix . . . Not gonna happen. So do we take these at 24? No. We go grab some merely excellent grapes down in Santa Ynez for two thousand bucks a ton less, and this year instead of making a classic we make an affordable killer that kicks ass on bottles twice its price—Chip heard steps behind him, turned, and saw Arthur. Who didn't seem depressed.

Arthur flicked a glance at the Vespasian Patch. "They're yours. We'll pick when you're ready."

The young vintner spent a second levitating, then came back to earth. "Ah jeez, Arthur, what did he hold you up for?"

"Nothing," Arthur assured him. "We worked it out."

"I won't let you get soaked. We've got options, we can—"

"Chip," Arthur advised, amused, "learn to take yes for an answer."

"Yeah." Chip grinned sheepishly. "It's just, I can't wrap my brain around what it'd take to move that bastard . . . How'd you do it?"

"We worked it out," Arthur repeated, still friendly, but quieter, and something changed in his eyes. The mousy-looking dude had some steel in him. The topic was closed.

Okay by Chip. Shazam.

Arthur, Chip, and Chip's girlfriend of the moment, Lweez, were celebrating at Yountville's foodie shrine of the moment, a restaurant where the arugula came with a biography and a mission statement.

The arugula was extraordinary. The celebration was heartfelt. Chip, a little lit and a lot ecstatic, was entertaining Lweez and Arthur with an enthusiastic, molecular response to Lweez's question about the exact physical process by which oak flavor got from the barrels into the wine.

"So wine is just chemistry," Lweez said.

"Not quite," Arthur disagreed, "or anyone could do it. It's chemistry plus talent."

"Chemistry *multiplied* by talent—no false modesty here," Chip giggled. "The shazam factor."

"And so," Arthur grinned, "we arrive at Chip's Theorem: Chemistry multiplied by talent equals magic."

"Arthur, awesome dude, if anyone at this table is a magician," Chip gave Arthur an impish significant look, "it's you."

"Not even close," Arthur demurred.

Magic had shit to do with it. Before going into business with anyone, Arthur did illegally thorough research on them, employing a felony nerd whose services Arthur occasionally required; he was the one who'd hacked into the Chicago police system and found Meelo, the face that matched Hector B's.

This time the felony nerd tapped and hacked his way into Fred Kaamp's phones and files. Turned out Kaamp had hidden some assets during his second and third divorces, which had stealthed them from the IRS as well.

Kaamp had calmed down considerably when Arthur leaned close and whispered the names and locations of Kaamp's offshore dummy corporations, and the serial numbers of those corporate accounts.

"I'm just a retired businessman who's glad to be here, doing what we're about to do." Arthur raised his glass. "Putting Chip's Theorem to work."

The celebrants drank to that. Chemistry multiplied by talent equals magic.

THIRTY-ONE

"Stop apologizing for how long it took. Just tell me it's double-checked."

The lab tech assured Mark it was and e-mailed the file. Mark copied it to Doonie. They reported to Husak.

"Green ink," Mark told the lieutenant. "Same shade as the snake."

"Tattoo ink?" Husak asked.

Mark shook his head. "Temporary tattoo ink. High-grade. A kind professional makeup artists use."

Mark and Doonie waited a moment while Husak worked it through. The evidence meant Darwahab had scratched someone with a temporary tat. Maybe of a green and red snake—or cow, or carrot. The artist who applied the tat could tell them. Except, if the tat *was* a copy of Meelo's snake, they were probably looking for a very dead artist. Look what happened to Ralph, who had only seen Oscar. This makeup artist had seen the shooter.

"Get going," Husak ordered.

The Illinois Film Commission didn't just have a list of Chicago's professional makeup artists who hadn't moved to Hollywood yet. They had it broken down by specialties.

Took Mark and Doonie a day and a half to get to all seven tattoo experts. None of them had painted a copy of Meelo's green and red snake on anyone. None of them had heard of any of their peers suddenly leaving town without a forwarding address.

All of them said the same thing about the type of ink required to stay on for extended periods but still not leave a stain on the actor when you removed it. State of the art, pricey hypoallergenic stuff, custom-made at a place in North Hollywood.

Ivo Foster, owner of Cosmetrix, would be happy to cooperate soon as he could confirm the voice on the phone was in fact a Detective Bergman of the Chicago Police Department. Mark supplied the necessary phone numbers. He also faxed an official request to Foster on Department stationery.

A couple of hours later Foster called back and said he'd supply the information soon as his lawyer cleared it; needed to be certain there were no liability issues vis-à-vis releasing business data about his clients. Foster was sure Detective Bergman understood how litigious the entire world had become.

Two days later, having received the necessary clearances from his attorney, the SEC, his priest, and his mommy, Foster forwarded a list of clients who in the last six months had purchased that ink in those colors.

Charlie Banza stood out. Banza had purchased a whole spectrum of the temp ink. Then ordered more of the green and red. Kind of like he'd been preparing for anything, then zeroed in on specific needs.

"Hello?"

"Hello, this is Detective Mark Bergman, Chicago Police Department. May I please—"

"My God! You found him?! Is he all right, where is he?!"

"Excuse me, sir, I'm trying to get in touch with Mr. Charles Banza. Are you—"

"This is Chazz."

"You're Charles Banza?"

"No, no, I'm Chazz Allen, his companion, why are you calling for Charlie, I thought . . ."

"Yes?"

"I thought you must be, must've known . . . sorry, I've been so . . ." The young man's voice caught.

"Take your time, Mr. Allen." Yeah. The rest of the conversation wasn't going to be much of a surprise.

Chazz Allen pulled himself together and launched into it. Said he'd been going nuts, wondering whether he should have filed a missing persons report by now.

About a month ago Charlie told Chazz he had a special gig for an extremely wealthy, very private client. Might have to go out of town for about a week. Two at the most. Couldn't say who he was working for or where.

Chazz wasn't buying. What the hell was so secret about a fake tat? He wanted to know what was really going on. Wanted to know who the fuck Charlie was seeing.

Charlie swore this was about jackpot dollars and . . . he couldn't say. Swore it was for a good cause. Begged Chazz to believe.

Chazz tried, but—big money *and* a good cause?! Oh pick some fucking excuses that at least go together . . . Chazz went into the kind of low-rent lavender rage he and Charlie never, never got into, all that bad dialog and screaming.

Charlie hinted he wasn't working for a rich *person,* it was . . . secret stuff someone had to do. He was working for the good guys. Which was already telling Chazz more than he should have, for God's sake Chazz had to trust him on this.

Way he said it, y'know, Chazz thought, my God, this is just too strange for Charlie to be making it up, like he's got a gig for "the good guys."

That's why Chazz hadn't filed a missing persons even though

127

it'd been a month now—Chazz was paranoid he might be screwing up something important by being paranoid about Charlie being gone.

Mark sighed, silently. The good guys. Jesus fuck. Someone sold Charlie Banza, showbiz pro, on the idea he was working for the Feebs or the spooks.

Mark thanked Chazz, offered his sympathy. Told Chazz he'd called to consult with Mr. Banza about a technical matter, because Mr. Banza had been recommended as an expert. Mark recommended Chazz file a missing persons report immediately. Mark suggested Chazz include as much detail as possible when he filed the report—for instance, had Charlie said anything or left any sketches or notes about what this mystery tat might be?

Zero.

Mark asked—out of professional curiosity—what date Mr. Banza had left, and how he'd traveled; if he'd driven or flown.

Chazz gave Mark the when: eight days before Willetts got whacked.

But not the how. Chazz, a digital transfer artist, had been at work when Charlie left home that day. Charlie's truck was still in the garage. Chazz had no idea if Charlie had called a cab or been picked up by the client or stepped through the looking-glass.

ASA Harrison Miller didn't think some fag makeup artist bullshitting his boyfriend constituted a suspicious connection to the ink from Darwahab's fingernail scrapings. Neither did Miller see anything intriguing about the fact the makeup queen disappeared eight days before the Willetts shooting. Though Miller did promise to check Banza's horoscope to see if the date held any hidden significance.

Lieutenant Husak allowed that while ASA Miller wasn't going

to win Miss Congeniality this year, the condescending butthole might have a point. Unless a corpse turned up, they had less reason to believe Charlie Banza was dead than he was real bad at making excuses when he snuck off for long romantic knob polish.

THIRTY-TWO

Mark caught himself hoping some normal murder would happen today so he and Doonie could go do something besides checking every black Explorer fender in the upper Midwest, or continuing to get their brains beaten in by whoever killed Willetts. Assuming it wasn't Meelo.

Assuming. Probably. Supposing. Maybe. If.

Fuck, he's sitting here in the squad room wishing for someone's simple violent death, as a diversion. Staring at nothing, not working, not knowing how to work this case any more. All around him cops and phones and computers and copiers and desks and chairs are doing their jobs, earning their paychecks, and he's so lost in frustration he can't think of how to think his way through this, he's so imploded that all this normal activity around him isn't quite real, it's right next to him but miles away. Maybe it's time to let go of this case.

"Maybe," Mark said to Doonie, "we put Meelo in the room again, beat a confession out of him, and be done with it."

"Okay," Doonie said, "but first let's call Arkansas."

Elizabeth Hackenmeyer had withdrawn fifteen hundred dollars from a bank branch in Heber Springs, Arkansas. Rock and fucking roll.

Doonie got on the line to the Heber Springs cops, and Mark called the Cleburne County Sheriff. Mark also got the number of the Arkansas state police from them. He hung up the phone, leaving his hand on the receiver, intending to wait a moment for the line to clear so he could get a dial tone. But a second after the receiver hit the cradle the phone rang. Mark answered it, trying not to sound impatient with the interruption.

"Bergman, Homicide."

"Hi," a friendly female voice greeted him, "I'm Betsy Hackenmeyer."

Pangburn, Arkansas.

Betsy sighted treasure. A turn of the century Greaves & Sons parlor stove. Cast iron, claw feet, ornamented firebox, blue and white faux Chinese tile on top. In B+ shape.

Claudeen, the seller, was a plump, pleasant granny with curly white hair and a little girl's wide, pale-blue eyes. Claudeen was asking twelf-hunnert an' fitty dolluhs for the pahlo stove.

When Betsy heard the price she just nodded, not reacting, and moved on. She hung around the vendors nearby, watched the reactions of other browsers to the price. Mainly snorts and laughs. Twelf-fitty was the highest ask on any item at the Pangburn flea market. Betsy had a feeling she could haggle it down by half. And if she couldn't move the price that far, no matter. Betsy could go a thousand on that stove and still double her money selling to a restorer; triple it selling to a homeowner at a big-city meet.

Betsy left Pangburn and hurried up the road to Heber Springs, site of the nearest supermarket that housed an American Fedbank sub-branch. She withdrew fifteen hundred and drove back to Pangburn in a shiny mood. Betsy, warrior goddess of the parlor stove quest. God, she enjoyed this game. Day well spent no matter how it turned out.

When Betsy returned to the meet she found Claudeen deep in negotiations with a kind of hard-looking biker-looking chick. Tall, rawboned, fortyish, short-chopped shocking yellow hair with chartreuse streaks, black leather vest over tight denim flares. A large square earring in one ear, six small hoops in the other. Nose stud. Tats on both arms and around her bare pierced navel.

As Betsy walked up she heard the biker-looking chick offer seven hundred. Claudeen sadly shook her head and turned it down—but hesitated just a sec before she did. The biker-looking chick sighed, frowned . . . then reluctantly went to seven-twenty-five.

Before Claudeen could reply—and possibly give in—Betsy introduced herself to both women. The tall, hard-looking, tattooed and pierced woman turned out to be just folks. Her name was Maggs, she had an easy, throaty laugh and she clearly hadn't popped a Tic-Tac after smoking a joint on her drive to the flea market. The bidding, while competitive, was friendly and chatty.

After they'd exchanged names Betsy apologized to Maggs, explaining this was just too nice a stove not to try for, and offered Claudeen eight-fifty. Hoping the large jump would end the bidding.

Maggs laughed, told Claudeen she had a feeling this was Claudeen's lucky day, and bid eight-seventy-five.

Betsy jumped it another hundred. Maggs again added twenty-five, bringing it to an even thousand. Claudeen, beaming, looked at Betsy.

Betsy pretended to think it over a while. Examined a bent hinge on the fire door. Betsy offered a thousand-fifty.

Maggs went to eleven hundred. Betsy topped that by twenty-five.

Maggs grinned. Told Claudeen eleven hundred was as much as she could spend, but she'd throw in free tattoos for Claudeen.

The three women laughed at the notion of Claudeen going under the needle gun.

Betsy asked Maggs if she'd had any luck swapping tattoos for goods. Maggs said you'd be surprised. Though of course she preferred working for cash. Gave Betsy her card.

Claudeen, concerned the tattoo artist's business card was a ticket to hell and Betsy was about to use it, said she could tell Maggs was a fine person, but Claudeen had grown up in a time when tattoos were associated with rough sorts, and in fact that might still hold some truth, look at what happened to that tattooed all ovuh felluh up near Joliet, you know, the one they pulled outta that polluted lake all, you know, done the way he was.

Maggs sighed, ruefully. Betsy shook her head; hadn't heard about it.

Claudeen was amazed Betsy had missed it—been on all the shows. Claudeen explained exactly how the tattooed all ovuh fella had been done, and how the police at first thought he was part of a drug gang in Indiana, and then it also turned out he was a tattoo ahtist—

"Which was not good for our professional image," Maggs admitted.

"—and this ahtist," Claudeen continued in a significant tone, "did a tattoo on a man who was ay-rested fuh the muhduh of some fancy architect in Chicago. The killuh—a Mexican—claims this tattoo felluh was a witness who could hep cleah him, and then he turns up done like 'at."

"Wasn't much of an artist," Maggs added. "Seen pictures of the tat—lame. Big dopey green and red snake going all the way up this Mexican kid's arm and onto his neck. Sloppy, real rush job, which you especially cannot do on a tat that size."

"*And,*" Claudeen interjected forcefully, reasserting control over what was after all her story, "that poor felluh up near Joliet might not be the only one done 'at way. The killuh also says there was anothuh witness who could alibi he was in this motel room at the time of the muhduh." Claudeen touched Betsy's arm and switched to an even more ominous tone. "Well, this othuh witness has dis-appeahed too."

The witness finished explaining how she'd tracked down the detective.

"Thank you, Ms. Hackenmeyer."

"Call me Betsy. You have a nice voice."

Mark thanked her again and asked her to provide some preliminary confirmations of her identity so he could ask her a few questions over the phone. Then Mark asked the big question.

Betsy gave him a medium-size answer. It was enough.

"Betsy, would you be willing to return to Chicago? The State's Attorney needs to depose you; your testimony is extremely important." The Department would send Mark down to Arkansas to interrogate Betsy and see if she could pick Meelo out of a photo array. But she'd be more convincing if she came here, answered everybody's questions, and picked Meelo out of a lineup. "The city will pay for your travel, and your expenses while you're here."

Mark was pretty sure he could get that authorized. Didn't care. Cover it himself if he had to.

"I'm on my way," Betsy assured him. You bet. This was more proof she'd made the right choice, to live free on the road, going where fate called. This was a chance for the warrior goddess to strike a blow for justice.

And who knows, if she helped clear that Garcia kid, maybe he'd be physically grateful.

And no matter how the justice thing or the young sex thing came out, she'd be able to get three grand for her newly acquired parlor stove at a Chicago antiques fair. Maybe more, if she got some publicity for testifying.

THIRTY-THREE

Way it worked out, Sy Vytautis didn't have to arrange a leak or schedule an interview to ensure he got credit for totally controlling the Willetts prosecution. All he had to do was show up late for a National Public Radio fundraiser.

The occasion was a dinner party for fifty at a Lake Forest estate. NPR had flown in its president, one weekday and one weekend anchor, and three of its best-known correspondents for face time with the Chicago area's heaviest donors. Sy's wife Millie was one of them; she was an hydraulics engineering heiress and a huge fan of public radio.

The cocktails and mildly exotic hors d'oeuvres hour was ending and the hostess was making her first attempt at herding her guests toward the dinner tables when Vytautis arrived, an hour late, because he'd stopped off on the way north for face time from his girlfriend.

Vytautis made his apologies to the hostess and scanned the room. Millie was chatting with Nathan Dougherty, managing editor of the *Chronicle,* and a slim, striking woman who had a glowing olive complexion and lush lips.

Perfect. All Vytautis had to do was go to Millie, kiss her, shake hands with the other two, and do the natural thing— apologize for his tardiness.

"My office is handling a pile of Murder Ones right now, and those require close supervision—even the cases that don't involve a famous victim."

The striking woman—Cerise LaVia, NPR's White House correspondent—took the bait. "You mean the Wilson Willetts case?"

Vytautis nodded. He noticed Nate Dougherty's gaze sharpen as the managing editor set his mind to record any juicy tidbits.

"Assuming you're permitted to discuss it," LaVia continued, "is there anything to that Grassy Knoll comparison the defense attorney was making last week?"

"Well," Vytautis deadpanned, "we won't know for sure until we complete our investigation of the defendant's alleged ties to the Mob, Cuban intelligence, and Howard Hughes."

LaVia had a rich, throaty laugh. Shame Millie was there.

"The lawyer also said something about a witness who could alibi the suspect," LaVia noted, with her pouty lips and reporter's persistence.

"Is this what White House correspondents think about while you're supposed to be analyzing the President's every hiccup?" Vytautis scolded, pretending to be displeased she'd thrown him another fat one down the middle. "Off the record—that alleged witness was registered at the motel but didn't spend the night there. That alleged witness is some sort of flea-market gypsy who lives in a truck and disappears on America's back roads for months at a time, which is apparently what's happened." Vytautis dropped into a grim, determined tone. "Wilson Willetts' death is not going to be turned into a carnival. We are not going to get ambushed or sidetracked, I—"

Vytautis stopped before he could overstep professional bounds—but he was just too damn passionate about this case to leave it there. Vytautis snapped a glance at Dougherty—a knowing, just between us Chicahgah guys look. "Let's just say I'm supervising the hell out of this one."

Vytautis saw Dougherty catch his meaning. Tomorrow morning the managing editor would be slipping a tidbit to one of his columnists—

The pager clipped to Vytautis' belt began nuzzling him. "Excuse me." Vytautis pulled out the pager. Saw Harrison Miller's number. "Excuse me," Vytautis repeated to Millie and the two journalists. "Catch up with you in the dining room."

Vytautis went out to the sculpture garden/swimming pool. Looked around to make sure he was alone. Took out his cell and called Miller.

"Garcia's alibi witness turned up, in Arkansas," Miller told Vytautis. "In her initial statement she put Garcia at the motel twenty-two minutes after the time of the shooting. She's on her way to Chicago."

When his boss didn't respond Miller filled the silence by bleating, "Hope I'm not interrupting dinner or anything, I paged you once before, about an hour ago."

Right, back at his girlfriend's house when Sy's pants were literally down, as opposed to now, when they were only drooped around his ankles in the professional sense. If this case—this case he'd just informed Nate Dougherty he's micromanaging—if this case blows up, one of Dougherty's snide *Chronicle* fucks will be writing how the State's Attorney got TKO'd by a witness he dismissed as a flea-market gypsy. On the splashiest murder case of the year. With the primaries coming up.

Screw that. He was not going into this election as Sy Vytautis, premature indicter.

Vytautis said, low and hard, "She'd better not be a credible witness," and hung up.

He knew Miller would correctly interpret that as an order to break the witness. He knew he'd worded the statement ambiguously enough to deny that's what he meant.

THIRTY-FOUR

She'd better not be a credible witness? Harrison Miller hung up his kitchen phone and stared into the microwave, which contained the gummy lumps of leftover gyros and souvlaki he'd been about to reheat for dinner. *She'd better not be a credible witness?* Well no fucking way she could be; Meelo's guilty as sin. But Sy, if you think, if it ever comes to that, I'm going to take the heat for you ordering me to . . . *She'd better not be a credible witness?* Oh, that is clever, Massa Vytautis, you're a fucking genius, the fucking Prince of Plausible Deniability. Oh yeah, Sy. You and Henry II.

Remember Henry's *Will no one rid me of this meddlesome priest?* Followed by, "Oops, Becket's dead, don't blame me—it was a rhetorical question."

That's you all over, Sy, Henry the fucking II—you weren't ordering me to trash the witness, by whatever means necessary—you were just voicing a sentiment. Real credible.

Fuck it. Doesn't matter. Miller was planning on taking this witness apart anyway. Because Elizabeth Hackenmeyer had to be wrong about the time. Emilio Jesus Garcia was the perp. Miller and Vytautis weren't the heavies here, they were on the side of the angels . . .

Hmm.

Miller started the microwave. Went to the living room and got out his VHS of *Becket*.

Needed to study Richard Burton's performance. The scenes after Becket becomes the Archbishop of Canterbury. Implacable,

138

relentless, utterly in the right, God's own enforcer on Earth.

Let's see how Elizabeth Hackenmeyer stands up to that tone. Shit, maybe if I'd hit that Burton/Becket tone with Darwahab, our conversation about that fucking imaginary scratch would have had a more positive outcome . . .

Miller began replaying his exact words to Darwahab, trying to imagine how they'd sound in terms of plausible deniability. Would his phrasing provide any better ass coverage than Sy Vytautis', or Henry II's . . . ?

Miller was saved from dark thoughts by the microwave bell. He parked his dinner plate on the coffee table, cued the tape, and began working on his Richard Burton.

THIRTY-FIVE

Mark wasn't surprised that Miller watched as he and Doonie interviewed Betsy Hackenmeyer, or that soon as the cops were done, Miller went at Betsy. What did catch Mark off guard was the ASA's tortured manner. Miller seemed to be struggling with something that was maybe just a lethal hangover, or maybe a midlife breakdown.

Miller kept fixing Betsy with a tormented gaze, knitting his brow and flaring his nostrils. His voice was odd; he kept muttering through his nose, and sometimes elongated random words in a way that was a strange blend of moan and duck call. Several times Miller abruptly burst out in a near-yell, biting the words off sharply and pitching his voice up, as if he were trying to bark an opera.

Didn't keep Miller from putting some dents in Betsy and her time line.

Betsy said she knocked on Meelo's door at 11:17 p.m. She was certain of the exact time because she'd looked at the digital clock-radio in her room right before going.

Mark didn't think the shooter could have made it back to the motel by that time. Darwahab said he'd automatically glanced at his dashboard clock when he pulled up outside Willetts' house; remembered it as 10:54 p.m. That jibed with neighbors' accounts of hearing shots at about 10:55. Which put the shooter driving away in the cab at 10:56 or :57 p.m.

Mark and Doonie had done multiple test-runs, driving at

140

that time of night from the crime scene to where the cab was dumped. The shortest run had taken nineteen minutes. Which would have made it 11:16. Then, at the fastest, it would have taken the shooter a minute to do the thorough wipedown of the cab. So he's out of the taxi and walking at 11:17 at the earliest.

Getting from where the cab was abandoned to the motel, moving at a fast pace without breaking into a run that would attract attention, took six minutes. So the earliest the shooter could've been back at the motel was 11:23 p.m.

Six minutes after Betsy's chat with Meelo in the doorway of Room Eleven.

But six minutes was not a fail-safe alibi. The neighbors put the shots at "around" 10:55. Could've been a few minutes earlier. Then the shooter could've broken some speeding laws and run a few red lights; not the smartest way to flee a murder scene, which made it believable behavior for Meelo.

Then there was the clock-radio in Betsy's room. Was it slow? No way to check that now; impossible to know how many guests might have reset the time since the night of the murder.

Murder! was what Miller suddenly erupted in bark-song about, reminding Betsy to remember this was a *Murder!* investigation when she answered his questions.

Betsy said of course she would.

Mark thought she was enjoying herself. Getting off on being part of a *Murder!* investigation.

Miller pointed to Betsy's wrist. She wasn't wearing . . . a *waawtch*. Miller turned that last word into a drawn-out honk. In some odd accent that was maybe . . . Turkish?

Betsy was pleased to admit she almost never wore a wrist-watch since her accident. Time was not something she let be the boss of her any more.

Miller nodded sympathetically and assured Betsy there was no reason she should.

But she instantly ruined Miller's mood by pointing out that even if the clock had been fast or slow, she'd been hearing the young man next door yelling in pain and banging around for a couple, three minutes. That's why she'd gone to check if he was okay. He'd been in there a while making noise before she went and knocked, at 11:17 p.m.

Miller furrowed his brow and gazed at Betsy as if he feared for her soul. He reminded her she'd said the TV and stereo in the next room had been blaring, sometimes at the same time. *Could!* she be *certain!* it wasn't the TV she'd been hearing.

Well yeah, it was live shouting and banging, not TV shouting and banging.

Lowering his voice as far as it would go and moaning through his nose, Miller regretfully but sternly inquired if Betsy was still taking painkillers as a result of her terrible accident.

Nope. Been off those over a year. Took Prozac for a while after she got out of the hospital. Had some nasty side effects. So now she took Xanax.

Miller established Betsy had had one beer with dinner earlier that evening, and noted her claim she hadn't taken any recreational drugs. "And what is the name of the bar you went to after you left the motel?"

"Coobie's."

"How many drinks did you have?"

"No more'n I could handle."

"Why didn't you return to the motel that night?"

"Met someone at Coobie's."

"Do you mind revealing *who!* that person *wwaahhs?*"

"Don't mind, exactly, but . . . what's it got to do with what time I saw Mr. Garcia at the motel?"

"We need to contact that person, verify you went to that bar, at the time you said, and were as relatively sober—no more than a beer and a Xanax into the evening—as you said."

Betsy pondered that. Finally said, "I thought a person's private life is private . . . but saving a young kid from an unfair murder charge . . . Coobie's customers were all, y'know, so low-grade . . . I went home with Coobie." Betsy grinned shyly. "Coobie's my first-ever woman. And my first bartender in a real long time—swore off 'em back in my twenties."

Assistant State's Attorney Miller was so delighted by all the ammo Betsy had just handed him that he slipped out of Richard Burton and into his own voice when he thanked Betsy for her cooperation. And begged her to understand he had to ask one more question. Had she ever known or even seen Emilio Garcia before that night, had they had any sort relationship, whatsoever?

Betsy was sure she'd never laid eyes on Meelo before exactly 11:17 p.m. that night. She was also sure their one-minute chat in a doorway, nice as it was, was not what she would call a relationship.

Betsy said that last thing with a coy, dreamy hint of a smile. Mark glanced at Doonie to see if he'd caught it. He had.

So. One of Meelo's wildly unlikely claims turned out to be true. The woman who knocked on his door that night had the hots for him.

Betsy left the room. Mark and Doonie looked at Miller. The ASA gave them an approving nod, then stacked the legal pad containing his list of questions on the legal pad containing his notes on the interview, and opened his briefcase. If Miller had any thoughts on how Betsy's answers affected the case he wasn't sharing them.

Husak, who'd been watching from behind the glass, came in.

"Tomorrow good for you, Meelo standing a lineup for the witness?" Husak asked Miller. Meaning it was time to notify Meelo's attorney Betsy had been located—so Obed could question Betsy and attend the lineup. After which Obed would probably inform the press he had proof Meelo wasn't the shooter, and demand Betsy be placed in the witness protection program to save her from Jack Ruby Jr.

"Set it up," the ASA replied. Miller was, for him, in a chipper mood. He looked as dour as usual, but as he packed his briefcase he was humming, under his breath, the theme from *Lawrence of Arabia*. (None of the music from *Becket* had stuck with him.) Miller snapped his briefcase shut and stood.

"Bye," Miller said to the room in general, vaguely, as if distracted by vast thoughts on matters of profound import.

Miller was reaching for the door handle when Mark stopped him by declaring, "Betsy Hackenmeyer just blew 'beyond a reasonable doubt' all to shit."

Husak tensed. Doonie relaxed, looking forward to the show. Wished he had a beer.

"Thanks for the legal advice." Miller wasn't annoyed. He was pleased Mark had asked to be pissed on. "But in my own humble opinion, testimony about the exact minute she did something, coming from a frowzy, traumatized, medicated, alcoholic, bisexual backwoods barroom slut who doesn't wear a watch because she won't let time be the boss of her, is not testimony I trust."

"Some of the jury will trust Betsy," Mark said. "She has this—invincible serenity. Even if it's only from the Xanax."

Miller shook his head sadly. He again started to leave. Stopped, relishing a parting twist of the knife.

"When the Pocket Pal puts Hackenmeyer on the stand I'm gonna demolish her so bad, Obed's next move will be to beg for a plea. This one ain't gonna go to a fucking jury, Detective Darrow."

Wrong, Mark thought. Obed might be willing to bend over and grin, but the strength here was the sister. Angela Garcia wasn't going to let her brother plead guilty. Not with Betsy, warts and all, dead certain Meelo was at the Golden Door Motel. *Only way this case doesn't go to a jury is if the State's Attorney drops the charges.*

Mark didn't say anything.

Miller interpreted Mark's silence as a surrender. He flashed a victorious Flynn-Grynn and left.

Mark and Doonie looked at Husak.

Husak scowled. Didn't have anything to say.

"Lieutenant," Mark asked, "you ready to write off Betsy's story, on top of everything else?"

Husak shook his head.

"So," Mark said, out loud, making it official, "we'd like to make some discreet inquiries about other people who might have motive."

Rich, connected people. Out of state. Huge can of poison worms they'd be opening. Even if the press didn't get hold of it.

Plus which Superintendent Blivins would have to be willing to piss off State's Attorney Vytautis. Who someday might be governor, or worse.

"I'll think about it," Husak said. Officially, procedure said this was Husak's decision. "Fast as I can," he promised, and left. Meaning this wasn't a decision Husak would be forgiven for making on his own, so he'd get on the phone to Downtown and start the process.

It was the first time Mark had seen Husak look embarrassed.

"They gotta give us the go," Mark muttered, trying to sound convinced.

Doonie stared at Mark. Eventually said, savoring each syllable, "Invincible serenity."

"Yeah, so?"

"Not bad. One a ya grandmas musta known an Irishman."

"As long as she didn't know Harrison Miller. Is it possible

145

he's getting weirder?"

"It's what happens when ya live alone too long," Doonie advised.

"Thanks, Phyl."

"Hey, she's right about some things, even if she married me."

They left the interrogation room. Walked to their desks in silence. When they arrived Mark asked, "Am I getting strange?"

"Not yet. But you don't wanna be that fuckin' lonesome when you're that fuckin' old. I'm thirsty—let's grab some lunch."

THIRTY-SIX

"Don't bother ordering squid-ink risotto in this country. You can get an edible one, but it will never taste the way it did in *Venezia.*"

"I've been finding that out. I'm actually tempted to fly back to Venice for dinner—how decadent is that?"

"Not at all, as long as you resist the temptation," Arthur said, doing a droll impersonation of himself.

"I may be driving up here again for lunch, though. You were right, these seafood sausages are amazing."

"The kitchen doesn't make them very often, be sure to call ahead."

They were in a cozy gourmet outpost a young Swiss chef had established in Cayucos, a Central Coast beach town that was mutating from working-class to recreation-class. Arthur's new home was nearby, about twenty-five minutes inland, perched in the spectacularly sculpted hills above Paso.

For Dina it had been a pleasant three-hour jaunt up the coast from L.A. But not nearly as pleasant as the lunch itself, as being with Arthur for the first time since the job. Dina could tell he was glad to see her. She was delighted with how delighted he'd been with the exquisite Murano vase she'd brought him. Shame the reason they were here was to deal with the shit that was beginning to fly.

Dina had been waiting for Arthur to retire and finally let her into his life. Lovers, husband and wife, one-night stand.

Anything. There was something between them, had been, always. They'd never spoken about it. Hadn't had to. She knew Arthur. Knew she wasn't deluding herself. There was something. Eventually they'd have to find out what kind and how large. But they never would while Arthur was still working and Dina was still sometimes his co-worker. Romance was a mind-altering drug Arthur didn't allow during office hours. Which ran 24/7, in a business where the downside included life imprisonment or execution. Arthur had been clear about that—as he had been about everything else—right from the beginning.

Dina and Arthur met the night they both showed up to kill the owner of a San Diego Jaguar dealership—Todd Denbow, an affable man, tall, lean, with silver-gray hair and pretty much the same boyish face he'd worn to prep school.

Dina was eighteen and putting herself through community college, slowly. She taught herself to look and sound more mainstream than the hard place she'd come from. She'd gotten a temp job as a receptionist at the dealership. She was pretty, sharp, worked hard, and was neither shocked nor seduced by the thrillingly profitable scams the staff ran on the customers. Dina was all business. She turned down offers from the salesmen. She turned down offers from the upscale clientele. She was offered the job full-time. She accepted, and registered for night classes.

One morning Dina was asked to deliver some papers to Denbow, who was on his boat in La Jolla. He'd been living on the boat since separating from his wife. When Dina got there Denbow was eating breakfast. He asked her to join him, said he hated eating alone. Asked how she liked her job, asked her opinions of procedures at the dealership. He wanted to know if there was anything she thought could be improved. He wanted to know about her. He approved of her determination. He said some of his clients were college administrators. He said he was sure he could help her get a scholarship to a four-year school if she kept her grades up. She thanked him. He raped her.

First he kissed her. She pushed him away. He wrapped her up in a bear hug. She kneed him. He put a knife to her throat. Pulled handcuffs out of a drawer next to his bunk, cuffed her hands behind her back.

Afterward Denbow warned Dina not to go to the cops. He'd checked up on her. Knew she'd been in foster homes since she was fifteen. Knew her father was unknown. Knew she'd been raised by an unmarried mother who claimed the semen donor was a Greek sailor. Knew Mom was a spic crack whore who'd been sent up for tricking out her daughter at age fourteen.

And by the way, if Dina did try to deny their belly-bump had been consensual, tried to shake Denbow down, the cops would be on his side. Know why? There was an extra three hundred dollars in Dina's checking account. Deposited there yesterday. Worth every penny, too. And there'd be more, if she was smart.

Dina didn't quit the receptionist job. Showed no change in her demeanor, except for making sure not to get caught alone with the owner. Just walked away without acknowledging it whenever Denbow copped a feel. Meanwhile she used his three hundred bucks to buy a gun. Unregistered, from a survivalist in the parking lot at a gun show.

Dina practiced. Waited for Todd Denbow to leave town on business. Went to his boat the night he was due to return. Sneaked aboard and went below to wait for him. But as she stepped into his cabin some fast violent force bent her arm behind her back and pinned her face-down on the bunk. A man's voice warned her not to struggle. She tried anyway. The man's thumb pressed below her ear and the pain erased her will. The man's thumb eased off. He found and removed her gun. Whispered, "If you shoot him you'll get caught. And I won't get paid."

Won't get paid.

Face still pressed into the mattress, Dina asked, "Oo ong oo kyu im?"

The man loosened his grip enough for Dina to shift her head. "You going to kill him?" she repeated.

"He has no future."

It was the coldest thing Dina ever heard. But not entirely frightening; there was a solid, factual, trustworthy quality. After a moment she asked, "What about me?"

Instead of answering, the man asked, "That morning you visited him here . . ."

The hair went up on the back of Dina's neck—the man had been watching Denbow for weeks—

". . . what happened?"

"Knife. Handcuffs. Rape." Trying to match the man's dispassionate precision.

After what seemed like a long time, the man inquired, "Did anyone see you come aboard just now?"

"Don't think so. But I don't know for sure."

For the first time Dina heard the man breathe. One deep, slow breath. Then in one motion he let go and was off of her.

Dina stood, slowly. Waited for his instructions. There weren't any. Dina turned and looked at him.

He was a bland-looking man. Dressed in a dark linen sport coat, white polo shirt and jeans, expensive glasses; dead match for a prosperous boater, except for the latex surgical gloves he had on. There was enough light coming in from the marina to tell he had black hair and beard. Dina wasn't sure but she thought the hair was a wig and the beard was dyed. His hands were by his sides. Dina was sure the thing in his right hand was a gun with a silencer. She looked at it, then at him. A professional killer. Who'd let her see his face.

150

Right. Dina smoothed her hair, straightened her shoulders, and met his gaze. Waited for him to do it.

"We'll leave together," the man said, unscrewing the silencer. "No hurry, very casual. Chatting as we walk." He dropped the silencer in a jacket pocket and tucked the gun in the back of his waistband. "I'm your Dad. You're trying to convince me you need a new car."

It was a twenty-minute walk from the marina to Dina's battered Tercel. When they arrived the man looked around at where they were—an oceanside bluff.

It occurred to Dina this was a more convenient place for him to shoot her than the boat would have been.

The man glanced at the path leading down to the beach, then said, "You were going to untie the dinghy, motor out of the marina, beach the dinghy down there, and climb up."

Dina nodded.

"The gunshots might've drawn witnesses from nearby boats, and the marina's rent-a-cops, by the time you got on deck," he said.

"If that happened I was gonna put the gun to my head and do the distraught, suicidal orphan rape victim for a couple of hours, hope for some TV cameras. Then ask some women's group to defend me, get me a plea bargain."

"What if he didn't come home alone tonight?"

"I was gonna apologize for intruding, say I absolutely had to see him, so I came down to the boat. He's vain enough, that'd make sense to him. Then I'd ask could I please see him alone here soon. When we did I'd tell my dirty little secret: I like it even rougher than he did it the first time. Get him to bruise me up, then shoot him in self-defense, with this unregistered gun he kept near his bed, along with his handcuffs."

The man made no comment and Dina couldn't tell from his expression what he thought of her stupid plans. She was going to tell him, look, Denbow had to die, and if she got caught she got caught. But she didn't think she'd be telling the man anything he didn't know.

"Go home," he said. "Don't do anything different. Not at the job, not in private. Especially don't quit or change anything after he's gone."

Dina nodded.

"For now, no changes in your mood or the way you relate to him. The big temptation in your immediate future," he told her, "will be to look at Denbow as if he's already dead. To say something clever. Resist that temptation."

Dina did.

Four days later Todd Denbow turned blue, spasmed, gurgled, and expired in the back seat of a Vanden Plas while playing with the teenage daughter of an old friend. The autopsy revealed Denbow, who suffered from allergies and an occasional accelerated heartbeat, died from complications of anaphylactic shock and high blood pressure. The precise cause of the allergic reaction could not be determined. Ephedra, a natural stimulant associated by anecdotal evidence with strokes and heart attacks, was present in Denbow's system. Overly vigorous physical activity may also have been a contributing factor; the pathologist surmised Denbow had taken Ephedra in order to match speeds with his four-decades-younger partner.

Five months later Dina heard from the man. He asked if she wanted to do a small job for him. She would have to distract two security guards for two or three minutes. Several weeks' preparation would be required for those minutes of work. She would be well paid. But if something went wrong she would be convicted as an accessory to murder with special circumstances.

Dina said yes.

The man said to call him Bill.

Two years later, during a discussion about choosing the appropriate weapon, Bill told Dina what he'd been doing that night on Denbow's boat: adding one multivitamin tablet to the bottle in Denbow's medicine cabinet. The pill was low on vitamins and minerals but loaded with organic allergens and a natural stimulant. Denbow taking a sixteen-year-old girl the same day he took the pill had been pure coincidence.

Dina figured Bill's client had been Denbow's wife. Dina never asked, and Bill never said. Bill probably didn't know who the client was; Bill's agent never revealed Bill's identity to the client, and rarely revealed the client's identity to Bill. Not that Bill would have told Dina in any case. When it came to work, Bill divided all conversation into two parts: shop talk and essential information. Shop talk didn't exist.

Three years later Bill told Dina his name was Arthur Reid. By that time Dina had graduated from UC San Diego with a degree in psychology. She'd also graduated from being Arthur Reid's apprentice to the status of independent contractor.

Satisfying as it was to succeed on her own, what Dina liked best was teaming with Arthur. He'd taught her how to kill and how to live. How to arrange identities, logistics, finances. How to enjoy the world, and how to behave in it. How, when you knew it was time to retire, you got right to it and walked away clean.

After lunch Arthur and Dina walked down the beach, heading south toward Morro Rock, the worn nub of an ancient volcano, a fat rugged upside-down cupcake of splintered granite that rose six hundred feet out of the water. Checking out the Rock was the natural thing to do after lunch; it had been the neighborhood's main picture-postcard attraction since 1542, when Juan Cabrillo had spotted it from his ship and written a rave review.

Arthur and Dina strolled along the tide line, barefoot, arm in arm. He was forty-seven and looked it; she was twenty-nine and looked younger. Passersby would take them for father and daughter, or executive and trophy wife. Dina was determined that with Arthur's retirement their relationship would stop resembling the former and start resembling the latter.

But instead of discussing how sex and/or love and/or marriage and/or children might complement Arthur's mission to create the good life and a world-class syrah, they were discussing recent developments in Chicago. The clues that had surfaced were disturbing, but all of them, even the abridged version of Ralph Garn, had been ambivalent. So far the prosecution remained adamant they'd arrested the right man.

That would change if Meelo's alibi witness turned up and was credible. The police would have to start searching for Oscar, Heather, and the look-alike shooter. The look-alike shooter— Hector B—would be the one the cops wanted the most, and would be the easiest to find.

"I'll keep tabs on him," Dina said, without Arthur having to tell her that's what was needed.

"Be careful. He can't know it's happening."

"He won't."

"Don't underestimate him."

"I won't."

"If the time comes, you don't go at him alone."

"I know."

"And stop making fun of me."

"I may."

Arthur slipped his arm out of Dina's and faced her, standing close. He looked at her with a knowing empathy and—*milagro*—a distant, carefully controlled hint of yearning. For a moment Dina thought, *This is it, he's finally going to do it. Kiss me.*

All he did was remain Arthur.

"No stupidity," he advised.

No way, Dina thought. She'd been waiting nine years for their first kiss. After putting up with that much foreplay she wasn't going to blow it by getting killed or busted this close to the finish line.

THIRTY-SEVEN

After garroting the Indian's mistress Hector B snapped her neck. Not because he wasn't sure she was dead but to confirm his arm strength was back to where it should be. It was almost there, but not all the way; took a little more effort than he remembered the last neck did. Shit. He'd been pumping like crazy to get his tone back; for that real profitable but real pain in the ass Chicago gig Hector B had had to lose weight and definition, so his arms would look small and un-cut enough to pass for Meelo's.

Hector B stripped the Indian's mistress, placed her face-down on her bed, and wedged a photo in her butt crack. It was a snapshot of the Indian's wife and kids. Hector B's Mafia-affiliated employer thought that would leave a clear message—get with the program, sign up your sacred Native American casino with the right security firm—or your family is next.

Hector B wasn't so sure; he thought Chief Humps The Blonde might just as easily worry the photo was a message from his wife.

Of course, if those Mob clowns had their act together they wouldn't be hiring outsiders like him in the first place. The L.A. outfit had never played more than double-A ball, underfunded and thin on talent. The city had no densely packed Italian neighbs like back east, no community, which was why out here the blacks and La Raza grew the gangs that counted.

In his teens Hector B had dipped just far enough into gang

156

life to decide it was bullshit. They got busted and mutilated and killed too easy and too often for too little profit.

Hector B had gotten into enough marginally profitable trouble on his own by age seventeen to motivate him to enlist in the army. What started out as a quick way to get far out of town for a long time turned out to be the trade school he hadn't known he was looking for. He went in mean and undisciplined, and came out mean, disciplined, and skilled. He got his GED and learned computers. Learned how much more effective guns were if you aimed before pulling the trigger. Learned about cutting tools and explosives. Went to jump school. Put in for the Rangers.

Three days before Hector B would've completed Ranger boot camp he went AWOL, attended church, let himself get caught robbing the collection plate, and slugged the minister. Hector B got a couple of months in the brig and a dishonorable discharge. Which was the idea. He wasn't up for getting deployed someplace where he might get shot at for soldier's pay.

When Hector B got back to L.A. he contacted the few old homies who'd developed business smarts. He pointed out that since he had no gang record and no known connections to them he could supply a safe, efficient method for disposing of their business problems.

After Hector B passed a few auditions, one of the homies recommended him to a wealthy civic leader whose son had been busted for wholesaling coke. Hector B made a key witness disappear. The grateful civic leader recommended Hector B to some people who knew people. Hector B got known as a young reliable problem-solver who didn't charge like he was fucking A-Rod going free agent.

Then Bill showed up. Bill had a risky complicated fucked-up proposition, but a client who was offering too much to walk away from. Except there was no fucking point having all that

157

cash if all it got you was a government needle in your arm. Hector B said no.

Bill sweetened the deal. And offered to help Hector B step up in class.

Bill would hook up Hector B with his agent. The agent was this real careful dude, wouldn't meet Hector B until months after the Chicago hit, till he could see it had gone down right, that Bill and Hector B weren't trailing any shit.

The Chicago hit went down fine. Hector B was waiting for enough months to go by so he could meet Bill's agent.

In the meantime Hector B took this Mob gig because it was quick, easy, and those scratches on his arm were scarring up. Doing the Indian's mistress got Hector B back in the groove and would pay for a trip to Costa Rica for plastic surgery, so he wouldn't have to tap into the retirement fund he'd just laid down, the way Bill had advised.

When Hector B got back from Costa Rica he'd be cleaned up and ready for the big leagues. It wasn't just the money he was looking forward to. Had to admit some of the Chicago gig had been fun. The thoroughness and teamwork reminded him of the good parts of being in the infantry. Always working alone got old.

And the hardware had been outstanding. Bill had sources for the best guns, electronics, whatever, and all this fucking impeccable fake ID, world-class shit. And Bill knew how to launder cash. How to set up a business in the straight world, get yourself a respectable cover life.

Hector B would be hooking into all of that when he got with Bill's agent. Bill's agent had a slick system going where he provided first-class problem-solving for high-end clients, who paid serious money and kept their distance. Mostly. And if they didn't, like whoever had insisted on this shit in Chicago, the agent made sure the pay was so fucking huge . . .

Bill had better be telling the truth. And he better not be planning to stall on hooking Hector B up with the agent, just on account of some fucking little blip like that tattoo bitch Ralph getting found in that chemical pond, that pond was Bill's idea anyw—The fuck?—

Hector B looked down.

A cat.

The Indian's mistress' cat was rubbing up against Hector B's leg. Shit. Just had these pants cleaned, now he'd have to pay to have them done again; fucking cat-hair DNA could put him at the scene.

Hector B picked up the cat, stroked her, kissed her, and broke her neck too.

THIRTY-EIGHT

Betsy Hackenmeyer had no trouble picking Meelo out of a lineup. That was him, no doubt about it, that's the sweet boy who answered the door at exactly 11:17 p.m.

"That's uh, only twenty-two minutes after the shooting," PD Paul Obed apologetically pointed out to ASA Harrison Miller.

Miller's response was a sarcastic smirk.

Betsy didn't care for the gangly, almost kinda ghoulish prosecutor, but she kinda understood his attitude toward the defense lawyer. Obed was about as forceful as Jello dressed in a suit and tie.

The public defender nervously cleared his throat and looked down, apparently addressing his question to Miller's shoes. "So I um, assume you're ready to uh . . ." Obed's voice dropped to a timorous whisper. "Drop the charges?" He risked a glance at the ASA's face.

Miller gave him a blast of The Gaze.

"Or," Obed offered in a half-protesting, half-placating whine, "at least agree for bail to be y'know, set."

"See you in court, Counselor." Miller turned to Betsy and shook her hand. "Thank you, Ms. Hackenmeyer," he said, with an appreciative grin that could give small children bad dreams.

After Miller left, Betsy, who'd noticed Meelo wasn't wearing a bandage, asked Obed if Meelo's hand had healed.

"His hand?"

Poor Meelo. Betsy had told Obed about how she'd offered to

160

bandage Meelo's hand, when Obed had questioned her in detail. This morning.

Betsy wondered if she could afford to get poor Meelo a better attorney . . . Damn. Couldn't do that. It would only discredit her, what's the word—partialness—as a witness.

Paul Obed issued a release announcing the key witness in the Willetts case had been located. Her testimony would prove the defendant was at the Golden Door Motel soon after Wilson Willetts was shot, too soon to have been the one who'd done it. There was a six-minute gap in the police timeline—a Six-Minute Gap of Innocence.

The State's Attorney issued a release stating that the homicide detectives had gone out of their way to track down a witness the defense should have. Extensive questioning by the police and ASA Miller had determined the witness' testimony changed nothing. The People were looking forward to going to trial at the earliest possible date.

Due to a sudden, nearly alchemical confluence of plea bargains, dismissals, and continuances on a dozen of his other cases, Judge Settimo L. Santini's docket developed an opening in ten days.

ASA Harrison Miller informed Judge Santini the State was ready to proceed.

PD Paul Obed couldn't think of any more preparations he might want to make, and told the judge, Sure.

Mark and Doonie waited to hear what Husak heard from Downtown.

THIRTY-NINE

The notorious sensitivity of the State's Attorney wasn't what was hanging Elvin Blivins up. Sy Vytautis didn't count for shit in the Superintendent's calculations.

Sure, Vytautis would get his panties in a twist if he heard the police were checking to see if a mistake had been made. Start shrieking how his high-profile case, his fucking Wilson Willetts TV show, was being compromised by the police raising doubts, aiding the defense.

Fuck him. Vytautis was no friend of the Department. Vytautis saw cops the same way he saw everyone else—tools to get as much use out of as possible. And Vytautis wasn't an enemy Blivins feared. Blivins' ties to the Hall were as strong as that camera whore's; Blivins had made the Mayor who'd picked him look nothing but good.

Except for being black and in charge, Superintendent Blivins was a classic Chicago cop. A man of sense, strength, height, and width. He'd powered his way up through the ranks, excelling, leaving every one of his commands in better shape than he'd found it. He wasn't a man who had trouble making decisions.

Usually.

The hang-up with the Willetts case was every fucking thing about it. The new evidence wasn't conclusive—but there was just too much of it to ignore.

If Emilio Garcia had been set up, the crew who'd fucked him left no useful clues. So the detectives had only one move—to look at who had motive and means to hire that crew. But the M&Ms in this case were a couple of big-time architects and their patrons, the Who's-Fucking-Who of the La-La power grid. Word would get out—count on it—that the Chicago PD was sniffing around their platinum asses.

If it turned out Garcia *was* framed, fine; Blivins would be doing his job—and protecting the Department. Blivins was sick to fucking death of the Department's rep for sloppy investigations and coerced confessions, especially from minorities. Sick of convictions being overturned and the city shoveling out six-, seven-figure damages. But if it turned out this Willetts "evidence" was all coincidental bullshit and Garcia was as fucking guilty as he looked, Blivins would look like a publicity-hungry fool.

That shouldn't be a concern. But Blivins had worked too hard to get here, sweated too much blood climbing this fucking mountain. He wasn't going to blow it now because he got suckered by a pile of circumstantial crap.

Blivins decided he needed to talk it over. Not with senior advisors who'd read the same reports he had. Blivins summoned the detectives who'd written the reports, along with their supervising officer.

A minute after Husak, Doonie, and Bergman arrived at Blivins' office Bergman got beeped; unspecified new development. Blivins grunted for him to go find out. Bergman left to return the call.

Doonie supplied Blivins with what wasn't in the written reports—his read of the witnesses, and how ASA Miller had responded to each. Blivins occasionally glanced at Husak to see if the lieutenant agreed with Doonie's impressions; Husak did.

"What about the daughter," Blivins asked. Meaning Nina Willetts, as a possible suspect.

Doonie shook his head. "She inherits, but it won't change her life; she's loaded. We ran the financials with the lawyer, Solwitz. Soon's Nina had a baby, Daddy moved a bunch of his assets into a trust she can tap. Plus which this Italian professor she married comes from this family, they invented cheese and banks, got money they made in 1512 they ain't spent yet."

"Maybe she's spoiled. Daddy pisses her off about some little thing, Daddy dies."

"Word across the board was Nina loved him. Day we interviewed her she was hurting bad but holding it in. Kid was taking care of everyone else. Solid citizen."

"Willetts' brother?"

Doonie shook his head again. "Ted also has his own money and got along great with Wilson, the two brothers ain't thrown punches since they were kids and it was natural."

Shit. There really was no one to look at except the rival architects and their megabuck patrons.

"This woman from the museum you want to talk to, this—" Blivins glanced at the report.

"Florence Brock," Doonie offered.

Odd. Doonie enunciated the name carefully, as if diction suddenly mattered to him. "This Brock," Blivins continued, "how long would she keep her mouth shut about talking to us?"

"I think she'll stand up if we put it to her she can't let rumors get out, because that would only put Nina through bad shit for no reason." After a moment Doonie added, "But you never know."

Doonie gave Blivins a small sympathetic shrug. The two went way back; Blivins had been Doonie's training officer. They'd always respected each other but aimed for different things, at different tempos. Doonie had never looked to move up the food chain; chose to keep his choices simple. Doonie's shirt was frayed and stained but Blivins had the darker circles under his eyes. All those non-simple choices he'd taken on along with the rank.

So fucking make one, Elv, now. Yes or no. Or stall—send these guys back to work so you can commune with the circumstantial crap pile in private . . . Blivins was getting ready to go with that third choice when Bergman returned with news.

Charlie Banza, the makeup artist who'd bought the green and red temporary tattoo ink, was dead.

"Murder?" Blivins asked, hopeful.

Bergman scowled. "Ambiguous."

"Welcome to the Willetts case," Doonie said.

The caller who'd beeped Mark was in California.

"Sorry for bothering you with this," Detective Ernest Iniguez of the San Bernardino County Sheriff's office told Mark, "but we've got this dead junkie, a dump job. Charles M. Banza, of Los Angeles. His partner, Chazz Allen, told us you were trying to contact Mr. Banza."

"Yeah. We were looking to consult with an expert on makeup. The partner said he'd disappeared, I advised him to file a missing persons."

Which Chazz had done. The L.A. cop who took his report nodded politely and pretended to take notes on Chazz's tale of Charlie's tale of going off on a secret mission. Then the cop ran Charlie Banza's description against the unidentified stiff, prisoner, and loony list. Got one hit, a John Doe who'd been found in the Cottonwood Mountains, about a hundred-twenty miles east of town. Dry, steep, scrubby high-desert country.

The John Doe had been found behind a boulder not far from a jeep trail. First by coyotes, then by turkey buzzards, then by vigilant teens who'd spotted the buzzard traffic jam circling what had to be a sizable carcass, and fired up their ATVs to go check out the show.

The John Doe was nude. The only identifying marks were fragments of tattoos on the uneaten parts of both arms and one hip. Those plus the John Doe's size, age, and coloring were what rang the Charlie Banza bell.

Cause of death was a heroin OD. No indications of premortem violence.

By the time the missing persons was filed the John Doe had used up his thirty days lodging at the county morgue and been resituated in a potter's field. After the disinterment the San Bernardino County coroner urged Chazz to bring in Charlie's hairbrush and wait for DNA confirmation. Chazz insisted on identifying the remains.

When Chazz was able to speak again he insisted Charlie had never used smack and never would. Chazz was certain Charlie had been killed, murdered with a syringe. Had no idea why or by whom. No idea where Charlie had been or what he'd been doing.

The dump site was fifty miles from Palm Springs, a gay playground. Police there circulated Banza's photo; nobody had seen him. Website postings hadn't drawn any hits either.

"No credit card or phone trail from Banza after the day he disappeared?" Mark asked, sounding as if he was just making reflexive shop talk.

"Nothing," Iniguez said. "The Chicago police wanting to talk to him was the closest thing to a lead we had."

"I picked his name off a list," Mark said. Wasn't a lie.

Mark ran the Charlie Banza details for the Superintendent, Husak, and Doonie.

The more Blivins heard the more impassive he got. Mark couldn't read him; the Superintendent had a poker face hard enough to take off and hang on the wall. Mark wasn't optimistic. The Banza thing didn't play like he'd been murdered. It played like a guy goes partying at somebody's house, shoots up, and ruins the host's buzz by keeling over dead. A standard junkie faux pas. The host panics, takes the corpse out and dumps it in a hurry, less concerned with hiding the body than getting rid of it and getting the hell away. A standard junkie memorial service.

Mark finished. Nobody said anything. The detectives watched Blivins, who sat there, solidifying.

Mark was about to risk offering an opinion the Superintendent hadn't asked for, when his decent boss stepped up and did it for him.

"On the surface," Lieutenant Husak pointed out, "Banza being just another junkie OD is almost as obvious as who shot Wilson Willetts."

"Yeah," Doonie pitched in, "the MO on Willetts, Garn, and Banza all fit a perp who likes to make a hit look like something it ain't."

Blivins went granite. Mark wasn't sure the Superintendent was aware of their presence. Or was breathing.

"The other pattern here," Mark said, "is Garn and Banza, the two witnesses who could've fingered the killers, are dead. Betsy Hackenmeyer, the one witness the killers didn't know about, is alive."

Blivins' granite head moved just far enough for his onyx eyes to find Mark. "The theoretical killers."

Ah shit. Blivins is gonna say no.

So from here on Mark was going to have to work the case in secret, alone. Had to keep Doonie from finding out, because Doonie would be in the shit if he failed to report what Mark was up to—

Blivins' gaze shifted to Doonie.

"Go talk to . . . Florence Brock," the Superintendent ordered. "Carefully."

That "carefully" had spin on it. Yeah, and Mark saw some private thing pass between Blivins and Doonie. Blivins grinned slightly, and the granite man turned back into flesh and blood.

"Thank you, sir," Doonie sighed, with the rueful grace of a guy pulling a dart out of his chest.

Hail to the Supe—somehow Blivins had picked up on Doonie's thing for Aunt Flo. But Mark had no idea what piece of history that look between the Superintendent and Doonie was about.

Didn't care. The boss was on board. All fucking right.

After the detectives left, Blivins stared contemplatively at his phone.

Banza's death had sealed it.

Blivins had fought it off for a few minutes, fought going with an instant gut reaction, which always felt good, but, playing up here in the executive snake-pit league, could lead to fucking disaster. So Blivins broke it down, cold and logical, and got to: fuck this pussyfooting political shit.

Much as being Superintendent meant to him, he wasn't willing to bomb the job in order to keep it. He'd walked into this office a good cop. He wasn't going to walk out the sorry-ass kind who decided not to notice corpses piling up around an investigation.

And, now that he had to make the call, Blivins realized something else. He was going to enjoy breaking the news to Vytautis.

FORTY

Wolves were howling in Sy Vytautis' head.

He knew what this was about. He knew what was going on.

Elvin cocksucking motherfucker Blivins was not the naïve shit-for-brains he'd pretended to be on the phone just now. Compelling circumstantial evidence my ass. Actually fucking sat there and told me he was doing his job.

Blivins knew this "evidence" wasn't worth squat. Cockfucking mothersucker knows no evidence short of a smoking gun on videotape plus a priest, a rabbi, and a judge as eyewitnesses would be an excuse to pull what he's pulling. Lardass blue-suit clown knows *You do not embarrass a State's Attorney with an election coming up.*

Just doing your fucking job, Elv? No shit. Only question, who the fuck are you doing it for? Who gave you the job of making me into Sy "Supervising The Hell Out Of Prosecuting The Wrong Man" Vytautis? Who gave you the job of dicking my campaign? . . . Ah shit. The Mayor? Has to be—who the fuck else does Blivins answer to?

No, no, Hizzoner wants me to run—and the Mayor wouldn't want to piss off those LAFAM billionaires, wouldn't want his cops making murder suspects out of guys who are major donors to the national party. If the Mayor wanted me out of this race he'd find other ways.

So who is behind this, who'd—

Vytautis realized he had a more urgent priority: *What if it was true?* The cocksucker did turn up a conspiracy, prove Meelo was a fall-guy? Fucking billion-to-one shot, but . . .

Vytautis beeped Carrie Eli. She was out interviewing a witness on another case. Vytautis called Carrie on her cell and ordered her to get her ass to his office soon as she was done.

FORTY-ONE

"Nah, be better if you made the call."

"You sure, Doon? I mean . . ."

Doonie shrugged. "Nah, you're better at the smooth tactful shit."

A whole schoolboy side of Doonie Mark had never seen; a chance to talk to Aunt Flo and Doonie chokes. Mark innocently insisted, "Fuck, you'd do fine, in fact it'd have more authority, I mean, you're almost a coupla decades closer to her age than I am."

"Blow me."

Doonie picked up the phone. Dialed a contact number Florence Brock had given them. Shoved the receiver into Mark's hand and went to refill his three-quarters full coffee cup.

The number was for Aunt Flo's personal cell. A breezy young woman answered. Said she was Gale Michaels, Mrs. Brock's assistant. Asked who this might be.

"Detective Mark Bergman, of—"

"The Chicago police. Florence told me about meeting you and your partner. Said you're good-looking enough to be an L.A. cop."

"That a compliment?"

"Up to you. Hang on, I'm a bringing the phone to Florence—she's out unearthing what look like kitchen implements."

"Unearthing?"

"Well, Detective, when you dialed Florence's cell the call was rerouted to this satellite phone. We are, of course, in what has to be the most remote valley on the eastern slope of the Peruvian Andes."

Of course.

Traces of a small city had been discovered, a hideout where remnants of the Inca nobility had fled after killer robots beamed down from the Starship Conquistador and swiftly grabbed all the land it had taken Inca kings centuries to grab from their neighbors. The Brock Foundation was picking up a big chunk of the tab for excavating the find, so Aunt Flo had been invited to be live on the set to witness an archaeological money-shot: the unsealing of a tomb. After which she and Gale stayed on for the fun/useful stuff, getting down in the dirt with brushes alongside the grad students.

Florence got on the phone, as effusive and bottom-line as usual. "Detective, what an unexpected pleasure—what's wrong?"

"Probably nothing. Thing is, Mrs. Brock—"

"Call me Florence."

"Thing is, Florence, a new witness put the suspect at his motel, far from the crime scene, shortly after the shooting."

"Yes, that 'Six-Minute Gap of Innocence.' We've got Web access," she explained. "Is it actually true?"

"Well, the new witness hasn't provided unequivocal proof Meelo wasn't the shooter. However, at this point there are enough—ambiguities—about the case, so that we have to check out alternative possibilities . . . in as quiet and discreet a manner as possible."

"Alternative possibilities?"

Here goes. First time Mark would be saying any of this to a civilian. "Framing Meelo—if that's what happened—would've entailed sizable expense. The only people I know of who might have both the motive and means were Mr. Willetts' rivals for the LAFAM commission, and their patrons. Florence, is it conceiv-

172

able to you that—"

"Yes."

So he wasn't bringing up anything that hadn't already crossed her mind.

There was no place on the dig where Florence could speak at length in private. But she was willing to come to Chicago soon as she could get there. And she was down with how important it was to keep this very, very secret.

"Sounded like it went okay," Doonie commented. He'd drifted back to the desk to listen to Mark's side of the conversation.

Mark nodded, casually.

Doonie cleared his throat. "So, like, uh, she's gonna go someplace more private and call us?"

"Nah. She's flying in. Gonna take three, four days. First she has to get from East Shangri-La, Peru, to her Gulfstream, which is parked in Lima."

Doonie glowed. "She hops on her jet like my kids hop on their bikes."

"That plane's a smaller percentage of her net worth than those bikes are of yours."

"And yet she's after me."

"Absolutely."

"Hey, you're not the first guy in history could get more than one woman going at once."

"A fact." Though, far as Mark knew, Doonie's idea of more than one woman at once was sleeping with his wife while imagining Aunt Flo.

In the three-plus years they'd worked together Mark was unaware of any instance where Doonie had gone and behaved like a married cop. And if Doonie had screwed around on Phyl back when they were young, and casual sex didn't include an exchange of HIV test scores, Mark hadn't heard anything about it.

Wasn't like Doonie was demure. Told plenty of war stories about bending the law, like how he'd once used an M-16 as a drop piece, planting it in the closet of a mouthy smack dealer, so the smug bastard would get cracked for an extra ten-to-twenty. But when it came to sex, Doonie only reminisced about other guys' scores; cops who'd banged an alderman's daughter, a cardinal's mistress, a governor's boyfriend, each other's wives, murder suspects, a rock star, a Federal snitch and a whole lot of really ugly whores just 'cause it was free. Doonie never mentioned himself, never even joked—

Mark's cell rang.

"Bergman."

"Hey." It was Carrie. Big news in her voice.

"What's up?"

"We have to have a drink tonight."

"Okay."

"Someplace we won't run into anyone we know."

"Why?"

"Same reason I won't be dropping by your place for a while."

"You've fallen in love and you don't want your latest married boyfriend to worry you're betraying him?"

"No, this is actually amusing. It's—possibly even good."

FORTY-TWO

The wall-to-wall din was as oppressive as Mark remembered.

"Perfect!" Carrie, who was standing next to Mark, shouted at him.

They were in a bar off Milwaukee Avenue. A neighborhood sports bar full of young guys who walked in already talking loud and then started drinking.

Carrie scored a table. Mark scored them a couple of beers.

Safely hidden in a cloud of shouted laughter, shouted groans, and shouted insults at TVs showing a Bulls game, Carrie leaned close and confided, "Sy made me the new second chair on Willetts."

A whole bunch of things clicked into place. Starting with the sad fact this case now meant too much to both of them to risk damaging it in bed.

Mark eyed Carrie. "So that's why you and I won't be getting naked, for a real long time. And why you sound so pleased about it."

"Not pleased, but . . ." A guilty shrug. A pleased, guilty shrug. "It may not be that long."

"Sure it will, once you replace Miller as first chair." Mark took a long, pleasurable swig of beer.

Carrie blinked innocently. "Who can tell what Sy's thinking?"

"Anybody."

Vytautis was starting to worry Meelo might be innocent.

The original second chair Vytautis had assigned to the Willetts case was Nick Pellucci, the youngest, most junior hire in the office. Guaranteed to remain invisible.

But if the indictment against Meelo suddenly fell apart before trial—or worse, during it—lead prosecutor Harrison Miller would get bounced, hard. Had to. Miller was the nearest thing Vytautis had to a scapegoat. Miller would be fired nasty, the way you fire a rank incompetent. Abruptly dumped off the case, accompanied by leaks detailing how many ways he'd screwed up, and withheld key information from Vytautis.

Enter Carrie Eli. Seasoned prosecutors like her weren't brought in to replace some kid like Pellucci who didn't have enough seniority to be trusted with his own key to the washroom. Carrie was made second chair to get her up to speed so she could replace Miller the instant his head landed in the basket.

And, unlike Miller, Carrie had a solid camera presence. She'd be the reassuring new face of the Willetts prosecution. Proof the State's Attorney was a forceful administrator who'd instantly removed the deadwood and sicced a competent dog on whatever new, fat-cat defendant had perpetrated the frame-up.

Of course, a fat-cat defendant would have a squad of big-money hardball lawyers, who'd hire an army of investigators, who'd do workups on every cop and prosecutor guilty of going after their client. Mark and Carrie getting caught in the sack wouldn't prove anything. But it would embarrass and tarnish her as a prosecutor, even though the judge (probably) wouldn't allow it to be introduced in court. The defense would introduce it in the court of public opinion, where a big chunk of the jury pool would assume there had to be *something* dirty about the prosecutor fucking the arresting officer.

Presuming Mark did find the murderer and make an arrest.

"What are you grinning about?" Carrie demanded.

"The only way you get your hands on this huge, career-maker case is if Meelo is innocent. Right now Carrie Eli is praying my vague gestalt of hink turns out to be true."

"My only concern," Carrie admonished him, "is that the truth is determined and justice is done."

"Amen."

"Yeah. Now go bring me back a really big fish."

"Do my best," Mark promised.

Carrie put her lips to his ear and whispered, "When this is over, I'll do mine." She tickled his ear with a warm damp breath. Then she sat back, all primness and posture.

Mark frowned, hurt. "We've been fucking since junior year and I haven't seen your best?"

Carrie chuckled, low. She picked up her glass, drained her beer in one long, slow swallow. Put the glass down and gave Mark a sultry, enigmatic smirk. Which got somewhat ruined when she belched.

The old friends shared a fond grin.

Mark extended his hand. "Counselor."

"Detective."

They shook hands. Left the bar separately.

Shit. The number of women he could call up and climb into bed with had now shrunk from three to zero.

Still, on balance, a good day. He was going to be allowed to do his job without getting fired for it.

FORTY-THREE

"This motel witness don't mean a fucking thing, Bill," Hector B growled. "This Gap of Innocence shit ain't shit compared to the eyewitness, the gun. He's gonna get convicted. That's why the fucking DA is going ahead with the fucking trial. So this ain't a problem, you know it, I know it, your agent knows it, so it's time he and me hooked up."

Hector B was working hard to keep cool. Goes through all this coded-message, get an appointed time and go to a payphone shit just to get Bill on the phone and listen to bullshit why he can't go meet Bill's motherfucking agent yet.

"Soon as he's satisfied there won't be any fallout I'll hear from him and you'll hear from me," Bill said, doing that calm as shit act of his. "Right now is a good time for you to go get that little procedure done and relax on the beach."

"You think there's gonna be fallout, Bill?"

"No, or I wouldn't have taken the job."

"That's exactly right." You evasive cunt.

"But I understand why the agent is going to wait a bit longer, see if recent developments lead to anything. He's an extremely cautious, patient man. And he values those qualities in others," Bill counseled.

Fuck. What's Hector B supposed to say to that? The agent's *going to wait.* Done deal, fuck you Hector B, go away. But then that next thing, the agent values patience, so prove yourself by eating this agent dude's shit and not complaining . . . did make sense. Same way some of the suck it up and tough it out army shit made sense. And the motherfucker and his motherfucking agent were the key to the serious money gigs. So what does Hector B say here?

"I value not being lied to," Hector B informed Bill, delivering the threat as calm and cold as Bill would.

"That's good," Bill replied. "Bye." He hung up.

Fuck. Hector B wasn't sure if Bill's *That's good* was talking about what he'd said, or how his imitation of Bill sounded when he said it . . . Motherfuck.

Bill better be hooking him up with this agent motherfucker. Soon.

Shit. This agent motherfucker better exist.

FORTY-FOUR

"I followed him," Dina told Arthur. "He did get on the plane to Costa Rica."

Dina took a pensive bite of sea bass roe and duck dim sum. She and Arthur were lunching at a Pasadena restaurant noted for its revelatory Italian twists on traditional Chinese recipes, designed to pair especially well with the reserve pinot noirs on the wine list.

Arthur said nothing. Watched Dina's face work. One of his deepest pleasures was watching thoughts and moods travel across that face. Arthur rolled a sip of '95 Reynolds-Arnemann "Emma's Vineyard" across his tongue and waited for what he knew Dina was now going to propose, even though she knew what his response would be.

"I don't know about the hygienic standards in Costa Rican clinics," she said, suggestively.

Arthur was betting she already had a flight booked. "Nothing bad will happen to him in Costa Rica," he ordered.

"Even the simple plastic surgery he's undergoing could have dangerous complications," she pleaded.

"If he shows signs of infection after he returns, he'll be treated for them here." Debate over.

Dina arched an amused, skeptical eyebrow and took a long sip of wine.

That was as much of an argument as they'd ever had over procedure. Only, Arthur knew, it wasn't really an argument, or about procedure.

Unless the frame-up on Meelo failed, Arthur wouldn't sanction a preventive strike on Hector B; Dina knew that. Dina wouldn't waste time by starting a pointless discussion about it. Normally.

Dina was, Arthur knew, trying to protect—finalize—his retirement. Because once this Willetts job was over, closed out, the time would finally be here. Arthur and Dina would finally talk, fuck, and feel out the answer to the question that had been in the backs of their minds since that night she surprised him on the sailboat and he didn't kill her.

So this wasn't an argument about whether to eliminate Hector B, it was Dina signaling how much Arthur meant to her.

"How's your first world-class vintage developing?" Dina asked.

Arthur suppressed a grin; mentioning his syrah wasn't changing the topic, it was underlining it. Dina had never tasted a barrel sample of his previous efforts, because she'd never visited the Santa Maria co-op where he'd been making wine. And she hadn't visited Arthur's new home/winery. She'd never visited any place he lived. Just as he'd never visited her. That way their neighbors—and now, Arthur's household and vineyard staff—could never be used by a prosecutor to link Arthur and Dina. When he'd needed to get together with Dina to plan jobs and test equipment they'd always met at a secluded safe-house Arthur owned in the hills above Ojai.

Paranoid? Maybe. Functional? He'd never spent a minute in prison. Never been busted. So he wasn't going to change his rules now. If he and Dina were ever going to putter in the garden, it wasn't enough for only Arthur to retire. Dina would also have to close up shop.

Arthur knew Dina was willing to do that. Eager. He wasn't sure she wouldn't, in the long run, get restless. Walking away from the game wasn't easy, no matter how much you wanted to.

Dina was still young enough so the stresses of being a pro hitter hadn't spoiled the excitement. The power. The getting away with it.

Dina was also still young enough to believe crunching the numbers was optional. As in the eighteen-year difference between them. When Arthur was sixty Dina would be forty-two. Seventy, fifty-two. He might be wearing a colostomy bag while she was wearing downhill skis. And raising children. She was still young enough. So was he, this month. But by the time his kids were ten he'd be their grandfather. That matter? Compared to a wife, a family? Not just a wife. Dina. The banged-up, kicked-around teenage grownup on the boat that night who'd looked at the Walther in his hand then looked him in the eye. Scared. Ready. Someone his own size.

He'd known other women, intriguing women, impressive women, women he might have come to love. If he'd been with them for more than a blink. Couldn't do that; came with the territory. But Dina, when he met Dina that night on the boat, he . . . well, another man might have been lovestruck. Arthur was struck by three options.

Waste her.

Enjoy her for a night and disappear.

Teach her his trade. The one way it would be safe to keep seeing her.

Safe except for coming to love her, more than he'd assumed he was capable of. Now he'd have to decide what loving her meant. Did it mean damn the math, be together, make the most of however many years they'd have? Or did it mean shove her away so she didn't squander herself on him? But where would that leave Dina? Now that he'd taught her his trade, what chance did she have of meeting someone she could stay with?

Maybe letting her in was the only way to save them both.

Letting her in would get Dina out of the game; admit it, she would have the strength to stay straight, for him.

Letting her in would get him out of one day looking back at his life and wondering why he bothered having it, aside from making a syrah that got poured at the White House. Which getting married wouldn't interfere with.

Decision made. He wanted what she wanted. They were going to do this.

So what he had to do now was not give her a hint of it. Didn't want her judgment skewed by daydreams of impending bliss. Had to keep her head in the game.

"At this point my first serious cuvée is still grape juice," Arthur told Dina. "Extremely elegant grape juice. But there's no way to be sure how well it'll turn out. The one thing I can be certain of is that rushing it would ruin it."

FORTY-FIVE

How totally odd she would be so anxious for the approval of these two men, and so pleased when she got it. Florence Brock had thrown formal dinners for sixty showbiz and moneybiz celebrities, and intimate soirées for Presidents, with less indecision than she went through today over what kind of food to have in her suite when the detectives arrived for what might be a lengthy session. A full buffet? Snacks? Or should she merely have coffee available? Ask if they wanted something from room service? But what if it were unethical for them to accept a meal from a witness?

Get a grip. This is a murder investigation. A goddamn great artist has been killed. Your goddamn friend. And here you are worrying about what kind of impression you'll make on . . . cops. But there it was.

Florence ran on a bit when the cops arrived, assuring them she'd taken every precaution she could think of. Hadn't told a soul she was going to Chicago—except of course for her pilots, and her assistant Gale, who'd booked the suite, under her own name. Hadn't told Gale *why* she was in Chicago—though Gale, nobody's fool, must have a good idea—but not to worry, Gale Michaels was the daughter of close friends, a completely trustworthy young woman. And Florence had picked this hotel because she'd never stayed here before and wouldn't be recognized by the staff. Hoped the detectives didn't think she'd gotten carried away with the cloak and daggerness of all this.

"No. Impressively thorough," Detective Bergman, the younger one, told her. Without a trace of irony, or suck-up.

And the tension flowed away. These were confident, comfortable men, and Detective Bergman's tone made Florence feel included, just a little, in their very private, tough club. Put her at ease. She stopped wishing she knew what to offer them to eat and started wishing she could buy them new suits. Especially Detective Dunegan. He was a hefty unkempt shambles, but an attractive shambles. Sort of an Irish, rougher-edged, blonder, less noisy Diego Rivera.

Florence got to it, told them what they wanted to know.

For an architect, the total rebuild of the most prestigious museum in the western United States was a chance to create a world-class personal monument. A chance for the kind of fame that could last centuries. Much as Florence hated to say it, she could see an architect killing for that. Well, one of the other finalist architects anyway. Not de Suau.

Florence knew the detectives had to investigate every possibility, but in her opinion Juan-Mari de Suau was no more capable of murder than Wilson Willetts would have been. De Suau was a courtly Spaniard, a devout Catholic, a sweet-tempered man who would do the cooking himself when he invited you for dinner. Juan-Mari and Wilson were friends; in fact it was Wilson and Karen who'd introduced Florence and Ed—Ed was her late husband—to the de Suaus. In fact she'd heard a rumor Juan-Mari had to be talked out of withdrawing his LAFAM entry and publicly urging the design committee to choose Wilson's—though of course that's what a murderer might do to avoid suspicion . . . "Jesus God, Detectives, you have a job where you have to look at even the most decent behavior as, as . . ."

"But the upside is," Detective Bergman said, "we sometimes

get to see decent behavior that turns out to be exactly what it looks like."

"Yeah, Homicide ain't so bad," Detective Dunegan added. "You wanna see real wear and tear, check out the cops on the bomb squad or public relations."

My God, was Diego—Dunegan—flirting? *Well, he may not be as attractive as the young one, and he's wearing a wedding ring, but at least he's not a pompous prick about it like most of the men who've hit on me since—and before—Ed died. Captains of industry and Fauntleroys of inheritance who act like they're doing you an honor by offering a quickie. Artists who are passionately attracted to your checkbook. Shit. Stop it. Back to business.*

The other architect finalist was a wretched arrogant Scot, Eric Fairlie. Florence had no trouble picturing Fairlie butchering his rivals and impaling their heads on his castle gate. Hideous man.

Dunegan asked if there was any history of bad blood between Willetts and either of these other guys.

Nothing specific Florence knew of. As she said, Wilson and Juan-Mari were friends who admired each other's work. Eric Fairlie was bitchy to Wilson, but Eric was bitchy to everyone except his mirror.

In case the detectives wanted to speak to the architects, Florence had checked; de Suau and Fairlie were both abroad at the moment, but both would be in L.A. for the official public presentation of the competing designs. As would Wilson's associate, Carlton Bass, who'd be presenting Wilson's design, which was just so much finer than the others . . .

Florence took a moment to pull herself together.

"Yeah," Dunegan grunted sympathetically, "Mr. Bass was telling us how it gives the other two a big edge, being able to socialize with the committee."

"Christ yes," Florence told them, hoping her nose wasn't red.

"It's going to be brutal trying to push Wilson's design through now that he's gone. That's why I believe—if this street mugger turns out not to be the murderer—the real killer could be someone involved with the LAFAM competition. Killing Wilson would be the only way for some bastard to—almost—guarantee Wilson's design would lose."

Florence realized she was grinding her teeth. She looked away a moment and unclenched her jaw, determined not to let rage distract her or damage her gums. When she got a handle on her anger and looked back at the cops, Dunegan was gazing at her a little strangely. More than a little.

"Tell us about the bastards," he urged her.

"With pleasure. There are factions of the design committee backing each architect, but of course there's *one* committee member who's especially close to and personally invested in each finalist . . . No secret I've been Wilson's champion, I'm convinced he'd create the best museum—but, of course, each patron is convinced their guy's design would do that—but also, the thing is, sponsoring the winner will give that patron huge status—now, and possibly for generations to come . . . Next to being the architect, there's nothing like being the pharaoh behind an extremely large, famous, drop-dead gorgeous building.

"Now, Juan-Mari de Suau is being backed by . . ." Florence tailed off. Oh, this was harder than she expected. Saying it out loud was so very different than thinking it. Saying real names to real homicide detectives: *Yes, Tish could have someone murdered. Calvin could, too.*

"You're not accusing these people of murder," the observant young cop said. "We were the ones who decided they might be suspects and came to you."

"I'm accusing them of being capable of murder."

"Everybody is," Bergman assured her. "That's the one thing

we already know about them."

Right. Blunt, but right. Back to work. "Juan-Mari belongs to Tish Sand. Not belongs as in sex. As in, she's his patron; if he wins, she wins."

Florence filled them in on Tish: Born into a socially prominent Pasadena family, which is to say Rigor Mortis Snooty. But from age twelve Tish Jenway grew up in reduced circumstances, due to her father's poorly timed coronary. Tish had the social standing and the act that went with it, though, and when she was young, the looks. That was enough for Jordan Sand, a hustling, self-made real estate developer who was on his way to becoming a one-man conglomerate.

"He needed a wife who knew 'which wine went with which fork'—Jordy's joke. To be fair, he does love her. Seems to, anyway; only wife Jordy's had. Anyway, Jordy branched out into heavy construction, finance, insurance. Politically and socially wired all over the place, you know, on a home-phone basis with the mayor, the governor, God, and Jack Nicholson. Tish, Tish stayed home, raised the kids, and enjoyed the social wars. Made sure Jordy bought into the right charities and arts groups. As Jordy got wealthier, Tish became a power on every board she sat on. And she lives to let you know it—especially if you're female. Tish *cannot* lose to another woman. Tish is, Tish is like something from one of those nature documentaries . . . Tish will bite. Tish *likes* to bite."

Dunegan asked, "You know if she's ever done any violence?"

"Physically, no. Not so much as a whiff of Tish-slaps-her-maid gossip. But she will always get back at you if you cross her, and you cross her if you do anything other than what she wants. And she *wants* Juan-Mari de Suau to build the new LAFAM. It would be Tish's biggest coup, ever."

That sounded so much harsher out loud than it had in Florence's head. But not inaccurate. Not even a little.

Florence couldn't tell what the detectives thought about what she'd just told them. She was dying to know but resisted the urge to ask. No point, really, until she'd also told them about Calvin.

Calvin Hirschberg. Florence assumed they'd heard of him.

Bergman had; Dunegan hadn't.

"Calvin's the kind of man who gives vicious queens a bad name. He grew up in St. Louis, but not much. At twenty-two he inherited the family business, a holding company that owned department store and supermarket chains. He sold them and moved to Hollywood. As always when a rich child shows up wanting to buy into show business, the cannibals descended. Calvin ate most of them. Started with movies, got into cable TV early, got into video games early, turned his ton of money into a mountain of it. For Calvin it wasn't work, it was one long mean party. Amused himself by crushing competitors, partners, artists, employees, lovers. There've been ruined careers, mental hospitals, a suicide. As far as actual violence, well, twice Calvin reached out-of-court settlements with people who claimed they'd been assaulted by his bodyguards. The second time, the rumor was it had been Calvin, not the bodyguard, who'd done the damage. I do know when Calvin owned a disco in the 1970s some of his regulars were gangsters. Calvin and the gangsters 'got' each other—that wasn't rumor, that was Calvin's own word. So if Calvin did want to have something done, he might have connections."

"And the Scottish architect, Eric Fairlie," Bergman asked, "he belongs to Calvin the way de Suau belongs to Tish?"

"That way, and in the bedroom way, too, I'm guessing. Eric's famous for sleeping with clients—including other people's. Tish says she's not sure if she'd call Eric Fairlie bisexual or just pathologically ambitious. Eric's been married a couple of times, but in Britain who knows what that means? He's all bluff and manly with the husbands, makes passes at the wives, then goes all lisping Cambridge foofie when Calvin's in the room, and, at parties anyway, they're constantly putting hands on each other when they talk." *Oh Jesus, I'm sounding like a batty old gossip, turning this murder investigation into a hen party.* "I'm only bringing that up because you were speaking in terms of motive. Calvin deigning to let Eric touch him in public is less a sign of affection for Eric than a warning to the rest of us how important this LAFAM commission is to Calvin."

The young detective assured Florence she was being nothing but helpful. They wanted to hear anything she considered relevant.

Florence thought about it. Shook her head. "That's about it. Unless you have any questions."

"One or two."

That took an hour and a half.

When Bergman ran out of questions he glanced at Dunegan to see if his partner had anything. The large man pondered for a moment, staring at nothing and pawing absentmindedly at his tie. Florence wished she knew Dunegan well enough to demand he burn it and permit her to send him a dozen new ones.

Dunegan made a decision, looked at Florence, and asked, almost harshly, "Mrs. Brock, did you have a, uh—sex—thing with Wilson Willetts?"

Florence felt her cheeks blaze. *I should tell him to go—no, no, they need to know where I am in all this, if I'm a bereaved lover who may just be lashing out—or—Shit! Is that son of a bitch thinking I'm a suspect?! How dare—well, I do have the means, and if I were some loony jilted—and flying all the way up here to cooperate, that would be something I'd do if I wanted to cover up . . . So Dunegan's just doing his—No, no, he didn't* have *to ask it that crudely. Look at Bergman, he's stonefaced, trying not to react, but he's definitely not pleased. So screw you, Detective Dunegan. Screw you for being just another bullying prick.*

Florence glared at Doonie. Delivered each sentence as if it were a slap. "My relationship with Wilson began as client and architect. Then I—and my husband—became lifelong friends with Wilson. *And Karen.* I loved them both. And I love Wilson's work. I could not be more pained by Wilson's death or devoted to his cause if he and I *had* spent the last thirty years coupling like frenzied chimps."

As Florence snarled, Dunegan's expression melted into that odd gaze again.

"No offense meant, Mrs. Brock," the rumpled detective said in a surprisingly tender near-whisper. "Like you said before, this is that kind of job."

"Yes," Florence sighed, her resentment ebbing as quickly as it had flared. Pleased to be back on their side, to be included again. "I understand."

"Thank you," Dunegan said. Then confided, "I get stuck asking the messy questions, because Detective Bergman is kind of shy with women."

"I'm sure," Florence teased. "Listen, I'm sorry I got angry just now—"

"Don't be," Dunegan pleaded.

Detective Bergman cleared his throat. Then began making polite, sincere thank-yous. The session was over.

Shame. Florence was just getting warmed up. Thought this was the perfect moment to start pouring cocktails and talking in earnest. Create the right atmosphere for her to ask what the detectives thought about Tish, Calvin, and Eric as murder suspects.

Instead she was walking the cops to the door of her suite, wracked by curiosity but suffering a rare case of lockjaw. Didn't want to be annoying, prying for information the cops weren't allowed to give. But. But. But.

"Detectives?" The word popped out of her mouth of its own accord. Shit. Bergman and Dunegan looked at her. Waited politely for her to overcome her temporary paralysis. What the hell, they asked about her sex life, she could ask about their work. "So . . . If there's anything else I can do . . ."

"We'll call," Dunegan promised, earnestly. Squeezed her hand in both of his.

Bergman shook her hand politely, and the cops left.

Florence shut the door, wondering when she'd become such a wuss. "If there's anything else I can do" was no substitute for "Which one of those bastards do you think had Wilson's brains blown across the sidewalk?" Oh, well. No cocktails, no glory.

Florence realized she'd never asked Bergman and Dunegan if they wanted something to eat.

Halfway through a flute of Deutz, Florence realized something else. She was replaying that strange gaze Dunegan had given her. Twice. At the time she'd been so wrapped up in making sure to be helpful she'd refused to acknowledge what was going on in that gaze; it combined the look of a child fascinated by a magic trick and the look of a Rottweiler about to hump your leg.

My God. What did Dunegan think of her?

What did she think of him? She wasn't sure.

My God.

FORTY-SIX

And now, Mark thought as they headed north on Lakeshore Drive, homework. Contract jobs were tricky to prove. The best way to find out if one of these architects or philanthropists had bought him- or herself a corpse was to bust the contractors and flip one.

But it's kind of hard to identify the contractors when all you've got are descriptions of "Oscar" and "Heather" from someone as bright as Meelo. The one reliable description Mark and Doonie had was of the guy Meelo never saw—the shooter. He'd look just like Meelo, only a little older, taller, and more muscular.

So for now it was down to research on Juan-Mari, Eric, Tish, and Calvin, hoping you got lucky and something popped. Yeah, like a receipt for homicide services rendered . . . Mark's ruminations were interrupted by a contented sigh from Mr. Bliss, who'd been silent till then, sitting in the passenger seat staring blankly at the choppy gray-blue lake, lost in a haze of idiot contentment.

"Hell of a woman," Doonie murmured.

"Yeah," Mark said, keeping his tone neutral and his eyes on the road. Grateful his partner was bringing up the topic so he wouldn't have to.

"I don't think Aunt Flo caught on I was getting her angry on purpose."

"That maybe got by her."

"Just came out like a natural part of the interview."

"Uh-huh . . . But there's no way she missed that look you gave her."

"Didn't give her any look."

"Twice."

"There was no look, she didn't notice it, and she didn't mind it . . . Did she?"

"Even if she did," Mark muttered, "it'd take more than you flashing that . . . face-woody . . . to keep Aunt Flo from helping us nail the perp."

"What I figured," Doonie sighed.

"But," Mark suggested, "you never know, so, maybe you could dial it back next time."

After a moment Doonie asked, with a soft, awed grin, "She really didn't mind, did she?"

No, Mark didn't admit to Doonie, *I don't think she did.*

FORTY-SEVEN

Judge Settimo L. Santini gaveled the trial into existence.

Harrison Miller's opening statement lasted twenty-one seconds: "Emilio Jesus Garcia is guilty of murdering Wilson Willetts. A witness saw the defendant shoot the victim. The murder weapon and the victim's wallet were in the defendant's possession when he was arrested. Emilio Jesus Garcia is guilty of murdering Wilson Willetts."

The prosecutor sat down.

The defense attorney stared into space for a little bit, then shuffled through his notes, eventually stood, and faced the jury.

Paul Obed told the jury he was Paul Obed, and explained he was an attorney at law who was representing Emilio Jesus Garcia. Told them the evidence the prosecution was about to present was full of strange inconsistencies and ambiguities. Told them this was because the defendant was the second victim in this case. The victim of a powerful, shadowy conspiracy to frame him for the murder of Wilson Willetts. Why, no one could say. But that the conspiracy existed, there was no doubt. Because there existed, beyond a doubt, a Six-Minute Gap of Innocence in the prosecution's evidence. The jury would be hearing testimony from a witness who'd prove it was physically impossible for the defendant to have committed the crime. *Phy-sic-ly im-poss-i-bull*, Obed repeated, emphasizing every syllable. *Phy-*

sic-ly im-poss-i-bull. He asked them to please think about what that meant.

Miller put all his evidence to the jury and rested his case in one day. The brevity was the message: This case is so simple and obvious only an imbecile would waste your time nitpicking. An imbecile like the defense counsel. Me, I'm gonna get you out of here and back to your lives in no time.

This high-velocity tactic had been crafted by Sy Vytautis; a quick conviction would undercut the rationale for the cops to continue expending resources looking for an alternative perp.

If the police did keep going and eventually came up with a new murderer, Vytautis could then fit the cops for scapegoat costumes: The State's Attorney's office had done an efficient job with the evidence the police provided—evidence that was persuasive enough to convince a jury. It wasn't the State's Attorney's fault the cops fell for the frame-up, took months to unearth and properly investigate additional evidence, and finally track down the correct guilty party. Sadly typical performance by the Chicago PD. Hell, Vytautis could campaign on a promise to work with the Mayor to upgrade police procedures and standards.

Assistant State's Attorney Miller opened with Naguib Darwahab. Had him describe the shooting and point to the defendant. Never brought up the cabbie scratching the shooter's arm.

On cross, Public Defender Obed asked about the scratch. Darwahab confirmed he'd scratched the shooter, deeply, on the left arm. Obed had Meelo display his left arm for Darwahab. The grizzled cabbie said he could see no sign of scratches.

Judge Santini asked ASA Miller if he had any redirect. Miller didn't. Santini asked the witness to step down. On his way out, Darwahab paused briefly by the defense table, glared at Meelo, then sadly shook his head, as his anger buckled under the weight of the grief this young savage had caused. The old man's eyes were glistening as he left the courtroom. Jurors saw it all.

Obed requested that the judge instruct the jury to forget what they'd just seen. Santini did so. Only three of the jurors were rude enough to look at the judge as if he were nuts.

Miller entered into evidence a coroner's report stating the cause of death was a .38-caliber bullet that removed a valuable chunk of brain. Though the victim had already been fatally wounded by a slug vandalizing the right atrium of the heart.

Miller followed with Mrs. Nomsilp. She identified Meelo as the man who rented Room Eleven at the Golden Door Motel on the day of the murder.

Obed had no questions.

Miller put Doonie on the stand. Had him describe the evidence trail and the bust. Entered the murder weapon and Willetts' wallet into evidence. Had Doonie describe the drugs Meelo had in the room, and Meelo's admission during inter-rogation he'd ingested significant amounts of marijuana and cocaine. And beer. Had Doonie confirm the defendant's admission he owned the .38-caliber revolver found in the trunk of his car—well, not owned—the defendant admitted he'd stolen the gun from his uncle.

Obed asked Doonie if the defendant's left arm was scratched and bleeding at the time of the arrest. Doonie said nope.

Miller entered into evidence the paraffin and ballistics tests, which confirmed the defendant had fired a gun, and the fatal slugs had come from the defendant's stolen .38-caliber revolver. Miller walked slowly to the jury box, holding up the plastic bag with the murder weapon inside. He scanned the jury, looking each in the eye. Still looking at the jurors, with his back to Judge Santini, Miller said, "The State rests, Your Honor."

His Honor called it a day.

FORTY-EIGHT

Paul Obed's first witness was the lab tech who'd done the DNA analysis of the scrapings taken from under Darwahab's fingernails. The material consisted of human blood and flesh, and tattoo ink. The DNA and blood type did not match the defendant's. The tattoo ink was not the permanent ink used in regular tattoos; it was a temporary kind used by makeup artists. Obed entered into evidence a lab report stating the ink in the defendant's tattoo was permanent.

On cross, Harrison Miller asked the witness if tests could confirm if Mr. Darwahab's fingernails had scraped up the flesh and blood at the time of the murder. The tech said no, the material could have been under Mr. Darwahab's fingernails for up to eight hours. So the cabbie could've scratched someone at, say, 3 p.m. that afternoon? Yes.

Obed called Mr. Nomsilp, who testified that someone who looked just like the defendant but who wasn't the defendant was in the motel parking lot at 11:36 p.m., opening the trunk of the defendant's car. Obed asked if Nomsilp was certain. Yes, the witness was certain the defendant was not the man he saw.

Miller asked Nomsilp if he'd at first identified Emilio Jesus Garcia as the man he'd seen. The witness said yes, but it was from a photo. Miller displayed enormous blow-ups of Meelo's booking photos. Nomsilp confirmed those were the pictures he'd seen. So the man looked just like this, Miller asked, pointing to the giant picture of Meelo—same face, same tattoo, same clothing? Yes, Nomsilp replied, except a little taller and more muscles.

Just like this, except a little taller and more muscles, Miller repeated, throwing a small sarcastic glance at the jury. No further questions.

Obed recalled Doonie to the witness box. Asked if he'd retraced the killer's path from the murder scene to the motel. Yes. What was the fastest time the police had managed? Twenty-seven minutes. Which meant the very earliest the killer could have gotten to the motel was . . . 11:23 p.m.? Yes, approximately.

Miller asked the detective if, during his test runs, he'd exceeded the speed limit? No. Run any red lights or Stop signs? No.

On redirect, Obed asked Doonie if in his experience a murderer fleeing the scene would be likely to draw attention to himself by speeding and running lights? Doonie said, Yeah, lots of people who are stupid enough to murder somebody panic right after, and get even more stupid.

Obed blushed and sat down. The judge recessed for lunch.

Obed and Meelo spent the break in a small conference room, lunching on tamales Meelo's sister Angela made. Meelo was excited to be eating real food and pleased to hear Obed thought the trial was going well, but got kind of sulky when Obed told him no, he hadn't smuggled in any beers in his briefcase. Gringo tightass fuck.

The trial reconvened. Paul Obed stood, took a long, deep breath, gave the jury a pleased, promising look. *It's Perry Mason time.* The defense called Betsy Hackenmeyer.

Betsy, who'd purchased a new sweater and jeans and gotten her hair cut for the occasion, took the stand beaming with pleasure at being able to help right a wrong. She puffed out her chest and sat at a slight angle, so Meelo would get the full effect.

Betsy told the judge and jury the same thing she'd told the cops and the attorneys. She'd seen Meelo in his room at exactly 11:17 p.m.

A Six Minute Gap, Obed noted, between then and the earliest time police estimated the killer could've been there. The defense attorney gave the jury a *See, what did I tell you?* smirk, thanked Ms. Hackenmeyer, and confidently informed Harrison Miller, "Your witness."

But as the prosecutor stood, Judge Santini asked if his cross was going to be substantial. Miller nodded, said it might go on a while.

Santini closed up shop. Instructed the jury not to discuss the case with anyone and wished them a good weekend.

FORTY-NINE

Ms. June Dockyer went out on a date with Barry Keefe. Well, not really a date. Keefe was married. But the hottest young trader in the firm. And his wife was visiting her folks back East and Keefe had an invite to a gallery opening in Bucktown and he didn't feel like going alone and was ready to blow it off and go sit in front of the tube with a pizza if he couldn't find company. So Ms. June Dockyer wasn't Keefe's date, she was company.

The gallery opening was for a young lesbian video artist who digitized every minute of her waking and sleeping life, then edited and processed the footage into a diary where each month parodied a different art technique or movement: Dada, Cubism, Tex Avery (WWII Propaganda Period).

Keefe liked the video diary more than Ms. June Dockyer did. They drank a couple of dark blue martini somethings, and Keefe started to intimate his wife's trip to Philly was more like a kind of trial separation. Keefe mentioned this while gazing, semi-hypnotized, at a multiple-monitor 1960s Op-Art psychedelic semi-nude satirical lesbian argument over the high price of organic toothpaste—not really paying that much attention to Ms. June Dockyer, until he suddenly gave her this impish grin and suggested this video would be even more awesome if the two of them were in the same altered state the artist obviously had been.

Ms. June Dockyer wrinkled her nose. "This is fine," she told

Keefe, indicating the dark blue martini something.

Keefe spotted some players he knew. He shot the futures shit with them for a little while. Ms. June Dockyer couldn't believe the numbers Keefe was dick-measuring with. Even bigger than office gossip had said. Guy his age. Not that much older than she was and already light-years ahead.

They met an artist. Not the lesbian video artist. A painter who knew her. This like six-foot, striking-looking girl, miles of kill-for legs and long black hair. Green eyes, and like point-oh-two percent body fat. Looked fierce but it was just she had that killer arty deadpan; the painter was friendly, once they got talking.

Keefe made another joke about psychedelics. The painter said she had some X she could part with. Keefe threw Ms. June Dockyer a questioning look. She thought it over, thought about the numbers Keefe was trading already, wondered what the point was of going into commodities if you weren't going all the way. And what the fuck, it was Friday night.

They scored the X from the tall arty-deadpan painter. Girl said if they liked it she had a steady source. Some lethal Jamaican around now, too. Keefe told her ooh, he'd probably be in touch. Ms. June Dockyer said she definitely would; totally liked Jamaican doob. Keefe gave them both the impish grin (the married dipshit was thinking threesome—dream on, pal), and said yeah, least they could do was support the arts by funding a ganja grant. Keefe asked the girl if they could go back to her place and score some tonight.

Ms. June Dockyer said scoring weed could wait, didn't want to do a business transaction while tripping on X. Ms. June Dockyer asked the painter if she was with a gallery, could they go see her stuff. Girl said she was still in school, working her way through by waitressing, and a little psychoactive commodities brokering. Took cards from Keefe and Ms. June Dockyer, wrote her name and number on them and gave them back.

Lovely name. Really. Even before the Ecstasy came on, Ms. June Dockyer thought the painter/dealer had a lovely name.

Janvier.

FIFTY

The enormous room was an angstrom aquarium awash with sparkling dark chaos as purple haze pulsing from a vast ceiling jeweled with black lights, strobes, mirror-balls, and lasers was punctuated by flashes of exploding Day-Glo violence whose crashing clatter was muffled by slickbeat thunder pop-reggae from No Doubt roaring at floor-shake brain-melt decibellations from the bowling alley's sound system, on the occasion of Patty Dunegan's thirteenth birthday party. Eighteen of her peers, two older teen brothers, and seven adults occupied five throbbing lanes.

"I can't bowl for sh—anything!" Doonie shouted, for the fourth time in two frames, gesturing at a lane alive with barriers of hallucinogenic flicker between him and the fluorescing pink and pistachio bowling pins at the other end.

"What?!" Mark, Patty, and three of Patty's friends shouted back, also for the fourth time, in chorus.

Doonie sagged into a seat and stuck his tongue out at Patty, who returned the compliment. Doonie reached behind the seat for his Rolling Rock, but it was gone. He looked over at the next lane and caught strobe-shard glimpses of Phyl holding his swiped beer, giving him a behave-yourself smirk, and taking a swig. Doonie stuck his tongue out at her too.

Patty picked up a 2-5 spare.

Mark threw a 4-6-7-10 split. He turned and shrugged apologetically at his captain, Patty. She came up to Mark, grabbed his shoulders, and played coach.

"Concentrate! You have to concentrate!"

"Biologically impossible!" he shouted, indicating the maelstrom. "I'm over thirty!"

"You're eighteen!" Patty shouted back, "Mom says you're still eighteen!"

Mark scowled and pointed to the bench. Patty went and sat. Mark scooped up his ball from the return. Set, breathed, concentrated. Threw a gutter ball.

Mark plunked down next to Doonie, who opened a couple of diet sodas and handed one to Mark. They traded a weary look and swigged. Been a gutter ball and diet soda kind of week. Research on the LAFAM patrons and architects had sucked. The four possible suspects didn't have a decent prior between them.

In Aspen in 1983 Tish Sand had pled guilty to a DUI and making unkind comments to the ticketing officer.

Also back in the eighties, Calvin Hirschberg's boyfriends, personal assistants, bodyguards, and chauffeurs had been nabbed for nickel-dime drug stashes they swore Calvin knew nothing about.

Eric Fairlie had been sued by ex-wives in Edinburgh and London for unpaid child support, and by employees and subcontractors on three continents who'd been shorted on salaries and expenses.

Juan-Mari de Suau's big crime was not having performed any outright miracles, which was going to complicate the canonization paperwork after he was gone.

There was nothing that would earn Mark and Doonie a warrant to pry into phones and financials. Shit, on this case, without solid leads they weren't even allowed to risk the allowable—like contact Robbery-Homicide in L.A. and ask would they please canvas their snitches, see if there was any gossip about a hitter being hired by Tish Sand's butler or Calvin Hirschberg's personal trainer. Not that there was any guarantee the shooter had been hired in L.A.

Going at it from the bottom up wasn't getting anywhere either. There'd been no progress determining the perp in the Dead Headless Ralph investigation. Mark and Doonie had spent some more time in Hammond. Canvassed the neighborhood for anyone who might've seen anyone else leaving Ralph's tat parlor the night it blew up. Reinterviewed family, friends, associates. Insulted the Hammond FD and PD by getting permission for Chicago arson and crime scene techs to reevaluate the evidence. Dry hole.

Mark and Doonie requested authorization to fly to L.A. and backtrack the disappearance and death of Charlie Banza. Denied.

If nothing broke soon, they'd resume working their other ongoing, the endless Ms. June Dockyer–related hit-and-run. Mark and Doonie had handed off the hit-run to another team, with the understanding they'd take the case back if it hadn't been cleared by the time the Willetts thing wrapped up. Or froze shut.

Patty, concerned by their expressions, shouted at Mark and Doonie, "What's wrong?!"

"What!?" the detectives shouted back.

Mark and Doonie stopped thinking shop and concentrated on their party responsibilities. Doonie went to the bar and returned with cans of diet cola spiked with Jack. Mark bowled three amusingly awful games, during which he remained resolutely oblivious to the furtive conferences among clusters of thirteen-year-old girls who needed to debate and rate his precise degree of coolness, so they could determine if Patty's crush was justified or something she needed to be talked out of. Mark was impressed by how the girls managed to hear each other whisper in so much detail, inside a hurricane of Green Day and Linkin Park amped to parent-destroying levels.

The party moved into the bowling alley's deli/pizzeria for cake and presents. Mark's gift was a teal and black bowling shirt from Montreal; the embroidered name of the shirt's original owner was *Pascale,* whose team had been *Les Jets.* Mark found it in a vintage clothing store Janvier had once taken him to.

Mark was surprised how pleased he was by how pleased Patty was with his gift. He sometimes forgot what a small but world-balancing joy it was to make a kid happy.

Patty put the Les Jets shirt on over what she was wearing, swept over to Mark, and gave him a long, tight hug. Mark was surprised at how uncomfortable he was about his friend's daughter's body not feeling anything like a kid's, and with all those people looking on. Wasn't so much the grownups and Patty's brothers; it was being stared at by the fourteen thirteen-year-old girls and four thirteen-year-old boys. They put Mark right back in seventh grade; it was to them Mark wanted to protest, *We're not dating!*

Mark murmured, "You're welcome," to Patty and gently disentangled himself from her arms, moving her back so he could speak to her face instead of the top of her head. He was about to say something when he felt the buzz of his pager. He glanced at Doonie, who was pulling his own pager out. Mark returned his attention to Patty. "Glad you like it."

"I *love* it," Patty protested. *"Je suis Pascale."*

"Bon anniversaire, Pascale."

"Merci, Monsieur Mark . . . You're coming back to the house, to have a nightcap with Dad, aren't you?" *Pascale*-Patty innocently inquired.

Mark didn't quite burst out laughing. He looked at the coy little *demoiselle's* dad . . . who had a business face on.

"Pardon," Mark said to Patty as he pulled out his pager.

Patty waited with angelic patience, for two seconds, then repeated, "Aren't you?"

"Not tonight. Cop stuff," Mark confided, just between them, in a tone that said he was sure she was an insider who'd understand. "Happy birthday."

Mark kissed Patty goodbye, turning his face just quickly enough to avoid her planting one on his lips.

Mark told Doonie to stay at the party, he'd go check it out. Doonie nodded his thanks.

Ralph Garn's van had turned up in a Milwaukee police impound lot.

FIFTY-ONE

The trial reconvened. The Hackenmeyer bloodbath went pretty much as Harrison Miller had predicted to Mark, only worse. In addition to his previous motivations Harrison Miller was spurred by the sinister presence at the prosecutor's table of his thoroughly professional, supportive new co-counsel, Carrie Eli.

No mystery to Miller why the overqualified Ms. Eli had been made second chair. If it turned out Sy Vytautis had indicted the wrong man, Miller would be yanked off the case—and pilloried as an incompetent oaf by Vytautis, for having done everything exactly as that malignant weasel had ordered.

So Miller went after Betsy Hackenmeyer more savagely than even he fantasized he was capable of. The key for Miller this time wasn't to channel the spirit of some great actor. The whole time Betsy Hackenmeyer was on the stand, Miller was imagining Betsy Hackenmeyer was Sy Vytautis.

Miller gently asked (Sy) Betsy if she was absolutely certain her clock had said 11:17 p.m.

Betsy was absolutely certain.

Miller gradually shifted into attack mode, painting a picture of a woman who wasn't competent to read a digital clock, let alone remember weeks later what the numbers were. Miller submitted medical affidavits asserting anyone mixing Xanax and booze couldn't be trusted about detail. Much less someone with Betsy Hackenmeyer's murky, traumatic past.

Miller had gone to Catawba, Wisconsin, whipped out his

shovel and dug. He introduced Betsy's school records—she'd dropped out of high school in the middle of sophomore year. Her grades had always been terrible, she'd never been able to concentrate—not her fault, given the beatings she'd taken from an alcoholic father. And given her own drinking problem. She'd started, when?—age twelve.

Judge Santini got tired of waiting for the defense to object, so he interrupted the State's Attorney himself and asked how this tour of Ms. Hackenmeyer's youth was material.

Miller replied it was foundation to establish a pattern of instability, unreliability, fantasizing, and outright mendacity on the witness' part, due to her inherent intellectual limitations and a history of physical and emotional trauma. There were also plain old-fashioned issues of character.

The judge looked at Obed. Obed had been following the judge and prosecutor's exchange with the rapt interest of a well-informed spectator, and continued to. Waited attentively to hear what Santini would say next.

Judge Santini ruled the State could proceed.

Miller introduced depositions from Ms. Hackenmeyer's sister and friends. He had Betsy read the good parts to the court. How she'd gotten caught lying on job applications, credit card applications, her marriage license application. The year or two here and there when Ms. Hackenmeyer had become intensely devoted to this psychic or that medium. Ms. Hackenmeyer's insistence for three years, during her belief-in-reincarnation phase, that everyone call her Jo, because she was the reincarnated Jo March from *Little Women*.

Betsy testified, with invincible serenity, that when she saw *Little Women* on TV she was sure Jo had to have been made up from a real person. Many years later, in the hospital after her accident, Betsy finally got a chance to read the book. Right there in the foreword it said she was right—Jo was based on the author, who was a real person.

Miller thanked Ms. Hackenmeyer for that insight into her thought process. He then had her read the part of her sister Christine's deposition that told how Betsy had lied to protect her rude drunk of a husband. How after Betsy's husband left, Betsy often lied about her boyfriends being employed and/or single. How Betsy once got fired from a factory when she got caught punching the time-card of a boyfriend who was too hung-over to get in on time. How as children Christine and Betsy were trained to lie to protect their dad when people asked where the bruises came from. How Betsy, right from when she was little, took to making up lies. It was the one thing she ever showed a gift for.

Betsy, whose serenity had sprung a leak while she was reading the part about her dad, somberly explained all that was a long time ago. She was now a grown woman, a successful trader in collectibles.

Miller asked if she made a living at it.

Betsy said she made enough to get by, combined with interest from her settlement.

Miller asked if she could furnish tax returns to back that up.

After a sticky pause, Betsy shook her head No.

Miller asked Betsy to describe the accident she'd received the settlement for. Had her describe the pain. The painkillers. The emotional counseling. Asked if her mental and physical condition had been weaker since the accident.

Betsy, just barely audible, said her body was a little creaky, but she was more, um, clear-headed now than she'd ever been.

Miller gave her a sad, pitying smile. Said it would be a remarkable recovery, considering. He read to the court a list of the injuries Ms. Hackenmeyer had sustained. As he worked his way through the specifics of head-to-toe carnage the blood drained from Betsy's face.

Miller asked the ghostly pale witness if she would be so kind as to pull her hair aside and show the jury the scar on her scalp.

Obed started to get to his feet to object, but by the time Obed was standing Judge Santini had ordered ASA Miller to move on or sit down. The prosecutor sat.

The judge scowled at Obed. "Any redirect, Counselor?"

"Mmm . . . Not at this time, Your Honor."

The judge thanked the witness for her testimony and told her she could step down.

The witness didn't move. "Your Honor, I saw *him*"—pointing to Meelo—"at exactly 11:17 p.m. That's the truth," Betsy stated, with wounded, daffy serenity.

Santini thanked Betsy and begged her not to say anything else. He instructed the jury to ignore Betsy's last statement, and gaveled the day's proceedings to a close.

Meelo, who thought things had gone pretty well, gave his lawyer an optimistic look, seeking confirmation. Obed gave Meelo a rubbery imitation of an encouraging grin.

In the first row of the spectator's section, directly behind the defense table, Meelo's sister Angela was staring at the exiting jurors, transfixed, lost in the agony of criminal defendant calculus, trying to imagine how believable the jury had found the sincere, but undeniably odd, possibly loco Betsy Hackenmeyer.

At the prosecutor's table Miller leaned close to Carrie. Gave her a small, intimate Flynn Grynn and whispered, "Bet you a nickel the Pocket Pal jumps at forty-to-life."

FIFTY-TWO

The defendant's response to the plea offer went pretty much as Mark had declined to predict to Harrison Miller.

After the trial adjourned Miller invited Obed and his client to meet with him and Ms. Eli in a conference room down the hall. Obed said, "Sure," then looked at Meelo to see if his client agreed.

They got in the room, sat down and Miller told them the number. Take it or leave it, good for today only, right now, won't be a second chance.

The Pocket Pal was genuinely hurt by the offer of forty-to-life. Flatly rejected it. Went right at Miller. Bargained him down to thirty-seven-to-life, and urged his client to accept.

Meelo was a puddle of despair. Tried to speak a few times but just moaned and covered his eyes.

The three attorneys waited patiently for a while, then Miller grimaced at Obed. Obed made a placating gesture and leaned closer to his client, who was still trying to disappear behind his hands.

Obed asked, as if coaxing a reluctant puppy, "Meelo?"

His client moaned again.

Stern words erupted from voices on the other side of the conference room door—the cop standing guard, and a woman demanding to be let in. The cop made a placating noise, then knocked. Stuck his head in and said there was an Angela Garcia, wanted to meet with her brother and his attorney. Miller

Lenny Kleinfeld

and Carrie obliged; maybe the sister could extract a decipher-
able response from Meelo. The prosecutors went to wait in the
corridor.

Eight minutes later everybody in the corridor, and possibly
everyone on the fifth floor of the Cook County Court Building,
heard Angela yell, "NOW!"

The door banged open and Obed fled the conference room.
He gave Miller a helpless, apologetic shrug and plopped down
on a bench.

Fifteen minutes later a quiet, grim Angela Garcia invited the
attorneys back into the room. Meelo stammered his way through
an official rejection of the plea bargain and stated his wish to be
judged by a jury of his pierced.

"Despite the prosecution's sensationalistic and, um, sensational-
ist personal assault on our witness, the fact remains there is
now no doubt there is at least reasonable doubt," Obed
mumbled to the press.

Which consisted of two print reporters. All the other journalists had split soon as both lawyers declined to comment after
the adjournment. The print guys were the only ones who'd
watched carefully enough to notice the ASA conferring with the
PD as the court emptied, found out the two sides were meeting
and hung around to see if a deal got made. The print guys were
not only more experienced nuts-and-bolts reporters than their
video brethren, they were more motivated.

Dan Ditzler, the political gossip columnist for a free weekly,
had a three-hundred-word hole in his column he had to fill by
six p.m.

Bob Gilkey of the *Chronicle* was doggedly covering every
second of the Willetts case. He was thinking book.

"Any developments on the alleged conspiracy?" Gilkey asked.
"Police have any leads on who dismembered the tattoo artist?"

214

Obed ruefully shook his head. "No, not to my knowledge . . . But, now that the jury has heard the DNA results and what Ms. Hackenmeyer had to say, we're confident jurors must conclude, at the very least, it was physically—improbable—my client could have shot Wilson Willetts."

"Physically improbable," Ditzler wrote in his pad, trying to keep the glee out of his voice. "So you believe the Six-Minute Window of Innocence is still open?"

Obed nodded. He was too shaken to lie out loud. Jesus Christ. When he'd prepped Betsy Hackenmeyer he'd asked if there were any issues in her past the prosecution might bring up, and she told him no, nothing ever happened in Catawba.

"So there's no chance of a plea bargain?" Ditzler wondered, skeptically.

"No," Obed scoffed, hoping his confident grin was not as bilious-looking as it felt.

"*No* you wouldn't consider any offer you've heard so far," Gilkey asked, "or *no* you wouldn't consider any plea bargain, even if a better one came up?"

"My client is innocent. Innocent people with a strong case don't plea bargain."

Gilkey switched off his minirecorder and his official reporter tone. "Paul," he gently inquired, "have you explained to your client what happened in there today?"

FIFTY-THREE

Arthur checked into the San Francisco Marriott, a fifteen-hundred-room behemoth where he'd be as visible as an ant. Not that he'd used his own name.

He had hours before his dinner engagement. Plenty of time to hit the hotel gym—for the exercise, and to work up the appetite he was going to need. And plenty of time left after his workout to visit a cyber-café and read the Chicago papers.

There was news. Betsy Hackenmeyer, the "alibi" witness who put Meelo at the motel twenty-two minutes after the shooting, had testified. The prosecution had kicked big holes in Hackenmeyer's credibility.

After the day's proceedings wrapped up, the prosecutors met with the defendant and his attorney. Afterward both sides declined to confirm if a plea offer had been discussed. As if the meeting might've been about anything else.

The prosecutor's only comment was to reaffirm his strong belief Meelo would be found guilty.

The defense attorney backed off his earlier assertion Hackenmeyer's testimony was absolute proof of Meelo's innocence, retreated to a claim her story created reasonable doubt. If the reporter's accuracy could be trusted, the PD's exact words, voluntarily offered for public consumption, were that Meelo's guilt was "physically improbable."

Arthur didn't mistake today's news for proof he was home free, but he had to enjoy it for what it was worth. Especially considering the occasion. Arthur's long-time agent and advisor, Stephan Densford-Kent, was taking him to dinner, to commemorate Arthur's retirement and celebrate Arthur's future.

"Physical improbability," Densford-Kent warbled in wonder and delight. "He's planning to save his client with a defense based on *physical improbability.* Should make for a damn stirring closing argument. Damn stirring. In fact, not since 1938, when Neville Chamberlain got off that plane and announced he'd saved Europe by getting Hitler's written promise not to annoy the neighbors . . . Reincarnation, Arthur—it exists. We have the proof. This Paul Obed can be none other than Neville Chamberlain reborn."

"Can't argue with you, Stephan," Arthur admitted. "Your logic is as deep and convincing as your cellar." He drained a glass of 1897 Sandeman Port.

"Oh, I am going to miss you, Arthur. And the fat commissions you brought in with admirable regularity."

Arthur glanced at the decanter. "May I?"

"If you must."

Arthur refilled their glasses. Arthur and his host had repaired to Densford-Kent's penthouse on Russian Hill after the large, robust sixty-six-year-old Englishman had attempted to murder him with single-malt, Champagne, Puligny-Montrachet, claret, *auslese*, and a French tasting menu the length and weight of a German opera. They were sitting out on the apartment's corner terrace, where it was legal to light a cigar and safe to chat quietly about professional matters.

"Here's to a brilliantly healthy, dull, anonymous retirement, my boy," Densford-Kent toasted.

They clinked glasses. Arthur took a sip. Densford-Kent kept his glass raised and quietly added, "Most of all, may this be your only retirement." He drank. "May you get out and remain out."

"It will be my only retirement. Guaranteed . . . if you skip the gold watch and send me off with a bottle of this Sandeman."

"Perspective, Arthur. Never doubt it would be easier for me to watch you ruin your life than to part with an 1897."

They puffed. Sipped. Appreciated the magnificent Bay view Densford-Kent's lengthy career as a posh murder pimp had bought him.

"How about you, Stephan?" Arthur asked.

"Never. If retirement was the goal I would've kept the bloody government job. That's why I became an entrepreneur, found a game I like, which no one can force me to quit."

"You could decide to quit."

"Does the elephant quit? No. The concept of retirement does not apply to the elephant or Densford-Kent. We go on being who we are, doing what we do, until the moment we are culled, by God or some young bull."

After a small, thick silence Arthur asked, "Are you that hooked on the game?"

"Yes. Yes, I am." Densford-Kent ran a hand through his gray but still-full head of unruly hair. "Didn't have your timing and discipline."

"A lot of which I learned from you."

Densford-Kent raised his glass to his star pupil, drained it, and shattered it. Arthur did the same.

"Your retirement present," Densford-Kent informed Arthur, "shall be a pragmatic stainless steel watch, and two bottles of the '97 Sandeman."

Arthur eyed him. "1897 or 1997?"

"It's the thought that counts."

"True."

"The 1897, you suspicious wretch. My last two bottles . . .

So it would be unforgivably rude, even for an American, if you ever again called and asked for work."

"Thank you. I promise you will never get that call. And it is the thought that counts. I can't accept your last bottles."

"Would you prefer to take them with you tonight or have them chucked through your living-room window?"

Excellent. Stephan's insistence meant he had more of the '97 stashed away.

So Arthur could, in good conscience, accept the gift.

FIFTY-FOUR

Good news from Chicago. No. Better than good. Lucky. That Garcia chump comes up with a wild card that could wreck the scenario—a witness who puts him at the motel too soon after the shooting—and she turns out to be a delusional juicer.

Bye-bye the patsy's alibi. Bye-bye any immediate need for Del Sutton to put a team in place to grab, torture, and kill Stephan Densford-Kent.

If the frame-up failed the cops still wouldn't know who the shooters were, and might never. But if the cops somehow got their shit together and busted one or more of the shooters, a shooter could give up Densford-Kent, who was—probably—the only one who could finger Del Sutton as the man who'd issued the contract, and the name of Sutton's idiot employer, who'd paid for it.

And Densford-Kent was certainly the only one who could give Sutton the names of the shooters so Sutton could erase them.

Sutton had of course used an alias. But thanks to Sutton's idiot employer, who'd insisted on a goddamn idiot frame-up, Sutton had had to go through multiple sessions with Densford-Kent to settle the terms of the contract. The conditions were so risky and the payoff so suspiciously huge the agent had insisted on knowing Sutton's real name, who he was working for, and why.

So now the Brit might have to go. Simply whacking Densford-

Kent would be fast, easy, and enough of a cut-out to protect Sutton—assuming the agent had been as solid about not giving Sutton's name to the shooters as he'd been about not giving the shooters' names to Sutton. But Sutton wasn't about to bet his life on that assumption. Which meant, if things went south, snatching and breaking the wily old bastard. Another load of complicated crap.

So thank you blind luck and whatever else was keeping the Cook County prosecutors focused on Señor Patsy . . .

Shit. Sutton should've lied to his idiot employer, said the shooters refused to mess with staging a frame-up. Even for the fortune the idiot offered them.

Fuck. Sutton couldn't believe how much the shooters made off this compared to his own salary and bonuses.

FIFTY-FIVE

The '93 midnight-blue Astro had been towed after overstaying its welcome in Remote Lot B at Milwaukee's Mitchell International Airport.

Turned out the tags were stolen.

The VIN had been stripped off the dash. But not off the axle. The vehicle was registered to a Ralph Lewis Garn of Hammond, Indiana, and was amazingly popular. The Hammond cops were looking for it. So was the sheriff of Will County, Illinois. And the Chicago police.

The van was unnaturally clean. Almost perfect.

On the floor between the driver's seat and the door there was one fly-shit-sized dot of dried blood. Ralph had been type O. Meelo was type O. The blood dot in the van came up type A.

The blood in the scrapings under Darwahab's fingernails had been type A. The DNA comparison of the scrapings from the shooter's arm and the blood dot from Ralph's van would take several weeks. Meelo's trial probably wouldn't.

There was a partial right thumb-print on the underside of the rear-view, where someone had gripped the mirror to adjust it. The print was smeared; someone had tried to wipe it. It was the only inch of the van where someone had been less than absolutely thorough.

Computer cleaned up someone's partial as best it could and tried to read it.

Mark and Doonie handed the suspect's sheet to Husak and watched the lieutenant's face. Husak looked at the sheet, then at the detectives, then back down at the sheet.

The suspect's fingerprint was only a four-point match. Enough to intrigue the computer—but wouldn't stand up in court. And the suspect's only adult prior was petty theft and simple assault—a church collection-plate heist, which the perp, a grunt, had parlayed into a dishonorable discharge. Not a sheet that screamed professional killer.

Didn't matter. The booking photo was enough.

"Let me fax this Downtown," Husak said, "and show them why I think you two should fly to Disneyland and bring back Mr. Benvanides."

Ah, fuck. Unbelievable.

Sy stared at the sheet Superintendent Blivins faxed over. Tried to think if there was any way to squash this one. Didn't waste much time on that. No point kidding himself where this was headed.

Fucking Hector Luis Benvanides didn't look like Emilio Jesus Garcia's identical fucking twin, but from both the front and profile photos you could see how someone could mistake them for each other. Easy.

Vytautis called Blivins back to concur with the fat fuck's recommendations.

Hector Benvanides, aka Hector B, should be scooped up— quietly as possible—for questioning about the dismemberment of Ralph Garn and the murder of Wilson Willetts. Chicago cops should be present for the scooping and the interrogation. They should also be equipped with a court order to obtain a DNA swab. Extradition papers should be ready in the event Mr. Ben-

223

vanides' DNA matched the blood spot and the fingernail scrapings, so he could be escorted to Chicago to explain how he happened to be present in Dead Headless Ralph's van, and how he also happened to get scratched by Naguib Darwahab—most likely, Vytautis allowed, at the scene of the Willetts shooting.

Fifty-Six

Harrison Miller knew Sy Vytautis. Had a good idea why Vytautis had summoned him and Carrie Eli; the malignant weasel had read the trial transcripts. Sy now understood how thoroughly Miller had demolished Betsy, and with her any shred of a viable defense.

Yes, Vytautis sees the trial's a done deal, so he's in a hurry to get right with the victor. Make up for the insults to Miller by congratulating him—in front of Carrie, letting her know that being second chair, being Miller's over-fucking-qualified clerk, is all she'll ever be on this case. That treat would be Sy's special little peace offering to Miller.

When Miller and Carrie walked in to Vytautis' office the boss came out from behind his desk, gestured for them to take a seat on the couch. Sy's tone was all business, no clue of the praise he was about to deliver. Miller expected that. Sy wasn't one to gush. There'd be a single low-key compliment, with the understanding you should be honored the great man had doled it out. Miller was in fact less interested in hearing the congratulations than in deciding what one perfect line, what exact words, he would skewer Carrie with when they left Sy's office . . .

"Here," Vytautis said, breaking Miller's reverie. Vytautis handed Miller and Carrie copies of Hector B's sheet.

Miller stared at Hector B's mug shots. Tried to read the rest of the sheet. Couldn't. The floor was melting, the couch smelled

225

sour, and Miller's clothes suddenly went heavy, as if his suit and tie were pulling Gs.

Vytautis told them how he and Blivins had decided to proceed. Ordered Miller and Carrie to get the warrants and extradition papers drawn.

Carrie nodded and said, "Right."

Miller couldn't untighten the muscles required to nod or speak.

"Don't look so down," Vytautis chided Miller. "If this Benvanides' DNA doesn't match the material under the cabbie's fingernails, your case is still intact."

Vytautis' words hung there a moment between the three lawyers. Not the case, or our case. *Your* case.

Vytautis went back behind his desk. Meeting over.

When they left Sy's office Carrie told Miller she'd take care of the paperwork. He grunted absently.

Carrie took the documents to a judge, hovered until they were autographed. She delivered the papers to Detectives Bergman and Dunegan, and briefed the cops on the legal details of their trip to the Coast. Then they repaired to a quiet lounge, so they could hoist a sympathy toast to poor Meelo, who was still, for a little while longer, fucked.

The brass had agreed this new Hector Benvanides line of investigation was at too preliminary and fragile a stage to warrant being divulged to the defense, because Paul Obed would, very publicly, use it to demand his client's release. Which would warn Hector B it was time to get invisible.

So Meelo would have to remain in jail and his Murder One trial would have to continue, at least until the cops nailed Benvanides. Carrie assured the detectives that keeping the trial going, slowly, wouldn't be a problem.

The defense couldn't count on even one juror going to the

mat for Meelo based on anything that came out of Betsy Hackenmeyer's mouth. So Obed would now have to bring in Dead Headless Ralph and the snake tattoo, and show how they fit the conspiracy theory of Oscar buying Meelo a distinctive, easily copied giant ugly tat. The only way Obed could accomplish that was to put Meelo on the stand and have him relate the entire conspiracy epic to the jury, beginning with Heather picking him up outside Water Tower Place.

Then Meelo would be cross-examined, in excruciating detail.

If Mark and Doonie needed more time than that to locate Hector B, Carrie promised the prosecution would then drag in a parade of rebuttal witnesses—

Mark said not to worry, he and Doonie could locate anybody in the Lower 48 in the time it would take Meelo to recite his saga under courtroom conditions. Throw in the cross-examination, they'd have time to locate Hector B, Oscar, Heather, the rich fuck who hired them, and six major characters from *Little Women*.

FIFTY-SEVEN

Problem. Hector Benvanides aka Hector B seemed to have disappeared.

Superintendent Blivins had ensured serious cooperation by starting the process at the top, putting in a call to his opposite number. L.A.'s recently hired Chief of Police Donald Connaught had instantly grasped the situation. Connaught was even more concerned than Blivins that Hector Benvanides be taken as quietly as possible, and interrogated the same way. Connaught wanted nothing about this investigation, nothing linking the murder of LAFAM finalist Wilson Willetts to an L.A.-based shooter, to go public, unless and until hard evidence demanded it. There'd be special hell to pay if word of the investigation leaked—which was dead certain to start a full-on scandal orgy—and then the suspicions behind it came up false or unprovable. The reputations of the museum and its board would have been flayed for no reason. A board loaded with thin-skinned heavyweights wired into everybody that mattered: the mayor, the city council, the police commission—and Mrs. Connaught, who'd RSVP'd to the ceremonial unveiling of the LAFAM designs and was pressing Chief Connaught to attend with her.

So top-notch Detectives Teophilo Ochoa and J'nette Levaux were waiting by the phone when Mark made his initial contact. The L.A. cops planned to check out Hector B's residence, see if they could locate the suspect and keep him under surveillance.

But they wouldn't pick Hector B up unless he was about to pull a runner.

The plan was to avoid starting the clock until the Chicago cops got there, to give them the maximum amount of time with Benvanides while they awaited DNA results. The LAPD could hold him forty-eight hours for suspicion in connection with the Willetts shooting. Then use the Milwaukee forensics to tack on a few days for suspicion of disassembling Ralph Garn and abandoning a stolen vehicle in a high-cholesterol zone. The real hope was the L.A. cops would find some unlicensed hardware on Hector B and/or in his residence, so they could hang onto him by filing weapons charges.

That was yesterday's optimism.

This morning at O'Hare, Mark had put in one last call from the departure lounge before he and Doonie boarded their flight. Levaux gave Mark the bad news. The L.A. cops had scouted Hector B's last known residence. He'd moved out eight months ago. Canceled his bank accounts, utilities, e-mail, and plastic. No record of him opening new ones.

DMV check showed Hector B had sold his 2001 Chrysler 300M to a used-car dealer in South Gate. Levaux said South Gate was an incorporated armpit pretending to be a city; bad place to get top dollar for a cushy late-model sedan, good place to get paid a small amount by check along with a larger amount in cash, off the books.

That was where Hector B's trail ended.

FIFTY-EIGHT

Mark and Doonie were on an eleven a.m. flight. It was the earliest departure the Department travel manager could find bargain seats on.

Deferring to Doonie's bulk, Mark gave him the aisle seat and what little solace it offered in the way of leg room. The big man squirmed, searching for a position that might negate the physics of the situation. "Shoulda asked Aunt Flo to lend us the Gulfstream," Doonie muttered.

"Riding a private jet's the kinda thing makes you turn Republican," Mark warned.

"Sacrifice I'd make for the job. Private plane, we'd have the privacy to talk business. Plus, sittin' five hours in chairs the same size as people."

No shit. Mark settled for taking out a yellow legal pad and making a list of ways they might pick up Hector B's trail.

Lunch arrived. Mark and Doonie declined the trays of warm salty glue.

Doonie retrieved his carry-on from the overhead. Pulled out a couple of gallon-sized baggies containing quart-sized baggies containing roast beef sandwiches, apples, and pecan brownies.

"I love your wife," Mark informed Doonie.

"Yeah, well, don't let 'Pascale' hear about it. This one's yours," Doonie said, handing Mark the baggie that also contained a snapshot of Patty wearing the *Les Jets* bowling shirt.

Mark stared at the photo for a moment. Was about to say something to Doonie. But there wasn't a single joke or protest Mark could make to the father of a thirteen-year-old girl about the girl's crush on him that wouldn't sound like a lyric from the pedophile songbook.

"I know," Doonie said, empathizing with Mark's dilemma. "Raising a daughter . . . My advice, when you settle down and have kids . . . I was gonna tell ya, 'Only have sons.' But God's honest, I'm not sure which is worse."

Mark said, "Good sandwich."

Doonie, mouth full, grunted agreement.

They munched contentedly. Doonie paused, lowered his sandwich. "Wonder what kinda food Aunt Flo serves on the Gulfstream."

Shit. Mark was not getting sucked into comparing Phyl's menu with Aunt Flo's. If he complimented Phyl's roast beef again it'd be a shot at Doonie, Mark passing judgment on extramarital shit that's none of his business. But there was also no way Mark was gonna just go along, fantasize about the glories of Aunt Flo's cuisine, while he sat here with Phyl's life-saving sandwich in his hand.

"Fuck the food," Mark dodged. "You were right the first time. It's the seats and the privacy. The sardine thing." He pulled his legal pad out of the seat-pocket and handed it to Doonie. "Here."

"Yeah, that's the same ideas I came up with so far," Doonie said after reading the items Mark had listed. All three of them.

"Ah fuck, it really is the fuckin' sardine seats," Doonie said, knuckling the small of his back. They'd boarded on time at O'Hare. Then sat until the plane took off an hour late. Spent forty minutes on the tarmac at LAX waiting for a gate. By the time Doonie pried himself out of his economy-class slot it had

231

turned into a six-hour sit.

The past few years Doonie's back occasionally locked up tight. This wasn't that. He was just creaky. If there was serious pain Doonie wouldn't say anything.

They inched their way up the aisle to the forward door. Three-twenty-seven, local time. There'd still be time to get work done today.

Hopefully the L.A. dicks had already gotten to Item Number One on Mark's list: The Usual. As in checking Hector B's known associates and looking under his mom's bed.

Item Number Two: the used car dealer. Maybe Hector B had gone to a guy he was tight with, who knew things. A long shot. But the used car guy was the last person they knew of who'd seen Hector B in L.A.

Item Number Three: find out if the L.A. cops had snitches who knew where to hire a pro shooter. If Hector B wanted to make a living someone had to know how to contact him.

The problem was time. There'd be a fuck of a mess if they didn't nail Hector B before Meelo's trial wrapped and the prosecutors had to keep it from going to jury by admitting they had the wrong man . . . Shit, Mark and Doonie might not escape this plane before Meelo's trial ended . . . They finally shuffled past the attendants doing mechanically cheery goodbye duty at the cabin door, out onto the blessed telescoping exit ramp where actual walking was possible, and into the passenger lounge, where Detective Levaux was waiting.

Great cop.

Brought Mark and Doonie right back to life. She was maybe thirty. Five-eleven, sleek curves and sharp-cut muscle, lustrous deep brown complexion, hair cut in a tight, short, stylish retro-'fro, large wide-set eyes with a gaze that could burn holes if it wanted, liquid alto purr of a voice, sharply pressed black suit that was probably afraid to wrinkle while being worn by someone this organized and determined, who crisply shook her new colleagues' hands and said, "J'nette Levaux. Welcome to Los Angeles. We have the suspect under surveillance. We can hook him and book him soon as we get there."

Great cop.

FIFTY-NINE

J'nette Levaux was a dreamy kid who'd been raised by a relent-lessly methodical dad; navy lifer, aviation mechanic. He'd taught J'nette to get her scattered, drifting thoughts four-oh-and-squared-away by making lists.

J'nette took writing lists so to heart she began to think in lists. Still did. As she spotted the two hunting animals emerge from the ramp—

1] *The potato-shaped disheveled one must be Dunegan—but he seems relaxed, not lazy; old pro.*

A] *Checked out my holster bulge before my boobs.*

B] *Eyes didn't stop on the boobs.*

2] *Can't tell from Bergman's looks if he's Jewish.*

A] *Dude from SoCal with Bergman's looks would game it more—sharper haircut, up-to-the-second clothes.*

B] *Never looked anyplace but in my eyes. Knows a woman appreciates being treated professionally—then she'll start to wonder when he* will *get to checking her out.*

3] *Neither one went flinchy at me being—*

A] *A woman—*

B] *A black woman, and—*

C] *Even though these two knew who to expect, so many guys and so many whites would still have had that built-in butt-pucker moment.*

Each cop gave his name as he shook her hand, and—

4] *Neither one does the bonecrusher handshake shit.*

5] Welcome them and get right to what they want to know—

"We can hook him and book him soon as we get there."

The Chicago dicks didn't say a word. The partners traded a quick pleased eye-check, then Bergman gave Levaux a small grin and gestured for her to lead the way. As they headed down the corridor, it occurred to Levaux—

6] No L.A. jokes from either of them.

A] Better fucking not be, the service they're getting.

SIXTY

The smog was different—noticeably less bad than the other time Mark had been there, eleven years ago, a twenty-year-old who'd collected a BA and hit the road with no goal other than to keep the party going a while longer, stave off the onset of real life. Back then L.A. had been veiled in a cloud of pale diarrhea-brown air that tasted—mercifully—more like aluminum foil than like something earth-toned. Today the air was clear enough so that from the back seat of the unmarked cruiser fighting its way out of the airport Mark could see the ring of mountains that formed the coastal basin the city sat in, get an inkling of what a beautiful place this must have been a few million people ago.

Other than the improved smog Los Angeles seemed the same. Still didn't feel like a city to Mark. No part of town achieved a critical mass of people and buildings jammed against each other; not enough teeming density to create that sense of hive, a billion things going on all around, all at once. L.A. still felt like a suburb the size of Rhode Island. But that might be an illusion; Detective J'nette Levaux seemed big-city.

When they got in her car Levaux radioed her partner, let him know they were on their way. Detective Ochoa told her they had recent visual confirmation the suspect was still in his house. Did the Chicago detectives want him to move in if they didn't arrive before dark? Doonie asked Ochoa to hang loose, they'd keep checking in along the way. Ochoa signed off.

Before dark? Mark asked, "How long's the drive going to take?"

Levaux said it should be less than an hour. But you never knew. Hector B's place was in Sunland, way to hell and gone, over the Hollywood Hills, in the northeast corner of the Valley, thirty-five- or forty-mile drive, about as far from the airport as you could get and still be in Los Angeles.

Levaux switched to commercial news radio. A traffic report came on and Levaux goosed the volume.

Shit, Levaux thought—but not as the heading for a list—when it came to traffic she found it more productive to visualize the map and think in terms of flow. She'd planned to take the 405 all the way north to the 118, then the 118 east to the 5 and loop south on the 5 to Sunland. But the radio said there was a Sig Alert on the northbound 405 near Culver City; a convertible sofa had fallen off a pickup, causing a nine-vehicle daisy-chain as drivers braked and swerved to avoid the queen-sized sleeper-sofa that had suddenly popped open across the Two and Three lanes, its mattress neatly made up with official Mighty Ducks sheets. So the best new route would be to take the 405 south to the 105 east to the 110, and take the 110 north to the 5, even though that would mean crawling through the mess where four freeways collided downtown, because once you got past that tangle it was a straight shot up the 5 to Sunland.

There was no better alternative—if they left the freeway and tried to get to Sunland using surface streets, Hector B would be collecting Social Security by the time they arrived.

"Okay," she muttered. "Won't be a problem."

When they heard the traffic report, Doonie, in the front seat, turned and shot a wary glance at Mark. Mark raised an eyebrow: *Yeah, welcome to L.A.*

237

The radio said there was something called a Sig Alert, because some hockey fan had lost his couch on a freeway—the freeway Levaux had apparently wanted to take, because when she heard "405" she frowned and made a small sharp noise. Then she dropped into a trance for a few moments, then said, "Okay," mainly to herself. Informed the Chicagoans, "Won't be a problem."

Mark decided to trust Levaux on that, even though she got on the 405 south, after saying Sunland was north . . . Mark imagined Levaux making that small sharp noise many times in a row, fast . . . Shit. Put it back in your pants, Officer. Mark took care not to fall into the lust-fantasy thing when working with women. Not fair to them—and fucking stupid dangerous not to keep focused on the job. But now, with Levaux, wham . . . Pathetic. He goes anything over a week without getting laid . . .

As Levaux drove she filled Mark and Doonie in on the details of the Hector B stakeout, so they'd have some sense of the situation in case they had to make a decision while still on the road. Gave them the physical setup, described Hector B's house and the assets she and Ochoa had in place around it.

Impressive, how organized, clear, and complete Levaux's off-the-cuff briefing was. Moved from topic to topic as if working her way through an outline. When she was done Mark and Doonie had no questions.

With what they needed to know out of the way, Mark moved on to what they wanted to know. "What happened after we got off the phone this morning?" he asked.

"Ochoa and I made a lucky guess," Levaux said. "Hector B's disappearing act was so thorough we figured he wouldn't blow it by hanging with the homies. So we sent our secondaries to question the family and known associates."

"And you took the used car dealer," Mark ventured.

"Uh-huh," Levaux confirmed, glancing at Mark in the rear-view.

"He made a list," Doonie explained.

Levaux gave Mark a slightly longer, more appraising eye-check in the mirror. Mark wondered, *She likes that I make lists?*

"Ran a BCI," Levaux continued, "and the car dealer turns up the right kind of dirty. Long juvie sheet, chop-shop connections, first adult rap grand theft auto. Did seven months. The light bulb goes off, he decides it's safer and more profitable to steal as a respectable businessman."

Doonie gave an approving nod. "Just the citizen Hector B would go to for cash back under the table."

"Our thinking," Levaux confirmed. "And in fact the on-the-books transaction was five grand, for a year-old Chrysler 300M; Blue Book is twenty-three-and-change."

"So you've got something to maybe squeeze the dealer with, if maybe he knows something about Hector B."

"Uh-huh," Levaux nodded, as she zigged from lane to lane, working the gaps, making what time she could. "But South Gate's out of our jurisdiction. So my partner gets on the phone to his cousin Romelio—a sergeant on the South Gate PD, who can walk us in and front for us . . . But we never got there."

Mark and Doonie straightened a little. Levaux let herself enjoy the moment a little.

"While Teo was calling Cousin Romelio," she explained, "I checked on who'd bought the car next. Day after Hector B sold it to the used car dealer, the dealer sells this twenty-three grand car for a mere seventy-five hundred, to a Harold Anderson, whose address is a PO box in Las Vegas."

Mark felt the hairs dance on the back of his neck. "Anderson's Nevada license comes up bogus."

Levaux gave him an almost-grin in the rearview. "And?"

"This alleged Harold Anderson—not long after buying this

bargain car—sells it to a guy with a valid California license, who lives in—Sunland?"

"Gentleman named John Rosas," Levaux confirmed, "whose DL photo—"

"Makes him Hector Benvanides," Doonie finished for her. "You nailed him without leaving the office."

"The man loves his 300M," Mark noted, gratefully, "and was too cheap to spring for a new one."

What must have happened was, Hector B takes the five grand from the dealer, but takes no cash under the table. Next day he comes back with his bogus Nevada driver's license, buys the car for seventy-five hundred on the books, and slips the dealer a tax-free ten grand or so. Saves himself half off what a new 300M would've cost . . . and leaves a trail of data crumbs J'nette Levaux and Teophilo Ochoa followed right to his door.

"Why'd he bother with the Nevada scam?" Doonie asked.

"California plates stay with the car when you sell it in-state," Levaux explained. "This way Hector B's original Cali tags are voided by the out-of-state sale, and 'John Rosas' gets a clean set of Cali plates when he 'buys' the car from 'Harold Anderson' of Nevada."

They slowed to a crawl, then a halting crawl, entering a knot of freeways that converged alongside the modest cluster of skyscrapers that made up L.A.'s downtown.

Mark quietly asked, "Um, Detective, is th—"

"No," Levaux shook her head, "there isn't a quicker route." She seemed embarrassed.

"These days traffic's a bitch in Chicago too," Mark consoled her.

The beautiful cop gave a disinterested grunt.

Touchy. The gossip must be true. LAPD morale really did suck after fifteen years of highlight-reel ineptitude, corruption, cowboy-cop violence, underfunding, understaffing, and a string of administratively challenged police chiefs.

"There's bottles of water in a bag on the back seat. You should drink, you get dehydrated in this climate even"—Levaux paused, annoyed to find herself bringing up the topic she was trying to avoid—"when you're doing nothing."

Mark found a six-pack of half-liters in a grocery bag. Handed one to Doonie. "You want one?" he asked Levaux.

She shook her head.

"Thanks," Doonie said, and took a swig. "Was gettin' dry. Appreciate it."

"*De nada,*" Levaux said.

She radioed her partner. Ochoa informed them Benvanides/ Rosas hadn't left his house. Asked when they thought they'd be getting to Sunland. Levaux muttered she'd have a better idea when they got past downtown. She ten-foured.

"So," Levaux asked her passengers, changing the topic the hell off of traffic, "supposing your theory of the crime is correct—how do you think whoever was the brains managed to find a Chicago patsy who was a look-alike for Hector B?"

The question was one Mark and Doonie had chewed on, and were looking forward to asking Hector B about.

"Well," Doonie said, "whoever's running the show—we figure 'Oscar'—has Hector B and maybe a couple of other reliable shooters in mind. So maybe they hack into the Chicago PD mug files and run a face-recognition thing, see if they can download some moron with the looks they need."

Mark leaned forward. "Or maybe 'Heather' plays tourist, claims she's been mugged, sits down with our detectives and gives a detailed description of Hector B—and there we are, digging through our photo-array of small-timers, knocking ourselves out to find Oscar and Heather their patsy." Mark made eye contact with Levaux in the rearview. "You guys think of anything else?"

"We've only been on this long enough to come up with questions," she said. "Like, how could they count on finding someone who was such a dead-on match for Hector B *and* gullible enough to—no, forget that second part, finding someone dumb enough is always easy."

"Amen," Doonie affirmed.

"I don't think they were counting on a dead match," Mark said. "Close enough for rock 'n' roll would've done it. They just got lucky."

"Very," Levaux replied, sounding skeptical.

"It happens," Doonie teased. "Like you finding Hector B in your computer this morning."

"Hey that wasn't luck," Mark protested. "That was first-rate cop shit."

Levaux issued a wryly formal, "Thank you, Detective."

The freeway loosened up enough for Levaux to accelerate to a steady twenty miles an hour.

"Though," Mark added, "we do blame you, personally, for the Sig Alert on the 405 and the traffic jam downtown."

"Fuck you, Detective" Levaux said, amused.

SIXTY-ONE

Hard to believe city cops worked turf like this. Turf like this should be patrolled by Smokies in four-wheelers. Earps on horses.

Sunland was way past suburban. Sunland was steep, hilly semi-rural semi-desert, its narrow, dry beige folds dotted with everything from semi-modern McMansions with Saddlebreds corralled out back to trailer-trash semi-hovels with deceased pickup trucks rusting out front.

Then there was the sound of the place.

"I thought roosters only crowed at dawn," Mark said.

"Nah, not when you got a whole mess of them together, fighting birds, and keep 'em indoors. Just go batshit," Detective Teophilo Ochoa explained.

Fucking impressive racket those birds were making. The noise was coming from two hills over from Hector B's house. Here inside the surveillance truck the crowing was muffled to the point of being merely annoying. If you stood outside you could, even at that distance, determine the source—a run-down ranch house perched on a hill. For the birds' immediate neighbors the effect must have been right up there with living next to a flock of dental drills.

"Nature," Doonie commented, sadly.

J'nette Levaux's face was set in an impassive scowl.

Mark understood. Whoever was running that cockfight supply depot must have his neighbors intimidated—and be keeping

243

the local LAPD greased to ignore the neighbors' complaints. If Levaux was embarrassed about clogged freeways Mark didn't want to think how pleased she was about being associated with this hotbed of flagrant rooster graft.

"We owe you double," Mark told Levaux. "For finding Hector B so fast"—Mark turned to Ochoa—"and sitting through six hours of this, waiting for us to get here."

"No," Ochoa amiably disagreed, "the shmuck *vato* who owns those birds owes me." He gave Levaux a quick, reassuring look. "We'll bust his ass soon's this is over."

Mark didn't doubt it. Teophilo Ochoa looked like someone whose high school nickname must've been Toro. Mark's height, six-one. But with arms like legs, legs like pier pilings. A vast expanse of chest, with a relatively small roll of gut spilling over his belt; most guys his build, living on cop cuisine and Hispanic home cooking, would by age forty be well on their way to acquiring Doonie's silhouette. Ochoa must still work out like he was waiting for the NFL to call. Or Paramount. Maybe looks *were* an LAPD recruiting requirement. Ochoa's massive head was topped by gleaming dark brown hair, in elegantly casual layers; if he was on the take, it was freebies from a Beverly Hills stylist. His hawk-nosed warrior's features were tempered by a gentle voice, which signaled he would prefer understanding and befriending you to snapping your spine like a toothpick.

The four detectives and a communications tech were comfortably ensconced in the surveillance vehicle—a customized CalTrans repair truck whose interior was a lot roomier than the delivery vans the Chicago cops were accustomed to. The truck was parked on the shoulder of a twisty ribbon of blacktop, just out of sight of Hector B's place; letting the truck sit all day where Hector B could spot it would've been only slightly less suspicious than Ochoa knocking on his door and pretending to sell Girl Scout cookies.

Mark and Doonie had gotten a quick look at the place, driving past it when they arrived at the stakeout.

Hector B's house was tucked into a slope below the crest of a rolling hill. The only access was up a gated driveway, leading to a two-car garage. The house was a plain rectangular stucco box. It gave the occupant a nice view in all directions, of the road below and all the approaches to the house. In front of and on both sides of the house the ground was bare except for isolated outbreaks of short, spiky bushes. (Chaparral, Mark figured, or sage—one of those words they use in Westerns.) Behind the house there was a brick patio with a built-in grill. Past that was a stand of gnarled, tough-looking trees that went all the way to the hilltop.

When Levaux and Ochoa drove past that morning, a black Chrysler 300M had just stopped at the driveway gate, which began to open. The car's windows were down; Hector B was at the wheel. He drove up the driveway and into the garage, letting the garage door close behind him—there must be direct access from the garage to the house.

The L.A. cops set up a surveillance perimeter; there were three SWATs hidden in the trees behind the house, in case Hector B tried to leave that way.

The CalTrans truck crew had spent the morning surveying the road in front of Hector B's place, then moved to its current parking spot, after which several vans had taken turns stopping to repair cable TV wires, or break down with an overheated radiator, for a couple of hours apiece, in places where they had a view of the house. Several fiber-optic spycams had been attached to phone poles and were feeding monitors in the truck.

So far the watchers had gotten only one glimpse of Hector B. He emerged from the back door, which connected the kitchen to the patio. The watchers reported the kitchen door was thick, windowless, looked like it might be metal, and closed with a heavy thunk they could hear in the woods. Hector B dropped a large white plastic garbage bag in his trash can and went back inside.

Now that the Chicago cops had arrived it was time to decide how to collect their garbage—bash the door in and grab him, or wait for him to leave his hillside fortress and bust him outside?

Mark and Doonie came to the same conclusion Ochoa and Levaux had; the best option was to wait, and take the suspect when he tried to leave. They'd have a few seconds' notice— they'd know it was on soon as Hector B's garage door began to open. When his beloved 300M got to the foot of the driveway Hector B would have to wait for the gate to open. A truck would pull across the mouth of the driveway and block him in, as cops with pump-actions and M-16s—including SWATs coming from behind, out of the woods behind the house—would converge on the car.

Problem was, willing as the cops might be to sit here patiently watching the monitors and listening to the cocks crow and crow and crow, there was a limit to how long they could get away with it. What if Hector B didn't leave the house, spent tonight at home? Sunland was an area with no sidewalks, no businesses, no reason for anyone but residents to be hanging around after sundown. Strange vehicles parked on the shoulder of the road all night—let alone strangers spotted on foot after dark—would not be ignored. Ma would be on the phone to the local cops while Pa locked and loaded his Mac 10. The watchers' cover would get blown and this thing would turn into a siege situation drawing media crews; Mark and Doonie preferred to bust Hector B without his gun-buddies or their employer knowing about it.

The four detectives agreed that if Hector B didn't go for a ride before seven p.m. they'd pull back. The L.A. cops had planned for that contingency. If Hector B did emerge, the spycams would spot him. There'd be time to alert unmarked cars that would be cruising around the junctions at either end of the road. Whichever direction Hector B drove, the cars would tail him and the cops wait for a favorable situation to grab him.

That scenario wasn't Mark's favorite. Too many chances for things to go sideways. Starting with Hector B making the cars tailing him, which could be easy out here at the ass end of nowhere.

"Anybody got any ideas," Mark asked, "how we might persuade Hector B to go for a drive before sundown?"

"We could close our eyes and wish real hard," Doonie suggested.

"That won't work," Levaux informed him, "not unless you have a *Santeria Olorisha* sacrifice a rooster first."

"Maybe ten or fifteen roosters," Ochoa growled.

"Sir!" a communications tech yelped, pointing to a monitor. "Garage door is opening!"

So you didn't have to sacrifice the roosters. Just threaten them. Shame.

SIXTY-TWO

It was like magic, Hector B gloated, like when you were a little fucking kid and you wished that if you just thought about some shit hard enough you could make it happen. And it did.

He was on a roll, no shit, life was all of a sudden pretty fucking good. Costa Rica had been kinda fun, that warm thick damp air wrapped around you like head-to-toe pussy, and he met this giggly Minnesota bitch was also down there for some knifework, had her nose done before he got there and she was just hangin', waiting for her freckly cow face to heal up before she went home. All Hector B had to do was tell her she already looked real fine, and she put out like crazy, no charge. Even bought him a shirt. And his own surgery had gone perfect; doc erased the scratches from his arm like they were never there.

Hadn't had a gig since he got back but he wasn't sweating it. Cash situation was still good and the Mob guys were pleased with the work he did on the Indian chief's girlfriend. Said they'd be having more for him.

About the only thing he'd been pissed about lately was Bill still not getting back to him about hooking him up with the agent. Hector B had been checking the Chicago papers online. Meelo's trial looked to be over soon. Man, then it'd be time to hook up with Bill's agent, step up in class. Jesus fuck, the money at that level. Not every gig would pay as crazy as capping this Chicago architect did, but still . . . Shit, look at this house. Hector B really liked this house. Got some nice new furniture for it, and he wanted more.

Kind of a pain in the ass not being able to show the place off to the homies, but Bill made sense about how you gotta have a safe secret place of your own . . . Now if Meelo's fuckin' trial would just fuckin' end . . .

Last night had been wack. Spent the night with a pair of clean young whores over in Pomona. God he loved stackin' two of 'em and slidin' it from one to the other . . . Didn't get home till late this morning, picked up some groceries, sacked out a coupla hours. Made some food and coffee, blew a little weed, and was chillin' with his new flight program. Not some PlayStation shit where you blast the MIGs or strafe the rag-heads, this was serious simulator learn to fly a fuckin' Cessna shit. Hector B was thinking, he makes some real money off this agent, he's gonna sign up for lessons, get a pilot's license. Make himself even more valuable—he can fly off anywhere to do a gig, not have to drive cross country, 'cause after 9/11 you know there's not never again gonna be no way to get your guns and shit on a fuckin' airliner.

Using his head like that gonna fuckin' impress that fuckin' agent for sure—that was the exact thought Hector B was thinking when this month's disposable cell rang. It was "Heather." Asked was he interested in looking at real estate in Calistoga tomorrow—which meant could he meet her at Location C in twenty minutes.

Hector B didn't say yes or no, just asked what was happening in Calistoga. And— magic time—Heather says—real friendly, which she never was—"Found something good, just the kind of place you've been waiting for."

So Hector B said, "Okay, sure," trying not to sound excited, and Heather said, "Excellent," like she's all pleased, like all of a sudden Hector B is in the club. And she hangs up.

Because he was stoned, Hector B got extra careful. He knew the locations by heart but double-checked the list anyway to make sure of the code-C address, then wrote the shit down twice and stuck the papers in different pockets. He put his computer to sleep, slapped on some aftershave to cover the weed stank, and got in his car. Not only was it magic the way Heather had phoned about the agent the exact second Hector B had been thinking about the agent, but her whole act was different. Hector B pulled out of the garage and rolled down the driveway. Till now Heather'd only had eyes for that old prick Bill, she tried to hide it but you couldn't miss that shit, 'specially the way she'd shut Hector B down when he tried to get next to her. He pressed the remote and the driveway gate began to slide open. But on the phone just now, fuck, it was in Heather's voice, this respect, like Hector B was about to be some kind of made man, and Heather was letting him know she was ready to put out—he wasn't trippin' about this, her tone was fuckin' letting him know—

A CalTrans truck pulled up, the front end blocked Hector B from getting out his driveway, and some hardhat asshole got out and came—*hey wait, this*—SHIT—screaming COPS with rifles pumps kevlar he quick checked the rear-view to back up but there were SWATs coming around his house pointing M-16s . . . Fuck it stay cool do not pull your piece, he did what the bitches were shrieking for him to do, turned off the engine, raised his hands and pressed his palms against the car's ceiling. This fuckin' huge *vato* started to open the driver's side door but Hector B was staring straight ahead at this gringo fuck staring in, standing there right in front of the car, badge hanging on his breast pocket but no gun out, and Hector B knew why, recognized the face, the Chicago fuck, big hero who busted that dumb fag Meelo was now just hangin' out in front of the 300M, casual, but giving Hector B this look with these cold gray eyes,

that vampire cop look where they pretend they can see right
fuckin' through—

SIXTY-THREE

All right, they came through the bad moment clean, nobody's index finger had gone psycho and blown the suspect away before he could surrender.

Some cops never got the hang of going over the top and staying in control. During those couple of endless, nerve-ripper seconds where they were doing their beserker act, trying to shock the suspect into submission, Mark had been gripped by a strange ugly feeling. A couple of the L.A. SWATs had that thick-necked steroid-sucker look and the quivering, foaming-at-the-brain fury that went with it. *Sorry, Detective Bergman, I had to shoot the suspect because he was breathing in a threatening manner.*

But no. The thing passed, as instantly and irrationally as it arrived; Mark felt the kill-craze vibe unclench and dissipate.

Ochoa, pump shotgun looking like a Hasbro in his beefy right hand, was pulling the car door open with his left. Mark, who'd stepped directly in front of the black sedan, was looking into Hector B's eyes, saying hello, getting a read, starting the game, when a blast of scorch bit the edge of Mark's ear, the Chrysler's windshield spider-webbed, a dot dented Hector B's forehead, his head snapped to attention, the back of his skull parted and bits of lead, brain, blood and bone blew through the headrest and through the back seat into the 300M's remarkably spacious trunk. Hector B's eyes were still open and staring at Mark but there was nothing interesting to read in them any more, cops were yelling "Gun!" and hitting the dirt, the edge of

Mark's ear was stinging as he eyeballed the angle of the hole in the windshield and, using his index finger as a pointer, traced a line back to the bloody nick on his ear, turned and pointed it up along the imaginary line which led to the place that fucking impressive shooter must be, the ramshackle ranch house two hilltops away where indignant cooped-up bantamweights were trading shrill trash-talk.

"Rooster ranch!" Mark yelled and ran to the nearest unmarked car, which had its doors open and motor running—

J'nette Levaux, who, like everyone except Mark, had proned out, launched herself and dashed to the car, yelling "I'll drive!" at Mark –

Ochoa yelled "Stay down!" but Mark and Levaux were in the car and peeling off before they'd gotten its doors closed—

Doonie yelled "Wait!" at the departing car as he sprang upright, almost—

Ochoa yelled, "Anybody hit?!" because the sniper was using a silencer and might've fired more rounds—

Cops yelled "No!"—

Doonie grimaced, grabbed his back and groaned, staggered two steps forward and sagged to his knees—

"Officer down!" Ochoa yelled and ran to Doonie—

"Don't touch!" Doonie roared at Ochoa, through gritted teeth, "Not hit—eeeegh—just motherfucking old and god-damn—ahwwr—fat!" Doonie grabbed Ochoa's shoulder and levelly instructed the L.A. cop, "Fuck me, go back 'em up," and, wincing, shoved Ochoa toward the truck.

Levaux braked to avoid killing a squirrel and managed not to roll the car; small miracle, considering the speed at which they skidded sideways through the banked, downward curve the squirrel had chosen as the site for its suicide attempt.

253

"Sorry," Levaux muttered, after the car's shocks heaved it level.

"For what?" Mark asked, innocently.

Levaux glanced at him, taking her eyes off the road for the first time since they'd gotten in the car. "You're bleeding," she observed.

"Nah, it stopped," Mark said.

"Head wound?" Levaux demanded to know as she powered through an s-curve, fishtailed a little as she emerged from it, straightened, and accelerated uphill.

"Just kissed the edge of the ear . . . *Finally*," Mark murmured, referring to something up ahead—the rooster house, he could finally fucking see it again. He'd lost sight of it as they blasted along the twisty blacktop, taking the lone, circuitous route through a notch in the ridgeline between Hector B's place and the crest where the rooster house perched. For a minute there Mark had wondered if they wouldn't do better going straight cross-country on foot.

Levaux slowed and turned onto the rutted, rocky dirt driveway. As the car jounced to a stop about twenty yards from the house, Mark pulled his piece, flung open the door, and crouched behind it, aiming his gun through its open window and scanning the grounds. He heard Levaux doing the same on the driver's side.

The sun was beginning to set, but syrupy golden light and purple shadows were wasted on this place. It was an old-fashioned wood-plank ranch house that looked like it had been here since before talkies came in, and remained unlovingly un-renovated. Mark counted six windows facing Hector B's place; sniper could've used any one of them.

Ten yards past the house was an outbuilding shaped like a barn shrunk to one-quarter normal size. Living quarters for the gladiators, who were shrieking insults at the new arrivals, challenging them to come out from behind those car doors and fight like a chicken.

There were no other signs of life. Not natural, seeing as how there were three vehicles parked outside the house. The sniper was probably gone—would've put his ass in gear soon as he saw his hollow-point connect with Hector B. But where were the drivers of the shiny black Blazer, the chromed-out Camaro, and the ancient, rusted Datsun hatchback parked out front?

Levaux said, "I don't think we wait for backup."

"I could tell from the way you drove."

"We gotta go in, some of them"—referring to the owners of the vehicles—"might still be alive, need help."

Plus which the sooner they cleared the house the sooner they could get a search started for the sniper, who couldn't be that far away yet. "Right," Mark grunted.

"I go in the door, you take the back."

"No—my case, my door."

"You're out of jurisdiction."

"Only legally," Mark noted as he took off for the front door, bent low, using the parked cars for cover. He heard Levaux curse and start sprinting for the side of the house.

Mark got to the front door without anybody drilling him. He flattened against the wall alongside it. Tried the door. It was locked. Also dry, brittle, and flimsy. Doorframe shattered on the first kick.

Mark went in.

There was a small foyer that led to a living room crammed with beat-up couches and chairs, around an industrial spool coffee table. There were open beer cans and a plate of tamales and gorditas on the table. There was a corpse on one of the couches, sagged back in a corner as if lounging, bullet wound in the forehead, male, Hispanic, mid-twenties, black jeans, Los Tigres del Norte t-shirt: the chromed-out Camaro.

Opposite the couch there was an overturned, bloodstained chair. A blood trail led down the hall.

Mark followed it to a bedroom. The wall alongside the bedroom door was blood-soaked. The victim had leaned against it.

Mark followed his gun into the room.

There'd been a struggle. An exotic, tripod-mounted sniper rifle had been knocked to the floor. Alongside it was another corpse. Two bullet wounds in the chest, lacerations on the face, bruised throat, smashed nose, male, Hispanic, about fifty, faded cowboy shirt and jeans, expensive boots, bulky silver bracelet, rings, and crucifix: the shiny black Blazer.

There was a five-inch switchblade on the floor next to the body. Blood on the blade. The Blazer might have cut the sniper.

Mark left the bedroom and continued down the hall. There were widely spaced drops of blood on the floor. Score one for the Blazer. Mark followed the red dots into the kitchen. The sniper's leakage led to the kitchen door, but Mark got sidetracked by a muffled whimper that came from what looked to be a pantry or broom closet.

Mark went to the pantry or broom closet. Raised his weapon, yanked the door open.

Broom closet. Occupied by a female, Hispanic, early sixties, frayed apron over a frayed housecoat, wrists, ankles, and mouth bound with duct tape, gazing, terrified, at the strange man who was aiming a huge gun at her head, where blood from a nasty scalp wound was seeping through her white hair: the rusted Datsun.

Mark was almost as glad to find someone alive as she was that he didn't shoot her. Mark lowered his gun and eased the old woman out of the—

From some distance behind the house, Levaux, shouting—

First, "Halt, Police!"

Then, "Off! Off the bike!"

Then, "Down! Face down!"

Mark sat the bound, gagged, bleeding old woman in a kitchen chair. *"Lo siento,"* Mark apologized, "help will—uh, *Ayuda lo lleg*—be here—*pronto!"*

Mark stiffened as he heard, from the same distance and direction as Levaux's shouts, a gunshot—the thin, bright crack of a smaller caliber weapon than J'nette Levaux's 9mm Glock. As he bolted he heard another small-caliber round. As he got to the door he thank Christ heard the hard deep *blat* of a Nine return fire.

SIXTY-FOUR

Nice morning for a hike. The air was clear, fresh, and pleasantly warm; there was a Santa Ana blowing, but it was a light one, not one of those Mojave airblasts that turns the city into a convection oven.

Dina Velaros had tapped Hector B's phone and e-mail but she hadn't photographed his house yet. She knew this was a good morning for that because yesterday Hector B had used his phone to book a statutory sandwich in Pomona. He was paying for an all-nighter. Dina made him for a john who'd insist on his money's worth—no one allowed to sleep before dawn. She figured he wouldn't be waking up and dragging his ass home till noon, the earliest.

Dina showed up in Sunland just after dawn, toting a digital camera with a three-hundred-millimeter zoom. If she did get seen scrambling around the hills at that hour taking pictures of boring semi-suburban vistas, the term "camera nut" would explain everything.

If it turned out Dina had to (was allowed to) dispose of Hector B, she'd prefer to make the hit at some less problematic site. But she might not have a choice, might have to work fast; had to be prepared. Dina had already scouted the area to see if the terrain offered a hidden firing position from which she could nail him long distance. She'd have to catch him on the back patio, or in his car at the driveway gate. There was a view of the patio from the trees behind the house, but Hector B might not go out back for days at a time. There were some firing positions with viable lines of sight on the driveway out front, but they were inside occupied homes on the hills facing Hector B's place.

Doing him inside his house might be the prime option. Dina was getting three-hundred-sixty-degree photo coverage of the house, so she could study the best way in, best way out.

Dina took a break, sat back against a tree, had a snack, daydreamed about making wine and babies with Arthur Reid, wondered how the hell Hector B could've bought this place with those goddamn roosters shrieking every hour of the day and night . . . Money. Hector B must've gone for the whopping sonic torture discount this house came with . . . *Speak of the fucking cheapskate devil, here he comes now, home at 9:36 in the morning. Poor baby, the Pomona girls must've worn him out early.*

Dina slid behind the tree, watched Hector B pull up and wait for his gate to slide open. He was driving that black Chrysler 300M he'd told Arthur he'd ditch, but just switched the plates on—

A conspicuously plain Crown Victoria sedan came down the road, just as Hector B entered his driveway. The Ford slowed as it went by.

The Ford drove around a bend and pulled onto the shoulder. Waited five minutes. Did a U-turn, drove back past Hector B's. Dina, through the three-hundred-millimeter, got a look at the Crown Vic's occupants. Driver, big Hispanic guy wearing, even at this distance, a cheap sport coat. Passenger, black woman in a smart black cheap suit. Both of them staring at Hector B's unremarkable house as they drove by.

Forty-three minutes later a CalTrans truck parked across the road from Hector B's. Two guys in orange coveralls got out, took a cigarette break, took a long time to unload, and set up, and calibrate, and recalibrate surveying equipment, so they could then stand thirty feet apart and painstakingly measure the distance between their noses. Then they took another cigarette break. Then they played with spray paint, making important marks on the blacktop.

Okay, it's official. Hector B is under surveillance. Might get busted any time . . . What if this wasn't about the Willetts hit? Might not be, Meelo's trial was almost over, why would they be arresting Hector B for that? . . . Didn't matter. If things went bad for Hector B on any death sentence rap, he wouldn't hesitate to try to deal her and Arthur.

Dina had to kill Hector B right away . . . While he was surrounded by police. Shit.

Dina decided not to tell Arthur about it till it was over.

No time, anyway. Had to get home, pack a kit, hustle back here, and get set up, which was gonna take hours.

SIXTY-FIVE

Dina parked her Explorer behind some trees near a jeep trail. Unloaded her dirt bike. Put on her daypack. Got on the bike and went to work.

When she arrived she hid the bike in some brush on the reverse slope of the hill behind the rooster palace. Circled round on foot. Used binoculars to check out Hector B's house. Scary moment; the CalTrans truck was gone. Did they already bust him? But then Dina spotted a guy messing under the hood of a van parked in sight of Hector B's house.

Dina walked up the driveway to the ranch house, knocked. Arrogant young guy in a Los Tigres t-shirt answered. Looked her over. Liked what he saw.

Dina said Hi, said she'd been hiking nearby, heard the roosters—

The kid got surly—assumed she was going to complain about the noise, or, worse, was some animal rights hippie. Dina let him know she was a big fan of the sport. In fact, she was wondering if they had a bird for sale.

The kid wasn't sure he believed her, but obeyed his dick and invited her in.

The *patron*, the kid's father, was gruff but reasonably gracious, seeing as how he didn't believe anybody about anything. Dina was amused to realize he figured this was a sting, made her for a cop.

An *abuelita* brought beers and snacks, retreated to her

kitchen. Dina tried to convince the *patron* she was a fan of real sports. Cockfights, bullfights, boxing. She waited till both men had beer cans in their hands, pulled her .32, plugged the kid in the head, turned on the dad—who'd lunged out of his chair surprisingly fast—and put two in his chest, which sat him back down in the chair, which tipped over. She heard the *abuelita* come rushing down the hall—Dina whirled—the old woman froze, eyes wide—Dina aimed, Dina had a clear head shot, Dina . . . Shit, the *abuelita* had spent her whole life waiting on pricks like these, and their roosters, Dina was sure the old woman was the only one who actually lived and slept here with that constant racket—

The *abuelita* fled down the hall, shrieking. Dina caught up with her in the kitchen, threw her to the floor. Shushed her gently, gave her a sympathetic look, assuring her she wasn't going to harm her. Leaned down and whispered, in Spanish, "When the police ask, you tell them the intruder was *a man*, a man wearing a black ski mask. *You never saw the man's face.*"

The trembling *abuelita* just perceptibly nodded. Dina gave her one good bash with the gun butt to keep her unambitious. Put on surgical gloves. Taped up the old lady, stashed her.

Went to a window, checked the scene over at Hector B's. A familiar big dull Ford sedan drove by Hector B's house and around a bend. It pulled over behind a parked truck—the Cal-Trans truck. Two men and a woman—the black woman in the black suit—got out of the Crown Vic and went to the truck.

Dina hurried. Went to the living room, did a quick check of the father and son—no pulses. Patted them down fast, found their pieces, tossed them—an Arthur move, don't trust the dead. She wiped everything she'd touched. She grabbed her daypack, went to a small bedroom near the kitchen. Opened the window, removed the screen. Unzipped the pack, took out a black Lycra ski mask and slipped it on; just in case someone saw her when she left here. She reached into the pack, took out and unfolded a tripod, took out and assembled Erma, screwed Erma onto the tripod, calibrated her scope.

Dina called Hector B, gave him the code to go to Location C. He acted sullen, touchy. Dina made Hector B's day, implied he was finally about to get hooked up with the agent. Gave Hector B the cozy-voiced impression she was finally ready to ride his big one. Suddenly Hector B sounded real interested in getting his ass over to Location C.

Dina chambered a round, snuggled up to the tactical rifle's recoil pad, slipped her hand into the thumb-hole pistol-grip, and put her eye to the scope. Erma was ridiculously pricey but felt and worked like no other weapon Dina had ever touched. Goddamn Germans. When it came to mechanical objects they were da bomb, *Ja-Ja.* Arthur was right about that. Like—as—he was about most things. Guns, grammar . . . *And I am right to be taking out Hector B before the law gets their hooks in him. Arthur will agree, this is the right, the only, thing to d—*

Hector B's garage door slid up. Dina followed the 300M down the driveway. The light was good, she saw him clearly through the windshield, laid crosshairs on him as he stopped and waited for the gate to ope—what the fu—

The CalTrans truck pulled across the driveway, blocking— no, no, okay, stopped in time, the hood of the truck was low enough so she could shoot across it, the driveway was higher than the road so she could still see into the Chry—Shit!—A cop stepped right in front of the Chrysler, his head partially blocking her view of Hector B's head—

Hector B glanced back, saw the cops rushing up behind his car, and when he turned forward he shifted position just enough. She did it.

Hector B died. The cop flinched, touched his ear. The cop pointed at the windshield, turned slowly, and pointed at Dina, his face large in her scope. She recognized him. From the Chicago papers. This was about Willetts. They were here. She could drop him. Might slow them—no, not worth it. Hairy enough without killing a cop. The Chicago cop was running to a car and the woman cop was right behind him. Time to pack Erma and go. The cop's Ford burned rubber.

Dina started to unscrew Erma from the tripod—

She heard it and turned just in time to see the deceptively pulse-less *patron* fling his dead body at her, blade in his hand. She deflected his knife-arm but he piled into her and they went down and she ripped at his eyes and he stuck her in the arm and she twisted hard enough to free an elbow. She rammed it into his Adam's apple three times fast and he pulled back gurgling and dropped the knife but his bulk still pinned her and he grabbed her throat, crushing and leaning his weight on it and Dina couldn't get at her .32 but she smashed the heel of her hand into the tip of his nose and he died again. But didn't let go of Dina's throat. No wonder the neighbors were scared of the bastard.

Dina broke the bastard's clawed fingers, yanked them off her neck, and shoved him off her. She pushed herself to her feet and the pain in her left arm woke up. She leaned against a wall, took a couple of deep breaths, and yanked her sleeve up. The blade had gone in the underside of her upper arm. Not bleeding bad yet, but Dina didn't know how long she'd be able to use the arm.

Dina sat on the bed. She pulled her belt off, looped it around her arm, yanked it tight into a tourniquet, buckled it. Suddenly felt tired. No, gotta move. Stood up. It was work. Shit, fucking wound didn't look that deep—How long did this fight take, how long had it been since the cops started for here? Had to get moving, *now*. Shit. She'd have to leave Erma.

Dina slung the daypack over her right shoulder and hurried

down the hall into the kitchen, where she swerved around a kitchen chair and banged her wounded arm into the edge of a low-hanging cabinet. Pain went off in fireworks she could see and hear as well as feel. She almost fell. She had to pause to let the agony dim. It did, a little, and she pushed on, out the kitchen door, and as it slammed shut she heard a car pull into the driveway on the other side of the house. The roosters erupted.

Dina started to trot down the steep slope to the bushes where she'd stashed her bike. She heard the car stop. Her boot nicked a rock and she went sprawling. She skidded a few feet and lay still, listening for a sign the cops had heard her fall and were headed this way. She didn't make a sound, one of the hardest things she'd ever done; there was gravel in her wound. Her throat was sore and stiff where the dead man had tried to crush it.

But she didn't hear footsteps. She raised her head, saw no one. The cops were still on the other side of the house. Okay, the roosters going postal covered the sound of her fall. But thanks to the roosters Dina also couldn't hear if the cops were coming. She forced herself to her feet and the daypack slid off her shoulder. She bent to pick it up—couldn't leave it here, they'd spot it. She bent down for the pack and the pain in her arm blistered up across her left shoulder and down her spine. Shit. Couldn't waste strength or time on the pack. She left it. Moved steadily but carefully down the slope. She reached the bushes, ducked behind them, and looked back. Nobody.

Dina crawled to where she'd stashed the dirt bike, on its side. Lightweight Kawasaki, she'd never had any trouble picking it up, till now. First had to slide it out from under a bush. Then get it upright. Using one hand.

Dina tugged. The bike slid a few inches then got stubborn. Fuck this! Rage was her friend. Rage helped Dina yank the goddamn bike from under the bush. And lever the bike up onto its wheels and not care about the tears blurring her eyes and the groans she couldn't tamp down any more. She swung a leg over the bike, and somebody not too far behind her yelled, "Halt, Police!"

The woman cop, standing upslope of Dina, aiming at her.

"Off! Off the bike!"

Dina stiffly slid off, let the bike fall.

"Down! Face down!"

Dina went to her knees.

SIXTY-SIX

J'nette Levaux was about to end the debate with Bergman by running to the front door when the—

1] Sexist pig?

2] Stand-up guy?

3] Stand-up sexist pig?

—beat her to it, bolting from behind the passenger-side car door and zig-zagging his way to the front of the house.

Levaux spat out a "Fuck!" and took off. She ran to the side of the house, paused a moment before going around the corner to the back, listened. Couldn't hear anything but the mass rooster rage that had been blaring since the car pulled in—there was a crash, splintering wood. That'd be Bergman forcing the front door. Then it was back to hearing nothing but bird tantrums.

1] Someone might be in the barn—

2] Soon as we clear the house—have to clear the barn.

Levaux swung around the corner of the house and scanned the back yard. Wasn't actually a yard, just bare hillside, flat for about thirty feet, then sloping down. Levaux went to the kitchen door. She heard something and stopped—a scraping noise, followed by what might have been a soft moan. It came from somewhere down the slope, out of sight.

Levaux took a quick look through the window in the kitchen door; couldn't see anything happening. She quietly crossed the flat part of the back yard . . . noticed fresh blood-spatter. Followed it to the edge of the slope and peered down. Saw a backpack abandoned on the ground. Not far below it were some rocky outcroppings and thick bushes, about four, five feet tall. Something was moving in the bushes, crunching dead leaves.

Levaux almost yelled to alert Bergman, but—

1] She didn't want to distract him unless she was sure this was the sniper.

2] If this was the sniper she didn't want to give herself away.

Levaux stealthily picked her way downhill. She heard a small angry grunt—*it's a woman*—and the sound of a large metal object being jerked across the ground, and saw the bushes shake. Levaux moved faster. Heard labored breathing, punctuated by soft, pained sobs. Came around an outcropping and saw, downslope, a female—black Lycra ski mask, wounded left arm, safari blouse, ripstop cargo-pocket pants—starting to mount a dirt bike—

"Halt, Police!"

The suspect looked at her, froze.

"Off! Off the bike!"

The suspect, wincing in pain, slid off the bike, let it fall, and took a step back. She clutched her bleeding arm and rocked a little, moaning softly.

Levaux wasn't buying. "Down! Face down!"

The suspect sank to her knees, tried to lower herself face down but clutched her gut, gagged, and doubled over—"Can't," the suspect whimpered, began to dry-heave, and as she jerked forward, gagging, her right hand twitched toward Levaux and the gun in it fired.

The bullet took Levaux's leg out from under her. She went down hard, as another slug whistled past. Levaux threw a shot at the suspect and scrambled behind a boulder. There was a baseball of pain stuffed inside her thigh. She felt dizzy. Her leg was soaked—

1] ARTERY!—

A] COMPRESSION!

Levaux grabbed her leg, found the source of the flood, inside left thigh, tried to press the wound shut, paid the price, as she heard the kitchen door bang open, running steps, and Bergman bellowing her name—

The dirt bike snarled to life—

Levaux yelled, "Gun!" to warn Bergman but it didn't come out very loud, ah Jesus, she was literally leaking away here, that goddamn bitch—Levaux leaned out from the boulder, spotted the bike slaloming downhill. She fired another round, way short. Then three fast blasts went off behind Levaux and she saw the rider flinch and the bike slew sideways—

The bike stayed upright and accelerated, and Bergman slid to a halt next to Levaux, knelt, and said, "Lemme see."

Levaux nodded at her leg and told him, "Artery." As if he couldn't tell from the red river.

Bergman tore his belt off, made a tourniquet, slid it up above the wound, and yanked like both their lives depended on it. They heard cars pull into the driveway. Bergman shouted, "Officer down behind the house! Officer down behind the house!" as he pulled out a handkerchief, eased Levaux's hand aside, and pressed the handkerchief against the wound. He told her, "I'm bringing you dinner tomorrow—do not touch, do not look at, the hospital food."

Tomorrow . . . Great word. J'nette gazed at Mark. She was a weird kind of hollow-drowsy, as if her mind wanted to step outside for a brief break . . .

Oh no.

"Kiss me," she said, seeing how scared they both were she might die, and this might be her last chance, and he'd do.

They kissed. Or—

Lenny Kleinfeld

1] Maybe she only imagined it.
2] She thought they did, though.
   A] Sensation of lips, breath.
   B] His gray eyes, then—
3] She thought she heard him yelling, "No ambulance car NOW,"
   then—
4] "Suspect wounded green dirt bike that way," then—
5] "Two dead inside, female wounded kitchen . . ." and then . . .
6] There were only some sweet roosters, far back, trying to sing
   nice.

SIXTY-SEVEN

The 'Roid-Ranger SWAT was bull-necked, twitchy, throbbing-veined, and entirely rational—he'd had some paramedic training and he agreed with Mark about Levaux. She could bleed out if they waited for the meat wagon. They'd diverted the ambulance that had been called to Hector B's—it was headed here. But the way Levaux was spilling, any wasted minute could be the fatal one. If the ambulance wasn't out front by the time they got her to the driveway, they'd take her to meet it.

The SWAT tied off the wound with a proper tourniquet while somebody brought a blanket that they used as a sling to carry Levaux up the slope and around the house to the driveway, where they eased her onto the back seat of an unmarked car, and the SWAT squeezed in on the floor to hold her steady and compress the wound, while a second SWAT got behind the wheel. Another unmarked Crown Vic led the way. Both drivers hit their sirens and the two-car convoy let it rip.

Mark watched the unconscious Levaux slalom down the snaky road, taking the curves hard but with more caution than the conscious Levaux had. Though this time any squirrel pressing his luck would not get a good result.

She could make it. Bad as the bleeding was, it didn't come close to the gushers Mark had seen when major arteries had gotten blown out.

Okay, file it and get back to business. Mark was good at that. Just like Teophilo Ochoa, who was standing next to him, also watching the car carrying J'nette Levaux till it was out of sight. If it was hard for Mark not to go with her, how hard was it for her partner? No matter. File it and dive back in.

She could make it. It was bad but it wasn't a gusher.

While Mark and others had been tending to Levaux a cop had dashed down the hill out back, hoping to at least catch a glimpse of the dirt bike. Didn't.

Mark gave Ochoa a description of the perp and her bike. Ochoa put out an APB. He also alerted every trauma center west of the Rockies to give him a jingle the instant any female, about five-five, one hundred and twenty pounds, possibly wearing a khaki shirt and cargo-pocket pants, showed up with a knife and/or gunshot wound. Cautioned she might be armed and capable of mass slaughter.

Ochoa ordered a canvas of every house along the dirt bike's route, to find out if anyone had seen it or its rider on the way in or out.

While Ochoa was making his calls a cop brought Mark some towels. Mark found a hose by the rooster dorm, stripped to his shorts, and rinsed as much of J'nette Levaux's blood as he could off his body and out of his hair. Then he hosed off his suit, shirt, and tie, stuffed them into evidence bags and changed into the only available clean clothes—an LAPD SWAT t-shirt and orange CalTrans coveralls. Mark, wet shoes squeaking, went and found Ochoa.

They went to the kitchen, where a cop had cut the duct tape off the old woman. An ambulance had arrived and an EMT was field-bandaging her head wound. Her skin was gray and she looked faint. So far she hadn't said a word, wouldn't or couldn't even give her name. Which was Guadalupe Ramos; cop had found her purse.

Mark squatted by Señora Ramos' chair so he'd be eye-level,

said hello, told her his name and asked if she was able to speak. She gave him a tortured look and lowered her head, refusing to make eye contact. She'd been less afraid of him pointing a gun at her than she now was of him pointing a question at her.

Mark felt Ochoa touch his shoulder. He moved aside.

Ochoa took a knee. Introduced himself in Spanish. The *viejita* kept her head down and began to tremble. The linebacker-size cop took her hand, enveloped it in both of his, and murmured soothingly. Got her to look at him. Ochoa made— Mark had just enough Spanish to follow it—a grave apology for troubling her at a time like this, but Ochoa was sure she'd understand how important her help was to find the terrible woman who'd done this—

"*Un hombre*—a man," Guadalupe Ramos insisted, looking from Ochoa to Mark and switching to English to make sure she was understood. "It was a man, wearing a black mask, a man."

Ochoa glanced up. Mark gave his head a minute shake. No, no way someone would mistake this perp for a man.

Ochoa asked the old woman how many intruders there had been.

She saw just the one.

Ochoa asked if she could tell them what happened.

Tears welled in her eyes. "My head," she whimpered.

Ochoa asked if the victims were related to her. She shook her head.

"Were you eating with them in the living room?" Mark quietly asked.

"N—," the old woman started to answer, then frowned, panicky, unable to puzzle out what the safe answer was. She shrugged, forlorn, begging Mark to believe it was all a blank.

Mark asked, in a sympathetic whisper, "So you never saw her face?"

"No, she—it was a man, a black mask," the old woman lied,

and moaned, touching her bandaged head. She grabbed the EMT's sleeve and asked if she was going to die, and before he could answer began weeping and praying, and wouldn't look at any of them.

Ochoa thanked her, told her the paramedics would take her to the hospital now, and asked if she had any family he could contact for her. She pretended not to hear him.

Mark and Ochoa backed off and left the room before they scared Guadalupe Ramos to death.

"Why'd you ask Guadalupe if she'd eaten with the vics?" Ochoa asked.

"Three plates on the coffee table," Mark replied. "If plate number three wasn't the old lady, it was the shooter—she wasn't sitting there wearing a mask, doing small talk and gorditas."

Ochoa agreed. "Bet your ass the *viejita* served the food, saw the perp's face . . . Look, I think I can get her to talk, but—might take a few days."

Mark just nodded hopefully. Getting Guadalupe Ramos to talk that soon, or ever, would make Ochoa a genius, considering how terrified of the killer the old woman was, with such good reason. And considering how grateful she must also be to the killer, the woman who'd spared her. The woman—he couldn't be certain, but it felt right—who was known in Chicago as Heather. And was apparently not just another pretty face with a pair of average—*shit*—

A sketch. He could put Meelo with a police artist and get a—

No—not without telling the judge and the defense attorney what was up. Not worth it, especially since Mark wasn't certain the sniper was Heather. Or even related to the Willetts case. And even if it was, all they'd get was Meelo's version of what Heather looked like. Mark imagined Meelo describing and describing and describing his memory of his dream girl to a sketch artist.

Mark put the idea in his back pocket for use if there was nothing else left.

Mark and Ochoa did a quick check of the bedroom the sniper had shot from and had her hand-to-hand death struggle in. Didn't find anything with her name on it.

They went through her backpack. Bottle of water, first aid kit, one spare clip of 7.62 mm, two clips of .32, a disposable cell phone. Maybe they'd get lucky with prints or phone records. Or DNA; the sniper had bled plenty.

Mark decided, "I should get to a computer, pick us out a dirt bike."

"Yeah."

"Like to stop and collect Doonie along the way." Somewhere in the recent swirl Mark had noticed Doonie hadn't come up to the rooster ranch. Figured Doonie had stayed behind to get first crack at Hector B, his car and house.

Ochoa pulled out his radio. "Let's make sure he's still there—his back went out."

Yeah, of course. Good day for it. Damn near perfect. Fuck. Mark hoped Doonie wasn't hurt bad. Mark hoped Doonie was hurt bad enough to finally lose some weight and start working out with something besides a beer bottle.

Levaux could make it. It was bad but it wasn't a gusher.

When Mark and Ochoa arrived, Doonie and an LAPD guy were tossing Hector B's place.

"Hey," Doonie said, lifting an eyebrow, about to make a crack about Mark's orange costume, but then realized why Mark must've changed clothes. Doonie shifted into business gear. Said they'd been through Hector B's pockets. Found an address scribbled on a piece of paper. L.A. cop checked, made it an organic coffee house in Glendale. Maybe that's where Hector B had been headed.

In his house, so far, one possible score—an address book. The e-mail and a lot of files were passworded, have to wait for a tech to crack them.

Mark told Doonie to c'mon with him and Ochoa, they'd fill him in on the rooster house action while they drove.

As they walked to the car Mark said, "Somebody said something about your back."

"It was nothin', just this momentary, fucker went as fast as it came," Doonie scoffed. He was holding himself stiffly, with his right shoulder hunched, and walking in cautious, sideways crablike steps. "How's Levaux?"

"ER," Ochoa and Mark said, simultaneously.

The SWAT had called just as they'd pulled in at Hector B's. The doctors had stanched the flow and were transfusing her. Needed a refill before she could go into surgery. Doctors said she should make it.

Should.

SIXTY-EIGHT

Mark was surprised how shabby L.A.'s famous headquarters, the Parker Center, was. He wouldn't be surprised at any other cop shop being dilapidated. But this one had starred in so many movies. Stepping inside was the cracked aging drywall equivalent of being introduced to the cracked aging Norma Desmond.

The first two elevators they tried were out of service. Ochoa directed Doonie—not that Doonie's back was serious or anything—to an elevator in another corridor, while Ochoa and Mark walked up three floors to the Robbery-Homicide Division, Special Section I, and got down to business: briefing the CO, Captain Lund, on where the case was at. And how one of his detectives got shot.

Mark had been wondering if Ochoa was angry about what had happened; so far the massive cop had given away nothing. Ochoa might simply be saving it till the job was done, when he'd tear Mark's head off and beat him to death with it. But when Ochoa briefed his commander, he gave Mark credit for calmly identifying the sniper's location despite the minor but half-inch-from-fatal wound to his ear, and described Levaux as simply reacting faster than the other personnel, who all shared her response of wanting to get moving. Ochoa omitted mentioning he'd ordered everyone to "Stay down"—covering his partner's ass, and Mark's by association.

Mark briefed Captain Lund on the action at the rooster house.

Captain Lund was a pinched, sallow bureaucrat who tried to disguise himself with the aggressively bushy moustache that's a favored macho cop fashion statement the world over. Lund and his moustache listened to Mark's story, then, with a prissy scowl, informed Mark, "You—and Levaux—should've waited for backup."

Mark didn't say anything.

Ochoa said, "Going in fast, they probably saved the old woman—head wound, bleeding bad. And though Levaux paid a price, she almost busted the perp, and Bergman seeing the dirt bike is our best lead." Meaning, *my partner made her choice and I'm down with it.*

Lund processed that, accepted it without comment.

Well, well. Brother Ochoa has serious standing, here in this elite unit.

Lund stared stonily at Mark. "You and Detective Dunegan are here to observe and consult. No physical involvement, unless and until you take custody of a suspect for extradition."

"Yes sir," Mark replied. *Unless and until someone else shoots a suspect out from under me and I have a chance to nail him, or her.*

Lund dismissed the detectives, ordering Mark to get to work on the next priority—filling out forms attesting to the police emergency that justified him discharging a weapon two thousand miles west of the Chicago city line.

The limited-duty sergeant in command of discharged-weapon paperwork had already been summoned and was waiting outside Lund's office. The sergeant handed Mark a printout listing the required forms, along with instructions for where to find them in the computer. Mark looked at the list, then at the sergeant. The sergeant, aware Mark had discharged his weapon at someone who'd just shot an L.A. cop, whom he'd then helped keep from bleeding to death, and whose assailant Mark was now helping to find, said, "It'll keep," and returned to his desk.

Doonie, who'd arrived while Mark and Ochoa were in Lund's office, was also waiting for them. He asked, "How'd it go in there?"

"Griswald," Mark explained.

Lieutenant Susan Griswald, who'd preceded Lieutenant Husak as their CO, was Captain Lund's spiritual twin. Smaller moustache.

"Ah." Doonie nodded knowingly. "Speaking of which, I should bring Husak up to speed."

Ochoa pointed Doonie to an office with a door so he could brief his CO in private. Doonie gingerly ratcheted himself down into a chair and made the call.

Ochoa showed Mark to a computer. He advised Mark to start with Kawasakis. Kawasaki dirt bikes were green. Hell, Kawasaki dirt bikes were Team Green. Ochoa went to see if there was anybody interesting in Hector B's address book, and to monitor reports coming in from both crime scenes, and check again to see if any female stab-shooting victims had patronized a local ER.

Mark pulled up the Kawasaki dirt bike site.

Bingo.

Nearly. It was either the KLR250 or the Super Sherpa. One had a raised front fender, one had a low, tire-hugging front fender. Okay, visualize the event: low fender? high fender?

Mark visualized away. Got fucking nowhere. During the event he'd been staring down a gunsight, concentrating on the rider. When he (possibly) hit the rider and the bike skidded he'd started hustling downhill to Levaux, catching a glimpse of the rear end of bike out of the corner of his eye . . . C'mon, the image is stored somewhere back in there . . . Concentrate: low fender . . . high fender . . .

Fuck the fenders. Mark ran the registrations on every

KLR250 and Super Sherpa in the state. Sorted for women owners.

Got three hundred and twelve hits. Mark pulled up the driver's licenses for all those women, culled them for approximate height and weight. Got it down to one hundred and eighty-seven.

Though of course the bike might be registered to somebody else. So he ran all of California's motorcycle driver's licenses for women, sorting for the height and heft parameters. Winnowed it to eleven hundred and—

Ochoa got a call from the hospital. Levaux was out of surgery and out of danger. Bullet had nicked a medium-sized artery. And proceeded to damage more fat than muscle. Surgeon reported he'd done a brilliant repair job. There'd be a couple of (erasable) scars. No limp.

She made it.

An oversized, overweight gorilla climbed down off of Mark's back. Joined the parade of massive simians exiting Special Section I.

Mark noticed he was hungry and tired. Looked at his watch. 9:30 p.m., local time. 11:30 in his body.

Ochoa and Doonie—who'd been working with Ochoa— ambled over.

"C'mon," Ochoa said, "quick stop at the hospital, then we'll get you checked in and fed."

"You go," Mark told Doonie. "I'm gonna finish sorting—"

Ochoa said, "Someone else can handle it."

"I'll stay," Doonie told Mark. "You gotta get that ear disinfected."

Mark turned to Ochoa. "Got a first aid kit?"

"You two are done," Ochoa ruled, confiding, "you both look like shit."

"I always look like shit," Doonie protested.

"And your bags are in the trunk of our car, which is parked at the hospital," Ochoa pointed out, giving Mark a sad glance.

Oh. Right. He was still wearing the SWAT t-shirt and Cal-Trans coveralls. Looked like a slightly bloodstained orange popsicle.

A nurse told them Levaux was in the ICU, where they'd keep her till morning. Ochoa asked if he could see her. The nurse told him the patient was sleeping. Ochoa told her that was okay.

Mark and Doonie waited down the hall while Ochoa spent some time watching his partner breathe.

A resident examined Doonie, gave him a fistful of muscle relaxer samples. Told Doonie to take two pills right now, then one every four hours.

Doonie looked at the pills, asked if he could have a drink after taking them.

"No. Take the pills," the resident ordered.

Doonie asked if he could work after taking the pills.

"Try these," the resident sighed, handing Doonie a package of disposable strap-on heating pads, "and don't do anything strenuous—anything that hurts. At all."

"Right," Doonie said.

An intern cleaned the curious abrasion on Mark's ear, applied some ointment, and taped on a white gauze bandage fifteen or twenty times the size of the wound. Mark went from looking like shit to looking like a moron.

The stiff, hunch-shouldered midwestern bear and the CalTrans worker with the gauze mushroom on his ear checked into the New Hikune, a large, oppressively glossy downtown hotel. The place gave LAPD guests a rate and was (for non-Angelenos) walking distance from the Parker Center—no—no *the*—local cops referred to it as Parker Center—the New Hikune was walking distance from Parker Center.

Doonie and Ochoa grabbed beers from the mini-bar in Doonie's room while Mark showered and shampooed off the last of the dried blood and changed into non-orange clothes.

At 11 p.m. L.A.'s downtown was almost a ghost town. Ochoa drove them up a hill and across a freeway into Chinatown. Livelier. There were pedestrians on the sidewalks and some of the restaurants were busy.

The cops went to a seafood place. Doonie went to the john. Mark and Ochoa looked at menus. Mark and Ochoa looked at each other.

"J'nette would've done what she did even if you weren't there," Ochoa told Mark. "I recommend the garlic black bean crab."

"Thanks," Mark said.

SIXTY-NINE

The Chicago cops had a nightcap at the hotel bar but their hearts weren't in it. The bar was all pristine lacquered surfaces, including the walls. Even the bartender and waitresses seemed varnished. There were a dozen other guests scattered across the room's darkly gleaming terrain, mostly business travelers making half-hearted late-night efforts to impress each other.

Drinking out of a paper bag in the alley would've been an improvement, if Doonie had been comfortable standing up. Not that he was comfortable sitting down. He was even more exhausted than Mark. So the Chicagoans only stayed for two rounds and the few necessary topics.

"So how the fuck . . . ?" Doonie wondered. Referring to Oscar and Heather. How had they known the cops were closing in on Hector Benvanides?

Mark shrugged. "We don't know it was them, could be a whole other set of people Hector B pissed off."

"Martians."

"Yeah. Or maybe it *was* our perps, they got nervous after we found Garn's body, so they put Hector B under surveillance and spotted our surveillance."

"Or . . ."

Or they were tipped. Would've had to be someone in the Chicago or L.A. police who knew what was coming. "I don't know," Mark said. "Seems a long shot. If it was an inside tip, LAPD would be likelier—maybe one of the rich fucks from

283

LAFAM is connected to the Chief or someone in Robbery-Homicide."

"And how'd we check that?" Doonie grimaced.

"Ask Ochoa and hope he isn't the mole? Nah, forget it, Doon. If an insider tipped them we were on the way, they woulda whacked Mr. Benvanides before we got there . . . probably."

"Yeah," Doonie sighed, "we can wait to go down that alley if it happens again."

"Yeah. So, speaking of going down alleys . . ."

"No big deal, my back'll be fine in the morning."

"And if it isn't, you'll take the day off?"

"Speaking of fuckin' goin' down a fuckin' alley, next time someone shoots at you, ya gonna take cover?"

"Hey, you saw—that girl's a world-class shot. If she was shooting at me, I'd be dead, not walking around with this fucking doofus wad of cotton candy on my ear."

"If she decided to slow us up, she coulda dropped you, standing there like that, givin' her the finger."

"It was my index finger, and even if I had hit the dirt, if she wanted to slow us up she would've just waited and plugged the first cop to stick his head up."

"Which can't be you," Doonie explained, " 'cause if you get killed I'm the one gonna catch endless shit from Phyl—and Patty."

"Okay, Doonie, promise—next time there's trouble I hide behind you."

"Good." Doonie sucked down the last few drops of bourbon and chewed thoughtfully on the ice. "Tomorrow we gotta find somewhere to drink—this place is a fuckin' nail salon."

The message light on Mark's phone was flashing. It was a voice-mail from Carrie Eli, who'd heard about their suspect getting capped and all the other fun and games; Mark had to call her back, no matter what time.

Mark didn't. He got into bed, turned off the lights, and channel-surfed, looking for a rebroadcast of local 11 p.m. news. Wanted to see how the LAPD would spin the assassination of a professional hit man, the murders of father-son rooster entrepreneurs, the skulling of a senior citizen, and near-fatal shooting of a homicide detective, so that no mention of a Chicago connection came up.

Okay, there the story was.

Anchor gravely announced there'd been three mysterious, possibly linked shootings in Sunland.

Cut to a reporter standing in front of the police tape marking off Hector B's driveway: Police had been preparing to take the man living at this house into custody as a material witness in a criminal investigation when he was felled by an assassin's bullet. Police declined to specify the nature of the crime the victim was a witness to, saying it would jeopardize an ongoing investigation. Police also declined to identify the victim until relatives had been notified.

Cut to the same reporter in front of police tape marking off the rooster ranch driveway: Shortly after the fatal sniper attack police found two men dead inside this house nearby. The LAPD declined to specify how the men died but said the manner of their death indicated foul play. Speaking of "fowl play," it turns out, as viewers may have guessed by now from all the crowing, that this second, barn-like structure is home to a number of roosters—the kind employed in illegal cockfights. As of yet it's not clear if there's any connection between the illegal roosters and the homicides. Police discovered the dead men when they arrived to investigate this house as a possible site from which the sniper shot the other victim. They are not saying if this was indeed the sniper's "roost," or if the killings in this house were related to the sniper. There were unofficial rumors the deaths might have grown out of a power struggle in the illegal cockfighting industry, or were perhaps gang-related—according to sources, some local gang lords invest in illegal fighting roosters, the way Mafia chieftains traditionally invested in racehorses.

Mark clicked the TV off. Not bad. None of Wilson Willetts' blood would get prematurely sprayed on the LAFAM board.

Mark began to drift, fitfully, thoughts flicking through his mind at random . . . Hector B was dead but there was plenty of case to work here, especially with possibly-Heather wounded and on the run on her Team Green KLR250 or Super Sherpa.

J'nette Levaux was going to be all right.

Doonie's back might not. Have to keep an eye on him.

Hell of a first day. Felt like a week since they got off the plane. *Came to Hollywood to bust homicide perps and all I got was three corpses and this lousy SWAT t-shirt.*

He should return Carrie's call . . . For what? Wake her up to tell her he was too tired to talk? And the sound of Carrie's voice would remind him how many weeks it'd been since sex.

Fuck the number of weeks it'd been—this was about today. Mark hated sleeping alone at the end of a day when a bullet had blown past his skull.

Probably wasn't a good idea to go to the hospital and curl up next to Levaux.

But that kiss.

In the car soon after they'd met there had been a little flash between them, the old electric tickle. But the kiss hadn't been about that, hadn't been J'nette needing to get her lips on Mark Bergman. It had been about her being afraid she'd never live to kiss anybody again.

But that kiss.

SEVENTY

"This is your wake-up call," the phone cooed, except it wasn't the operator. It was Patty Dunegan.

"Shit . . . Wait, wait, you didn't hear me say that," Mark said, realizing he hadn't thought the word, he'd spoken it.

"Okay," the thirteen-year-old amiably agreed.

He squinted, forcing the clock into focus. "G'morning, why aren't you in school?"

"I am, in the girl's room, on my cell," Patty explained.

"C'mon Patty, the girl's room is for smoking cigarettes and dishing guys your own age."

"Have you *seen* guys my age?"

"Patty, if you're gonna run up your dad's long distance bill, be polite and do it calling him."

"And that word 'dishing,' " she sighed, "that's so old school."

"Thanks for calling and don't do it again, I'm working long hours and need my sleep. Bye."

"Mark—"

"Au revoir, ma petite," Mark snarled, with firm finality.

Patty chuckled with alarmingly adult satisfaction and hung up.

Mark put the phone down and started to get out of bed but the phone rang again. Ah, fuck. He picked it up. "Listen—"

"Why didn't you call me, a night you got shot at, you putz," Carrie Eli demanded to know.

"I didn't get shot at, Hector B did. G'morning. Can I call

you back? I gotta take a leak."

"Don't hang up—it's a good hotel, there should be a phone in the bathroom."

Mark removed the ear bandage, got dressed, and collected Doonie.

Doonie was still walking at the same angle as a crab. But slightly faster.

Robbery-Homicide detectives had worked all night and a new team was hard at it when Mark walked and Doonie sidled into Parker Center. The L.A. cops had assembled photo arrays of the hundred and eighty-seven women who owned the relevant Kawasaki dirt bikes, and the eleven hundred-odd women who had motorcycle licenses but didn't have a Kawasaki registered in their name. Ochoa had gone to the hospital to see Guadalupe Ramos; he took a bouquet of flowers and a laptop loaded with the photo arrays.

Mark and Doonie started working their way through the evidence.

Autopsy on Hector B determined a cause of death that didn't surprise any of the cops who'd been there. Mark and Doonie were also less than shocked the coroner found evidence of recent plastic surgery on Hector B's left biceps.

Hector B's address book was useful if you were looking to hook up with local Mob bosses, gang leaders, and a bent cop or three. L.A. dicks were out interviewing them. Others were running BCIs and knocking on the doors of the names they didn't recognize to see if any of them looked like someone who might be Heather or Oscar. No luck so far.

There were also two handwritten numbers that were for voicemail boxes, and two for disposable cell phones. L.A. detectives called the cells. If either belonged to Oscar or Heather, they weren't answering. The voicemail boxes had been disconnected—last night, within hours of Hector B's death. A check with the voicemail providers showed the boxes had been rented by people with phony names and addresses; paid for with postal service money orders.

Computer techs had cracked Hector B's files. Found his financials, including his offshore accounts. He'd been having a career year. His phone, e-mail, and pager records turned up nothing worse than the kinds of dealers and hookers the average law-abiding citizen kept in touch with.

Detectives and crime scene techs who'd spent the night disassembling Hector B's house had unearthed stashes of weapons and fake IDs. A call had been put in to the Feebs, to see if their specialists recognized the high-quality work on the passports.

Hector B's car had an unregistered .38 in the medical kit in the trunk; hadn't been fired recently. Semen, coffee, beer, and guacamole stains on the seats. A brochure for a flying school in the driver's side door pocket. (Just a lookie-loo. A call to the school showed Hector B hadn't signed up for lessons.)

The preliminary forensics from the rooster house weren't exactly a bonanza either. The sniper hadn't left any prints on her rifle, the scope, the tripod, her backpack, or its contents. Or, apparently, anywhere in the house.

The rifle was German-made, an ERMA SR100. One of the most accurate rifles on the planet, luckily for Mark. Retailed for nine grand; not a weapon for the casual weekend assassin. The serial number was gone. The Chicago and L.A. dicks agreed it was one of the coolest hunks of steel they'd ever seen. Took turns fondling it.

Bootprints behind the rooster house revealed the sniper was wearing Vasque Cyclone GTX hikers, size seven. Tire prints revealed she was riding on Michelin Sirac Dual Sports. Possibly-Heather shopped well.

Ochoa returned from the hospital, said he'd gotten nowhere.

Guadalupe Ramos liked the flowers. Offered a prayer when she was reminded a police officer had been shot. Expressed amazement when she heard two officers identified the masked shooter as a woman. Stuck by her story the sniper was a man. Said she looked after the roosters for the slain owner, but knew nothing about him, or any illegal activities the roosters indulged in during their spare time.

Ochoa assured Guadalupe the police didn't care about the roosters, only wanted to find the person who'd killed Guadalupe's employer and nearly killed one of the cops—who'd risked her life to save Guadalupe's.

The guilt about that last thing registered, but Guadalupe Ramos resisted it.

Ochoa then told her since she was the only one the killer had spared, and she was insisting the killer was a man when two officers had seen a woman running from the house, the police had to assume Guadalupe might be an accomplice. At that point she started wailing; her sister and nieces rushed in from the corridor and accused Ochoa of endangering a wounded old woman.

Ochoa told them that was the last thing he wanted. In fact he was authorized to pay for her to remain in the hospital so the doctors could keep her under observation. And he'd continue to post a uniformed officer to guard her room around the clock. Ochoa told the family that was to protect Guadalupe in case the sniper had second thoughts about leaving a witness alive. Guadalupe's family knew the cop was also there to keep them from spiriting her away.

Ochoa left, to let Guadalupe chew on the guilt and the threat. He'd return tomorrow with a material witness warrant in his pocket and take her into custody if she failed to cooperate.

Mark and Doonie wondered if it wouldn't be better to serve it right now.

Ochoa replied that if the cops merely played rock to the killer's hard place, Guadalupe would agree to look at the photo array and simply fail to recognize any of the faces. He wanted her to cooperate, not look for a way out.

Doonie nodded, told Ochoa to go with his gut. It was his partner who'd gotten shot.

"But if the old broad doesn't talk tomorrow," Doonie said, "we take her out back and beat the shit out of her, right?"

"I'll hold her arms," Ochoa promised.

"Think it'd help if Levaux visited?" Mark asked. "Let Guadalupe try to say 'No' to a woman in a wheelchair?"

"I'm not sure," Ochoa said. "Let me find out how she feels about blacks."

SEVENTY-ONE

After six hours of not getting any closer to the sniper Mark and Doonie went out for a coffee break so Mark could tell Doonie what he had discussed with Carrie this morning, and what he wanted to discuss with Aunt Flo this evening.

Sometime in the next day or two they'd get preliminary DNA confirmation Hector B was the man Darwahab scratched, right after Darwahab saw him shoot Willetts.

Carrie would have to go to Judge Santini and inform His Honor—along, unfortunately, with defense attorney Paul Obed—that Meelo was innocent. Carrie thought she could get Santini to play along with recessing the proceedings a few days without divulging the reason, in order to give the cops more time to operate beneath the radar in Los Angeles—if Obed and his client agreed to it.

Carrie thought she could persuade the Pocket Pal not to leap in front of the nearest news camera and warble a hundred choruses of "I told you so." The price would be her promise to drop the weapons and drug charges against his client. The free pass on those felonies would be conditioned on Meelo cooperating with the investigation by remaining quiet and in the lockup a few more days—and going through the twelve-hundred-plus California women's motorcycle driver's licenses to see if one of them was Heather.

Doonie shrugged his approval—of course he was for it, this was all obvious shit—and moved on: "And calling Aunt Flo is an even better idea—what're we calling her about?"

"Remember what tomorrow afternoon is?"

Doonie shook his head. "But is it something's gonna make her all angry and hot?"

"Probably not. It's the unveiling of the LAFAM designs. The architects will be there, and everybody on the design committee. One of us should go."

Doonie nodded. This might be their one chance to meet the suspects face to face; once the charges against Meelo were dismissed, the rich fuck who'd hired the shooters might get nervous and head overseas.

"I'm there," Doonie said.

"It should be me."

"Why?"

"I won't be grabbing my back and limping to the nearest chair every five minutes."

"My back is nearly fuckin' perfect."

"Another thing is, I got a cover story for being there."

"Like what?"

Mark told him. Doonie reluctantly agreed.

Mark would show up at the LAFAM press reception and be introduced to the suspects. Mark would be there as himself, a Homicide dick who'd worked the Willetts case—no choice, he'd been in the papers and on the tube—but he shouldn't be there on business. Mark's story would be that he'd met Aunt Flo's assistant, Gale, while working the case—and now he and Gale were dating.

If Tish Sand, Calvin Hirschberg, Eric Fairlie, or Juan-Marie de Suau got rattled by meeting the cop who'd worked the Willetts murder—even if said cop was just in L.A. to get laid—that might be the break the cops needed. And if none of the suspects blew their cool, Mark would at least get a read on them.

So now all he had to do was call Aunt Flo, see if she—and

Gale—would go along with it, on short notice.

Mark dialed Florence Brock's cell. This time she answered it herself. She was delighted to hear Mark and Doonie were in L.A. But a little surprised; to the outside world it looked as if Meelo's trial was rattling along to its preordained conclusion.

Mark told Aunt Flo that Meelo's trial was about to come to an abrupt halt. Told her he and Doonie were in L.A. looking for the real hit men—and their employer. Mark would like to attend the LAFAM event, in a semi-undercover capacity: As her assistant Gale's date.

Aunt Flo was sure Gale would be up for it. She asked Mark to hold on while she checked. Less than a minute later Aunt Flo got back on and reported Gale was ready to help find Wilson's killers any way she could.

Mark asked if it was possible to meet with Florence and Gale sometime that evening so he and Doonie could fill them in on the details.

Aunt Flo insisted on canceling her dinner plans and having the cops come to her place for a quiet meal and planning session, just the four of them. Mark said he thought he could talk Doonie into it.

Aunt Flo suggested 8 p.m. Mark asked if they could push it back till 8:30. That way Doonie could spend an hour in bed cuddling with a heating pad, and Mark could pick up a rental car and go honor his other dinner engagement.

SEVENTY-TWO

J'nette Levaux was gloriously alive, and not just in the sense of not being dead, which by itself would've made Mark's evening. Levaux was pleased to see him. Lit up when he walked in holding a bag from a downtown restaurant recommended by the hotel concierge.

"Hi"—three-hundred-watt grin—"you're a man of your word."

"Hmmf," Mark grumped, spotting hospital dinner debris. He lifted the metal cover and glanced at the plate. "You're breaking my heart, Levaux. And clogging your own with whatever substances were in this . . . beige glop." He gingerly put the cover back on the toxic, possibly radioactive plate and removed the hazardous tray from the room.

"I was hungry," Levaux explained.

"No excuse. Here," Mark sighed, handing her the bag. "Maybe you can bribe a nurse with this or something."

"Oh, thank you." Levaux pulled out one of the Styrofoam containers, opened it, and took a whiff. "No way I'm giving this away; they can microwave it for me later," she insisted. "And you can call me J'nette."

"I'll think about it."

"So, Mark, how's it going?"

Mark filled her in on the day's less than thrilling news, some of which she'd already heard from Ochoa.

"Unfortunately, I gotta go soon," he apologized. "Anybody

coming by to keep you company? Ochoa said your dad's deployed to the Gulf."

"Yeah," J'nette assured Mark, "my aunt and cousin drove up from San Diego this morning, and more people are coming tonight. Teo and his wife are gonna stop by . . . This has actually improved my social life."

"Yeah," Mark empathized, "know the feeling."

"You been shot?"

Mark nodded. "And not some puny little through-and-through in the leg."

"Yeah? Let's see."

Mark brushed that notion aside with a small dismissive wave.

J'nette scowled, demanding Mark show her.

He pulled back his jacket and yanked his shirt up, holding the shirt-tail in his teeth while he tugged the waist of his pants down to show J'nette the dime-sized bull's-eye scar on his right side.

Which was undoubtedly why the guy who walked in behind Mark grumbled, "Hello?" wondering who the fuck was exposing himself to the patient.

"Hey, Thad," J'nette grinned at the handsome black man wearing a midnight blue double-breasted Hugo Boss suit.

Mark spat out the tail of his shirt.

The handsome man leaned down to kiss J'nette, then turned to Mark and extended a hand. "Thaddeus Stevenson."

Mark shook his hand. "Mark Bergman."

Stevenson's expression warmed.

"Mark was just showing me where he'd been shot," J'nette explained.

"Well then, this was a peer review of relevant police data," Stevenson observed.

"Thad's my fiancé," J'nette bragged. Clearly adored the guy.

Right. Sure. You bet. J'nette Levaux, like many engaged

woman cops, didn't wear the diamond on the job. Sensible.

Thad Stevenson took Mark's hand again, this time in both of his. "Thanks, man," he said. "Thanks."

Mark hung out a while. Thad gave Mark his card, said to call him if there was anything he needed while in town, and made Mark promise to join him and J'nette for dinner before he went back to Chicago.

Thaddeus Stevenson. Fiancé. Lawyer. Nice guy.

Ah, fuck.

On the other hand, J'nette had avoided mentioning Thad would be visiting her tonight; she'd just talked about "people" and Teo and . . .

Give it up, Bergman. Yes, J'nette was enjoying the attention, the little flirtation. No, she was not the messing-around-during-the-engagement kind.

Neither was Mark. Yet another thing they had in common.

So what happened here, he made a friend. Maybe two.

Can't have too many of those.

SEVENTY-THREE

Like Sunland, Bel Air was hilly, steep, and accessed by a few narrow twisting roads. It was within Los Angeles city boundaries. That was it for similarities.

Bel Air was on the wealthy Westside, sandwiched between Mulholland Drive along its upper ridgeline and Sunset Boulevard below. Bel Air's main entrance, on Sunset, was guarded by grandiose, vaguely Gallic wrought-iron gates, in case the neighborhood's name alone wasn't enough to convince visitors they were entering Fontainebleau West.

Unlike the dun, semi-arid Sunland landscape Bel Air was green, dense with whole forests, whole jungles, planted and maintained by whole regiments of Central American gardeners. There were as many trucks per capita in Bel Air as in Sunland, but the only cargo these SUVs hauled was an extra three coats of wax. Nobody was raising roosters around here, though a few residents had raised spectacularly silly cock-waving mansions.

High up, occupying a promontory with views of the city and ocean, Florence Brock lived in a sweep of Wilson Willetts elegance that even elicited a quiet, respectful "Shit . . ." from Doonie.

Aunt Flo—*Florence*—when speaking to her they had to remember to call her Florence—answered the door herself, flinging it open, trilling an emotional "Welcome!" and wrapping Mark, then Doonie, in the grand, lost-soulmate hugs she'd almost given them that wet afternoon in Willetts' foyer in Chicago.

Mark hoped Doonie hadn't popped wood when Aunt Flo plastered herself against him. Probably not; looked like all Doonie's blood had rushed to his face. Hard to tell if Aunt Flo's embrace had aroused Doonie, alarmed him, or aggravated his back injury. Or all the above.

Aunt Flo showed them through the house. The place was a fine little museum, a tribute to what you could accomplish with a passion for art and a majority stake in a midsized oil services company. Aunt Flo noticed the way Doonie was walking and asked, "Detective Dunegan, what's wrong with your back?"

Doonie tried to dismiss it with a micro-shrug, a centimeter being as far as his shoulders would move.

Aunt Flo asked if he wanted to see a doctor—she knew several excellent orthopedists and an acupuncturist who was the next best thing to a magician.

Doonie said the back was just a little tight, no big deal.

Mark knew it was a pretty big deal, seeing as how on the ride over Doonie had been uncharacteristically quiet, in too much pain to relish his upcoming chance to provoke Aunt Flo into a titillating rage. But the night was young.

Aunt Flo led them to the kitchen, apologizing for the fact they'd be eating there because for the sake of secrecy she'd sent the staff away for the evening.

Doonie assured her the kitchen was just fine.

Mark had no complaints. The kitchen was roomier than his apartment, and standing at a granite-topped island unpacking recently delivered beef tenderloin dinners was the most intriguing young woman he'd seen since leaving that wounded engaged cop at the hospital an hour ago.

So this was who went with the voice on the phone from Peru. It wasn't just that she wasn't ugly, in a five-ten, unassistedly blonde hair pulled back in a twist, high-cheek-boned, plush-lipped kind of way; it was the self-possessed intelligence and deadpan playfulness with which she assessed the cops, deciding how they matched the detailed descriptions Aunt Flo had certainly given her.

The young woman said, "Hello, I hope you're not vegetarians."

"He is," Mark said, indicating Doonie. "But he hides it well."

Aunt Flo slid an arm around the young woman's waist. "Gentleman—my wildly overqualified assistant, Gale Michaels. Gale, this is Detective John Dunegan, and your date for tomorrow, Detective Mark Bergman."

"A pleasure, Miss Michaels," Mark said, shaking her hand.

"Yeah," Doonie concurred.

"Gale," she instructed. "My dates usually call me Gale."

"We appreciate your cooperation, Gale," Mark said. "And your willingness to let people believe you're going out with a cop from the Midwest—in a day or two the investigation will be public and you can, y'know, correct that impression."

"Correct the impression a man flew two thousand miles and attended a museum P.R. function just to be with me?"

During dinner Mark and Doonie gave the ladies a general idea of what was happening and why. Gale didn't seem to have any second thoughts about getting into this, so Mark gave her the opportunity.

"What we need you to consider is, as what happened to Hector B shows, this is a hardass bunch. Now, I seriously doubt they'd come after anyone except an eyewitness who could put them away; you cooperating in this little charade shouldn't make you a target. But, if you have any—"

"I don't."

"Okay . . . Well, we have to get our story straight, so let's keep it as minimal as possible."

Gale nodded. "The less history we have the less likely we are to give contradictory details."

"Exactly. We met, briefly, in Chicago, during the investigation. Liked each other, but never had a chance to go out."

"Florence and her damn hectic schedule, destroying my social life."

"So—I got some time off, decided to come to L.A. You suggested I join you and Florence for this event, seeing as how it involved the man whose case I worked."

"Got it," Gale assured Mark.

No doubt about that. "Is there anything I should know about you?" Mark asked.

She thought it over. Very seriously informed him, "I don't spell my name with an 'i.' It's G-a-l-e."

"Like Gale Sayers." Doonie nodded approvingly.

"Just like," she said. "That's who my dad named me after, when Mom wouldn't let him name me after Ernie Banks."

"Thank God," Aunt Flo said.

"Yeah," Doonie agreed, "you don't wanna handicap a kid, naming her after a Cub."

"So you're from the North Side?" Mark asked.

"Just my name. And, obviously, my dad."

"You still got folks there?" Doonie wanted to know.

"Couple of cousins. My father's family moved out here when he was in high school."

"But by then," Mark sympathized, "he was stuck rooting for Chicago teams."

Gale tapped her heart twice with two fingers, kissed them, and gestured heavenward, Sosa-style.

"I don't understand this thing people have with teams," Aunt Flo sighed. "I don't get sports in general."

"Think of it as performance art, with beer," Mark suggested.

"And betting."

That tickled Aunt Flo. She beamed delightedly at Mark. And Gale. At Mark and Gale, together. With the look of a woman engraving wedding invitations in her mind.

Doonie, except for being a guy, and instead of a smile having the pinched expression that comes from struggling not to wear your back pain on your face, was looking at Mark and Gale with a similar benign dopiness.

Mark recognized the look. It was love at first sight. Not between the parties involved, but on their behalf, by the married and/or older people observing them. When Mark was younger he'd found that look irritating, a sentimental intrusion by the old folks. In recent years it struck him as sad—a wistful yearning by the old folks for a vicarious taste of new-bloom romance. Tonight romance didn't strike Mark as the world's worst idea. Hell, way he was feeling, marrying Gale Michaels if she'd agree to sleep with him sometime soon seemed like a reasonable deal.

Though, if he had to pick, Mark's first choice would've been for Teophilo Ochoa to get lucky with Guadalupe Ramos.

It was Doonie who got lucky, with Aunt Flo.

He'd been quiet. Aunt Flo made several attempts to draw him out. Wasn't daunted by the lack of response.

Mark was pretty sure Aunt Flo was just being her usual self— but he also sensed she was a little disappointed Doonie hadn't given the least hint of flirting with her the way he had that afternoon at the hotel, and she was campaigning to regain Doonie's interest.

The one sign of life Doonie showed was to shift in his chair from time to time in an unsuccessful hunt to find a tolerable position. The third time he did it, Aunt Flo offered to get him a pillow, a painkiller, a doctor. Doonie thanked her, he was fine.

Aunt Flo offered to refill his wine glass. He declined. She asked if he'd prefer something else, speak right up, you name it, she had it.

Doonie allowed he wouldn't mind a bourbon. Aunt Flo excused herself, returned with a bottle of some single-cask Kentucky joy juice with a hand-numbered label.

When they finished the main course Aunt Flo suggested they move to the den for coffee and dessert; much more comfortable place to sit.

Soon as Doonie finished his chocolate-hazelnut biscotti and organic Gaviota strawberries with hand-whipped cream, Aunt Flo informed Doonie his back was killing him, she recognized the body language; her late husband Ed had had back trouble and been as stubborn as Doonie about trying to ignore it. She asked Doonie if he'd let her give him a massage—she'd taken classes after Ed hurt his back, it was no substitute for what the acupuncturist could do, but she still had her massage table and guaranteed Doonie would at least be able to sleep easier when she was done with him.

Doonie gave Aunt Flo a long, warm, pleased, infinitely regretful look. "I really appreciate that, Florence, but . . . I'm kinda runnin' out of steam."

As they drove out the Bel Air gate onto Sunset, Mark asked Doonie, "You need to see a doctor?"

Doonie scowled.

"Knew you were hurting," Mark explained. "Didn't know how bad until you turned Aunt Flo down."

After a moment Doonie told him, "Wasn't my back . . . I was never lookin' to do more than look."

It was Mark's turn to launch a skeptical glance.

"You're right, my back's killin' me," Doonie muttered, not bothering to make it sound like more than an excuse. He stared at the passing scenery, pretending to be interested in the mansions whizzing by.

After a while, Doonie said, "There was this cop bar, on Belmont across from the Nineteenth—this is before your time. Me and Phyl were married, three, four years. I useta screw around a little, nothin' crazy, just the usual . . . Mostly Phyl never knew, but . . . after the second one she found out about, she . . . So I'm workin' late one night, stop in for an unwinder and I run into Elvin Blivins, who useta be my training officer—didja know that?"

Mark nodded.

"Right. Well, so, me and Elvin are at a table in the back, the good Lord was with me that night, 'cause if it had been anybody else, or even another cop with us, or a table in the middle of the room, I woulda had ta quit the job . . .

"But it's just me and Elvin, catchin' up a little, and he looks up like someone he knows is walkin' in and I turn around and it's Phyl, headin' straight for us and she's got this look—not like she's crazy-angry, or—just this look, I'm not sure what . . . And she just walks up to us and stands there, and I'm askin', 'Hon, something wrong,' because like Kieran's maybe eighteen months at this point, Phyl wouldn't leave him alone, musta dropped him off at her mom's or had the old bag come over . . . But, Phyl just says 'Hi Elvin.' Then stands there lookin' at me a minute . . .

"Says t' me, 'Next time you fuck around you dumb Mick son of a bitch, I'm fuckin' around—starting with Elvin.' And Phyl looks at him and says, 'Wouldn't turn this down, wouldja?' and opens her trench coat, and there is my old lady, stark fucking naked under the coat, in a cop bar, showin' her stuff to Elvin."

So, Mark thought, that's what that jam-packed look Blivins had shot Doonie had been jam-packed with.

"And this was Phyl," Doonie went on, "so, you know . . ."

"She meant it."

"Yeah. But like I said, 'cause of it's the last table in back, no one but Elvin sees. And Phyl just shuts the coat and walks out . . . So then, I'm . . ."

Doonie took a long, slow deep breath and shook his head.

"I can shoot her. I can shoot me. Or I can admit I love the crazy bitch enough not to hurt her again . . . And lose my kids . . . And have to share her with Elvin Blivins." Doonie gave a ruefully amused little snort. "Even if Elvin is one stand-up guy."

Hugely; if there's one thing cops are bad at it's sitting on cop gossip. Blivins keeping a story like that confidential for fifteen years was a standard by which Mark would now have to measure himself.

"And, so," Doonie concluded, "that's, that's . . . that's why I'm gonna pass on all the other women in the world for fucking ever, including the hottest richest woman who was ever after me."

"Ah," Mark commented.

After a moment Doonie said, "Don't let this scare you off marriage."

"Okay."

"Marriage, greatest thing there is . . . Even if you don't make it legal, I mean, it's that thing of having a thing with the one woman, that's the thing you really need most, it's the one that counts. Can't do without it. I'm not sayin' it's easy. It's like every other fuckin' thing. There's no free lunch."

No. Never. Not even a little.

SEVENTY-FOUR

"I had to do it."

Those were the first words Dina had said to Arthur when she called to tell him she'd killed Hector B and shot a cop and been stabbed in the arm and shot in the leg and needed help, fast.

Those were also the last words she was saying to him here at the airport, sitting in a wheelchair at the metal detector, wondering if they were the last words she'd ever say to him, because she'd never be seeing him again.

"I had to do it."

Arthur continued to not talk. He'd been doing a lot of that. Taking care of what needed to be taken care of. Saying as much as he had to. Nothing else.

Dina had never been as frightened or angry as she was right now, sitting here wearing an excellent blonde wig that matched photos of her in a passport and driver's license identifying her as "Julie Knott," a scarf covering her bruised throat, one arm in a sling and one thigh heavily bandaged beneath her long loose skirt, both wounds throbbing through the thin dose of painkiller she'd limited herself to in order to keep her mind clear, determined to remain in front of this goddamn metal detector, refusing to move until Arthur up and told her he loved her and would join her as soon as he could, or that he was going to be a stupid ice-man asshole and blow off their whole life together just because he was pissed she'd gone and blown discipline and done what needed to be done without clearing it with him because she loved him enough to risk getting shot or busted in order to keep Hector B from getting busted and giving them up.

Dina would accept it if Arthur ended things here. But she was not going to let him get away with doing it by not saying a word.

The attractive young possibly Hispanic blonde grimaced, grinding her teeth as she levered herself out of the airline wheelchair, stood, and stared with anxious, hungry ferocity into the eyes of the mild, balding middle-aged gent who'd wheeled her in.

The bullet had just grazed the back of her thigh, but by the time she'd ridden the Kawasaki back to her truck Dina felt as if someone had sliced the leg open, poured lighter fluid in and lit it. That and the stab wound in her arm made controlling her bike the most physically difficult thing Dina Velaros had ever done.

Up to the moment when she had to lift the goddamn bike and heave it into the truck.

Which she did not a moment too soon. By the time Dina slid behind the Explorer's wheel, the hills were alive with the sound of mad Dopplering sirens. As she pulled onto the freeway Dina saw a police chopper swoop down to eyeball a biker. Whose bike happened to be green.

Dina dragged herself into her house, in a quiet part of Chatsworth, at the far northwest edge of the San Fernando Valley. She limped into the bathroom, sat on the toilet, and used her latest disposable to call Arthur on his latest disposable.

He said, "Hello."

She said, "I had to do it."

From Dina's tone and the short silence that followed she

307

knew Arthur understood what "it" was. But to make sure she used the code word, telling him she'd just made a purchase. Told him she made the purchase seconds before a couple of tourists from Chicago were about to grab the item she had her eyes on.

Then she told Arthur the drive home from her shopping trip hadn't gone well. Had two problems. A front tire and a rear tire had both gone flat; a puncture and a blowout, in the same day, if you could believe it. She'd need a tow; she was too rattled to handle it on her own.

Arthur said he was in Paso; asked if it was safe to leave her car where it was till he got there, or did she need it towed right away.

Dina said she could hang on till he got there.

Arthur said, "Okay."

Dina said, "I love you."

Arthur hung up.

Dina washed and bandaged the wounds as best she could.

She managed to get her emergency cash and a couple of sets of IDs out of the hidden safe under the floor under the oven. To get to it she had to open the oven door, remove the bottom panel, then the floor tile beneath, so the whole time she was head-first in the oven like the Witch in "Hansel & Gretel." Which is where Dina had gotten the idea for where to put the floor-safe.

Good thing Arthur wasn't there yet. If he saw her butt sticking out of the oven he'd be tempted to do a Hansel, shove her in and slam it shut.

By the time she finished, both wounds were oozing more heavily than when she'd begun and she was dizzy with pain. Shit. No way she could pack her clothes. She'd just bleed all over them and/or pass out. Best she could do was try to sleep until Arthur got here . . .

The doorbell rang, waking Dina up. She looked at her watch; Arthur had made it in under three hours. She called out for him to wait a moment. Her arm and leg had stiffened into angry concrete tubes. She hobbled to the door, unlocked it, and stepped back. Arthur let himself in and locked the door.

"Welcome to my house," Dina said.

Arthur had of course never been there.

Arthur of course said nothing. He gently took her arm and tried to walk her into the bathroom. Dina stopped him, hugged him, apologized for bleeding on his jacket, then let him take her to the john.

He inspected her wounds, said, "Ugly, but you'll be all right," and did a better job of cleaning and bandaging than she'd been able to.

While he was working on her he asked what had happened. Dina ran it down. She paused after telling Arthur about not killing the old lady; he didn't say or show anything. Dina apologized again for ruining his jacket, a gray sport coat, a nubby silk-linen blend.

Arthur rigged a sling for her arm. Said he'd take her to his place in Ojai, but first they'd have to go to the home of a reliable bent doctor he knew in Long Beach. Meant a lot of time in the car but there was no way to avoid it. Dina needed stitches, shots. Had to make sure her wounds weren't more serious than Arthur thought, get her patched up enough to travel.

Zurich. Arthur had a contact there who'd escort her to a discreet clinic, where she'd be cared for by brilliant Swiss physicians who would not question the assertion her stab and gunshot wounds had been self-inflicted cooking-related kitchen mishaps.

As Arthur was backing out of Dina's driveway her neighbor

from three houses down, Mindy James, came barreling around a curve in her somewhat battered Suburban and clipped the rear bumper of Arthur's pristine Toyota 4Runner.

The Suburban skidded to a halt. Arthur got out, glanced at the minor damage to his rear bumper, and walked to the other truck. It had a fresh crunch in its front bumper and a shattered turn-signal lens, to go with the collection of older dings the vehicle sported, front, back, and on the passenger side.

Mindy James got out and wobbled a little. Arthur swiftly caught her arm and graciously inquired if she was all right. Mindy James announced her neck hurt and the accident was his fault. Arthur asked if she wanted to call the police and have them administer a sobriety test, gauge her speed from her skid marks, and have her insurance company informed of the results . . . Or accept five hundred in cash from him now and forget this happened.

Mindy James looked at Arthur, looked at the 4Runner—Dina was too stiff to slide down in her seat, but kept her head turned away, hoping it was too dark for Mindy James to recognize her profile. Dina wasn't sure what Mindy James was capable of perceiving; depended how many martinis into the evening her horse-, gossip- and gin-loving neighbor was.

Mindy James inspected her own bumper; the new damage wasn't as bad as some of her truck's older, untreated ow-ees. She looked at Arthur and said, "Seven-hundred-fifty."

This was too public a place in which to kill her so he gave her the seven-fifty.

It was 11:30 p.m. by the time they got to Dr. McWherter's home in Long Beach, way down at the south end of L.A. County. It took a little over an hour for Dr. McWherter to examine and dress Dina's wounds, and a few more minutes for Arthur to kill Dr. McWherter and his girlfriend Lori, who was watching a DVD in the den.

Shit. Burning an asset as valuable as a reliable bent doctor was something else for Arthur to be pissed about.

It was well after two in the morning by the time the 4Runner pulled into the garage of the secluded little house in the hills outside of Ojai, in Ventura County, about ninety minutes north.

Dina woke up as Arthur slid her out of the passenger seat and carried her inside. She could've walked, but was not about to break off the longest, closest physical contact they'd ever had.

Arthur took her to the guest bedroom, tucked her in.

A little before dawn Dina woke up from a combination of thirst and bladder pressure. She drank two glasses of water from the pitcher Arthur had placed on the bedside table, shuffled into the john, and sat.

Arthur's jacket was hanging from the shower nozzle; he'd soaked the parts Dina had bled on.

She noticed a few crumpled, bloodstained pieces of paper in the wastebasket. She fished them out.

They were test-print labels for wine bottles; Arthur must have had them in his pocket when she'd called him. The labels were for Arthur's new syrah, the first he'd ever made from world-class grapes, at his own winery.

The winery was named "A. Reid."

The wine was named "Cuvée Dina."

Dina took one bloodstained label back to her room, flattened it, put it under her pillow, and made a wish. First time she'd done anything like that since she was fourteen and Mami put her on the street.

At breakfast Dina tried to get Arthur to discuss her decision to whack Hector B. True, Hector B had only known them as Bill and Heather, but he could describe them and he had seen vehicles they owned. The *pendejo* had to die, and once the cops grabbed him, arranging that would've been infinitely more complicated.

Arthur gazed at Dina a moment, then told her he'd booked her a first-class seat on a flight leaving at 2:55 p.m., so they'd have to get to LAX by noon. He asked if she needed help getting dressed.

She shook her head.

When she was getting ready to leave she took the bloodstained wine label from under her pillow. Almost put it in her purse. Crumpled it and flung it across the room.

Made her other wounds hurt like hell.

"I had to do it."

Arthur didn't respond, so now they were standing here in the Bradley International Terminal, enraging the citizenry by flagrantly blocking access to a metal detector. Arthur gently moved Dina aside so the passengers behind them, who'd been in line for almost an hour, could get through.

Dina and Arthur stared at each other for a few more miserable hour-long seconds.

"I know," he finally said.

The Sphinx speaks! And it's still fucking useless! Because he's still Arthur fucking Reid speaking in that fucking bland unreadable he should be the one living in Switzerland teaching graduate seminars in neutrality Arthur fucking Reid voice, so no one, not even Dina, could tell if he's saying he loves her or saying she's something he needs to scrape off the bottom of his fucking shoe!

"We had a deal," Dina growled at him. "We have never once in all these years said a word about it, but it exists, it has existed since the minute we met on fucking Denbow's fucking boat, and now you *are* going to say a word about it . . . Yes or no, Arthur. Yes? Or no?"

Son of a bitch took his time before saying, opaque as ever, "You'll have to stay out of the country a year, maybe more."

Then he vowed, softly, but powerfully, as if letting loose a lifetime's worth of yearning, "I'll bring you some of this," and handed her a Cuvée Dina wine label.

And kissed her.

Many hours later, over the Atlantic, Dina took the wine label out and gazed at it for the umpteenth time.

Did he mean it? Or had he just said and done what was necessary to make her get on the goddamn plane and out of his life forever?

Dina decided he meant it. Had some evidence he meant it.

That kiss.

SEVENTY-FIVE

Carrie Eli and Harrison Miller were walking to the Cook County Court Building for that morning's proceedings when Miller confided he had a sure-fire plan to slow up the trial for at least twenty-four hours: "I can collapse in the courtroom."

Carrie grinned; wasn't much of a joke, but it was the first Miller had made since she'd joined him on this case.

"I can do this, make it convincing," Miller assured her. "The gasp, the clutch, take a nice little fall . . . Santini grants a recess so I can be taken to the hospital for observation, turns out it's just stress and overwork. Maybe even buy us a two-day delay."

My God, he's not kidding. He wants *to do this. He has . . . rehearsed.*

"Oh yeah, it'd work," Carrie said, trying to sound as if she were pondering the tactical implications. "But I think we should keep it in reserve, in case we run out of rebuttal witnesses before the DNA tests on Hector B come back."

Miller shrugged, trying not to let his disappointment show.

Carrie touched his arm. "We save it for after the defense rests, the day we're supposed to do our close. Maximum impact. Much more dramatic moment."

Miller stared daggers at the patronizing cunt but said nothing.

They were heading down the hallway to the courtroom when they spotted Paul Obed standing by the courtroom door, chatting up *Chronicle* reporter Bob Gilkey. Fucking reporter had given more ink to the cops and the Pocket Pal than to Miller, right from the get-go.

"Hiya, Bob," Miller cheerily called out. As the newsman looked up and recognized him, the prosecutor stiffened, made shuddering hiccup-like noises, clutched his left arm, dropped his briefcase by opening his left hand and holding his long bony fingers spread out wide and stiff, stared down at his outstretched fingers so onlookers would know what they were supposed to look at (this, Miller knew from studying thespian web sites, was what professional actors referred to as "giving focus"), then took one stumbling step forward, sank slowly to his knees and sagged sideways, supporting himself with one hand so he slid into a near-prone position without banging his head even though he was wide-mouthed and pumping for air like a wrinkled, pinstriped guppy who'd been dumped out of his bowl.

Miller's co-counsel, Carrie Eli, seemed too stunned to react, so the *Chronicle* reporter—who knew a vivid first-person column opportunity when one collapsed at his feet—dashed to the fallen prosecutor's side, yelling, "Medic! Medic!" and cradled Miller in his arms, playing Mary to the old guy's Jesus in an improvised Courthouse Hallway Pieta.

Miller sneaked a look at Carrie, letting her know he was fucking aware the DNA could come back any minute now and end this trial, so he was damned if he was going to pass up this opportunity.

Then Miller's attention shifted to more urgent matters, as he had to pretend to recover just enough to fight off Bob Gilkey's attempt to give him the Kiss of Life.

Too late. Gilkey pinched Miller's nose shut, yanked his jaw open, locked lips and huffed hard into Miller's mouth. Which is how Miller discovered Gilkey had recently breakfasted on a bagel with lox, cheese, and onion, heavily sweetened coffee, and two cigarettes.

SEVENTY-SIX

"I met the detectives on that case," Ms. June Dockyer told Janvier.

They were watching the evening newscast. There had just been a report about how that day's session of the Willetts trial had been cancelled, because an Assistant State's Attorney had collapsed in the hallway outside the courtroom and thrown up in the mouth of a *Chronicle* reporter who'd gone to his aid, triggering a chain-vomiting incident among onlookers, including several jurors.

Ms. June Dockyer was rolling a joint, chilling on Janvier's couch after work, as she did more and more lately. Ms. June Dockyer's affair with Barry Keefe had lasted one cosmically dull night—the Ecstasy had been first-rate but the erotics had been less than ecstatic. Keefe's hygiene had been nearly as deplorable as his performance and attitude, so he and she both, being no-bullshit, cut-to-the-chase brokers, had been pleased to leave it at Keefe throwing a few trades Ms. June Dockyer's way and calling it a relationship.

But she'd been hanging with Janvier ever since. Janvier was totally cool, had fine dope, and knew about all sorts of artsy bars, shops, and gallery openings with which Ms. June Dockyer could score status points around the office.

And though Janvier wouldn't front Ms. June Dockyer an ounce of whatever Jamaican or Humboldt or other fucking amazing, pricey weed she had in stock, Janvier was always good for a free joint. These artistic types didn't sweat the small stuff.

"You were involved in the Willetts case?" the artistic type asked.

"No, but the night it happened, these two homicide detectives, Bergman and Dunegan, were at my apartment—I'd uh, been kind of a witness—not a witness, I was . . . *near* this hit-and-run thing, and the cops kept trying to get me to say I could identify the driver, which I honestly could not. Honestly," Ms. June Dockyer emphasized. She took a long, thoughtful toke. Exhaled philosophically, gazing at the smoke. Christ *almighty*. Praise Jah for dis Ja-makin, mahn. "Shame this stuff is a grand an ounce."

"No, it's great it's a grand an ounce," Janvier disagreed, as her guest belatedly passed her the j. "Waitressing pays the rent, but this is tuition and art supplies . . . So, what were this Dunegan and—Bergstein?"

"Bergman."

"What were these cops like?"

"Well Dunegan's just this fat old pig, but Mark, Mark's a hottie."

" 'Mark'?" Janvier wondered, in a way that clearly meant, *Did you do him?*

Ms. June Dockyer gave her a small rueful grin and shook her head. "Hasn't happened—yet."

"Yet?"

"He'll be back. Son of a bitch tried to bribe me into describing the hit-run driver, by offering to take me out— to the ballet."

Janvier grinned, Cheshire-deep, when she heard that.

"I know," Ms. June Dockyer went on, "cop/ballet, doesn't compute. But—claimed he knew somebody who works at American Ballet Theater."

"He does—I mean, I'm sure he does," Janvier frowned, grop-

317

ing her way through a well-baked thought. "I mean, he's a cop, working a homicide, he's probably not stupid enough to claim he can get ballet tickets unless he can."

Janvier stubbed out the roach, nudged the baggie of weed in Ms. June Dockyer's direction. "Roll yourself a j for home."

"Wow. Thanks."

As Ms. June Dockyer busied herself rolling as big fat a j as she figured she could get away with without looking like a big fat parasite, Janvier asked her, "So this cop, this—hottie?"

"Totally."

"What happened with you and him?"

"Well, after I kept telling him the honest truth—that I was just *near* this hit-run, it was dark out, didn't get any real look at the driver, like I was pretty freaked, so I honestly don't have any sharp memory of the event—the cop starts inviting me to the ballet, but makes it clear it isn't on unless I describe the driver. I cannot honestly do that, so Detective Bergman gives me his card and they leave—then later that night on the tube I see him and the fat cop at the Willetts thing, then, y'know, their names are in the paper when they bust the killer, and they get a press conference on TV . . ."

"But you haven't heard from him since?"

"Well . . . There was something there, y'know, between me and Mark, I could tell, so I'm just gonna chill till he calls me, no bullshit about me testifying, cause, um, y'know, if I call him and say 'Let's hook up,' he's gonna try to play me, get me to talk about the hit-run, and y'know, I cannot, cannot get involved in all that . . . um, especially, since . . . I didn't get a good look at . . . anything."

Janvier studied Ms. June Dockyer for a moment. "I don't know if I see you and Mark—you and a cop—being a fit."

"Oh," Ms. June Dockyer scoffed, "just a one- or two-nighter, he's just some healthy, uncomplicated—"

"Uncomplicated?"

"Yeah, nobody serious. But a whole lot more useful than Barry Keefe, self-centered premature-ejaculating farting drooling blows his nose on the pillowcase married asshole," she chortled. "You know?"

Janvier nodded. "Sounds like you could hook up with the cop for sure if you could describe that hit-run driver to him."

Ms. June Dockyer stiffened—*Is Janvier implying I'm lying about not seeing the hit-run—That bitch, who's she think she's accusing—Whoa, control yourself, Junie, this bitch is the one with the stash of Jamaican.*

Ms. June Dockyer collected her stoned wits and modulated into a cooing, girlish tone. "Honest, I didn't see the driver. Can't describe him . . . Don't you believe me?"

Janvier's face just did that cool blank thing artistic types do to make themselves look above it all, just *examined* Ms. June Dockyer as if she was trying to decide if the broker trainee was a subject worth painting, or was just some drab drone she wanted the hell out of her crib . . .

Janvier grinned and the room warmed. "Chill, girl. I trust you. In fact . . . you know anyone around your office who could afford the Jamaican?"

Whoa. What's up? Ms. June Dockyer nodded, cautiously. "Maybe."

"Well," Janvier said, lowering her voice to a droll conspiratorial whisper, "I can't front you an ounce, but I will front you four ounces."

"Uh . . ."

"You sell three, priced so they pay for your one, and maybe a couple of bucks left over. That's what I do, it's the only way I can afford this quality."

You want me to deal dope, Ms. June Dockyer thought. *No fucking way . . . but, shit, this weed . . .*

319

"Hey," the artistic type teased, perceiving exactly what was going through Ms. June Dockyer's mind, "you're a commodities broker, right?"

Oh fuck oh fuck oh fuck, this Jamaican was just billowing through her brain, pillowing through her body, Ms. June Dockyer was too high to make this kind of decision now . . . *A whole ounce of this shit, for free—and if I charge fifteen hundred an ounce this is free plus I've got, uh, five hundred left over, tax-free . . . But, shit, if, if, if . . .*

"Hey," Janvier giggled, "you worried I'm gonna tell Detective Mark Bergstein on you?"

SEVENTY-SEVEN

"Tell me a little bit about yourself, Detective."

Not an unreasonable request. A classic one, in fact, in this situation. The deep late hours, three fucks into the night, taking a damp, drowsy breather, wanting to stay awake for more. Wanting to know who you're enjoying this rented bed with.

"Which little bit would you like to know?"

"The usual. Where you're from. How'd a nice boy like you end up in a job like this. Do you adore me for myself or are you just a pushover for women named after Chicago Bears."

"When I'm with a woman named after a Bear I never discuss other women named after Bears."

"Fair enough. Nothing personal, then. Just tell me about your family, your childhood, friends, school, career."

Tempting. Gale was one of those rare people Mark instantly felt comfortable with. So much so he didn't automatically distrust the feeling. He was sure he would've had that feeling even if he weren't lonely, horny, and frustrated when he and Gale went on their interesting first date.

And they had to talk about something besides their interesting date. Mark wasn't free to discuss an ongoing investigation with a civilian, even if she was helping him get next to his homicide suspects, and to humanize this heavily lacquered hotel room.

Gale had picked Mark up at the New Hikune; it would've been

321

simpler for Mark to meet her at the museum, but it would be a more convincing impersonation of a date if Gale and Mark showed up together.

The Los Angeles Fine Arts Museum was a campus of bulky rectangular buildings from the 1960s, which Gale called the Three Ugly Cartons. But they were spacious and well-lit on the inside, which Mark thought was the basic requirement for displaying art. Gale explained these days a museum couldn't be a true Event Destination unless the building itself was an Event.

The debut of the three proposed versions of the Event was held in a ground-floor gallery of one of the Ugly Cartons. Before trying to fight their way through the media surrounding the architects and the wall of society flesh surrounding the key design committee members, Mark and Gale took a quick tour of the architectural models.

The design by Eric Fairlie (the Scottish architect Aunt Flo had described as a client-fucking, toxic narcissist) was a jumble of narrow rectangular tubes; looked like a pile of giant pickup sticks dropped by a mammoth child.

On the wall behind the model were huge panels containing yards of text and drawings and charts, all by Fairlie, ranting about how a building composed of a pile of intersecting rectangular tubes expressed his integrated theory of anthro-esthetics, sensory-bio-social pan-sequential art encounter, moral-tactile-structural-neurological foot-traffic flow essence, and low-cost environmentally synergistic anti-paternalist utilities configuration. Fairlie's book-length wall essay plunged into ever denser thickets of estheti-babble, with clauses, adjectives, and neo-thoughts strewn as randomly as the components in Fairlie's design.

Mark stopped reading and looked at Gale.

"Oh yeah," she confirmed, "you could tranquilize rhinos with this drivel."

"Does it work on the people who make the decision? I mean, reading this wouldn't make me eager to commission a building that looks like that," Mark said, frowning at Fairlie's aggressively awkward design. "Let alone risk setting foot in it."

"Especially in an active earthquake zone."

"How did this get to be a finalist?"

Gale gave him a shrewd look. "You now understand just how much clout Calvin Hirschberg has."

They moved on to Juan-Mari de Suau's model. This was a building Mark wouldn't have minded stepping inside of; a massive, swooping, science-fiction cathedral-fortress. Handsome . . . but kind of bulky and foreboding.

Gale said, "De Suau's building looks like it wants to exalt and armor the art, not invite people in to enjoy it."

"Yeah, well, Spain's hosted a bunch of wars the past few thousand years."

Mark and Gale went to the Wilson Willetts model, the array of four elegantly but playfully sculpted buildings connected by ramps, with parkland in the center, that Mark had seen in Willetts' office. Mark had liked it then. Now that he'd been in and around Los Angeles a few days he liked it more. The buildings' flowing curves riffed on the local topography and the Streamline Moderne moves of Hollywood's long-gone stylish period. It was the design Mark would've picked to build. Its architect wasn't the one Mark would've picked to shoot in the head.

Gale seemed gripped by the same mood Mark was, somberly contemplating the Willetts design.

"You ever meet him?" Mark asked.

Gale nodded. After a moment she asked, "Do you ever develop a sort of intimacy with the victims whose deaths you investigate?"

"Not intimacy—the relationship is kind of one-sided for that . . . You meet a corpse. Then you go poking around in his or her life, get a feel for who they were," Mark nodded at the model, "what they were capable of . . ."

A hearty voice boomed. "Gale! And—Detective Bergman! This is an unexpected pleasure."

They'd been spotted by Carlton Bass, Wilson Willetts' associate, the architect who'd shown Mark and Doonie the model back in Chicago. Bass came over to them, delighted. Kissed Gale, pumped Mark's hand.

"You here on business?" Bass asked.

"No," Mark lied. "Had some time off, and . . . Well, during the investigation Gale made the mistake of giving me her phone number."

Bass grinned. "I see."

"How's it going, what's the response been?" Mark asked.

"Lots of heartfelt condolences. Lots of effusive praise about Wilson's design—though, if Wilson were alive, there'd be the exact same praise—that's all you ever hear at these things. We won't have any useful feedback until the media coverage comes out—and we get our intelligence from Florence on the design committee buzz—which, officially, Mrs. Brock is not supposed to be divulging," Bass teased. "I assume we can trust you, Detective."

"Mostly," Mark deadpanned.

A LAFAM press rep interrupted, her steel-plated smile sweeping aside all obstacles as if it were the prow of an icebreaker. She merrily apologized for the intrusion and informed Bass he was needed for another interview. He told her he'd be there in a moment. The press rep chirped, "Great!" then bubbled her way back to a waiting TV news crew.

Bass studied Mark and Gale for a moment with a practiced eye. Gave them a small, rueful grin. Confided, "Wilson would be amused and pleased by how you two met. He hated waste." The portly architect put on his game face and marched off to engage the camera.

Mark felt as if he and Gale had just received Friar Tuck's blessing to go make babies. Ah well. Mark was certain Gale, being a bright, attractive, outgoing twenty-four-year-old woman, was as used to getting subjected to nonstop matchmaking as he was, being a thirty-one-year-old man who bathed regularly. Or maybe he was being unfair to Carlton Bass, who was grieving, and grasping for solace by trying to find anything good that might come out of his friend's death. Didn't know Bass well enough to say.

Right now Mark had to go do his job, which was to get to know people who weren't grieving Wilson Willetts' death.

SEVENTY-EIGHT

Took a while to work through the scrum surrounding Calvin Hirschberg and Eric Fairlie. Hirschberg, being a showbiz mogul, was more interesting to the media than any architect, so Fairlie was staying glued to Hirschberg. When the initial wave of interviews petered out, Hirschberg escorted Fairlie to a corner of the room for a private moment. The five-foot-ten Scot, doughy, ruddy-cheeked, with scraggly pale brown curls, somehow seemed smaller than the sleek five-foot-six silver ferret he was huddling with.

Mark and Gale headed over to them. Gale predicted the silver ferret would be sociable to her but the dough-boy would pretend not to recognize her.

As they neared the two men it became obvious Hirschberg was quietly but sternly correcting Fairlie for some gaffe he'd committed with a reporter. Hirschberg spotted Gale and smoothly switched gears, breaking out a lethal smirk and giving Gale a quick peck.

Fairlie was so relieved to be saved from the scolding it took him a moment to remember to not know who Gale was; he was leaning forward to kiss her cheek when he caught himself, frowned, and asked if they'd met.

"You know Gale," Hirschberg declared, continuing Fairlie's spanking. "Florence's assistant, you've met her many times."

"Oh. Right," Fairlie sighed, giving Gale a sour half-grin. "New hair color, isn't it?"

Gale, whose hair wasn't dyed, ignored the question and introduced Mark. As instructed, she said Mark was from Chicago and left it at that.

Hirschberg frowned. "I've seen your face," he told Mark. "On camera."

"Oh. Are you an—actor?" Fairlie gave the noun a medieval odor, as if it were a synonym for dung.

"No. A cop."

"The Willetts case," Hirschberg announced. "You were one of the detectives who arrested Wilson's killer."

"Oh. Poor Wilson," Fairlie muttered, irritated another architect was being discussed. "Bloody shame. You going to"—he attempted a sneering Bogart—"send him to the chair?" Managing to sound both utterly indifferent to the fate of the faceless urchin who'd murdered the inconsequential Willetts, and condescending to the barbarian Americans and their death penalty.

"Capital punishment has been suspended in Illinois," Mark said, with a faint tone of regret, looking Fairlie in the eye. "And the trial isn't quite over yet."

"But this clown you busted," Hirschberg asked, "he is going to be convicted?"

"That's what it looks like."

"Good," Hirschberg declared. He fixed Mark with a frank, curious gaze. "What brings you here?"

"Needed a break. Had some airline miles. And I like architecture."

Fairlie didn't bother to repress a snort.

"And," Mark told him, "I like Gale. Met in Chicago."

"Oh." Fairlie packed the syllable with faint amusement and vast disdain. Though he did give the two little lust-monkeys a lascivious sneer before he muttered, "Oh. There's someone," and left.

"Eric's a complete shithead," Gale volunteered, "but at least he's not talented." She grinned at Hirschberg, unafraid of speaking truth to mogulhood.

"That's not fair," Hirschberg admonished, amused by her challenge. "Eric is an immense talent."

"Oh." Gale imitated Fairlie's arch delivery of his favorite word.

"Gale, you can't blame an artist if his work is a bit more advanced than your sensibilities." Hirschberg gave Mark a conspiratorial smirk. "The curse of genius."

"But," Mark innocently inquired, "if the genius's work goes over the head of someone like Gale, how is the general public going to relate to it?"

"Good question," Hirschberg said, in a tone that said it was a Mickey Mouse question. He rolled out his standard response. "Eric's design is equal parts advanced and spectacular. The public will be drawn to it by its sheer boldness, and as they grow accustomed to it, learn to love it. The de Suau and Willetts designs would, over time, just grow dull—no disrespect to the dead."

"Speaking of which, you think Willetts' death helps or hurts his chances?"

The silver ferret's eyes darkened and Mark felt himself being inspected with new interest; Hirschberg had the gift of making the person he was looking at feel like prey.

"Both," Hirschberg answered. "Obviously there's a sentimental urge to honor Wilson's final effort. But there's also the pragmatic downside of these proposals being at a very early conceptual stage, with years of modifications to go. Picking a firm whose lead architect is alive makes a lot more sense . . . Not that anyone wants to win that way."

"I get the impression Mr. Fairlie could overcome his disappointment at his anthro-esthetic sensory-bio-social pan-sequential masterpiece winning that way, or any other."

Hirschberg half-grinned, spent a moment selecting a reply. Said, wry, "I haven't met many Jewish cops."

"Come to Chicago, I'll introduce you to some. Me, I'm Lutheran by birth. Atheist by choice. And part psychic—bet you a dollar Wilson Willetts wins this competition."

Hirschberg's lip twitched. He reached into his jacket as if reaching for a weapon and came out with an antique silver card case. Thumbed it open, withdrew a business card, and handed it to Mark.

"After the announcement's made, you can send your dollar there."

Mark gave Hirschberg one of his own cards, winked, took Gale's arm, and strolled away.

When they were out of mogul earshot Gale asked, "What just happened?"

"You tell me. Quietly," he added, ushering her down a corridor and into a deserted gallery.

"I thought," Gale said, regarding him curiously, "you're not allowed to discuss the particulars of your investigation."

"I'm not. And won't."

"Ah."

As Gale considered what she was going to say she chewed thoughtfully on her lower lip. Mark resisted an urge to help her chew. Damn. She had this healthy, happy, in her prime and eager to eat the world quality that Mark found irresistible. And a little dismaying. He felt about a century older than Gale.

"Well," Gale started, then paused.

Mark saw she didn't want to say anything flaky that might make him think less of her. *So this buzz is flowing two ways.* "Go on," he teased. "Everybody loves playing cop. And I won't be grading you."

"Sure you will."

"So?"

"So okay . . . Eric Fairlie's this pale damp grub of a human, a world-class example of the sad truth that talent is not a moral fact."

"What kind of fact is it?"

"A physical one; talent's something you're born with, like big feet."

"And how did Bigfoot respond when he found out I was a detective who'd worked the Willetts case?"

"He didn't. You were just another unfamous, unrich, uninfluential irrelevant creature consuming perfectly good oxygen without being any help to his career. Worse, you were using oxygen to discuss Wilson instead of discussing him . . . But, Eric didn't act guilty—not that he'd feel guilty if he'd had Wilson killed—but he'd be wetting himself if he'd done it and you turned up here today. I don't see Eric Fairlie having the nerve to commission a murder," Gale concluded, "or the willingness to shell out that much money—he doesn't pay his bills, you know."

"Yeah, that's what Aunt Flo—Florence—told us."

"Aunt Flo?" Much amused.

"Its what Nina Willetts called her, and . . . You are never going to tell your employer Detective Dunegan and I think of her as Aunt Flo, right?"

Gale enjoyed a moment of enigmatic silence, then went back to playing cop. "Calvin Hirschberg, well—he recognized you— means he's following the investigation. But I don't know if that means he's keeping tabs on a murder investment—just because Wilson is dead doesn't mean he isn't a threat to Calvin's boy Eric, so Calvin might simply be keeping track of the publicity the competition was getting—which is why I assume you asked him if he feared Willetts getting sympathy votes."

Mark didn't answer or change expression.

"Well," Gale went on, "Calvin mentioned that Wilson being dead makes him difficult to work with—but if Calvin were guilty, would he announce his motive to a detective?" Gale shook her head. "The only thing I'm sure of is Calvin tried to run a flattering/bonding thing on you by that remark about you being a Jewish cop, and you flipped it by proving him wrong *and* making the bet about Wilson winning—to see if you could press Calvin's buttons."

Mark silently acknowledged she might be right about that.

"You got him a little angry," Gale said. "But it'd take a whole lot more one-upsmanship than that to get Calvin to lose it."

"So what's your bottom line?"

"If Calvin was the one who did this, meeting you didn't rattle him into giving anything away—not anything I could spot." Gale leaned closer to Mark and whispered, "How'd I do?"

It was Mark's turn to flash an enigmatic grin.

SEVENTY-NINE

Getting to meet Juan-Mari de Suau and Tish Sand was easy; Aunt Flo was chatting with them. Aunt Flo spotted Mark and Gale, waved them over, and introduced Mark as a simply fabulous man she and Gale recently met in Chicago.

"Fabulous is the least I expect of Florence—and Gale," Juan-Mari de Suau confided to Mark, as he kissed Gale's hand and then shook Mark's. The Spaniard was short, dapper, charming, and wearing a black ribbon pinned to his lapel, which, he explained, was a tribute to his fallen friend Wilson.

Tish Sand restricted herself to one quick venomous glance at the black ribbon, exerting every bit of her breeding to keep from ripping the ribbon off de Suau's chest and ordering him to stop mentioning Wilson. The small, trim, surgically smoothed matron was equal parts regal confidence and tight wrapping; a serene time-bomb. Her enunciation was flawless even though she spoke without parting her firmly clenched teeth.

"Florence has an incredible gift for meeting interesting young people," Tish cooed to de Suau, with a hint of wistful compassion to underline the implication that the Widow Brock was reduced to purchasing youthful companionship. Then she focused her cold, charming grin on Mark. "Are you an associate of Mr. Willetts?"

"Only in a roundabout way. I was one of the detectives who investigated his death."

Tish frowned daintily, a trifle confused. "You're a private detective?"

"Public. Chicago police."

"My apologies, no offense meant," Tish assured him.

"None taken," he assured her.

Tish flicked a glance at Gale, silently complimenting her on acquiring a midwestern brute who could supply refreshingly bestial sex and yet was sufficiently obedience-trained to bring to upscale civic functions off his leash.

Gale flashed a minute, grin-like sneer at Tish: *Thank and screw you.*

So, Mark thought, *this is how girls or sports cars feel when guys show them off to each other.*

"Detective Bergman and his partner," Aunt Flo informed Tish and de Suau, "were the officers who arrested the man who—" Aunt Flo hesitated.

Please just say *shot*—

"—who's on trial for Wilson's death," Aunt Flo said.

De Suau looked at Mark with mournful appreciation. *"Gracias."*

Tish wasn't quite as touched. Too busy assessing Aunt Flo's hesitance.

"Is there any doubt he's the killer?" Tish asked. "I thought a witness identified him as the man who shot Wilson."

"Uh-huh," Mark nodded, "And we found the murder weapon and the victim's wallet in his possession. I believe the trial will end in a day or so." All true.

Aunt Flo was blushing, embarrassed at the possibility she'd aroused Tish Sand's suspicions about the purpose of Mark's visit.

She had. But about something far more important than the murder trial.

"So," Tish inquired of Mark, "you've come to Los Angeles to

visit Gale, and lobby for Wilson's design?"

"Lobby? Well, I'm a hometown fan of Mr. Willetts' work, which in Chicago I get to see every day, and I do admire his LAFAM entry—but I'm also enormously impressed with yours, Señor de Suau."

De Suau gave a grateful, guilty shrug and his hand unconsciously went to the black ribbon on his lapel.

"But, while I'm rooting for one of those two designs to win," Mark assured Tish, "I doubt my opinion would be of any interest to the design committee."

"Every intelligent opinion is of interest to us," Tish told Mark. She turned to Aunt Flo. "Just please tell me you haven't been forcing Detective Bergman to talk to the press."

"Relax, Tish," Aunt Flo purred, seizing the opportunity to recover from her stumble and go on the attack. "You won't be seeing any stories about how the officer who arrested Wilson's killer flew out here to honor his memory and urge Los Angeles to choose Wilson's design."

"Flo, dear, I would never suggest you'd indulge in something as tawdry as exploiting Wilson's death like that."

"Sorry," Aunt Flo countered, arching an eyebrow, "I must have misunderstood what you meant by 'forcing Detective Bergman to talk to the press.' "

Mark traded quick glances with Gale and de Suau, and, yeah, the three of them agreed this might be a good moment to take a few steps back to avoid the blood-spatter.

"I was," tight-toothed Tish explained to Aunt Flo, gently, slowly, as if to a dotty, distracted elder, "simply expressing a wish that this officer to whom we're all so grateful for his fine work in this, this violent, painful, horrible situation—honestly, Detective, I don't know how you deal with these things day in and day out and retain your good nature—I was simply trying to make certain Detective Bergman's vacation was exactly that, nothing but pure relaxation." Tish grinned benignly at Mark and Gale, generously assuming that Florence's assistant was indeed doing her duty in that regard.

Mark said, "Thank you, Mrs. Sand—"

"Tish," she insisted.

"Mark," he reciprocated.

Tish gave Aunt Flo a small victorious glance.

"The few days I've been here have been terrific. Met some amazing people," Mark said, absentmindedly scratching the small red mark on the edge of his ear.

"Well, there are at least two more you must permit me to introduce you to," Tish simpered, suddenly gone girlish. She waved at someone behind Mark, took possession of his arm and turned him so his back was to Gale and Aunt Flo, and he was facing the two large men who were obeying Tish's summons.

Mark recognized both from photographs. The one in the dark blue suit was Jordan Sand. The one in the dark blue uniform was Los Angeles Police Chief Donald Connaught.

Jordan Sand was sixty, prosperously beefy, and did a passable imitation of a down-to-earth, ordinary, decent guy who just happened to be worth two-point-eight billion more than you.

Donald Connaught was a sharp-eyed, crisp, accomplished son of the Boston streets who'd risen to command of the police department there. Los Angeles had recently hired him to clean up the messy scandals and organizational deficiencies the LAPD's previous chief had been hired to clean up, after the chief he'd replaced had failed to clean up the mess his own predecessor had been hired to clean up. The Mayor, and much of the rest of the city, was hoping that, at the least, some of Connaught's tidiness would rub off on the Department.

Mark was impressed with how coolly Connaught played it when Tish informed Jordan and the Chief who Mark was; Connaught gave no hint of knowing Mark was in town to possibly arrest one of the people in this hall, and had already been in the vicinity of three killings and the wounding of an LAPD homicide detective.

Mark, for his part, made sure not to show any response to the possibility Chief Connaught might be a pal of the husband of one of his suspects. The Chief might just be making nice with the heavy hitters; from what Mark had heard, Connaught was an operator but not a whore.

Before her husband or Connaught could ask, Tish explained Mark was in town to see the debut of the LAFAM models; she omitted any mention of Gale, implicitly taking possession of Mark and credit for introducing him to the people who mattered, like her husband and the Chief.

"Well this is an unexpected and very real pleasure," Jordan Sand declared, with the genuine friendliness of a born salesman. But his heavy, authoritative baritone wasn't selling, it was stating certainties you would not be wise to dispute. "Tracking and busting the bastard who shot Wilson within hours of it happening, that's law and order efficiency."

"Well, I was working with a veteran partner," Mark pointed out, "and the suspect was pretty easy to find."

"He's been convicted, right?" Jordan asked.

"Trial's not quite over."

"How's it looking?"

"I wouldn't want to be the defendant."

Jordan Sand nodded shrewdly and turned to the Chief. "Don, why don't you and I take this young man to dinner, see if we can recruit him for the LAPD."

"Good idea, Jordy," Connaught deadpanned. "But, thing is, luring promising young officers away from their home cities takes more than a feed at the Ivy. Now, if you were to endow a fund that would disperse recruitment bonuses and pay moving expenses . . ."

"The Chief is on to something here, Jordy," Aunt Flo asserted, putting a hand on Mark's shoulder, so he was now bookended by Florence Brock and Tish Sand, with his ostensible date, Gale Michaels, relegated to handmaiden status. "The private sector ponies up for cultural talent, why not for law enforcement?"

"C'mon Florence, you know Tish has already allocated all my cash reserves for the arts, medical research, and designer clothing. You'll have to take the lead on funding this one."

Aunt Flo gave Mark a playful look. "Maybe I will."

"This is very flattering," Mark protested, "but Chief Connaught was pulling your leg. Private funding of police officers is a dangerous practice. We're even trying to discourage it in Chicago, lately."

Jordan Sand chuckled, then asked, measuring Mark, "You got so intrigued by Wilson's work you came out just for this?"

"And to have dinner with Miss Michaels, whom I had the good fortune to meet during the investigation."

"*Whom*," Jordan boomed, delighted. "A cop, from Chicago no less, who uses *whom.*"

There was a sudden buzz of voices and movement from the doors. The Mayor and his entourage had arrived.

Mr. and Mrs. Sand excused themselves, scooped up Señor de Suau and hustled off toward His Honor. They arrived two steps behind the sprinting Calvin Hirschberg and Eric Fairlie.

"You're not going to ferry Carlton Bass over to the Mayor?" Mark asked Aunt Flo.

"No, we'll let His Honor come to us, over there," she said, indicating the table where Willetts' design was displayed.

So the Mayor would be photographed offering his condolences to Wilson Willetts' partner, next to the model of Wilson Willetts' entry. Way to go, Aunt Flo.

"Do you mind if I borrow Detective Bergman for a moment?"

Connaught asked Gale.

Gale shook her head. "I'll be over there with Florence and Carlton," she told Mark. She gave Mark a kiss on the cheek and accompanied Florence over to the Willetts model to await the Mayor.

Connaught grinned, putting on an expression that would make onlookers think he and the Chicago cop were making small talk, and lowered his voice. Referring to Gale's kiss, Connaught inquired, "Is that fine young woman just providing cover or is this a real date?"

"Just providing cover, but a guy can dream," Mark confessed. "Don't know the last time you were briefed, sir, but as of this morning we're still waiting for Hector Benvanides' DNA to come back. And Guadalupe Ramos, the old woman from the rooster ranch, was still refusing to look at photos of women who own Kawasaki dirt bikes, so I took this opportunity to get a little face time with some possible suspects, people I might otherwise never get near."

Connaught nodded once. "Any of them go hinky at the sight of you?"

"Tish Sand, but it wasn't about Willetts getting killed, it was about me possibly being here to campaign for him."

"Sounds about right. Any initial reads?"

"I don't see either of the architects issuing a contract."

"Calvin or Tish?"

"I'd keep their names on my list. And, considering he's married to Tish, knew the details of the arrest, but got me to talk about the trial by saying he thought it was already over, Jordan Sand is someone *whom* I'd add to the list."

"Be nice," Connaught grinned. "And be careful," he added.

Yes sir. You bet.

After the reception Gale drove Mark downtown, dropped him

at Parker Center.

Mark thanked Gale for her cooperation. And company.

Gale told him he was very welcome. She invited him and Doonie to join her at the dinner Aunt Flo was hosting that night for Carlton Bass and the other Willetts staffers who were in town.

Mark thanked her and said he and Doonie had a working dinner planned. Which was true; tonight it would be room service, a heating pad for Doonie and a chance to bullshit with him about the day's events.

"Well," Gale asked, unmistakably, "what are your plans for after dinner?"

Shit. Maybe there was a God.

EIGHTY

So here they were in Mark's relentlessly glossy hotel room.

Gale had—a woman's work is never done—taken the conversational lead and filled the first few bed-talk gaps. She'd given Mark her read of his encounter with de Suau and the Sands. As with her analysis of Fairlie and Hirschberg, Gale nailed the important details and resisted leaping to conclusions.

Later, having run out of harmless murder talk, when the repeated afterglow was especially warm and sex was somehow leading to intimacy, Gale volunteered some detail about her life. A shameless *I'll show you mine if you'll show me yours* ploy.

Gale eased into it with a seemingly innocent revelation. "Just want you to know my attraction to you isn't purely physical. You and I have a great deal in common spiritually."

"You're a Cubs fan?"

"Well, that too—I don't think my father would have fed me if I'd tried to root for the Dodgers."

"Sounds like a reasonable guy."

"He is. But what I meant we have in common, spiritually speaking, is my father is Jewish and my mother's Catholic French-American, so in self-defense I went agnostic."

"But not all the way to godless soulless atheist."

"Well, I go to holiday services and Masses, because I like the rituals. And I think it'd be rude to enjoy the show but deny the possibility it has an Executive Producer. Or insist that a lot of good-hearted people are dead wrong about it."

"That *is* very polite of you," Mark allowed.

And from there it was off to the races.

Gale Michaels had led a reasonably happy, remarkably un-tough life. She wasn't sure why she should be sounding apologetic about that—any more than she would have to apologize if she'd had a miserable childhood—but there it was.

Her parents were academics. Dad was an economist turned businessman; he was a partner in a niche software company that created classified applications for the region's aerospace heavies.

Mom was a professor of Art History at USC. Wrote books that required spending significant time in the loveliest parts of Europe.

Gale had a two-years-older sister, Aurélie (named after their maternal great-grandmother), who was an MBA and raising two children and nearly unbearably perfect.

There was a younger brother, Michael (named, depending on which parent you asked, after the guy who played for the Bulls or the guy who painted for the Vatican). Michael was a senior in high school and contemplating a career as a musician/actor/video-game designer/oceanographer/activist.

Gale admired her parents' lives. But she didn't possess enough of their scholarly grit to make it all the way to PhD-land. Gale scored a Master's in Lit, then wrote, and rewrote, and rewrote and rewrote the first fifty-three pages of a novel she didn't like. Her parents were willing to support her a while longer, but they'd raised her with too much Catholic Jewish agnostic guilt for her to live like a trust-fund flake. So she took her Master's degree out for a spin, landed the usual temp office jobs, and worked her way up to art gallery sales associate.

Florence Brock saved her. One of Florence's favorite hobbies.

Gale's parents had been friends with the Brocks for ages,

since Ed Brock invested in Dad's start-up. When Florence's previous assistant fell in love and moved to New Zealand, Florence offered Gale the job—informing Gale that if waiting hand and foot on an imperious old broad didn't drive her to a real career and/or marriage, nothing would.

So far the job had been a dream. Taking care of Florence Brock's personal logistics hadn't been aggravating or demeaning. The two of them spent a lot of time bopping around to some of the coolest places on Earth, meeting incredible people who were doing worthwhile things. Then there were the less than incredible people who were merely wealthy or powerful and made worthwhile and/or dreadful things happen; totally interesting.

And so while, yeah, life as a paid secretary/companion would eventually get too trivial to bear, it was, right now, a hell of a ride.

"For instance," Gale pointed out, "if it weren't for 'Aunt Flo' I never would've met you."

"I don't even qualify as one of those less than incredible people."

"You're not wealthy?"

"I'll be getting a dollar from Calvin Hirschberg after Wilson Willetts wins the competition."

"Watcha gonna buy me?"

"What makes you think I'm gonna blow my fortune on you?"

Gale showed him.

Afterward, in the floaty quiet, she murmured a request for him to tell her a little bit about himself. The little bit about family, friends, school, career.

Mark licked some sweat off the nape of Gale's neck and thought about how he might put it.

Mark might tell her how he grew up on Chicago's North Side,

in quiet, mid-middle-class West Rogers Park. Had a brother, Ben, three years older. Their father managed a hardware store. Their mother was a nurse. When Mark was nine they got divorced. Neither parent ever saw a reason to tell the boys why.

Ben never asked. Ben went to the U of I Circle campus in Chicago, drank, dropped out, drank some more. Drank with a girl from Indianapolis whose father and uncles owned a tire store. Ben got married, moved to Indianapolis, sold tires, had two kids, and drank less, most of the time.

Mark went to the University of Wisconsin at Madison. Majored in European history. Senior year he received an unsolicited offer of a scholarship to grad school. It was from a professor who invited Mark to become his research assistant. Mark asked what a research assistant did. The professor explained there was no teaching or grading of papers involved. All Mark would have to do was assemble the research materials for—and write the rough draft of—the professor's next book.

That June Mark collected his diploma. Didn't apply to grad school. Wanted some time off. School had been his full-time occupation since age four. And he wasn't ready to commit to spending the rest of his life there by becoming a professor. He was a little too street for the academic life. A little too intellectual for the street.

So now he had to find a way to temporarily make enough of a living so he wouldn't have to live at home for however long it took to figure out what the hell you do with the fifty or sixty years after you've been freed from homework.

Mark's parents, separately but nearly verbatimly, told him he needed to pick a career, get at it, and stick to it. A week would be plenty of time to think it through.

Mark's maternal grandfather advised him to take the summer off and hit the road. Grandpa handed him an envelope containing a graduation present that made it possible.

Europe called like the Sirens, but Mark wasn't a Greek warrior-king-adventurer-gloryhound, he was a midwesterner who didn't want to halve the length of his odyssey by blowing a big chunk of his budget on transatlantic airfare during peak tourist season. Mark put on hold his dream of visiting the continent he'd studied and sleeping with its women.

Mark headed up to the Rockies. Met some people, slept with an American woman who improved his camping skills. Loved the mountains, but realized he was, for better or worse, a city boy.

Mark headed down across the desert, which was impressive, physically and in the way it seemed to attract so many extreme people. Slept with a way older woman (thirty-four) who owned more guns than any guy Mark knew. Taught him to sight-in a scope.

Mark headed to the Pacific, which was how he came to visit Los Angeles, briefly. The air was depressing, Hollywood Boulevard was depressing, he wasn't interested in amusement parks, he didn't know how to surf, he couldn't get into the supposedly hot clubs because the doors were guarded by Fashion Inspectors.

Mark headed north. Big Sur was beautiful but expensive. Mark met a blissful young macramé artist who made hairy, itchy-looking wall hangings. She took him home; said before she could meld chakras with him they'd have to spend a chaste night on her healing bed, which had a drawer full of crystals in the frame under the mattress. Mark spent the night on her couch.

San Francisco was also beautiful and expensive. Had good music bars with people who liked to talk, but who had rigid requirements about being hip and politically aware and got angry with anyone who brought up facts. Mark continued north, figuring he'd pilgrimage up the coast to the grunge Mecca, Seattle.

He stopped in Eureka, where the damp, steep fern and redwood forest climbed straight up out of the sea into the sky. Mark headed into the mountains, camped by a small lake. Mugged a trout, when one of his casts hooked the fish on the side of its head. Climbed a real big tree. Tried to do some serious thinking. Watched the stars. Watched satellites streaking across the night sky. Wondered if he'd blown it by turning down the corrupt scholarship deal. Masturbated.

He hiked down to the nearest road, hitched a ride back into town with Zelda and Roberta, who were not only from New York, they were a band: the Generous Dykes. Zelda played bass and Roberta played keyboards. They'd decided to get as far away from the East Village as possible, get their music together, and not come home from the wilderness till their chops were sharp as sushi knives.

Mark actually told them a little about himself. Zelda and Roberta totally got what Mark was going through. They invited him to crash at their place, which was this surprisingly cushy three-bedroom cabin overlooking the ocean. (Zelda's stepdad owned twenty-seven Burger King franchises on Long Island.)

They built a fire and did mushrooms. The Generous Dykes jammed and Mark sat in on tambourine and cowbell and conga. When they got too high to play, the Generous Dykes lived up to their name and took Mark to bed. Improved his woman-touching skills.

They crawled out of the sack the following afternoon, made coffee, rolled a joint. Zelda asked Mark if he wanted to hang with them a while, rehearse, maybe turn into their drummer. Roberta laughed and said, "Yeah, we're gonna totally turn you into a Generous Dyke."

Mark went Hmmm, took a looooong toke. Wow. As a

temporary thing to do while not living at home and figuring out what to do with his life, this was like having a wet dream come true.

They drove into town to pick up groceries. Mark went to a pay phone to call Mom. Figured he should let her know he'd be in the aptly named Eureka for the foreseeable future.

His mom told him his dad had had a serious stroke three days ago.

Mark flew back to Chicago.

When it became clear Mark's dad would need care for the rest of his life, the woman Mark's dad had been living with left him.

Mark's mom took her ex-husband back and hired a caregiver. Didn't work out. Dad and Mom weren't getting along, Dad and the caregiver weren't getting along.

Mark took over as caregiver, but, fact was, Dad was deteriorating. Sooner rather than later Dad would have to move into a facility. Which Dad's insurance wouldn't cover, and Mom couldn't afford if she was going to have a penny or a life of her own.

Down in Indianapolis, Mark's brother Ben had just had his second kid; the only help Ben could provide was the occasional free set of tires.

Mark looked around at what work was immediately available and paid decently. He stopped doing drugs. When his system had cleared enough to pass the blood and urine tests he took the entrance exam for the police department.

He took to the job.

Four years in, his dad had another stroke and Mark's original reason for becoming a cop got swallowed by a cemetery in Schaumburg.

Mark's friends urged him to return to school or look for something more lucrative. Well, all the women did. Some of the guys kinda liked having an old friend who was a cop, that testosterone-by-association thing; assumed he'd move on but kinda hoped he'd keep the gig.

Mark was going back and forth on the topic himself, when he met Molly and they became engaged for six hours. When Molly demanded he give up the job or her, Mark kept the job. Didn't even think; just knew.

One night Mark was off duty when he walked out of a bar off Damen, heard gunfire from around the corner, and found a robbery in progress that had turned into a shootout with a couple of cops. One of the cops was trading bullets with three perps holed up in a jewelry store, and the other uni was down, bleeding and groaning, in the fucking middle of the fucking crossfire. Mark yelled and flashed his shield at the healthy cop, tore ass to the wounded uni, and dragged him to cover, then things went black. Woke up in Northwestern Hospital with a .38-caliber body-piercing.

When Mark was fit for duty the Department gave him a little something to pin on his uniform and asked if there was any assignment he'd like. Mark said he'd like to ditch the uniform and work Homicide. They gave him the gold badge, put him on Robbery for six months to make sure he wasn't just a lucky reckless idiot, then handed him over to Detective John Dunegan.

Mark didn't put it that way to the perceptive, achingly sweet and lissome young woman he was lying next to. What he said to Gale was, "I have some family, I have some friends, I got a liberal arts degree which was just as utilitarian as yours. Then I got this job as a cop in Chicago whose greater cosmic purpose was obviously to lead me to meeting you . . . Details to follow, sometime when we're both awake."

"How about tomorrow night?"

"Probably not. Tomorrow's gonna be hectic."

Gale looked at him. A little concerned. Trying not to show she was wondering if she should be disappointed. Or angry.

"That's not a brush-off," Mark said, quietly. "It's a fact. Stuff is happening. Another fact: You will be seeing me again."

True and true. Stuff *was* happening.

That afternoon, when Gale dropped him at Parker Center after leaving LAFAM, Mark had caught up on everybody else's day.

Doonie wasn't at the office; his back had gotten so bad he'd actually gone to see Florence Brock's acupuncturist.

Teo Ochoa was in—just gotten back from the hospital. J'nette Levaux was doing well. And Guadalupe Ramos was ready to cooperate. Sort of.

Guadalupe's deceased employer had not been entirely unconnected to the *Eme*, the Mexican Mafia. Who apparently were as interested as the cops in any help Guadalupe might provide in identifying the shooter.

That morning two gentlemen had shown up at the hospital to pay their respects. Despite the bouquet one carried, something about their shaved heads and gang tats caused the cop guarding Guadalupe's room to ask the gentlemen to wait while he asked if she wanted to see them.

She didn't. Moot point. When the cop went back out into the corridor the bald gentlemen were already gone. Having left the flowers on the cop's chair.

Guadalupe got a phone call. From out in the hall the cop, who was Hispanic, heard the old woman pleading with the caller to believe she had not seen the killer. When he went into the room to see if she was okay, Guadalupe quickly hung up. The cop called Ochoa.

Ochoa as usual brought the photo arrays. But this time he ordered Guadalupe to look at them. Told Guadalupe he'd know if she was lying and pretended not to recognize the shooter.

Told Guadalupe if she lied, he'd let the *Eme* hear she *had* seen the shooter; then he'd remove the cop from her door. But if she cooperated he'd protect her by putting the word out she hadn't seen the shooter.

Her choice.

She made the right one.

Ochoa started her off with the photos of women who owned the relevant dirt bikes. But ten minutes in, Guadalupe was laid low by a fierce headache and dizziness. Couldn't focus on the pictures.

Ochoa checked with her doctor; the symptoms were common for that kind of head trauma, and Guadalupe's chart showed she'd been suffering identical symptoms for several days. The doctor told Ochoa to try again in the morning.

Tomorrow would also be the third day since the lab had gotten Hector Benvanides' DNA sample. The preliminary results would be back by noon.

Mark couldn't go into any of those specifics with Gale.

"Don't know whether I'll be free tomorrow night," Mark told her. "But we will be seeing each other again." He kissed her. "And again."

They didn't have any more sex that night. They fell asleep in each other's arms. And woke up that way.

To the sound of Doonie pounding on the door. It was 7 a.m., Doonie's back was feeling a lot better and he wanted Bergman to get his ass in gear.

EIGHTY-ONE

Del Sutton didn't think his boss was being paranoid. And in fact it took only a couple of hours to confirm this wiseass Detective Bergman was not really in town to bang that juicy piece who worked for Florence Brock.

Sutton had gotten a call from his boss, who was at the LAFAM reception, saying this Chicago cop had shown up with Gale Michaels on his arm, the cop and the snotty niblet acting all hard and wet with each other.

Easy enough to believe any guy would've flown out here just to sling the niblet's legs around his shoulders. Except this Bergman happened to be one of the Homicide dicks who'd busted their patsy, Meelo. The coincidence smelled bad, no?

Yes. Sutton got a couple of people over to LAFAM quick. The boss fingered Bergman. Sutton's people tailed the cop when he and Michaels left.

The juicy niblet drove Bergman to Parker Center. Not exactly vacation central. But who knows, maybe Bergman was making a courtesy call.

Sutton's people spotted Bergman leaving Parker in an unmarked cruiser driven by a big Hispanic in plainclothes. They drove to St. Joe's in Burbank. Went to the hospital's fourth floor, where they visited a black woman, a wounded LAPD cop. One J'nette Levaux, the detective who'd gotten shot during that odd triple murder up in Sunland.

So, shit . . . What had that Sunland thing been about? And

how was this dick from Chicago connected?

The large Hispanic dude dropped Bergman back downtown, at the New Hikune. Bergman went to the eleventh floor, let himself into a room; couple of minutes later he went to the room next door where an older guy let him in. Room service delivered two dinners.

The second room was registered to a John Dunegan; Bergman's partner, the other detective who'd worked the Willetts case.

An ID came in on the Hispanic plainclothesman: Teophilo Ochoa. Homicide dick. Levaux's partner. Had been there for the triple-whacking in Sunland. Sutton put some people on finding out exactly what had been going on there . . . Though from the newspapers Sutton could make the outline. The guy in the car with a bullet through his head, that was a hit. The two dudes in the house where the shooter had been, that was collateral damage.

Sutton wanted to see a picture of the vic. Newspaper report made him Hispanic, male, twenty-five to thirty years old. Sutton wanted to know how much the dead man resembled Meelo . . . His ruminations were interrupted by a late report from the New Hikune.

Bergman had gone back to his own room a little after ten. Half an hour later Gale Michaels showed up at his door.

Shit. Son of a bitch was here to fuck with the Willetts case *and* bang the juicy niblet. Sutton's kind of cop.

Sutton called his boss, said they needed to talk in person, now. Went to the mansion, briefed the boss: If the vic in Sunland was the Meelo-look-alike shooter, it meant the other shooters were cleaning house. Which meant they knew the cops were onto something. Which meant Meelo's trial in Chicago was a sham . . . Was that possible? . . . Didn't fucking matter. If the shooters were worried about the cops busting them it was time for Sutton and his boss to worry: The murder agent, Stephan Densford-Kent, knew Sutton's name and the boss'. If the shit was hitting the fan Densford-Kent now had a good reason to give their names to the shooters, since Sutton and his boss were the only potential witnesses against them.

Prudence dictated doing unto the shooters before they did unto us.

First priority was to scoop up Densford-Kent, persuade the crusty old fuck to give up the names of the shooters. Then bury him.

The boss concurred. And ordered Sutton to also stop or at least slow down the Chicago cops' progress. No way should Sutton let those detectives get to the shooters before he did.

Sutton thought that was a dicey proposition but kept the opinion to himself.

The boss frowned thoughtfully for a moment; came up with a plan to intimidate the cops.

Shit. Silence was no longer golden. Sutton had to say out loud the plan was too risky and would probably backfire.

The boss asked if Sutton had a better plan.

Sutton said not yet, but he'd work on it.

The boss ordered him to grab the Brit *and* make the intimidation move on the cops. Right away.

Sutton wanted no part of the cop thing. Said so.

A cold moment. Then the boss wrote a dollar figure on a piece of paper and showed it to Sutton.

It was a brain-jamming, bowel-clearing number. Sutton could not turn that number down. But he tried; told the boss he wanted half up front.

The boss nodded. No hesitation.

Fuck. Just what Sutton had always wanted: Too much money. Fuck. Okay. He'd take the risk, wrap this up, cash out, and walk the hell away from this megalomaniac. Forever.

EIGHTY-TWO

When Mark opened his room's door just a crack Doonie's eyes lit up, because Doonie knew what the blocked view of the bed meant.

"Meet you in the coffee shop," Doonie said, before Mark could tell Doonie to meet him in the coffee shop.

Wasted discretion.

Mark and Gale were showering when the phone rang. Doonie, calling on his cell. From the coffee shop. All he'd done was lift a fucking coffee cup and his fucking back fucking tightened up so bad he couldn't get himself out of the fucking chair he was fucking wedged into at the fucking counter. Manager offered to call a fucking meat wagon but fuck that.

When they got downstairs Doonie was trying to fucking banter with a concerned waitress but was holding himself rigidly with his elbows propped on the counter, pale, a wince cemented on his face.

As Mark knew it would, the sight of Gale improved Doonie's mood; Mark and Gale had gone and fulfilled the fantasy Doonie and Aunt Flo had had on their behalf.

The sight of the rigid man being eased out of the stool and into a hotel wheelchair by a young couple with wet hair and clothes clinging to their damp bodies also raised the spirits of the coffee shop staff and patrons, who had little doubt where Mark and Gale had been when the phone rang.

Mark wheeled his partner out into the lobby and paused.

"Hospital? Acupuncturist? Or," Mark suggested, "Chicago?"

Doonie scowled. "Even if I was ready ta quit on ya, I couldn't last five hours in some fuckin' airline sardine seat."

"Won't have to," Gale said, touching Doonie's shoulder. "You can take Florence's plane, stretch out in a bunk. And there's bourbon."

Mark gave Doonie a significant look. "The Gulfstream. Dream come true."

Doonie tried to shake his head. Flinched. "Just get me to the fuckin' doctor," he muttered, disgusted. "Let's see what the fuckin' drugs do."

"I'll get the car—" Mark started to say, but his cell rang.

It was Teo Ochoa. Prelim DNA was back. It was now a scientific probability (certainty would take another week) that Hector Benvanides, the man whose partial print had been found in murdered tattoo artist Ralph Garn's abandoned van, was also the man whose arm Naguib Darwahab had scratched, immediately after the man had shot Wilson Willetts. Ochoa suggested Mark join him and Levaux at the hospital to help lower the boom on Guadalupe Ramos, make her identify the woman who shot Hector B.

"Get to work," Doonie instructed Mark. "I'll take a cab."

"I'll drive you," Gale told Doonie.

"Nah, ya don't haveta do that," Doonie said.

"Like you have a choice," Gale scoffed, grabbing the handles of the wheelchair.

"Yes ma'am," Doonie demurred, giving Mark a small sly glance: *You have met your Phyl, buddy.*

Gale kissed Mark. "Call me when you can."

Gale wheeled Doonie out. The door shut behind them.

"Yes ma'am," Mark murmured.

Mark phoned Lieutenant Husak and let him know crunch time

had officially started.

Husak would inform Superintendent Blivins, who'd inform State's Attorney Sy Vytautis, who'd let Harrison Miller and Carrie Eli know it was time to get an adjournment from Judge Santini, so they could try to work a deal with PD Paul Obed and Meelo to keep things under wraps another day or two.

After Mark finished with Husak he put in a call to Carrie. Got her voicemail. Left a quick heads-up. Told her he'd e-mail the photo arrays of the twelve hundred women who owned the relevant Kawasakis and/or had motorcycle licenses. Told Carrie even if she couldn't cut a deal with Meelo to stay quiet and in jail a few days more, she had to get Meelo to look through those photos and find Heather. Sooner the better.

Because Mark wasn't expecting anything but migraines, double vision, and dizziness from Guadalupe Ramos.

EIGHTY-THREE

"Ella," Guadalupe said. Reluctant, but certain. *"Es ella."*

They'd been through all one-hundred-eighty-seven Kawasaki owners' photos, gotten no hits, and were some three hundred head-shots into the motorcycle DLs when Guadalupe stopped. Stared at a photo. Looked away. Closed her eyes. Opened them, looked at Ochoa, who was standing alongside her bed. Looked at Mark. Looked at J'nette Levaux, who was sitting in a wheelchair; looked at J'nette a while. Then reluctantly pointed at a photo. Hand trembling. *"Ella. Es ella."*

"Seguro?" Ochoa asked. Somberly. Demanding honesty.

The old woman sighed and sadly, gingerly, tapped on the photo. *"Sí."*

Ochoa looked at Mark and J'nette.

They both nodded imperceptibly. Yeah, Guadalupe was telling the truth. She wasn't faking how guilty—and terrified—she felt about fingering the shooter who'd spared her life, and might now be looking for revenge.

Shooter named Gloria Blair, according to her motorcycle license.

No need for Guadalupe to have taken it so hard. Gloria Blair had a real motorcycle DL but a fake address, phone number, and social security number.

The fake address was in Culver City, which was south and west. Mark and Ochoa got a search warrant and rendezvoused down there with a backup team, which seemed sensible considering how extremely armed and dangerous the young woman had proven herself to be. Except neither she nor anyone else was living in the abandoned storefront that matched the address on her license.

Mark and Ochoa checked with the local post office; Gloria Blair had posted a change-of-address notice so her mail was forwarded to a commercial mail drop in Encino. Which was north.

They drove up the 405. For Mark, a Walter Brennan flash: the dang trail was jammed solid, so Ochoa moseyed off at Montana and took Sepulveda on up over the Pass down on into the Valley. Where they found the commercial mail drop. A box was registered in Gloria Blair's name, with her fictitious address and nonexistent phone number. Records showed she'd paid cash.

Dusted the mail box for prints. Dang thing were blanker 'n a banker's conscience.

Mark called Doonie. Woke him up; he'd had a breakfast of muscle relaxers. Gave Doonie a quick rundown of the morning's fun and told him to go back to sleep.

Mark and Ochoa continued their freeway-intensive day. Mostly the traffic moved better than in Chicago, but the monster mileage felt all wrong—this was like driving to Milwaukee and back without leaving town. Now they were heading east across the Valley, back to Parker Center. Not talking much. Ochoa driving, Mark contemplating the photo of Gloria Blair, aka Heather, aka who knows how many other aliases, with good paper to back them up.

Meelo had described Heather as having long brown hair and brown eyes.

Gloria Blair had short black hair and green eyes; wig,

definitely, and contacts, probably. Looked Latina, but could pass for a lot of ethnicities. Young unlined glowing-flesh pretty, but fully adult—sturdy, wolfishly confident. Gazing coolly into the camera with an almost playful, challenging knowingness— Mark suddenly felt he knew what Heather/Gloria's expression was about. At the instant her picture was taken she'd anticipated this moment, a cop studying this photo . . . *Stare all you want, Officer. Never gonna lay a finger on me.*

Mark imagined those eyes, brown, intense, peering through the scope of the ERMA SR100, the back of his head filling the left side of the field of view, the crosshairs right on the edge of his ear, past which was Hector B's forehead.

Those eyes, brown, intense, peering out of a black Lycra ski mask, the crack of a .32 automatic—

—J'nette Levaux sprawled on a rocky dry yellow-dirt slope, bleeding out. That kiss, alive with fear and defiance and pure longing to be touched, to be known. The deep-gut relief of going to the hospital every day and seeing J'nette alive . . .

Oh man, how do people live with being married to a cop . . .

Gale Michaels. Shit. Word "marriage" goes through his head and next image up is Gale, pungently scented and sweetly exhausted, curled against him . . . Fuck, he had a bad case of it, he could get really nuts about this girl really fast . . . But that wasn't love. Yeah it was a connection, it was real. But love— trust—wasn't fast, at least not for Mark . . . How did regular humans do it—be flat total gone in love? Get to the point where they could just jump out of that airplane? . . . Maybe there was nothing wrong with him. Maybe he was just honest, and he honestly hadn't yet met—

His cell burbled. He flipped it open. "Bergman."

Carrie purred in his ear: "Mark, there's something I need you to know: I was the only one near them who didn't puke."

"Huh?"

"The Harrison Miller Vomit-Fest didn't make headlines in L.A.? Never mind, I'll explain later. The real headline: Meelo took the deal."

"No shit," Mark said. Get cracked for weapons/dope and spend a year in the can, or spend two more days inside and then walk; there's a sensible decision even Meelo could make.

"Better yet—the other reason I called—about eight hundred faces into the photo array, Meelo spotted Heather."

"So did our witness. Gloria Blair. It's a fake. Dead end."

"Gloria Blair," Carrie said, sounding for some reason dryly amused. "Hold on a sec."

Mark heard computer keys tapping.

Then Carrie, pleased: "Holy shit. It's her again."

"Again?"

"Just pulled up your Gloria Blair. Except for the green eyes and that godawful black wig—the blunt-cut Dutchboy thing is all wrong for her—she's a dead ringer for the face Meelo picked out: brown-eyed, brown-haired Elena Esquivel. You want Esquivel's address?"

EIGHTY-FOUR

So Heather had two motorcycle licenses, two names. Right.

Another warrant, another SWAT team. Better result.

It was early evening when they arrived. Unlike Heather/Gloria's, Heather/Elena's address was attached to a residence. In Chatsworth, at the far north end of the Valley. Nicely restored two-bedroom 1950s ranch house behind a tall hedge. Comfy, private, inconspicuous, perfect home for a single professional killer.

The single professional killer didn't answer her mellow chiming doorbell, so Mark and Ochoa used their warrant and a two-hundred-and-fifty-pound SWAT with a ram to let themselves in.

There was a trail of bloodstains leading from the garage through the kitchen and into the bathroom. Someone had cleaned up the bathroom just enough to smear the fingerprints and shoeprints off the bloodstained fixtures, walls, and floor.

In the garage there was a Volvo C70 convertible, and a Ford Explorer with a green Kawasaki Super Sherpa in its cargo bed; bloodstains in the SUV and on the bike. Ochoa ran the plates. All three vehicles were registered to a corporation, Chatsworth Alliance, headquartered in a post office box.

The garbage in the kitchen can was fragrant, a couple of days overdue to be taken out; the top layer was bloody towels and bandages.

The bedroom showed signs of someone having packed in a hurry.

A quick toss of the house turned up no address books, no documents linking Gloria/Elena to family, friends, or places. A file drawer in her desk had been emptied and the hard drive had been removed from her desktop computer. A more thorough search uncovered a floor safe under the oven; stash contained some guns and ammo, but no documents relating to Heather's many identities. Someone had removed all the significant shit. Gloria/Elena looked to have lost too much blood to have managed that by herself.

Mark had an idea who the someone was. Like Meelo said ten or thirty times during his epic confession, *That Oscar thinks of everything.*

Crime scene techs lifted prints and swabs from the house and vehicles, and hustled back to Parker Center.

It was dark when the cops canvassed the neighbors, see if anyone had noticed a wounded Elena Esquivel coming or going.

Three houses up the road, in a mock-Tudor mansionette, Mark and Ochoa met the Wonder Drunk.

Mindy James, with her slightly stained stretch-fabric blouse she should've stopped wearing fifteen pounds earlier, her desperately girlish ponytail that had partly escaped its pink scrunchy, her blowzy cocktail breath, her permanent alcohol sullenness poking through her mock-friendly demeanor, was the woman of Mark Bergman and Teo Ochoa's dreams.

The Wonder Drunk had several evenings ago been driving down the road when, "Some maniac backs out of that Esqvel's driveway maybe, what, fifty, sixty milesanhour, damjizz my bumper. Sixty milesanhour.

"A truck. Dunno what kine-a truck . . . Shiny . . . Very shiny, beige, a beige truck. Little smaller than my S'burban—but doing fifty, sixty milesanhour, backasswards.

"That Esqvel wasn't driving, she was inna passenger seat, din't even get out. This little guy—not little, this just sorta nothingy guy gets out, and—No, don't remember what he was wearing, it was gettin' dark and I was in shock from this accident—he was kinda bald, nothingy little moustache, maybe forty, fifty, he was like early middle-age years old—and he gives me sev—uh, three hundred bucks to just forget about it, and he's kind of— *mean*—allofasudden *mean*, nasty, so I just took the cash . . . And I got his license plate, just in case, y'know, the three hundred din't cover my bumper damjizz.

"No, I din't write it down, I mesmerized—whoops, mem-orized it. Always been good at minonics, y'know where you mesmerize things with minonic devices?"

Ochoa ran the plate number Mindy James was certain she'd mesmerized.

While Ochoa was doing that, Mark showed Mindy James a police sketch of Oscar based on Meelo's description.

"Imagine him without the beard," Mark suggested.

The Wonder Drunk studied the sketch, scrunched her nose in concentration. Shrugged.

But if her visual abilities were limited, her mathematical skills were up in pickled idiot savant range; the Wonder Drunk got better results from minonic devices than Mark had ever managed with mnemonics.

Plate came up a beige Toyota 4Runner. Registered to a corporation called Ojai Associates. Headquartered, of course, inside some fucking PO box.

They put out an APB on the truck and ran the Ojai Associates incorporation papers. President was one William Pacelli, who resided in the same mailbox his firm did.

DMV search turned up three William Pacellis. William Dante

Pacelli was seventy-four and lived in Truckee. William L. Pacelli was nineteen and lived in La Cañada-Flintridge.

William Pacelli, no middle initial, was forty-three, lived in San Francisco, and quick online map check showed his address was in the middle of what was now a parking lot for Pac Bell Park.

Ochoa got on the phone. Ojai Associates had purchased the 4Runner at a Toyota dealership in Oakland. After the five-thousand-mile service the truck had never been back for maintenance or repairs, even the free warranty oil changes and tune-ups. And, of course, the address William Pacelli had put on the repair forms was the Ojai PO box. Along with a bogus phone number.

Mark had an idea. "Esquivel's front is the Chatsworth Alliance, and she and her vehicles live in Chatsworth. Pacelli's front is Ojai Associates, so let's say he keeps his truck in Ojai. The 4Runner is three years old, and the Wonder Drunk said it was cherry, so . . ."

Ochoa nodded and glanced at his watch. It was twenty after eight. "Tomorrow morning. Good thing tomorrow's a Saturday."

Mark grunted his agreement; if tomorrow was a Sunday they'd be fucked. This way, first thing in the morning they'd start checking the maintenance records at Toyota dealerships in the Ojai area, see if they got a hit on the 4Runner whose tag numbers had been mesmerized by the Wonder Drunk.

Mark called Doonie, to update him and see how he was doing. Phone was busy.

Later that evening Mark and Ochoa were putting in overtime at Parker Center filing paperwork when they got a call from one of the techs. She'd lifted three sets of prints in Esquivel's house. Gotten one hit. Big hit.

Dina Velaros.

Dina Velaros had a juvie jacket from San Diego County. Busted at age fourteen, prosty. Pled guilty, did three months, went to a county home, then a series of foster families.

Mother a crack whore, OD'd while Dina was doing her ninety days in the joint.

Father unknown.

Dina graduated high school with good grades; county records ended there. Computer search turned up a model citizen, Dina Velaros, who'd gotten her shit together and graduated—3.78 GPA—from UC San Diego, BA in Psych. Then she disappeared. Not that anyone had filed a missing persons. Dina Velaros' paper trail just stopped.

Ochoa's fax spat out a copy of fourteen-year-old Dina Velaros' booking photo.

It was her. Gloria/Elena. At just a touch older than Patty Dunegan was today.

So pretty. So young. Looked more twelve than fourteen—though she already had Gloria Blair's eyes, doing that statement stare right through the camera: *Go ahead, bring it.* But unlike in the Gloria Blair and Elena Esquivel photos, fourteen-year-old Dina still had a lot of kid in her, in that photo taken the day she was busted for fucking and blow-jobbing losers in alleys.

EIGHTY-FIVE

Mark left Parker Center around 10:00 p.m. Walked to his hyper-gloss hotel. Called Doonie from the lobby, asked if he wanted to go find a real bar.

Doonie said no, told Mark to come to his room.

Mark hurried. It wasn't just that Doonie had turned down a drink. It was how neutral and grim he sounded. Ugly. This wasn't about back pain.

When Doonie opened the door he was moving stiffly but was oblivious to his physical condition. He nodded for Mark to sit. Asked, too quietly, what Mark and Ochoa had found today.

Mark gave him the update. Then asked, softly, "What?"

Doonie muttered his way through the facts, fast and simple.

When Phyl got home from work today, house seemed empty. Kieran and Tom were away, they and their pals had driven down to Champaign to catch a Bears game, would be gone for the weekend. But Patty should've been home from soccer practice.

There was an envelope on the kitchen table.

There was a photograph inside. Patty. Asleep in her bed, stripped . . . legs spread. Back of the picture said BACK OFF WILLETTS OR PATTY'S PHOTOS GO PUBLIC.

Phyl ran to Patty's room. Found her unconscious. Zonked out, drugged.

Phyl got Patty dressed, called Doonie. He called Lieutenant Husak, who sent over an unmarked car to take them to the

365

hospital; didn't want a meat wagon fuss, neighbors asking questions.

While that was happening Doonie called Kieran and Tom. They were okay; he told them to get home. Then Doonie called Mark's mom, made sure she was okay. Told her there'd been a threat made relating to a case, told her not to worry, but be careful. Asked if she'd mind having a bodyguard a few days.

She would mind. Doonie told her all right, but phone right away if anything suspicious happened.

Phyl called from the hospital. Patty was unharmed. Hadn't been molested.

Patty didn't remember much. Just she got back from soccer and there was something odd about the house. Then somebody grabbed her. That's all.

The intruders must've been waiting. Must've doped her with something that had amnesiac side effects.

So far Patty was only a little freaked. But that would get worse soon as the drugs were totally out of her system and she had time to think. Then there was what it would do to her if those pricks put pictures of her on the Web or something. For now Doonie and Phyl weren't telling Patty she'd been photographed.

Phyl was holding it together like always, but . . . Phyl kept saying our house has been violated, our house has been violated . . . Like, y'know?

Yeah. Mark knew. Like Phyl couldn't bring herself to say Patty had been violated, even if she hadn't been raped. Even if these scumbags didn't follow through and post the naked shots of her . . .

Doonie'd arranged for a patrol car to sweep the street in front and alley behind Mark's mom's building once an hour all night. "You should call her, tell her she should let us put a bodyguard on her."

"Uh-huh," Mark nodded. "And you should get on a plane."

Doonie shook his head. "Phyl can handle it."

"Doon, you should be wi—"

Doonie's lip curled back. "I'm fucking *here.*"

Mark didn't say anything. Knew better than to argue when Doonie got like this. Not that Mark had ever seen him quite like this.

"Told Phyl my back is too screwed to fly," Doonie went on. "I'm going to work tomorrow—and we don't tell anyone—*anyone*—in the LAPD about this, not till we know who gave us away. Husak is with me on that."

Mark didn't think they should keep this from Ochoa, but nodded.

"Gonna find out who ordered this done to my family," Doonie grumbled. Leaned forward a little. "I'm gonna shoot his dick off. Then kill him."

"I know," Mark said. Then: "How about we get a bottle of Jack from room service?"

Doonie said, "No."

Mark returned to his room, phoned his mother, woke her up. Told her there was a small problem, asked would she please put up with having a bodyguard for a few days and not finding out exactly why until he got home. Mark said he had no reason to believe there was any threat to her, but someone they were investigating had sent a message to Doonie, at home. So this was just to be on the safe side.

Mark's mother, sleepy but sharp—she had a nurse's ability to go from zero to sixty as needed—said a bodyguard couldn't come to work with her, he'd scare the patients, who wouldn't believe she'd have a bodyguard if there was no danger.

Mark said the guard could sit at the nurse's station.

Mark's mother wanted to know if Mark was in any danger.

He told her, "Not at all," and she pretended to be reassured.

There were some situations in which Mark was grateful for his family's fanatical impassivity.

Mark phoned Gale. She was awake, offered to come over. Mark thanked her, said he was beat. Had a dawn start tomorrow. Stuff happening. Couldn't tell her about it. Just called because he wanted to say goodnight.

Gale said, "I miss you too."

Took Mark a while to get to sleep. Trying to figure what he was going to do about Doonie. Doonie, who'd taken the time to put security on Mark's mom before he'd even heard back from the hospital how his own daughter was. Doonie, who hadn't been blowing smoke in that threat he just made. Mark recognized the tone. Patty's dad meant to make good on every word. Verbatim.

Mark liked the idea. But he also had to make sure it didn't happen.

That should be fun.

EIGHTY-SIX

Mark, Doonie, and Ochoa were at Parker Center dialing Ojai numbers at 7 a.m., the minute live people start answering the phones at dealership repair departments.

The three Toyota dealerships in the general area had no record of servicing a truck with those plates.

The cops starting calling independent repair shops. Ochoa got a Miguel Terkassian, owner of Mira Monte Foreign Auto Specialists. Terkassian knew the shiny beige 4Runner the cops were talking about. But since Ochoa was just a voice on the phone, claiming to be a cop, Terkassian wasn't about to divulge any information about one of his clients.

Ochoa gave him the number of Parker Center and waited. Terkassian didn't call back. Ochoa called the Ojai PD. They sent a couple of cops over to Mira Monte Foreign Auto Service and informed the owner about the downside of impeding a murder investigation. Terkassian gave them a name—William Pacelli—with an address, and three phone numbers from three different repairs.

The address was a sham, and two of the phone numbers were for expired disposables. But the third was from a residence in the hills just outside of Ojai. Gotcha.

Ochoa got in touch with the Ventura County courts and had valid paper by noon. He and the two Chicago cops were barreling up the 101 to rendezvous with the Ventura SWATs when Mark's cell went off.

It was Carrie. With big, if unsurprising, news. Mark thanked her, hung up, and told the others, "That was Chicago. Meelo just ID'd Pacelli's DL photo. William Pacelli is Oscar."

Ochoa gave a small pleased nod. "We are headed to the right place."

Mark grunted his agreement.

"Pacelli and Velaros could still be there," Ochoa continued, "holing up while she recuperates."

"That would be too easy," Mark warned. But, yeah, the case had finally cracked, things were moving. Felt right.

Except for Doonie, sitting in the back seat like a large, glowering black hole, sucking all the energy out of the car.

Ochoa couldn't fail to notice. But if he wondered if Doonie's mood was about anything more than back pain, he'd been too polite to ask. So far.

Ninety miles north of L.A., Ochoa hung a right; within minutes of the car exiting the coast-hugging highway and heading east the air went from ocean cool and damp to desert warm and dry.

Ojai, nestled in a pretty valley in the steep foothills of the Santa Ynez Mountains about a half-hour inland, was a farm town that had been repurposed as a SoCal lifestyle statement. Its modest main drag and meandering side roads were dotted with luxury spas, cute restaurants, storefront galleries featuring therapeutic candles and traumatic ceramics. There was also a police headquarters where Ventura County SWATs were saddled up and ready to go. They led the way up a serpentine two-laner, on a ten-minute drive into the mountains.

Once again Mark strapped on LAPD kevlar so he could go ring a doorbell.

Once again there was no sign of anyone being home.

Once again the cops vandalized the front door and surged in.

Once again a quick toss turned up nothing unusual, except a complete lack of a personal documents. There was a DSL hookup but the computer, apparently a laptop, was gone.

Ventura County's small forensics unit was occupied working two violent crime scenes, and this wasn't their case anyway, so they agreed to let LAPD guys process the house. So while the L.A. techs were en route, Mark, Doonie, and Ochoa had time to make another, more careful toss. Especially for signs the wounded Dina Velaros had been there.

Bathroom had been scrubbed to death. Kitchen garbage can was empty and stank of Lysol.

Ochoa took the master bedroom; Mark and Doonie went over the guest bedroom.

Doonie poked around in an armoire. Mark was examining the bed. It had clean sheets but there was no mattress pad; odd, for a place this meticulously maintained. There were no bloodstains on the mattress. Mark lifted it; there were bloodstains on the underside. Dry but recent. Someone—Pacelli—had removed the blood-soaked mattress pad and turned the mattress bloody-side down.

"Hi, Dina," Mark said.

Doonie grunted. He was on his knees, bent low, at who knows what cost, reaching under the armoire.

"You guys find something?" Ochoa, appearing in the doorway.

"Dustballs," Doonie muttered, as he slowly, creakily pulled out from under the armoire and cautiously straightened up.

"This." Mark, at the bed, lifted the mattress, showing the maroon-splotched underside. "Bet it's hers."

Ochoa nodded. Doonie seemed less than interested.

Odd. Or maybe not. Maybe it was the back pills, dulling him. That would be a good thing right now.

The crime scene techs arrived. While the residue brigade

processed William Pacelli's house, the detectives canvassed what there were in the way of neighbors. The nearest lived a quarter-mile away.

Three of the locals were familiar with the beige 4Runner driven by a phenomenally average guy. Two knew him by the name of Bill. Pleasant, polite, quiet, very private man. Seemed bright and kind of formal. Like a lawyer or a professor, but not arrogant.

No one actually knew what Bill did for a living, or where he went when he wasn't in Ojai. Nobody recalled seeing him for months, which was not unusual, or informative; Bill might've been out of town, or been there the whole time.

They grabbed some dinner on the way back to Parker Center. By the time they got there forensics on Pacelli's house had begun to trickle in. The place had been scrubbed unnaturally clean, no prints anywhere, not even on the toothpaste tube. Then the techs did an inch-by-inch of the house and discovered two hidden caches. In the garage's concrete floor a disguised hatch led to an underground armory. Weapons. Silencers—most probably milled on the excellent metalworking tools in the garage. Ammo. Video surveillance and eavesdropping gear. Cash, in used bills. No ID papers of any kind.

The second cache was behind a wall in the master bathroom; a hidden closet packed with neatly arranged and labeled stage makeup, including wigs, noses, latex, tinted contacts.

The techs pulled some partials off of a couple of .307 hollowpoints in one of the many preloaded clips Pacelli had stockpiled. They also pulled two complete prints off the surface of the cream inside a jar of cold cream in Pacelli's makeup stash. The prints matched several found in Dina Velaros' house in Chatsworth. Ochoa had already run those, hadn't gotten a hit; if those prints were Pacelli's, he'd never been arrested, or served in the military, or been a cop.

Dina's prints weren't found in Pacelli's house, but the blood stains on the mattress provided DNA the techs were running against samples from Dina's house and the rooster ranch.

They called it a night. Ochoa said they'd made some real progress, they were getting close, he could feel it. Mark agreed. Doonie gave a token nod, his mind elsewhere.

Eighty-Seven

When they got back to the hotel they went straight to their rooms; Doonie said he needed to talk to Mark, but first he had to check in with Phyl. Mark said to give his love to Phyl and asked if it was too late for him to give Patty a call. Doonie said, no, that'd be nice, the kid would like that.

Soon as Patty said hello Mark started ragging on her about how *this* was the time of day you called someone in another city, not the crack of dawn.

Patty said any time you needed to talk was the right time to call.

Mark launched into an ongoing riff of theirs, said it was not a law of nature you had to be on the phone and/or messaging your friends every second you were awake.

Patty said it was too a law of nature, obviously, 'cause everybody did it. She and Mark talked trash about it, almost like normal.

Mark didn't ask how Patty was or make any reference to what had happened. Told her hey, last time he saw her, her birthday party, he was totally embarrassed by how lame he bowled. Soon as he got home he was gonna take her and her friends bowling—at some alley that wasn't lit like the inside of a dance club in a video game set on another planet. He was gonna spot her fifty pins a game and kick her ass anyway.

After a moment Patty said, very quietly, "Everybody's too

nice to me. You don't have to suddenly be nice to me."

Mark said, "I've always been nice to you. Nothing's changed."

After a long silence during which Patty's breathing changed a few times, she asked Mark which stars he'd seen so far. Mark said none of them, and asked which ones it was most important for him to see. Patty sorted through the variables and finally settled on Colin Farrell and Jennifer Garner.

Talked twenty minutes. Mark never got a laugh out of Patty. A first.

Patty said Mom was off the phone with Dad and wanted to say hi. She handed her phone to Phyl.

Mark asked Phyl how she was doing. Phyl said, "Okay." Not very convincingly. Asked Mark to hold on a minute. She went out into the yard so she could talk in private.

When Phyl was alone, she quietly inquired, "How is he?" Meaning Doonie. Meaning, *I know what's on his mind.*

"Don't worry," Mark told her. Quietly. Firmly. Meaning, *I won't let him do it.*

Phyl sobbed, once. As if it were a luxury she was permitting herself.

Mark went back to Doonie's room. Doonie thanked him for calling Patty. Said Patty and Phyl were doing okay, considering . . . Well, shit, last night, Patty, Patty, the kid wet her bed. So humiliated by that, worse than from getting grabbed and spiked and waking up naked . . . Y'know?

Yeah. Mark asked if Kieran and Tom were back.

The boys were home safe. Everything was locked tight. Superintendent Blivins had called Phyl himself. Put twenty-four-hour surveillance on, ordered volunteer off-duty cops to bodyguard all three kids, Phyl, and Mark's mom. So the barn door was closed, now the horse was fucking gone; cocksuckers could post those pictures of Patty any time they felt.

Mark asked how Doonie was doing.

Doonie indicated a latex glove that was sitting on his desk, then nodded at his jacket, which was slung over a chair, and in a dark, dry, empty voice said, "Right-hand pocket."

Mark pulled the glove on and reached into Doonie's jacket pocket. Pulled out a crumpled, bloodstained piece of paper.

A wine label. From a place called the "A. Reid Winery," in Paso Robles. And the wine was named, "Cuvée Dina."

"Found it under that dresser, in Pacelli's place," Doonie rasped.

Yeah. That's why he'd been so quiet. "What're you planning," Mark asked, as if he didn't know.

"Go to this winery, have a private talk with this Reid guy, who I bet looks just like Pacelli and Oscar. Gonna ask what he knows about what happened to Patty; if he didn't order it, who's he think did? You go into work tomorrow, tell Ochoa I couldn't make it 'cause my back is fucked again."

"Your back *is* fucked. Paso Robles is a couple of hundred miles up the coast, I think. You're in no shape to make that drive, forget take on this guy."

"So you come with. But only if you want. This ain't on you."

"Yeah, right, Doon, we phone Ochoa and say we're both taking the day off, it's against our religion to work Sundays."

"I'm fucking doing this."

"No, Doon, I'm doing this, you're fucking going to show up for work bright and early, tell Ochoa I uh, I came down with the raging shits, was up all night, took a sleeping pill at dawn . . . That's the only way it'll work."

"It might be your badge."

"Yeah."

Doonie regarded Mark balefully. Wondering how far to trust him.

"I'll do what's necessary to open the guy up," Mark promised his partner. "But even if it's him, I ain't shooting his dick off.

That's all yours."

Doonie closed his eyes. For a moment Mark thought Doonie was about to get rational—or at least guilty enough about getting Mark involved—to call it off. But then Doonie opened his eyes and said a low, hard, "Okay."

Mark returned to his room, fired up his laptop, and went looking for the A. Reid Winery. No web site; an unusually shy winery. But Mark did track down a phone number and address, in the online yellow pages. Sherlock Holmes lives.

Sherlock stretched out on the bed. Tried to get a few hours' rest. Tried to imagine how much time, logic, and bourbon it'd take to talk his distraught, concrete-headed partner into settling for finding the perp and merely beating him half to death. Failed on both counts. All Mark could do from here on was make sure he got to every suspect before Doonie could.

At 5 a.m. Mark got into his rental and headed for Paso Robles.

EIGHTY-EIGHT

"No, we're not going to punch down the cap more frequently."

"We're not extracting fast enough."

"Chip, this juice is brilliant."

"Which is why it would be a sin to retard it."

Arthur Reid and Chip Bozeman were in the heart of the A. Reid Winery, a converted barn. The two men were standing by one of the facility's three six-hundred-gallon stainless steel tanks, having their first serious philosophical dispute.

Before being transferred to the elite barrels that were stacked at the far end of the room (Gamba barrels—French oak, crafted by Italian coopers, seven hundred dollars a pop), the wine would ferment in the steel tanks for six months. Question was, exactly how much should that fermentation get massaged?

Arthur drew a sample from a tank, sipped, swirled the juice across his tongue. Tried to extrapolate what this raw young semi-fermented syrah would be like when it grew up, given proper guidance. Or proper lack of it.

"It's already showing sizable fruit and lushness. Doesn't need any manipulation. That's why I got you these Vespasian Patch grapes and made sure they were picked the day you wanted," Arthur said, reminding Chip whose wallet this winery was standing on.

The passionate young winemaker was undeterred by that irrelevant data. "You have to take the juice where it wants to go, and this juice is begging for intensified maceration."

"It's going exactly where it should. You're the one who keeps saying syrah wants oxygen more than it wants phenols."

"I stopped saying that two weeks ago."

Arthur was all sympathy and no threat as he laid down the law, disguised as a suggestion. "Let's make the wine we planned to."

"We planned to make a great wine! The way to get the greatest possible wine out of this juice is to macerate the carefully monitored shit out of it!" Chip was grinning, enthusiastic, pacing across the winery, flinging his arms, gesturing at the gleaming steel tanks, preaching to his employer/congregation. "It's got the backbone to take on the extra size! Power up without losing grace! Arthur, we are gonna make a fucking elegant monster—Syrahnasaurus Rex!

"That," Preacher Chip concluded-pleaded-vowed, "is the greatest greatness we can get out of these grapes."

True—given a young man's definition of greatness. Arthur's went in a more austere, complex direction.

At the beginning Chip had been on the same page with Arthur. The intent was to make a restrained, aristocratically dry syrah. Full but firm, a wine meant to incandesce with fine food. An American homage—and rival—to the Hermitages of French classicist Louis Chave.

But the past few weeks, with each tasting, Arthur had seen Chip get more and more seduced by the plush fruit's promise of voluptuous glories. The kid was dying to start punching down the cap two, three times a day.

The cap was the glop of grape skins and stems that continually floated to the top of the tank; punching those skins and stems down forced them back into contact with more of the juice, which extracted more of the phenols from the solids. Which resulted in a plumper, more bravura wine. Which might only match up with a narrow range of food. Or possibly with none at all. A plump, bravura soloist of a wine.

Arthur liked Chip, looked forward to working with him for years. If Arthur flat overruled him, Chip would feel his artistic integrity had been violated and start looking for purpler pastures. So if it was at all possible Arthur didn't want to command, he wanted to cajole. He wanted consensus.

For starters he reexamined the possibility Chip was right. Took another taste, from another tank. Shut his eyes and played chemist-artist-fortuneteller . . . No. Plumper wouldn't be greater, it would be a flashy waste. A novelty act. Not a wine that would ever appear on a White House dinner table alongside a roast.

Besides, plump was not a direction he could go with a wine named Cuvée Dina.

Dina.

That last night together, in the Ojai house.

It had been an hour since Arthur, stretched out fully clothed on his bed, had heard Dina come out of the bathroom. Heard her bite back a gasp of pain as she eased into bed. Heard Dina's breathing become softer and more regular as she finally drifted.

Arthur went silently to her open doorway. Matched his breathing to hers. Stood there with the most desperate, stinging, mournful hard-on of his adult life as he tried to logically, rationally slog his way through the biggest decision of his adult life. A decision he'd already made, but couldn't keep from going over and over.

Arthur slipped into a silent debate with the sleeping Dina.

"I had to do it," the unconscious woman insisted.

"Behind my back?"

"There wasn't time for us to argue the merits. And I trust you. I trust you know why I did it."

"Then there's how you did it. Not making sure that bastard

with the knife was dead."

"A mistake."

"Not one you've made before."

"Not one I'll make again."

"Failing to finish him with a head-shot was careless. But leaving the housekeeper alive, that was—if you did this for us, to make sure it was safe for us to stay in this country, to raise a family—"

"And safe for you to keep your winery."

"Then why did you leave a witness alive?"

"You've already guessed the reason."

"Your earliest memory."

In Arthur's mind Dina nodded, Yes.

Arthur continued. "The look on your grandmother's face. You're four. Your grandmother catches your mother stealing from her purse. Your mother pulls a knife. The look on your grandmother's face when she saw your mother point a knife at her."

Dina didn't respond. Just defiantly held his gaze through her shut eyelids.

"You killed three people for us, to make us safe, then risked everything because the housekeeper had the same scared look as your grandmother."

"I loved her."

"No excuse. Not in this business."

"We just got out of this business."

"But I can't trust you any more."

"You can forgive me."

"This business, which we can get out of but never get free of, doesn't leave room for that."

"This business doesn't love me. You do."

"I . . ."

Arthur wasn't sure what came after that. Like so many others, who usually had versions of this argument out loud with conscious partners, Arthur gave up in frustration and walked out of the house.

Half-moon, lots of stars. Arthur gazed at the stars for a while. Got as much insight out of them as an astrologer does.

The cool night air did the job. His emotions and erectile tissue receded. His mind returned to its normal rigorous compartmentalized state. Got back to work:

Dina had just plain melted down. This close to the wire, she melted down.

But none of this would've happened if *he* hadn't taken this Willetts gig, this insanely complicated . . . No, the pressure of the job hadn't gotten to her.

It was worse than that. It was the pressure of him putting her off all these years. He'd driven her nuts with every kind of desire. For his approval, for his company, for his touch, for his love, for a life. If he'd let it happen, she never would've done this. She wouldn't have needed to do this and dare him to not forgive her.

Or maybe, if they'd become lovers, they simply would've gotten distracted and sloppy and busted. Or dead. Not maybe. Probably. Which was why they hadn't risked it.

Irrelevant. Irrelevant whose fault it was. Fact was Dina had cracked. Dina could no longer be relied on. Dina had to get on a plane and leave. For a long time.

Then, when the investigation finally, decisively dead-ends, and Dina is safe, what happens between Arthur and Dina when—if—she returns? Could they . . . No. It was over.

Was it? He still loved her.

Couldn't count on her.

Could forgive her.

No. The thing they'd chosen isn't about forgiveness. It's about survival.

It's not about love. The lethal wild card. Lets people make irrational demands that have to be honored. Puts them both in so much danger just because of that look on her grandmother's face . . . And now there's a witness who can give the cops Dina's face.

So, Dina's face, before she comes home, if she ever comes home, will have to be altered . . . Even if he did see Dina again, he'd never see her face again.

Arthur was surprised how much that hurt.

Irrelevant.

It's over.

Of course, Dina refused to put up with that. Right there in the goddamn airport, in line at the goddamn metal detector, she gets out of the goddamn wheelchair, reiterates "I had to do it," and just stands there refusing to goddamn move. As if this were the perfect time and place to have this little chat.

He had to get her on that plane. He just needed to tell her one little lie. Yes, I love you, we're still on, lifetime, stuck with each other. Now go, and we'll fix everything. He—

He couldn't say it. Couldn't lie to her. She'd screwed up but she'd never lied to him. There it was—another of those goddamn demands people you love can make on you that have to be honored.

What the fuck was wrong with him? He'd always been able to do the necessary, done things that had given even him nightmares, and now he couldn't tell one small profound lie.

But, as always, he had a fallback plan. In this case, a silent lie.

He pulled out a Cuvée Dina label and handed it to her. Let Dina misinterpret it. Let her think the label meant as much and held the same promise as it had before she'd broken discipline—

He kissed her. First time ever. Hadn't planned on it. Just

happened. And for an instant he saw himself rushing to the counter, grabbing a ticket, and flying away with her.

Instead he watched her pass through the metal detector and disappear into the terminal. As he watched her go he felt a cramping in the calf muscles of both legs. Was amused at what a strange place that was to be feeling this kind of loss.

On the drive home his calves continued to ache for Dina. And California seemed strangely empty . . . Arthur had a total of two friends in the world. He'd just lost the closest one . . . He wondered, how many people's best friends had he killed? . . . Jesus, put that pathetic adolescent crap away and get to work.

Arthur, slowed by sporadic attacks of cramping calves, cleaned up the Ojai house. Decided it was time to sell it.

Drove back to Paso that night. To his dream home, the winery. Put Dina behind him.

If he needs to love something, pour his hopes into something, he's got it. The syrah.

Arthur finished contemplating the wine sample. Opened his eyes.

Chip was grinning at him, trying to appear confident Arthur had come to the obvious, the only possible conclusion about punching down the cap. But Chip's grin, like the rest of his body, his being, was eerily motionless, frozen in the space between heartbeats as he waited to hear the decision that would determine the fate of the most important vintage of his life and maybe the universe.

Arthur imagined informing the kid this vintage meant even more than that to him, and explaining why.

Instead he quietly told Chip, "We're not going to punch down the cap any more than we already do. We're going to let this wine make itself."

Chip caught the finality in Arthur's tone. Disliked it.

Accepted it. Mastered an urge to make a last-ditch plea. Mustered a degree of grace. "Fucking tragedy, but not a fucking disaster. Make a different wine, but still a great one . . . The wine," Chip admitted, "that you—we—planned to make."

Not bad. The kid wasn't all talent, brains, and idealism. Had some spine. Who knows. Someday Chip Bozeman might be Arthur's third friend—

"POLICE! FREEZE!" a voice barked from somewhere behind Arthur, who looked over his shoulder and saw a plainclothes cop in the doorway at the other end of the winery.

"Whoa! Chill, dude." Chip, who was facing the man, stayed cool, as if having a gun pointed at him was no hassle. Assumed this was some prank or bizarre error not worth tripping over.

Arthur recognized the cop's face: Detective Bergman, from Chicago. Alone.

"Hands on your heads! NOW!"

Arthur nodded for Chip to obey. They both started to raise their hands. With one hand Arthur flung Chip toward the cop, as with his other hand he pulled his gun and fired. Knowing the cop wouldn't shoot back, with Chip between them.

Arthur squeezed off two rounds in the direction of Chip and the cop, and dove to the nearest cover, behind the middle steel tank.

EIGHTY-NINE

A half-hour earlier Mark had exited the 101 at Paso Robles and easily found—all hail MapQuest—a narrow country road that roller-coasted up, down, and around fat, undulating, mustard-colored midget mountains. On the lower slopes there were a few modest homes and some crapped-out semi-abandoned farms. But tucked into the shadier, woodsier hillsides were mini-Taras, with horses posing in pastures framed by fragrant stands of eucalyptus. And on some of the upper, steeper slopes there were vineyards. Some of the vineyards had wineries.

One had a sign out front so modest it was easy to miss. Mark drove past the curiously bashful A. Reid Winery. Parked in a pullout a quarter-mile down. Walked back. Found cover. Took out compact binoculars.

The place was set thirty yards back from the road, behind an idyllic front yard; some kind of weeping willowish trees, rose bushes, antique well and arbor. The main building was a two-story remodeled Victorian. Three-car garage on the left. Up a path to the right was a remodeled barn.

All three garage doors were shut. There were two vehicles parked under trees alongside the driveway. An old Neon. A new Dodge pickup.

Two men came out of the house and headed up the path toward the barn. One man was young and short. The other man was Bill and Oscar.

A middle-aged Hispanic woman emerged from the house and

called out. The men stopped walking and she went to them. She said something to Bill/Oscar, gesturing in the direction of the Neon. Bill/Oscar took something out of his pocket and handed it to her.

The men went into the barn, the woman back into the house. A minute later a garage door opened and a beige 4Runner pulled out, with the woman at the wheel. The truck was wearing the tags that had been minonically mesmerized.

The 4Runner drove away. Mark waited. Didn't see anyone else on the property except for the army of bare gray crucified vines.

And in the house? No way to tell. Could be nobody or anybody. Maybe Dina Velaros.

First things first. Mark moved in on the barn or wine-shed or whatever the hell the building was officially designated in its present incarnation.

They were arguing about their syrah; life and death shit. Mark overheard enough to find out the young guy's name was Chip. And Bill/Oscar's name was—surprise—Arthur.

Mark stepped inside and announced the bad news.

Suddenly the young guy was launched toward Mark, staggering, flailing, in the line of fire between him and Arthur. Mark couldn't shoot.

Arthur did, twice, and lunged behind a huge steel tank. Mark got one clear glimpse and snapped off a shot. Missed Arthur, hit the tank, put a hole in it. A hard stream of red liquid spurted out.

Mark took semi-useless cover behind a stack of empty wooden wine barrels. Saw Chip, with a miraculous lack of bullet-holes in him, standing slightly hunched over, arms birdwing-wide for balance, eyes cartoon-wide in disbelieving terror, frozen in that odd position, as if standing dead still would render him invisible and bulletproof.

"GET DOWN!" Mark roared.

Chip considered the suggestion a moment then abruptly tried to go from dead still to a dead run, slipped on the wine-wet floor, tripped over his own feet, hurtled jaw-first into one of the thick steel uprights of a small fork-lift. Went down hard, unconscious before he hit the ground. But not dead, judging from the soft moaning.

Mark yelled for Arthur to toss the gun and come out with his hands on his head.

Arthur had no angle from which he could shoot at Mark without exposing himself. But he could stick a hand around the curve of the tank and fire blind in the general direction of the young guy splayed on the ground. Two bullets smacked the floor near Chip, spraying him with splinters of lead and concrete.

Mark held his fire.

Arthur threw another blind shot in Chip's direction. Missed him by an inch.

Message received. Mark could hang back and watch Chip get shot, or he could rush out and get killed trying to drag him to cover.

Mark muttered "Shit," just loud enough for Arthur to hear, then rushed out toward Chip—and immediately dove hard to his left—

Arthur surged out from behind the tank—

Four shots. Two apiece.

Arthur's first missed Mark. The second gashed Mark's upper right thigh.

Mark's first missed Arthur and punched another hole in the steel tank. Second shot tore through Arthur's midsection. He doubled up, a marionette whose strings had been slashed, and his momentum carried him butt-first into a wall. He bounced off and fell face-down. Lost his gun, but he was done with it anyway.

Mark scrambled up and started to hurry to check on Chip, and that gave the hot pain in his leg just the boost it needed to overwhelm his endorphins. Mark stiffened—Fuck-fuck-*fuck!*—but hobbled over to Chip—keeping his gun and one eye on Arthur, who, making a Herculean effort, was rolling onto his side and levering himself upright enough to sit sagged back against the wall.

Mark got to Chip. Kid still had a pulse and a lack of bullet holes. Jaw looked broken. Neck felt like it wasn't.

Mark went to Arthur, who, bless the tough fucker, was gutshot and flooding blood but still alive enough to talk. When Mark went to pull Arthur's hands off his abdomen so he could inspect the wound, Arthur shook his head once.

"Done."

Mark pried Arthur's hands open. Saw the damage. Arthur's diagnosis was correct. Any minute now.

Mark asked, "Who ordered that thing in Chicago yesterday?"

Arthur, not looking at Mark, just gazing across the winery, murmured, with some difficulty, "Don't know. F-first I heard. Nothing—with me."

What Mark figured. Pro shooter wouldn't be stupid or spendthrift enough to go after a cop's family. "Who hired you to kill Willetts?"

"Don't know. Done thr—" Arthur grimaced, gathered what he had left, ". . . c-cut-outs." Kept staring across the room, not in agony but with immense regret. As if the pain from Arthur's wound was nothing compared to the sadness of some other loss he was preoccupied with . . .

The leaking wine.

Okay. "Who hired you," Mark demanded.

Arthur didn't seem to hear him.

Mark fired a bullet into one of the other tanks. Another fountain of red juice erupted into the room.

"No," Arthur ordered, with a quiet force that was kind of remarkable for the living dead.

Mark looked at him.

"Don't know," Arthur insisted. In a papery whisper. Running on empty.

Mark aimed his gun at the third, final, tank. Arthur groaned, except it was a growl, the sound of a dying predator threatening to come back from beyond the grave and punish Mark if he shot his last tank of wine.

Mark put a bullet into the final tank—up high, so only the top quarter would leak out. Glanced at Arthur, then extended his arm, aimed at the lower half of the not yet fatally wounded tank.

"Promise," Arthur gasped. "Promise you—tape t-the holes."

"Deal."

"Del Sut-sutton . . . chief—security for Jordan Sand."

"Del Sutton, Jordan Sand," Mark repeated, to make sure he had them right.

"*Duct tape*," Arthur moaned insistently through gritted teeth, nodding in the direction of an equipment cabinet.

Mark didn't move. "One more thing—where's Dina?"

Arthur broke out in a subtle, wistful grin. Tried to explain; shuddered. Locked eyes with Mark. Made a soft noise Mark couldn't decipher.

Mark leaned down, put an ear close to Arthur's mouth.

"My calves are cramping," Arthur confided, and died.

His calves are cramping? Another addition to the list of mysteries Mark knew he'd never solve. But an inspiration for Mark to prepare a decent set of last words, just in case.

He closed Arthur's eyes. Spent a moment watching Arthur's blood blend with the tide of exotic red juice swirling down the drain in the winery floor.

Limped over to the door, sneaked a look at the house. If Dina was in there she would've heard the shots. Mark had to go check, see if Dina was there and if he could do a better job of taking her into custody than he had with Arthur.

But first Mark limped to the cabinet where Arthur indicated the duct tape was stashed. Arthur ponied up, now it was Mark's turn; keeping deals is what makes the world work. It'd just take a minute—second tank was the only one Mark could rescue. The first tank was almost bled out. And there was no way, with this leg, Mark could get up a ladder to tape the hole high up on the third tank. Which wasn't going to lose much anyway.

Armed with a roll of silvery tape Mark hobbled back to the second tank. Struggled to get the tape to stick to the wet slippery steel and staunch the tremendous pressure, spraying generous amounts of wine on himself in the process—

Chip groaned, unconsciously reprimanding Mark for not doing his duty and calling for medical assistance.

Sorry Mark had to clear the house before he could do that. Mark half-hoped Dina wasn't there; that way he could call 911 and be gone before the local cops and EMTs arrived. If Mark stayed, he'd have to turn over his weapon until Arthur/Bill/Oscar was declared a righteous shoot. And then he'd have to explain what the hell he was doing there, out of jurisdiction, alone, busting suspects known to be armed and dangerous, after tracking them down using a key piece of evidence he'd concealed from his LAPD liaison, Teo Ochoa, who was stand-up and didn't deserve Mark pulling this shit on him.

Mark managed to bandage the wounded tank. He pulled his gun and sloshed over to the barn door. His shoes were wine-logged, his clothing soaked, red and pungent. A big improvement over being drenched in J'nette Levaux's blood, but still not quite looking or smelling the way he should while representing the Chicago PD. Beer-soaked would've been more like it.

Mark paused at the winery door, scanned the house carefully for a sign Sniper Girl was lurking behind one of those windows. As if she'd be careless enough to give herself away.

Shit. No sensible way to go at this, beyond limping over there fast as he could. No choice. Had to clear that house, bandage his leg and borrow a set of dry clothing from Arthur, who owed him that much.

Mark took a few deep breaths and squished out of the barn.

As Mark stepped through the door a large man grabbed his gun hand as another, even larger dude drove a lineman-sized fist into Mark's solar plexus.

Wasn't so bad. The glue on the duct tape across his mouth fouled his tongue, but the drug they'd shot him up with was a mother; he resented being curled in the trunk of some car with his ankles taped together and his hands taped behind him, but didn't mind it. The pain from the gash on his leg detached from his body and floated away. He got some sleep.

NINETY

Yes, things were getting a little hairy, but, all in all, Jordan Sand was enjoying himself. Unlike his dour chief of security, Del Sutton—Sutton's job, after all, was to deal with worst-possible-case scenarios—Sand's life was about success. About making best-possible-case scenarios come true. You couldn't get there by being pessimistic, unhappy, small.

Big Jordan Sand didn't worry about not succeeding on the first try. He just had to keep his eye on the goal. Stay smart. Tenacious. And lucky. He was, he had to admit, blessed. The cosmos seemed to like him.

Take, for instance, his attempt to intimidate the Chicago cops by arranging that little photo shoot of underage police-daughter snatch. To Sand, his plan seem an easily comprehended combination of visceral impact and rational negotiation. The message was, *You are out-manned, out-funded, up against a vastly superior force that can reach into your homes at any time. Yet we have neither hurt nor sexually assaulted the girl. Be reasonable, and we never will go that far. Be unreasonable, and we can ruin her life by publishing the pictures, without even having to come back and get physical. Though if you push us, we can get nasty as we like, any time we like.*

Anyone capable of simple cost-benefit analysis would back off.

Sutton had argued the cops were capable of that analysis—and their bottom line, based on centuries of experience, was no police department could enforce the law if police families were targeted. That's why the traditional response to an assault on a cop's family had been ultra-violent off-the-books retaliation.

Sand felt that made sense on a local level, but surely the cops would see this elimination of a lone architect was a special, one-time-only situation which was not truly their concern, would not affect their ability to police their city—and they were up against an opponent who was way out of their league.

Sutton didn't directly tell Sand he was wrong; just declined to take part.

Then Sand wrote a number on a piece of paper and Sutton decided going into a cop's home was an acceptable risk.

But, as it turned out, Sutton had been correct; the photo-shoot hadn't stopped or even slowed the investigation. Which—the cosmos smiles on Jordan Sand yet again—turned out to be a good thing, because Sutton had hit the wall on Priority Number One: scooping up Stephan Densford-Kent.

Densford-Kent should've been the only one able to identify Del Sutton and Jordan Sand as the men who'd taken a contract on Willets; the shooters shouldn't have been told their names. But now that the shit had hit the fan, Sand wasn't about to bet his life on a murder agent's business ethics.

It was time to grab the old gasbag, slice the names of the shooters out of him, then eradicate him, and them. Problem was, Densford-Kent had disappeared. Left the concierge of his building a note saying he'd be out of town an extended amount of time. No word where he'd gone or for how long.

And no chance to search his apartment for him or for clues. Densford-Kent had left the place in the care of house-sitters. Three hard guys with thick Irish accents. Just who you'd hire to water the houseplants and walk the dog.

Didn't make a difference whether the old bastard was holed up in his apartment or in Katmandu. They'd have to wait him out. Which is why it was so nice of the Chicago cops to stubbornly put law enforcement ahead of their own families' safety and sanity. With Densford-Kent unavailable, those midwestern plodders were the only ones who might lead Sutton's crew to the shooters.

Sand ordered Sutton to put round-the-clock watchers on Bergman and Dunegan. And tap their hotel phones.

The taps paid off big (and Sand got surprising enjoyment out of listening to the tapes; there was a kind of godlike thrill in secretly observing the cops' earnest, oh-so-serious strivings—and messy personal lives). The cops were making real progress. The victim in the Sunland shooting—the cops called him Hector B—was the Meelo look-alike, the shooter who'd done Willetts. The other two shooters, "Oscar" and "Heather," must've whacked Hector B—and warned their agent, Densford-Kent, to make himself scarce.

Following the cops had been a hoot—beat hell out of following sports. Two days ago they'd broken into a house in Chatsworth. Belonged to an Elena Esquivel. Sand was betting Esquivel was "Heather." But she was gone.

Next day the cops hustled all the way up to Ojai and busted down another door. This time the property trashed by the boys in blue belonged to a William Pacelli. Once more they were a day late and a dollar short.

That night both Chicago cops made interesting calls. Dunegan spoke to his wife, who wanted him to come home. Dunegan told her his back was still too painful for him to move around. A lie; he'd been along for the Ojai raid. Sand agreed with Sutton's interpretation: Dunegan, the enraged dad, had fantasies of taking revenge on whoever had taken the photos of his not beautiful but undeniably attractive daughter.

Meanwhile, Bergman had been on the phone with the creamy young bud. Bergman was making nice, trying to entertain the kid. And ignoring the way Patty was flirting with him. What a tantalizing waste; even with Sand's power and position, nothing that young and fresh ever had the hots for him any more. The sweet, yearning sensuality in the girl's voice made Sand wish he'd ordered Sutton to make a video of her in addition to the stills.

Then at some godawful hour early this morning Sand was awakened by a call from Sutton. Bergman had left the hotel—alone—and headed north in his car. Why?

Intrigued, Sand drove over to Sutton's office and joined him while he monitored Bergman's journey up the 101. The team tailing Bergman reported via an encrypted wireless uplink. Sand had to admit he got a kick out of this remote-control spying on the cop's journey up the coast. Like being in the Ops room of his own little CIA.

Bergman just kept driving. The morning got even more intriguing as the cop blew past Ventura; Santa Barbara; San Luis Obispo.

Maybe Bergman had gotten a line on Densford-Kent and was hustling up to San Francisco—no, he would've taken the 5, much faster than the 101. And why was he going alone? Sand offered the opinion that maybe this was evidence Sutton was right about cops' responses to threats on family; the atavistic sons of bitches meant to massacre everybody who might have arranged the photo-shoot. Which would, of course, include him and Sutton.

Sutton just shrugged and said, "Possible." He wasn't going to agree with the notion that Sand's insistence on the photo shoot had backfired—even if it was Sand himself who was bringing it up.

Sand enjoyed that; Mr. Tougher-Than-Thou Del Sutton tiptoeing around anything that could sound like I-told-you-so criticism of his boss.

Then the morning got even better. Bergman stopped in the hills west of Paso Robles. Ditched his car, snuck back to a winery he'd passed. Shot the owner. Guy named Arthur Reid.

Sand ordered Sutton to grab Bergman. Sutton's men wrapped up the cop quick and easy. Then they photographed Reid's corpse and e-mailed it.

Reid was bald and had a small moustache instead of a beard, but otherwise fit Meelo's description of Oscar.

So, two dead and two—Esquivel and Densford-Kent—to go. Sand's cosmic luck was holding.

Sand told Sutton to take the Chicago cop someplace private and do whatever was necessary to find out what else he knew. Sand instructed Sutton to perform the wet-work alone; didn't want Sutton's men to learn any unnecessary details about the Willetts killing.

Sand was tempted to help Sutton slice up the cop, or at least be there to witness it; it was one exercise of power he'd never had a chance to taste, and quite probably never again would . . . Nah. He and Tish had a rare, already twice-postponed private night at the cottage penciled in for tonight. Tish didn't need to be serviced all that often but there was hell to pay whenever he got too busy for too long and Tish began to worry he'd permanently lost interest. And Jordan didn't want to think about what kind of ten-figure sum there'd be to pay if Tish ever opted for a divorce.

Patty Dunegan. Tonight he'd think about Patty Dunegan.

And tomorrow he'd find out where to buy one.

NINETY-ONE

"Unh," Dunegan grunted, when Ochoa asked him to sift Bill Pacelli's financials. Surly, grunted "Unhs" had been Doonie's main form of communication this morning.

What was it with these Chicago cops? When they showed up they seemed to be smart, solid dudes. Then the case gets into gear and Bergman wimps out; he's up all night with the runs, takes a damn sleeping pill, and will be snoozing till who knows when. Worse, Doonie's back locks up and he doesn't wimp out. Seems to be in pain like he should be taking disability retirement, but he insists on limping into work and slowing things down. The one treatment Doonie seems to have gotten is a personality transplant. Was real amiable when he arrived; now the back pain—Ochoa surmised—had turned him into a sullen lump.

Bad enough Ochoa was working a Sunday—missing Mass and *comida* with his family, after a week of not being home in time for dinner, or even to say goodnight to the kids—but with the Chicago guys the way they were, and J'nette still in the hospital, Ochoa was going to have to carry the ball alone.

He immediately began kicking himself for complaining about his good health. Said a quick silent prayer for the recovery of his three co-workers . . . It was just, much as he loved being a cop, each year he was more bothered by seeing not nearly enough of Mandy and the kids. Since making detective he felt as if he'd mainly spent time with his daughter and son at birthday parties, weddings, and other big family get-togethers. Watched more of their sports matches and school plays on tape than in person. It was the kind and amount of time he'd spend with them if he were their uncle and lived in Fresno.

Ochoa stopped brooding and went back to the other point-less thing he'd been doing—sifting the reports on Bill Pacelli's house. The serial numbers had been filed off of every weapon. There were no photos of Pacelli or family or friends or anyplace he might have worked or vacationed. No numbers in his phone's auto-dialers. And Pacelli's phone records contained no calls to anyplace besides local retail establishments.

"Anything there?" Ochoa asked Doonie, about Pacelli's fi-nancials.

"Unh-unh," Doonie grunted. "Tax returns say Pacelli's a 'consultant.' Incorporated in the fuckin' Caymans."

Ochoa nodded. Made a note to have a forensic accountant start banging his head against that brick laundromat—

Got a call from the Paso Robles police. Regarding the APB on Pacelli's well-maintained beige Toyota 4Runner.

They had the truck.

And the driver—a forty-four-year-old female Hispanic. Said she was the housekeeper at the A. Reid Winery. She'd never heard of William Pacelli. Far as she knew the 4Runner belonged to her boss, Arthur Reid. Then the Paso cops showed her Pacel-li's driver's license photo. She said Pacelli's face belonged to Reid, too. Reid was at the winery right now and would be all day. Only other person there was the young winemaker, Chip.

Paso cops asked if they should go pick up this Pacelli/Reid. Ochoa asked them to hold a second. Told Doonie what was happening.

"This guy's dangerous—they should go slow, maybe keep the place under observation till we get there," Doonie suggested, perking up—but in an odd, wary way. "How long it'd take us to get there?"

"Three-hour drive," Ochoa told him. "The Paso guys should be careful but go grab Reid soon's they can."

Doonie mulled that for a moment . . . nodded, kind of reluctantly. Said, "Gonna give Bergman a call."

"You sure? He's not in any shape for a three-hour drive," Ochoa said.

"Nah, he'd want me to wake him," Doonie insisted.

Ochoa advised the Paso cops to surveil the winery and not go in till they scrambled the San Luis Obispo County SWATs. He got off the phone just as Doonie hung up his phone, looking troubled.

"What?" Ochoa asked.

"Nothin', uh . . . I uh couldn't wake him up."

"That's all right."

"Yeah," Doonie agreed. But sounded concerned.

"Hey, not unusual a sleeping pill might knock Bergman out so a phone wouldn't wake him—and maybe he turned the ringer off altogether—"

Ochoa's phone rang. Paso 911 had gotten a call from some guy who sounded bad—both ways—he was in big pain, and his mouth was damaged.

Operator who caught the call could barely make sense of the caller's words. She asked the caller if by "dea'," he meant "dead," as in somebody's dead. The caller made an affirmative grunt. When she asked the caller where he was he said something like "ee einery."

The computer was no help; traced the number to a cell belonging to a Chester Bozeman, home address in Atascadero. The operator asked if he was Chester Bozeman. He was. She asked if he was home and he replied "O, I ah Ee Einery—" then dropped the phone and the connection broke.

The operator contacted the cops.

The Paso duty sergeant yelled out a question to the room at large, asked if anybody remembered which wineries had a long "ee" in their names, and if anybody recognized the name Chester Bozeman.

Arthur Reid's housekeeper did, partly. Bozeman was the last name of the young man, Chip, who made wine for her boss.

So screw surveillance and SWATs—the two nearest units, one Paso car and one CHP—were going in to the A. Reid Winery soon as they could get there. Paso cops promised to update Ochoa soon as they had it locked down.

Ochoa thanked them. Filled Doonie in.

"Hunh," Doonie replied—though this time it was an energized, nearly manic grunt. He hastily dialed his phone again, frowned, hung up.

Ochoa asked, "Bergman?"

"Tried his cell," Doonie nodded. "Got that one turned off too, probably."

"If you wanna run over to the hotel, bang on his door—"

Doonie shook his head.

Shit, right, he doesn't wanna walk. "I'll go—"

"Nah, nah, let him sleep," Doonie insisted.

Odd, Ochoa thought. *Doonie calls Bergman twice in two minutes, really wants him involved, but now he won't let me go wake him . . . Something is strange here.*

"So," Ochoa asked Doonie, "we got a corpse at the winery—any bets who the hell it is?"

The Chicago cop got very still. Pale. Looked like he had a whole bunch to say but didn't want to. Finally just shook his head, grunted an ambiguous, "Unh," and started a slow, pinch-backed tactical retreat to the men's room.

Oh yeah. Something was way the fuck strange.

★ ★ ★ ★ ★

A real long forty minutes later the Paso cops checked in. Ochoa put it on the speakerphone.

The Paso cops had found one dead—Arthur Reid, gunshot.

(Doonie exhaled heavily, seeming relieved, when he heard that.)

Chip Bozeman was wounded—badly broken jaw, severe concussion, going in and out of consciousness. Had trouble articulating, but managed to scrawl some answers on a pad before the EMTs bundled him off. When asked who shot Reid, Bozeman wrote, *"Cop."*

(Doonie stiffened.)

When asked if he knew the cop's name, Bozeman shook his head. Wrote, *"Cop tried arrest. Arthur tried shoot me!!!"*

They asked if he knew where the cop was. Bozeman wrote, *"Men t"* and passed out.

Bozeman slept through his ambulance ride and his arrival at the hospital, where he was shot up with painkillers. Hustled in for X-rays and CAT scans, determine if there was any damage to his skull, brain, neck, or spine. Paso cops said they'd keep someone at Bozeman's bed, try to get more out of him soon as he was awake and coherent.

The Paso cops asked if Ochoa knew who or what *"Men t"* might refer to. He did not.

Ochoa hung up. Looked at Doonie. Who'd turned chalk-white.

"What the hell are you hiding?" Ochoa quietly demanded.

Sounding calm, all business and sick to his stomach, Doonie said, "The cop is Bergman. His rental car is a late-model burgundy Mazda sedan. We gotta get the plate number and put out an APB."

Ochoa did that. Then stared at Doonie.

Doonie grunted softly. Gave Ochoa a quick rundown on what

had happened to Patty.

Shit. No wonder. Ochoa said, "You should've told me."

Dunegan said they would've, but—at the museum Chief Connaught came walking up, pals with the husband of one of the suspects. Doonie and Bergman didn't think it would turn out Connaught was leaking why they were in town—but this was Doonie's child, he wasn't taking any chances the perp would find out what steps they were taking.

Ochoa asked what that was. As if, at this point, he didn't have a pretty good idea.

Doonie got quieter; admitted he'd found an A. Reid wine label at the Ojai house. Early this morning Bergman went up there to check it out.

"And that's the whole reason Bergman's freelancing? Worried the LAPD might tip the perps?" Ochoa pressed, letting Doonie know it was time to level. Past time.

Doonie evaded the question. "We never thought it might be you or Levaux." After another moment he said, "Mark was only gonna push Reid, find out what Reid knew about who did this to my daughter." Added, quietly, "Mark's no murderer."

"No. If the story the Paso cops got from the witness holds up, it was a clean shoot . . . What about you, Doonie? You planning on murdering somebody?"

Defiant silence.

Ochoa examined his conscience, his feelings, and his professional obligations. Decided honesty was the best policy. "You can't," he explained to Doonie, "kill a suspect. And whatever else you do to him . . . Can't do it in front of me."

Doonie growled a barely audible, sincere, "Thanks."

"I got a girl and a boy, eleven and eight . . . Try Bergman's cell again."

They did. No answer. Shit.

NINETY-TWO

Mark woke up bad. Eyes weren't working. Eyes hurt. Everything did. Leg was on fire. Stomach felt crushed. Head grinding, a sour chemical crash. Clothes were clammy and he stank of stale wine and tire rubber. Sitting upright. Couldn't move. Bound. Someone ripped the tape off his mouth. Poured some water in. Mark didn't gag all of it out. His eyes began to focus. He was in a room. Taped to a wooden chair. Sunset light coming in from a large window behind him. A man looking at him. Beneath the odor of wine-rubber Mark scented salt air. Listened. Yeah. The pounding wasn't all in his head. Surf. Close. Outside the window behind him. Mark rolled his head, to loosen his neck and look at as much of the room as he could. Wood walls, expensive vacation-home stuff. Big picture-windows. Room was empty, furniture cleared out. Floor covered with plastic drop cloths. Wasn't a good sign. Especially given the tray table set up next to Mark's chair. A set of surgical tools laid out on it. Next to a neatly folded rubber apron. And, on the floor, a large car battery; attached to the terminals there were cables with nasty-looking clamps. A man was standing about six feet away, looking at him. Didn't care that Mark saw his face. Wasn't expecting Mark to live long enough to ID him.

"Good morning," the man said, despite the fact it was sundown.

The man was about fifty. Straight, flat steel gray hair. Matched his steel gray five-o'clock shadow. And his bushy eyebrows, which were too big for his eyes. Or maybe his eyes were too small for his face. His thin-lipped mouth was tiny, fish-like, especially considering the stair-step jaw beneath it. He was wearing a management-grade black suit over a body of military-grade muscle. His nails were manicured and his knuckles were scarred. He was looking at Mark as if Mark were a minor problem that'd be easy to destroy.

"Tell me everything you know about Elena Esquivel," he advised Mark.

So she wasn't in the house at the winery. And the steel gray man doesn't know her real name is Dina Velaros. There's one small satisfaction Mark could hold onto when the steel gray man started slicing flesh and electrifying genitals.

"She wasn't home." Mark pretended to weigh his options for a few moments. Asked, "How much you get paid to kill a cop?"

The steel gray man pretended to take the bait. "If you want to know how much you're worth," he said, "do what you have to to put yourself on my payroll."

"All I know is she's disappeared."

The steel gray man was disappointed. "You're not as good a liar as you think."

"That's 'cause I'm telling the truth."

The steel gray man studied him a moment. "What's my name?" he asked.

How long were the goons who grabbed me listening outside the winery—shit, no difference. Tell the man his name. "I'm guessing Del Sutton. Head of security for Jordan Sand."

Mr. Sutton acknowledged that with a small nod.

"So," Mark said, "now you know what I know."

"You got a problem you need to outgrow fast, sonny. You're local talent. You think like local talent. You think my job offer was some bullshit interrogation technique, something you and Dunegan—Doonie—would run. You think I'd be afraid to let you go because you guys have your hearts set on killing me."

Sutton grinned. A threatening sight. But a welcome one. Arrogant bastard liked to play with his food. Be a few more minutes before the actual torture began.

NINETY-THREE

Paso cops called Ochoa. Bad news. The missing letters from *"Men t"* were *"ook."* Detective Bergman had been kidnapped.

In the hospital Chip Bozeman had come to long enough to ID a photo of Bergman, then answer questions by typing on a laptop. But the first thing Bozeman typed was a question about the wine—he remembered waking up wet on the winery floor, being relieved when he realized it wasn't blood, it was wine. Wasn't till just now at the hospital he realized *There must've been a big spill*—he typed, WHAT HAPPENED TO MY WINE TANKS!?!?

Paso cops told him one was drained, one half-full, one had been taped and was just oozing a little.

Bozeman refused to answer questions till the cops called a winemaker friend of Bozeman's, told him to get over there and seal the drips, *NOW!* Then Bozeman finally started typing.

Wrote that after he hit the forklift he'd drifted in and out of consciousness. Heard some kind of scuffle, someone getting dragged—and voices, low, sounded like two, three guys. One of them checked Bozeman out—he played unconscious—no problem, the guy kicked Bozeman and he passed out for real. When he came to, they were gone. But his body started working, he could move again. Just a little. Got his cell phone, hit 911. Talked a minute. Passed out again.

Paso cops' initial sweep of the crime scene supported Bozeman's story. Judging from wine-stain footprints in the farmhouse, someone who'd been sloshing around in the winery had then done a quick toss of the house. No sign Dina Velaros had been there.

That same someone also may have taken Reid's gun; there was no weapon found in the winery. Did find one piece of evidence on the winery floor suggesting a cop had been there: a handcuff key. It was in a wine puddle, hidden from view.

The cops combed the area, found no sign of a burgundy Mazda sedan; if Bergman did get snatched, the perps must've taken his car too.

Ochoa thanked the Paso cop, hung up. Looked at Doonie.

The terrible, quiet rage that had possessed the Chicagoan the past few days had been replaced—well, joined by—a terrible dread.

Best keep things as normal as possible. "Gonna order in some lunch," Ochoa said. "Waddaya want?"

Doonie shook his head. Too knotted up to eat. Then, looking down, studying the fascinating top of his desk, muttered, "Shoulda gone with him."

"Three hours in a Mazda," Ochoa scoffed, gently. "You wouldn't have been able to get out of the damn car."

"Yeah," Doonie grunted. Then, raising his eyes and looking at Ochoa: "He went . . . to keep me from . . ."

Ochoa nodded. Thinking, *make that terrible dread plus terrible guilt. Good. Might keep Doonie from crippling whoever it is when they finally bust him.* Unless, of course, Bergman's dead. Then Ochoa would have to disarm Doonie.

Meantime, Ochoa ordered two lunches.

Ochoa and Doonie ate, and waited.

Paso cops forwarded Reid's phone records. They were every bit as useful as Pacelli's had been.

Ochoa sent the Paso cops Dina Velaros' various driver's

license photos. Arthur Reid's housekeeper came up blank; never seen the woman.

Ochoa and Doonie waited.

J'nette Levaux called, just to say hi, let Teo know she was getting sprung from the hospital tomorrow morning. And to ask if something was up—she hadn't heard from anybody the last day and a half.

Ochoa gave J'nette the basics. Promised to update her, when and if.

Ochoa called Mandy, apologized, told her he wouldn't be home for dinner. Asked her to put the kids on so he could catch up with them a little.

Ochoa and Doonie waited.

J'nette rolled into the office in a wheelchair pushed by her fiancé, Thad. J'nette said she was well enough to drive a desk, handle the phones if anything broke.

Ochoa, Doonie, and Levaux waited.

Got a hit on Bergman's car.

Couple of squad cars from Central Traffic were clearing a six-car daisy-chain and fistfight on the 10 east, just south of downtown. Freeway was jammed with drunks—a Lakers game had just let out. Eastbound traffic was stopped while the unis got the combatants separated and their vehicles pulled off onto the shoulder. A uni setting out traffic cones spotted a burgundy Mazda stuck dead center in the gridlock. She ran the plates, got the hit, called it in.

The Mazda was trapped, about a mile from Parker Center.

NINETY-FOUR

For Augie Pugh it had been a whole goddamn day of pissed-off motherfucking hurry up and wait, and now this. Three shitty miles from the chop shop where he was going to ditch the Chicago cop's rental Mazda, and Pugh's trapped—locked solid—on the 10. Nothing to do but sit here sucking fumes from all the fuckheads didn't have the sense to switch off their engines—and to stew about how much of Del Sutton's shit he'd been eating all day—all this year—ever since he put on a few pounds and Sutton started calling him Butter Boy.

Hey Butter Boy, lose the Mazda and lose it right, I don't want so much as a goddamn seat spring ever coming back.

Like Pugh doesn't know what the word "lose" means, a fucking member of Sutton's heavy team. Trusted with shit like snatching a cop.

When they left the winery, Pugh, driving the Mazda, had followed Pyotyr and the snoozing cop to Jordan Sand's new "ranch" on the Central Coast. Ranch, Pugh's ass—fifty spoiled, pure-poodle-bred cows lounging on hundreds of acres of prime oceanfront—with the cattle fenced off so they couldn't drop their registered champion turds within a half-mile of the "ranch house." Place was some tax-loss scam Sand hadn't even stayed at yet, on account of how that arrogant fuck and his snooty bitch had to "renovate" that "ranch house" mansion on the edge of the bluff before the two of them could risk spending a night.

Pugh and Pyotyr entered through the main gate on Highway 1, headed up the "driveway"; eight minutes to drive to the house. Stashed their vehicles in the six-car garage, unloaded Rip Van Winkle from Pyotyr's trunk. It'd be four, five hours before the cop woke up. Plenty of time for Sutton to drive up from L.A.

By the time Sutton arrived Pugh had already tried to contact the two chop shop guys he could trust with this. One had a body shop in East L.A., other one had a junkyard near Brawley, way the hell down by the border—but neither of them were around. East L.A. fuckoff even had a pager but he wasn't responding.

But Sutton sends Pyotyr home, then turns to Pugh and gets all, *Butter Boy, get your chubby ass in gear and lose that car NOW.*

Yessir, Darth Vader Jr., anything you say. Shit. Wasn't like he could dump the goddamn Mazda with just anybody, not with that fucking Jap shitmobile connected to a missing cop.

Pugh finally got hold of the fuckoff in East L.A.; fuckoff said it'd be a couple, three hours before he could do it.

Fine. Three hours was the time it would take Pugh to get down there—and grab a quick lunch on the way—nothing at the goddamn ranch but cattle feed—nah, fuck, better skip lunch, just dump the car, stay to make sure they get it stripped thorough, then get dinner—though shit, it'd be the middle of the goddamn night by then, right before he finally puts his used-up ass to bed—so all the calories were gonna stick to Butter Boy like glue.

But that's not enough. Now there's this unbelievable traffic crap. Pussy-ass Lakers can't close out the fucking Wizards till the final buzzer—so it's one of those rare games where everyfuckingbody leaves the Staples Center at the same goddamn instant—and there's not just a Sig Alert slowdown—it's a daisy-chain accident and a fight and those dipshit LAPD bozos clos-

411

ing the damn road—The fuck? *Shit.*

That big Mex dude in a suit walking down the 10—got fucking plainclothes written all over him and the prick's looking right at *me*—

Ochoa and his men approached the car on foot.

The suspect—white male, forty, large, black suit—spotted Ochoa, got out, and started to run down the narrow lane between the gridlocked vehicles, but pulled up short as he saw other detectives hustling toward him from every side, hemming him in.

The suspect attempted to escape by scrambling across the trunk of the car he was next to, a chopped and channeled '64 Impala convertible. He leapt onto the Chevy's high-gloss trunk and slipped, doing a knee-drop into the trunk lid, denting it, steadied himself by grabbing the top of the rear seat, which is when the rear seat passenger, a fifty-five pound pit bull, buried most of his teeth in the suspect's right wrist and refused to let go, while the suspect frantically, awkwardly, tried to pull his gun from a holster on his right hip with his left hand, as the car's two outraged human passengers stormed out of the front seat, armed with a sawed-off bat and a steel pipe, and began dissuading him.

The cops arrived seconds later, disarmed the car customizers, and, thanks to Ochoa's size, strength, and fearlessness, detached the pit bull from the suspect with a determined yank on the dog's privates.

They disarmed the suspect, cuffed him, ignored his screams about the effect on his shredded wrist, hustled him to their car parked on the shoulder, threw him in the back seat. Where Doonie was sitting. Doonie asked the suspect where Bergman was. The suspect didn't say anything. Doonie didn't repeat the question.

They drove to an abandoned factory east of downtown. Ochoa pulled the suspect out of the car by his collar, dragged him across the factory floor, yanked the lardass upright as easily as if he weighed about the same as the pit bull, slammed him into a wall and asked where Bergman was.

Suspect said he didn't know what Ochoa was talking about.

Doonie put on latex gloves. Ochoa uncuffed the suspect, spun him around, recuffed him with his hands in the front.

The suspect got technical. "I want a lawyer. A lawyer!"

"This is Bergman's partner," Ochoa informed the suspect.

Doonie unzipped the evidence bag containing the car customizer's steel pipe, which already had the suspect's blood on it. Doonie took out the steel pipe. Raised it. Aimed at the dog bite.

NINETY-FIVE

"Truth is," Mark confessed to Sutton, "I'm not sure yet who we got our hearts set on killing. I was betting Sand."

"Why?"

"The consistent amateurish idiocy. Pro wouldn't have risked all that ricky-tick shit setting up a fall guy in the Willetts shoot. Would've left it an unsolved street crime, walked away clean."

Sutton verified Mark's conjecture with a hint of a world-weary shrug: *I'm like you pal, a working stiff stuck taking orders.*

Mark gave a knowing flex of the eyebrows to indicate his blue-collar solidarity. "Then, to top it by going into a cop's home, messing with his family—now we've got an idiot on a roll."

"Yeah. The photo session was another Jordan Sand brain-storm."

"Then he's the only one we want."

"So why'd you waste Reid?"

"Second Reid saw me he started cranking; I was just looking to bust him."

A sly, conspiratorial edition of Sutton's poisonous grin. "Then why'd you go up there alone?"

"Needed a private word with him, find out who his idiot client was."

"So you and the outraged Daddy aren't out to whack everyone who got a peek at that bright pink little pussy."

"We're not Colombian."

"So I don't have to be afraid you'll kill me."

"Not because you trust what I just said. You're not afraid of me killing you, period. Local talent."

Sutton seemed pleased by that answer. "You got potential. You could make it to the bigs. The real world, the real money."

"So this doesn't have to get ugly. This really could be a job interview."

"Do the math, sonny—mine and yours. Mine: If a homicide detective disappears, there's going to be a hardass investigation. Ninety-nine percent chance it goes nowhere—but a hundred percent is better.

"If you live, I've got an asset; man with a badge is useful. After a couple of years, you've had time to prove yourself to me, and it's been long enough so it's safe for you to retire without anyone connecting it to the Willetts case. You sign on with me—through a dummy corporation, so there's no direct link between you and the Sand organization."

"But I don't get to kill Sand."

"That's right, sonny. Your math: Making me happy is what keeps you alive. Tonight and forever."

Mark took a moment, pretended to show the strain of doing the math without a calculator. Finally nodded his head, once. "Thing is—I don't have shit on Elena Esquivel. We know she went back to her house in Chatsworth, and Reid picked her up there. After that, *nada.*"

Sutton walked up to Mark. Stopped. Selected a measured response. Elbowed him in the chest, so hard Mark and the chair went airborne for a second. The pain was literally blinding. Blue flare agony. But he could still breathe. And the chair's crash-landing loosened the tape around his legs. A little.

The steel gray man squatted so he could inquire, face-to-face, "You could have your life and a job, but you choose the scalpel and the twelve-volt?"

"I—" Mark coughed, gasped for breath.

"Take your time," Sutton offered, reasonably.

"I-I've . . . been dead . . . since your goons heard Reid tell me your name and Sand's . . . O-only reason you risked grabbing a cop . . . was . . . t-to shut me up."

"Damn, you're smart. Pop quiz: Where's Esquivel?"

"If I knew I'd tell—why'd I . . . wanna go through . . . the 12-volt if you're gonna kill me anyway? . . . Trade you anything I got for a quick bullet."

"That's one theory. Other one is, you're pissed 'cause I'm gonna waste you no matter what, so you're yanking my chain. Either way, we gotta find out, don't we?" Sutton moved behind Mark, grabbed the chair. "So fucking smart . . . You lead me to the boss shooter, eliminate him for me, and—this is your slickest move, sonny—set yourself up to be the fall guy when Elena Esquivel gets killed." Sutton pulled the chair and Mark upright. "Prime suspect's gonna be Detective Mark Bergman, the rogue cop who murdered Arthur Reid, then dropped from si—"

Mark jerked up onto his feet and twisted violently, the chair's back legs bashing Sutton's legs out from under him.

Fighting a doomed battle to maintain his balance, Mark lurch-hop-staggered at the window. Flung himself into the window hard as he could, being hunched over in a chair with his legs still loosely taped together.

Tried to hit the window chair-first.

Hoped he hit hard enough to smash all the way through.

Hoped what was on the other side wasn't a hundred-foot drop. Or a balcony.

NINETY-SIX

Mark was in free-fall. Long time. Almost forever.

Landed about ten feet below the window. Chair shattered but Mark didn't. Sandy surface.

Sandy, but not level. Mark tumbled down a slope, through patches of sand, ice-plant, and loose gravel, with the pieces of smashed chair still taped to him clattering like tormented rhythm sticks until they began to snag and tear free.

Mark slid to a halt at the bottom. A beach. He flexed things. Didn't seem fractured or dead. Didn't sense any bad cuts from the window—in him or the fucking tape. His arms were still bound behind him. He was on his back, looking up. At a rocky bluff. In the rapidly decaying twilight he could make out a large, dark, T-shaped house perched horizontally across the top of the bluff and dripping vertically down its face. The room Mark had flown the chair out of was on the lowest story. Sutton appeared in the shattered window, glared down, spotted Mark, and aimed a gun.

Mark rolled away hard, as three bullets quick-marched after him, kicking up sprays of murdered silica and succulents. The loosened, shredded duct tape on his legs finally tore and Mark propelled himself to safety behind one of the gnarled, boulder-sized eruptions of sandstone the beach was decorated with.

A door slammed. A second later there were heavy, rapid footfalls from somewhere above Mark. He looked around—just visible in the gloom were the bottom steps of a stairway switch-backing down the bluff from the house to the beach; broad steps cut into the slope, the vertical face of each step secured by a railroad tie.

At the moment Mark couldn't see Sutton, which meant for the moment Sutton couldn't see him.

Mark inched up the boulder and wedged himself to his feet. Wrenched at the tape binding his wrists, trying to yank them apart. Useless. Hurriedly felt the rock behind him, found a small jagged outcropping, snagged the edge of the tape on it, yanked and rubbed viciously at it. The duct tape tore partway, loosened. But the goddamn tape fought back—tore the outcropping right off the boulder.

Sutton's footsteps were closer.

Mark hurried back into a dark rocky fold in the base of the bluff. Tried to twist his wrists apart. Stubborn shit-head tape stretched but didn't give.

He rolled onto his back, curled up tight, bunched his knees against his chest and managed to slide his hands down past his backside and wedge them under his feet. He repeatedly straightened his legs, fast, jerking his feet against the tape. His shoulders tried to leave their sockets. The tape broke.

Mark heard Sutton slow down. Mark froze.

Mark heard Sutton stop. Sutton must've heard Mark's thrashing. Must be listening carefully, peering into the heavy shadows, trying to pick Mark out.

Sutton began moving carefully down the stairs. Mark, sticking to the shadows and matching his footfalls to Sutton's, moved along the base of the bluff. Mark crouched in the dark, shadowy fold of the final switchback, where the stairsteps were about five feet above the beach.

The footsteps stopped again. There was a soft crunching sound—Sutton was swiveling, scanning the rapidly deepening darkness below him.

The pattern resumed. Steps. Pause. Crunch. Directly above Mark. All Sutton had to do was shoot straight down, put one through the top of Mark's skull.

But Sutton didn't look straight down. He resumed his cautious descent. Mark lunged up and grabbed at Sutton's ankles from behind, meaning to haul Sutton's feet out from under him, but Sutton heard Mark move and was beginning to twist away as Mark grabbed—

Got both hands around one of Sutton's ankles and yanked, whipping Sutton sideways—

Sutton flew off the stairway, landed on his back, and rolled up onto his feet, facing Mark, who was already charging into him, butting him under the jaw and grabbing Sutton's gun hand in a simple judo hold, local talent stuff, his thumb planted in the back of Sutton's hand, twisting the hand back and snapping the wrist.

The gun went west. The men went north, thudding down in a feral frenzy of punches, chops, knees, gouges, then Mark jammed an elbow into Sutton's ribs simultaneously with Sutton driving bent fingers into Mark's kidney and the two men wrenched away from each other, roaring with pain.

Both started to scramble to their feet. Mark was wobbly, slow. Sutton was faster but stiffened abruptly, lanced by pain from broken ribs. Sutton fell, jolted down onto his knees; the ribs stabbed him again and he pitched forward, catching himself on outstretched hands, including his broken right wrist. The steel gray man bellowed but didn't go all the way down, remained hunched over, propped on his good hand.

Mark was woozy, his long day catching up with him. Nothing left in the tank. Was just able to stand and punt Sutton in the ribs. The impact folded Sutton up but also knocked Mark off his feet.

Mark rolled away, stagger-crawled in the direction the gun

had gone. Heard the world-class beast behind him snarling, forcing itself to move. Mark caught a glint of dark metal in the sand just as Sutton landed on his back, tearing at the left side of Mark's face with his left hand and burying his teeth in the right side of Mark's neck. Mark got his fingers around the barrel of the gun and slammed the butt into the back of Sutton's hand. Bones crunched and Sutton's hand shuddered loose. Mark jabbed a finger in Sutton's eye and bashed his elbow into Sutton's shattered ribs and twisted out of Sutton's bite. Sutton took some flesh with him but there was nothing spraying out of Mark's neck, which meant it was no biggie, Sutton didn't have any of Mark's blood vessels stuck between his teeth.

Mark made it to his knees, got the gun turned around so he could use it as something besides a club, and aimed it at Sutton, who, with a broken wrist, broken hand, broken ribs, and bloody eye, was yowling in enraged anguish, eyes clenched shut, willing himself up onto his knees, from where he would somehow head-butt Mark to death.

"Del," Mark said, trying to get Sutton's attention. "Del. Stop."

Sutton opened his eyes. Saw the gun aimed at his forehead. Gave Mark a twisted, surly half-grin. Playing the world-class tough guy, ready to relish a bullet to the brain. Fucking drama queen.

Mark scowled. "Tell me where the fuck Jordan Sand is tonight."

Sutton spat a bloody tooth at Mark. Who didn't respond with a bullet.

"Th'matter," Sutton lisped through the red-gushing gap in his teeth, "never thot a man inna fwont?"

"Much as I want to, Del, fun as it would be, I don't plan to shoot you or your boss. I plan to get to Sand before Doonie does, and *bust* him, because if I don't Doonie will shoot his dick off—for starters. And the thing is, Del, if Doonie kills Jordan

Sand, he's fucked. And so are you. You've lost the one honkin' huge Moby Dick of a fish you could offer a prosecutor—you got no deal to cut. Look, with Esquivel missing, and the other shooters and Jordan Sand all dead, you're the only one left to prosecute for the murder of Willetts—and Garn, and Banza . . . Do the math."

Sutton sneered, winced, coughed up a little blood. Sneered harder.

Okay. Let's try Interrogation Technique B.

Mark lowered the gun's muzzle to Sutton's crotch. "Or, I can shoot *your* dick off, claim it happened during the struggle for the gun, let you live, and protect Doonie by convincing him the main job's done—Sand isn't our guy—I circumcised Del Sutton, the idiot who ordered the photo session—then bragged to me about seeing that sweet little girl's bright . . . pink . . . pussy."

Sutton studied Mark's face a moment. Paled.

So did Mark, because, to his mild disappointment, he was fucking done with the law. Down to revenge. Ready to shoot the unit off this son of a bitch and enjoy it.

Fed up, exhausted, Mark muttered, "I'm gonna count to two. One. T—"

NINETY-SEVEN

Sutton barked out a short, sharp cry of capitulation before Mark got to the end of that one-syllable word; the steel gray man was ready for a bullet to his brain, but not to his joy toy. Mark had to settle for putting him through the agony of dragging his fractured ribs back up the steep steps to the house.

Found a roll of duct tape in the kitchen, treated Sutton to a semi-mummification.

The mummy told the cop which drawer his gun, badge, and cuffs were stashed in. The keys to the handcuffs were missing; must've lost them at the winery. No matter. Mark's concern was getting them on Jordan Sand. Someone else could get them off.

And Sutton had some good news about Sand; Jordan and Tish would be alone tonight in a "cottage" at the upper end of their compound in Montecito, a ninety-minute drive from here. Their security staff would be in the main house, well away from the cottage. Jordan and the old lady went there, Sutton informed Mark with a collegial leer, when they wanted to spend some quality late-middle-aged time together.

Mark asked if Tish had been in on the Willetts killing. Sutton said far as he knew, it was all Jordan.

Before leaving, Mark used the bathroom. Scared himself a little when he looked in the mirror. Mark had pulled dead guys out of car crashes who looked and smelled better than he did.

Good. The more horrific he was when he barged into Sand's love nest, the better. Even with Sutton's testimony, Mark wasn't optimistic about getting a conviction against someone as mega-wealthy and influential as Jordan Sand. Least Mark could do was put the cocksucker through a few pure nightmare minutes. Then get him safely into custody before Doonie could get at him.

Mark drove slowly down Highway 1; he was stiffening up, starting to feel almost as shitty as he looked, so he was taking special care not to bash into any of the other vehicles or send Sutton's Mercedes off a cliff for a swim in the Pacific. Fine car. Had tinted windows, so other motorists wouldn't see Mark's face and freak. A GPS computer that drew a cheery green line from here to Montecito. And a hands-free cell phone. But, fighting his training and instinct, Mark resisted calling Ochoa and Doonie until he arrived at his destination; at this point, after all he'd already done to keep his partner away from Jordan Sand, he wasn't taking any chance of letting Doonie know the address and having him get there first.

Plus which (he hoped this wasn't his weariness and tranq hangover talking), Mark did believe going in alone he had a better chance of actually putting cuffs on Sand. A squad of cops politely pressing the front gate buzzer would get stalled by Sand's security guys. By the time the cops got past the main compound and up to the cottage, Sand would be halfway to Switzerland, or surrounded by a wall of hundred-foot lawyers.

Mark arrived at Montecito, a wealth preserve at the south edge of Santa Barbara. The "city" consisted of a mile-wide strip of lavish Pacific-bucolic suburb—few sidewalks, massive greenery, shingled mock-rustic mansions with whimsical mailboxes—which started at the beach and climbed two-thirds of the way up a mountain slope. The top third of the mountain was part of a National Forest that rode hundreds of miles of coastal ridgeline. The Golden State's glorious front yard.

He found Sand's address. It was on a gatepost at the uphill end of the longest street. He drove a few hundred yards past the gate to where the pavement ended. Parked. Dialed Ochoa's number at Parker Center.

J'nette Levaux answered.

Mark was pleased to discover J'nette was out of the hospital. J'nette was pleased Mark wasn't dead.

Mark asked her to tell Ochoa and Doonie where Sutton could be picked up. J'nette informed him Ochoa and Doonie were already at the entrance to the ranch—they'd nailed one of Sutton's men trying to ditch Mark's car, found out where Mark was being held, then choppered up the coast, picked up some CHP backup and were about to bust in.

Mark told her to let them know Sutton was alone and trussed up, in the kitchen, eagerly awaiting medical assistance and a chance to dime his boss—whom Mark was about to arrest. Mark gave J'nette the Montecito address, told her he was about to cash in a one-in-a million opportunity to surprise and bust Sand.

J'nette started to order Mark to wait for backup but he cut her off, saying a quick "Gotta go—" and hung up.

Hell. Of all the things he'd been through today, being rude to J'nette bothered him the most. Go fuckin' figure.

He got out of the car and limped onto a dirt trail. Found the fork that led to a five-foot-high wooden fence that marked the boundary between the bottom edge of the National Forest and the top edge of the Sands' weekend getaway estate.

Ninety-Eight

Hauling himself up and over the fence was the worst thing Mark had ever done. Just the agony from the twelve-hour-old, untreated bullet gash in his leg would've qualified, without any help from the swollen, stiff, head-to-toe mass of cuts, contusions, bites, bruised organs, and strained ligaments he'd collected since. He tried to carefully lower himself down the other side but landed with a clumsy jolt and sagged against the fence. It took a minute for him to gather enough breath and will to start walking, and when he did he moved like a man searching for a pair of lost crutches.

So there was no reason not to keep going and bust that smug bastard.

Sutton said the cottage was tucked into a wooded copse at the top end of the property, well away from the main house. Mark had no trouble spotting it; there was a waxing moon, starry sky, more than enough light for someone whose right eye was barely bruised and left eye was swollen only halfway shut.

Nestled in the trees was a pristine replica of an English yeoman's cottage, complete with an undulating, mushroom-cap roof. Except the cottage felt kind of hulking, too tall, windows too large; the owner had ordered the architect to lovingly duplicate Old World charm, then supersize it.

There was smoke curling from a chimney and firelight glowed in the windows of a large corner room. Mark painfully made his way to that corner of the cottage and got two pleasant surprises.

The first was that on the side of the house there was a small veranda, accessed by French doors. This was a sixteenth-century cottage with a veranda and French doors.

The second surprise was what Mark saw when he peeked in a window. Tish and Jordan Sand were in a sitting room furnished with Edwardian couches and chairs and antique silk rugs. But they weren't sitting. Tish was dressed in a 1920s-era split-skirt riding dress, complete with gleaming boots and a leather crop, with which she was slowly, peevishly lashing her husband's buttocks. Jordan was down on all fours, wearing a white peasant shirt, dark green corduroy breeches pulled down around his ankles, and a fine English saddle strapped across his back, and his wrists were bound with a human-scaled pair of leather hobbles, the kind used to tether a horse's front hooves. With each stroke Tish would moan, "Oliver-r-r," and Jordan would yelp, "Constance!"

Beautiful. Caught him with his pants down and his hands already cuffed. And a French door was about the only variety Mark, in his current condition, was certain he could kick open.

Mark's confidence wasn't misplaced. Even though the kick hurt him way more than it did the doors, they crashed open with a satisfying bang and Mark lurched in, a badge-and-gun-waving cop zombie who'd recently been beaten to death but was too crazed to admit it.

Tish shrieked, almost as loudly as Jordan.

"Police! Don't move!" the bloody apparition croaked. "Jordan Sand, you're under arrest for the murders of Wilson Willetts, Ralph Garn, and Charlie Banza, sexual assault on a minor, plus the kidnapping and attempted murder of a law enforcement officer." The ghoul's bloody mouth twisted into a sick grin. "Feel free to give that officer a reason to discharge his weapon."

The Sands remained still as they could, Jordan on all fours

playing trembling horsy, Tish on her feet but cringing away from Mark, arms clenched against her chest, hugging the riding crop as if it were a teddy bear.

In a quavery whine, Jordan implored, "Please, calm d—"

"It's over, Jordy." Mark took out a set of real handcuffs. "Sutton rolled on you. Tonight's your one chance to confess and cut a deal." Most preposterous Hail Mary of Mark's career, but at this point what the fuck.

As Jordan tried to decide on a reply, Tish's hard gaze traversed from the horrific cop to her husband, her fear washed away by a small tsunami of rage.

"You *asshole*," Tish brayed and kicked him near there, knocking him flat.

"Stop!" Mark ordered Tish, sharply raising his arm and pointing at her. The sudden gesture made him dizzy. Shit. He hoped the quiver in his arm looked more like him trying to control his anger than his balance. Waves of exhaustion were hollowing him out.

Mark switched his attention to Jordan. "And you, Seabiscuit, stay down. Gonna remove the hobbles, put these on." Mark pulled out the handcuffs and started forward. But the air suddenly got sleepy and the room started to close its eyes. Mark wobbled, dropped his gun and the cuffs, almost passed out but caught himself on a table, knocking a lamp off of it. Leaning heavily on the table, he remained on his feet and forced his eyes open, refusing to run out of consciousness at such an inappropriate moment. Hadda get back to work, fast.

It was Jordan who moved first and fast, rolling away and yanking hard on the hobbles—the leather strap snapped, easily—shit, it was rigged to do that, their big finale must be an aroused Oliver bursting his bonds and ravishing Lady Constance—and Jordan was on his feet, tugging up his drawers with one hand and yanking open a drawer with the other.

Mark had a plan. Was going to straighten up and push off from the table, propel himself at Jordan. By the time Mark completed the straightening-up part Jordan was pointing a gun at him. Spiffy nickel-plated .32 automatic.

"You're alone," Jordan complained. "This isn't an arrest, you're deranged, out for blood."

"Nah, it's business. We've got Sutton and your other employees who kidnapped me—I'm gonna look great on the news, huh?"

"I don't know what Sutton's been up to or why."

"Think the world or a jury is gonna believe that? Believe it's Del Sutton who cares so deeply about who gets the LAFAM commission? Cares more than you—and your wife?"

Mark watched Tish rapidly grasp the concept of what a plausible co-conspirator she'd make. She began to yell, "God-*damn* it Jor—"

Jordan tried to abort the scolding by shooting Mark.

Mark felt a small fist punch his left side, then a fiery sting, which bloomed into what felt like a cloud of tiny red-hot fish-hooks expanding inside him. His knees began to buckle. Tightly clutching his midsection and his dignity, Mark staggered sideways and eased himself into a defiantly upright sitting position on a couch, from where he immediately slid straight down onto the floor, splayed out with only his head and shoulders propped against the couch. Shit. He dodges bullets from two pro shooters in one day, then gets drilled by an amateur wearing a saddle.

"How could you do this to me!" Tish hissed at Jordan.

Jordan, keeping his eyes on Mark, snapped at Tish, "Just making sure you get what you want—as always."

"I didn't want Wilson murdered! And this, shooting a cop right here in our—"

"It's just meat, it'll be removed. Don't worry; this never happened."

"Oh right, Jordy, nothing to worry, because you're sure no one will find out about this—just like *he* didn't find out you're the moron who killed Wilson!"

"Clam dow—*calm* down and think! *He*"—Jordan jabbed the gun in Mark's direction—"doesn't have a case! If he did there'd be real cops here, with a warrant!"

Tish hesitated while she pondered that.

Jordan took advantage of her silence. "*Think*—he's bluffing—the murder trial in Chicago is about to go to the jury."

"Uh-uh," Mark groaned. "Charges against Meelo are being dismissed."

Tish snorted at Jordan. "Asshole," she reiterated, and paced away in frustration.

Jordan kept his .32 pointed at Mark but turned to look at Tish; couldn't satisfactorily argue with his wife without making eye contact. Safe enough; Mark had dropped his weapon miles away, behind the couch.

"Tish, don't you walk away from me," Jordan growled.

"Once this gets out," Tish explained, teeth clenched, "trial or no trial, we're destroyed. We're nobody. *All we'll have left is money.*"

"This won't—and if the worst did happen—which it won't—"

"They have Sutton!"

"I'll handle that! No jail time for me, never! But okay! Say there's a scandal, and I, we do get—why did any of it happen, Tish? *Why?*" Jordan glared at her. "This was all for you."

"I never asked—"

"Never asked!? *Never asked?* It's the goddamn biggest thing in your life!"

"I would've won without having Wilson murdered!"

"Really, Tish? You sure?"

Tish preferred not to answer that. But if Jordy was going to start flaunting bottom lines here, she had one of her own.

"*You didn't get away with it,*" she said, biting off each individual word. "And don't you say it was for me. It was for you, everything is always about you."

"You forced this on me, sweets."

"I *what!?*"

"You are Mrs. Jordan Sand; when you go after something this big, this public, Mrs. Jordan Sand cannot lose, because the only thing that means is *Jordan Sand* lost, and *Jordan Sand* does not lose the big public ones, even the silly ones—"

"*SILLY!?*"

"—because that costs me credibility, costs me invincibility, when I go after the shit that fucking matters, you fucking pretentious cow!"

Tish stood silent, rock-still, eyes blazing hotter than the custom mix of Tennessee hickory and Utah juniper logs in the fireplace.

Buoyed by landing a blow that reduced the pretentious cow to frustrated silence, Jordan returned his attention to Mark. And was disappointed by what he saw. "You still with us?"

"Always," Mark darkly promised. Always or maybe five more minutes. He was getting cold.

Jordan shook his head, disgusted. "What you trough-hogs in the public sector don't understand—no, do understand but don't give a damn about—is that time is money." He recited it again in slow sing-song, a grown-up patiently teaching a child a last lesson before shooting him again. "Time . . . is . . . mon—"

"Ass-*HOLE!*" Tish snarled as she swung an eighteenth-century Venetian lion's-head-handle fireplace poker at the asshole's head. She missed, striking the back of his neck, but it was a monster two-hand overhead slam delivered with psycho Zen purity. Jordy pitched forward and crashed down flat on his face, losing his gun and a meatball-size chunk of his back, torn out by the poker's iron hook.

Jordy wasn't moving but he was breathing. Tish stalked forward and stood over her prostrate husband, eyes wide, incisors bared, wet red fireplace iron raised, ready to answer Jordy's next smart remark.

"Tish," Mark whispered.

Tish held her at-bat pose, turned her head just enough to stare down at Mark.

"Thank you," he said, feebly but sincerely. "Please call nine-one-one."

Tish scowled.

"For me," Mark clarified.

Tish thought it over, regarded him shrewdly.

Ah fuck, she had terms to settle first.

"I—" Tish stopped abruptly as Jordan let out a mournful groan and began to squirm—not going anywhere, still unconscious, and unarmed, his .32 had skidded away when he hit the floor—but Tish whacked him again, another two-handed slam, this time on target. Jordy wouldn't be dishing out any more insults tonight. Or tomorrow. Too much of his gray jelly speech-control lobe was soaking into the Aubusson.

Tish slowly closed her eyes, regained herself. Opened them and calmly informed Mark, "I had to hit him again—he still had the gun, was about to shoot you."

"Exactly," Mark nodded. "Saved my life. Maybe. Nine-one-one," he urged. Who knows, this neighborhood, the meat wagon might get here before he bled out.

Tish dropped the fireplace iron, went to an early-nineteenth-century worm-holed cherrywood map case with brass fittings, opened it, took out a cordless phone, pressed the 9, and, finger poised above the 1, paused and looked at Mark.

"Also," she politely suggested, "during my conversation with

Jordy, I never said anything about myself, I never sa—"

"No problem."

Undeterred, Tish resumed where she left off. "I never said, 'You didn't get away with it,' or anything else about Jordan or myself, or being socially ruined."

"Got it," Mark gasped. He tried to turn a grimace of pain into a reassuring grin. *Dial the fucking 1-1.*

"In fact," Tish continued, "my only reaction was horror that Jordy had caused Wilson's death."

Shit. Shot by an amateur wearing a saddle, dies debating the best way to preserve Tish Sand's social status.

Mark gritted his teeth for one last try. "If I'm dead you can't save my life . . . *and* I can't confirm you . . . weren't in on Willetts . . . Your only chance to come out . . . looking good."

Now that was a valid, persuasive point. "Just wanted to make sure we were clear on the details," Tish cooed. She pressed the 1. Started to press it a second time. Paused.

"How do I know I can trust you?"

The .32 was on the floor within Mark's reach, but he just didn't have the strength to pick it up and shoot her. Fuck. Had to settle for explaining why he would've kept his end of the deal if she'd called 911 in time.

"I'm from Chicago."

Not the greatest last words, but Mark closed his eyes and let go, reasonably satisfied. Beat going out with a report on the condition of his calves.

NINETY-NINE

Mark Bergman's death was punctured by a strange, hazy frag-
ment of awareness. Either there was an afterlife, featuring a
purgatory which bore a spooky resemblance to an ICU—or
Tish Sand had finished dialing 911 in time.

The awareness went away and took Mark with it.

When Mark woke up for real he was in a top-floor suite at the
UCLA Medical Center. He'd been stabilized at a trauma center
in Santa Barbara, then choppered to Westwood and passed along
a re-assembly line of surgeons. The .32 bullet had torn through
his intestines, skated up his pelvic bone, and come to rest near
his spine. The first surgery was a very careful excavation of the
slug. A few days later his vandalized disposal system was spliced
back together. The .40-caliber gash in his leg had been sewn up;
he might want to think about plastic surgery, depending on how
fond he was of the scar.

It was a little while before Mark found out about that stuff.
At first he had more pressing concerns. His eyes were gummy
and didn't want to open all the way. He needed to say
something, get some help with this.

He made a sandy whistling noise, and coughed. Someone put
a straw to his lips and held his head while he sipped water.
Then, before he could ask, she wiped his eyes with a damp
swab.

Now he could see. The out-of-uniform nurse who'd just

wiped his eyes: his mother. And, around his bed: Carrie Eli. J'nette Levaux. Gale Michaels.

"Hi," Mark croaked to Mom and the chorus.

Mark's mom delivered a feathery tap to the top of his head. Given his condition it was as much of a spanking as she could give him for nearly getting killed, again. He knew it would also be the only comment she'd make on his recent busy day, unless he brought it up.

Carrie, on the other side of the bed, searched for an unbruised spot, touched her lips to his cheek. J'nette, who was on crutches, blew a kiss.

Mom looked at Gale, cautioning her to be brief. "They need to monitor his vitals."

Gale nodded.

Mark's mother, Carrie, and J'nette left the room, so Gale would have a few minutes alone with him before his vitals got monitored.

You hit thirty and the matchmaking never stops.

Doonie called. Apologized for not being there. Said he'd stayed in L.A. until the doctors swore nobody would be having to buy Mark the nice suit and the pine box. Then Doonie'd headed back to Chicago—Phyl and the kids really needed him.

Mark said don't apologize.

Doonie thanked Mark for all the stupid reckless shit Mark did, in order to, y'know, keep Doonie from going and . . . So, now, he was stuck owing Mark any fucking thing Mark ever needed. Lifetime. Like brothers. Like actual never-ending pain-in-the-ass family.

Mark said he needed Doonie to start rooting for the Cubs.

No fucking way.

ONE HUNDRED

Try to get a travel authorization when you're investigating a murder, it's like pulling teeth. Put one bullet in a murderer and the day after you come out of your coma two Internal Affairs guys get flown in from Chicago to do the obligatory postgame interview.

IA had no problem with Mark laying Reid down: self-defense. Arthur Reid had shot first. Mark had Chip Bozeman to verify that.

And Superintendent Blivins was taking responsibility for the decision to withhold evidence from the LAPD.

The procedural shit was where it got sticky for Mark.

Why, immediately after the shoot, hadn't he called for an ambulance for Bozeman?

Mark said—just like his handcuff keys (true)—his cell phone (false) must've fallen into some dark wine puddle during the shooting. When Mark couldn't find his cell he started for the main house, where he presumed there'd be a phone.

Before heading for the house, why did he take the time to tape the bullet hole in the wine tank?

It was a deal with a dying man. Only took a minute.

What the hell was Mark's rationale for attempting to take Jordan Sand into custody, out of jurisdiction, without a warrant?

Mark said there were ample grounds to make an arrest for murder, kidnap, attempted murder—and a unique, one-night-only opportunity to physically get to Sand without his security

435

staff intervening.

Why didn't Mark request backup while he was driving to Montecito, or wait for backup as Detective Levaux ordered him to when he was outside Sand's estate?

Mark couldn't tell IA the big truth—one of the cops who showed up would've been Doonie, looking to administer a 9mm neutering. So Mark told a smaller truth—he went solo because he believed one man had a better chance of slipping in fast and unnoticed than a whole squad would've.

One man in the beat-to-shit condition Mark was in at that time?

Well . . . Good point, guys. He'd been shot, assaulted, drugged, threatened with torture, smashed through a window, taken a ten-foot fall, rolled down a hill, then engaged in life-or-death hand-to-hand combat. Might have affected his judgment.

Superintendent of Police Elvin Blivins issued a statement. Said an evaluation of Detective Bergman's actions would be made according to strict, impartial procedure. Running with a theme Mark established, the Superintendent did note that during the events in question the officer had been subjected to extraordinary physical and pharmaceutical stress.

Blivins assumed Bergman's real reason for going cowboy was what had happened to Patty Dunegan. If Bergman had gone out to shoot the fuck behind it Blivins didn't give much of a shit, as long as Mark did it without getting caught. Blivins especially didn't care if the fuck got killed by his own wife, and all Mark did was to somehow provoke it.

Down at the Hall neither the Mayor—nor Mrs. Mayor, who'd been pals with Wilson Willetts—was inclined to bounce a detective who'd solved the murder of a great Chicago-American artist, shot and slugged it out with professional killers, brought down a seemingly untouchable billionaire sociopath, and, in doing so, rescued a poor ethnic street kid from being railroaded. This was not a cop the public wanted to see punished for coloring outside the lines.

The Mayor did not discuss the matter with Superintendent Blivins, who then did not have a private talk with the officer who'd be presiding at Bergman's hearing, after which Blivins didn't say anything to Lieutenant Husak, who didn't pass the word to Doonie, who called Mark to let him know what the deal was.

Two-day suspension. No reduction in grade. No reassignment out of Homicide.

One Hundred-One

Mark's surgeon seemed insulted by the notion anyone would voluntarily leave California, especially to return to Chicago. Made it clear Mark being ready to leave the hospital wasn't the same as being ready to hop a plane. He instructed Mark to refrain from travel for at least two weeks; in fact he hoped Mark would be sensible enough to complete his recuperation here, instead of rushing home to the rains and harrowing sub-fifties temperatures of autumn on the Lake Michigan shore.

Gale invited Mark to stay at her place for the two weeks. A coach house in Santa Monica.

The first two nights Gale slept on her couch, fearful she might accidentally bump into Mark in her sleep. The second night Mark shuffled into the living room and squeezed in alongside her.

Mark wasn't prone to falling in love. But he fell into domesticity with Gale in nothing flat. His third morning there, while squeezing oranges, it occurred to him that since he wouldn't be able to go back to work for at least a couple of months, there was no reason not to spend some time here, waking up next to Gale. If she really did want him to stay.

He mulled it over another few days, to see if he kept feeling that way.

He did. So he put the question to her. "Would you mind—"

"No."

"You don't know what I was going ask."

Gale shrugged.

Problem was, Mark's wounds did eventually heal.

Gale was prepared. Had a plan. Mark would go home alone. He needed, she informed him, breathing room, so he could deal with reentry into his "normal" life without her around as a complicating factor.

Gale said she was looking forward to how quickly he'd realize how much he missed her.

Mark kissed Gale.

Gale tore Mark's shirt off. Pulled him down to the floor and bounced him around as long and hard as she could. No use. No concussions, no spinal trauma, no ruptured incisions. He was still healthy enough to board a flight.

ONE HUNDRED-TWO

Stuff had happened in the meantime.

Meelo got a call from Betsy Hackenmeyer, who wanted to congratulate him—and, as he'd daydreamed about during the dull parts of his murder trial—take him to bed. Spiffed up for court, Betsy actually looked better during the day than she had at night. Cleaned up nice, for her age and weight.

Betsy was also flush; she'd sold the parlor stove for $6,170, on consignment at a Kinzie Street antique shop. Betsy picked Meelo up in her truck and they checked into a room at the Drake. An hour later they were in love.

Ms. June Dockyer sold two ounces of Jamaican to a hottie bonds analyst who turned out to be a hottie narc.

In the unmarked car on the way to the lockup she tried to cut a deal, offering to give them her supplier. *(Sorry Janvier; it's me or you.)*

Narcs weren't interested. But even with the rigid sentencing guidelines these days, Ms. June Dockyer would probably get no more than twenty-four months. Easy bit, the hottie assured her, with a nasty grin.

The narcs stopped talking, let Ms. June Dockyer meditate on that easy twenty-four months.

When they arrived the driver cut the engine but neither cop opened his door. Ms. June Dockyer and the narcs sat there in silence, the two men looking at her. She began to wonder if they were expecting her to offer sex in exchange for letting her slide. She was about to make an exploratory comment when one of them said a detective wanted to have a word, before they booked her.

Before they booked her. Sounded significant.

The narcs got out. A moment later a beefy man wearing a frayed shirt and a stained tie got in and sat next to her. Detective John Dunegan. The Cro Magnon, from the hit-and-run thing.

"Wanna look at some pictures?" he asked.

Architect Juan-Marie de Suau withdrew from the LAFAM competition and demanded the museum select Wilson Willetts' design.

Eric Fairlie (defying instructions from Calvin Hirschberg), declared that, due to his vast respect and affection for Wilson Willetts, he was remaining in the competition.

Calvin stopped returning Eric Fairlie's phone calls. Planted rumors in the media and chat rooms that Fairlie had grown increasingly unstable the past four years, that Fairlie's junior associates had in fact designed his recent buildings.

Florence Brock introduced a motion for the design committee to endorse Wilson Willetts' design. The motion passed, unanimously.

The project was budgeted at three hundred million dollars. Members of the board pledged a hundred. Public funding would have to supply the remaining two hundred mil.

Wouldn't have been a problem in the late 1990s, when the project was initiated. But by early 2003 every level of government was in deficit. There wasn't a city, county, state, or Federal dime to be had.

LAFAM announced its rebuild was indefinitely postponed.

Wilson Willetts remained permanently dead.

Del Sutton fingered an alleged ex-spook, a Brit named Stephan Densford-Kent, as the murder-broker who'd fronted for the shooters. Police arriving at Densford-Kent's condo on Russian Hill found the place had been cleaned out.

British intelligence had no record of any former employee by that name, they said.

The search for Dina Velaros also came up empty. Maybe because she'd died of her wounds. Maybe not.

Arthur Reid turned out to be a pseudonym. The identity went back seventeen years. There was no trace of who the man using the name had been before that. No indication he'd ever existed.

There was enough wine left in the tanks for Chip Bozeman to make two-hundred-twenty-seven cases of Cuvée Dina.

Retasting the barrel samples when he got out of the hospital, Chip decided Arthur, even if he'd tried to shoot Chip, had been right about how to handle the juice. Chip went for the more restrained style.

The syrah won several gold medals. Its quality and scarcity, combined with the notoriety attached to it, meant the initial release sold out in two hours, at six hundred dollars a bottle.

A. Reid Winery's Cuvée Dina syrah was never poured at any official White House function.

UNINDICTED
CO-CONSPIRATORS

Constructive deconstruction of the first draft: La Jaffe, Uncle Sheldon, T-Kaz, Mighty Mike, and Motorcycle Jim.

Judicial restraints: Dr. LL Cool Law and Pisces John.

Danke schön pour l'espagnol: Mandy of Bow-Wow.

DNA sequencing: The Daughter of Potkin and the Father of Crow.

Grape-ology: Hammack The Photographic Palate and Estrin The Esthete. (*RIP*, Mr. E.)

Cover concept conceptualization: Kev The Shakespearean Cowboy.

Lastest but not leastest, The Childe Lucille, my agent and fellow parishioner at St. Wrigley's: *Wait till next year.*

ABOUT THE AUTHOR

Lenny Kleinfeld began his career as a playwright, in Chicago, where he was also a columnist for *Chicago* magazine. His articles, fiction, and humor have appeared in *Playboy,* the *Chicago Tribune,* the *New York Times* and the *Los Angeles Times.* In 1987 Mr. Kleinfeld sold a screenplay, went out for a drink and woke up in Los Angeles. He currently resides there with his wife, National Public Radio correspondent Ina Jaffe.

Shooters and Chasers is his first novel.